Susan Carlisle's love affair with books began in the sixth grade, when she made a bad grade in mathematics. Not allowed to watch TV until she'd brought the grade up, Susan filled her time with books. She turned her love of reading into a passion for writing, and now has over ten Medical Romances published through Mills & Boon. She writes about hot, sexy docs and the strong women who captivate them. Visit SusanCarlisle.com.

Born in the UK, **Becky Wicks** has suffered interminable wanderlust from an early age. She's lived and worked all over the world, from London to Dubai, Sydney, Bali, NYC and Amsterdam. She's written for the likes of *GQ*, *Hello!*, *Fabulous* and *Time Out*, a host of YA romance, plus three travel memoirs—*Burqalicious*, *Balilicious* and *Latinalicious* (HarperCollins, Australia). Now she blends travel with romance for Mills & Boon and loves every minute! Tweet her @bex_wicks and subscribe at beckywicks.com.

REDEEMING THE REBEL DOC

SUSAN CARLISLE

TEMPTED BY HER HOT-SHOT DOC

BECKY WICKS

MILLS & BOON

Published in Great Britain 2018
by Mills & Boon, an imprint of HarperCollins*Publishers*
1 London Bridge Street, London, SE1 9GF

Redeeming the Rebel Doc © 2018 Susan Carlisle

Tempted by Her Hot-Shot Doc © 2018 Becky Wicks

ISBN: 978-0-263-93343-7

MIX
Paper from
responsible sources
FSC® C007454

REDEEMING
THE REBEL DOC

SUSAN CARLISLE

MILLS & BOON

To Jeanie,
I couldn't have asked for a better sister-in-law.

CHAPTER ONE

"RETRACTOR!" SNAPPED Dr. Rex Maxwell.

His surgical nurse quickly placed it in his palm.

"We need to find this bleeder. Suction." With a gentle movement, Rex lifted the liver as his assistant, standing across the OR table from him at Metropolitan Hospital in Memphis, Tennessee, obeyed his command.

Rex watched intently for any sign of red liquid. This patient had come through the emergency department the night before and one of his colleagues had patched the man up but the patient wasn't recovering as he should. His midsection had swelled. There was internal bleeding. Rex was known as the "go-to man" who handled hard-to-find problems like this. He didn't disappoint. Confident in his skills as a surgeon, his success rate had proved him more than competent. Except in one case.

His heart jumped as he spotted the problem. "Found it. Sutures."

"That figures. You find them when no one else can," the anesthesiologist said, admiration in his tone.

Rex looked over his mask at the man. "Thanks."

Over the next few minutes Rex repaired the leak. He was almost finished when the phone on the wall rang. A nurse answered. Seconds later she hung up. "Rex, you're wanted in Administration as soon as you're done here."

He muttered a word that his mother would scold him for using. Polite people didn't use words like that. But, then, to her, life was about always making the right impression.

An hour later he trudged down the wide tiled hallway toward the hospital administration offices. With a patient in surgery prep who had been pushed back hours because of the bleeder, Rex should be back in surgery, not on his way to a meeting he wasn't interested in being a part of. Hadn't he spent enough time in the last twelve months with Dr. Nelson, the hospital administrator? Being arbitrarily summoned to Nelson's office should have stopped when the unpleasant malpractice suit had been settled.

Rex had endlessly replayed the details of that night and that surgery in his mind and had told lawyers the tale of what had occurred more than once.

He'd been called in late on a Saturday night after having been to a club on a date. Since he had been on call he hadn't been drinking and when he'd arrived at the hospital the patient had already been prepped for surgery. It hadn't been until after he was in the OR that he'd learned his patient was Mr. Royster, the man who had been both his father's best friend and chairman of the board of the country club when his father had filed for bankruptcy. Royster was also the father of Rex's ex-girlfriend, who had dumped him because she'd been ashamed of being seen on Rex's arm after his family's financial downfall had become public knowledge.

The situation with Mr. Royster's perforated stomach had by now deteriorated to the point that he'd had little chance of surviving even with surgery. The repair hadn't been difficult the chance of serious infection had been high. Less than twenty-four hours post-op Mr.

Royster had steadily been going downhill. In another forty-eight, he was gone.

Devastated and grief-stricken to the point that they couldn't accept what had happened, Royster's family had lashed out by filing a malpractice suit against Rex, accusing him of not taking the necessary medical steps to save Royster's life in retaliation for how he and his family had been ostracized all those years ago. Powered by the family's money and influence, the case had gone further than it should have. The most damage had been done by the Roysters' manipulation of the media, which had dragged the hospital into the nastiness.

The relationship between Rex and Dr. Nelson had been contentious at best while the hospital had been faced with the possibility of paying millions in damages. Rex's career, as well as his and the hospital's reputation, would still take years to repair. Thankfully, though, both he and the hospital had come through the experience bruised and battered, and both were still in business. So what could Dr. Nelson possibly want now?

Opening the glass door of the administrative suite, Rex went straight to the assistant's desk. "Marsha, please let Dr. Nelson know I'm here."

She nodded toward a closed door. "Go on in. He's waiting on you."

Relief washed through him. At least he didn't have to waste time waiting. He checked his watch as he entered Nelson's office. He was determined to get to his patient sooner rather than later. As Nelson looked up from his chair behind the desk, Rex closed the door.

Dr. Nelson waved him toward a chair. "I'm glad you could make it on such short notice."

Rex dropped into the seat, elbows resting on his

knees, and looked squarely at Dr. Nelson. "I have a patient waiting."

"I won't keep you long. After the unpleasantness of the last year, the hospital's reputation has taken a hit. The community is left with the impression the hospital doesn't provide quality service."

Without thinking, Rex uttered that foul oath again. Dr. Nelson's eyes narrowed. In turn, Rex straightened in his chair. "Everything about my service is high quality. Was and will be in the future. I'll put my skills up against any surgeon's."

"The question is, does the public believe that?" Nelson countered. "This is a serious situation. I'm sure you've noticed the downward turn in your workload."

"Yes, but I'm still very busy." Rex was confident people would soon forget about the long-drawn-out court case. Especially since it was no longer nightly news. Time was the secret. After all, he'd lived through scandal before and survived.

Dr. Nelson's face sobered. He leaned forward, placing his arms on his desk and clasping his hands. Maybe there was more to this meeting than Rex had originally thought. He gave Mr. Nelson his full attention.

"Because of the situation, the board of directors has decided to bring in a public relations firm to help minimize the fallout. With the hospital accreditation committee planning a visit at the end of the month, we need to bolster public opinion as much as possible. Since you were involved in the lawsuit they want your cooperation in the matter. The idea is that if the public perception of you improves then so will the hospital's and vice versa."

Rex held back a frustrated groan. Nelson must be joking. There wasn't time in his day for PR stuff. Instead of voicing his real opinion, he said, "Do you really think that's necessary?"

"It's not what I think but what the board has decided. However, I agree with them. I expect your full cooperation."

Rex started to open his mouth.

Dr. Nelson raised his hand. "The board knows you're a talented, dedicated doctor. They want to keep you but the hospital's reputation must improve. If you plan to continue working here, I highly recommend you go along with this."

Rex was invested in Metropolitan Hospital. With his surgical skills he could work anywhere, but that wouldn't be enough to get him the promotions he craved and if he were to leave it was highly likely that any hospital he applied to would take a dim view of him, given the malpractice lawsuit, even though he had been legally cleared.

He'd been able to start work at Metropolitan as his own person without the worry of the negative connotations of his family name. He'd been exceptionally successful, despite being what some would call a free spirit. There had been no issues until this recent incident and he didn't anticipate any more problems in his future. His intention was to achieve the position of departmental head in this hospital.

Now he was being pressured into unnecessary PR nonsense with no say in the matter.

Just like when he had been a teen and his family had become the subject of too much outside attention.

After his family's fall from their high-society status, he'd vowed he would never be forced into putting on a façade to impress people. However, it seemed that that was what it was going to take if he wanted to achieve his goals in medicine. Even though experience had taught him that putting a pretty face on an ugly reality could backfire badly.

His mother and father had lived that way. The best clothes, nice cars, private school for their children, big house and membership to an exclusive country club. The problem was that they couldn't afford it. Everything had been outward appearance and no substance. When Rex had been seventeen it had all come crashing down. His parents had been exposed and the family had gone bankrupt.

Reality was a too-small apartment on the other side of town, a ten-year-old car, cheap clothes and no more country club.

Most of Rex's friends had turned their backs on him because they'd no longer had anything in common. What had really hurt, though, had been the girl he'd been in love with ending their relationship. When he'd been snubbed by country club snobs, she'd declared they had no future. He wasn't enough for her. So much for love.

Rex had promised himself then that he'd never judge someone by where they lived or what they drove, neither would he ever put on pretensions of wealth and social status to impress again. He was who he was. People could like him or not. That was one of the reasons he wore a T-shirt, jeans and boots to work. He might be a well-paid physician, but his open, honest lifestyle had nothing to do with his salary, his brain or his skills in the OR. He would not tolerate pretense in his life.

Forcing his attention back to the dilemma Dr. Nelson had just created for him, he decided that during this new PR push he'd just lie low and concentrate on his patients. Refuse to get any more involved than he absolutely had to. He had nothing to prove to anyone and nothing to hide.

The moment Rex sighed, satisfied with his decision, Nelson punched a button and told his assistant to send in Ms. Romano.

Tiffani Romano waited apprehensively in the outer office of the administrator. She'd already seen Dr. Nelson but he'd asked her to wait while he spoke to Dr. Maxwell in private, then he would introduce them.

When her boss at Whitlock Public Relations had asked her into his office and explained that Metropolitan Hospital wanted to hire the firm to improve their image she had been excited that he was putting her in charge of the job. Tiffani saw this as a once-in-a-lifetime opportunity to advance in the company. Success in the campaign would give her the two things she desperately wanted—a promotion that would move her to the corporate office in another city and the chance to no longer encounter Lou, her ex-boyfriend, daily.

The only glitch was that she had no respect for the medical community. She knew from personal experience that doctors were only interested in themselves and cared little about the patients whose lives they ruined instead of healed.

When she'd been a child her father had been crippled in a motorcycle accident and he had lost one leg completely and part of another, condemning him to a wheelchair. The situation had made him a very bitter man. To this day, he insisted the doctors had done nothing to save his lower limbs. With his lack of mobility had gone his desire for life—his only joy to be found at the bottom of a bottle or in the comfort of prescription drugs. These tragedies had been underscored by his sullenness, all making it impossible for him to hold down a job.

Her mother had supported her father's vendetta. Suf-

fering through her father's recovery and attitude about
his life, the lawsuit he'd pursued against the physicians
and hospital, and having little money, she had been
almost as unpleasant as her husband. She'd soon di-
vorced Tiffani's father and the once happy household
had changed to one of permanent misery. Nothing had
been the same after that fateful day.

Her father still complained about how he had been
mistreated. Today he was wasting away at an assisted
living home, spending more of his time in bed than out.
It made Tiffani miserable to visit him and see him like
that, but he was her father and she loved him.

Would Dr. Maxwell, with whom she'd have to work
closely, be any different than the doctors who had destroyed her father? From what she had read and seen
on the news about the malpractice case, she'd believed
Maxwell guilty. Nevertheless, he'd been cleared of all
charges. She wasn't surprised. Like all physicians, she
was sure he'd played God with someone's life with no
thought to what would happen to the patient afterward,
or the effects on the family. Her father lived in pain daily
because of hasty decisions and half-efforts his doctors
had made. Though her father had survived, unlike Maxwell's victim, his life and the lives of his family had
been destroyed.

Regardless of Dr. Maxwell's devil-may-care attitude,
his surgical success rate was above average. That could
be used to her advantage if she could keep him in check
long enough to achieve the "you-can-trust-me" crusade
she envisioned. Her intense month-long strategy was
to boldly make him the face people associated with the
hospital. It was an ambitious plan and she had no time
for indecisiveness or uncertainty.

She would keep her opinions on the medical field to

herself and convince him that it was in his best interest, and the hospital's, to cooperate with her plans. The board expected positive results and she intended to deliver. Doing so was too important to both her career goals and her sanity.

She gripped the business satchel lying on her lap tighter. The merest hope of never again seeing Lou's smug face fueled her determination. Unfortunately, fate had chosen Dr. Maxwell as the key to making that flickering hope her reality.

A young doctor walked past without glancing at Tiffani and sidled up to Dr. Nelson's assistant's desk. With a warm smile, he asked for permission to see Dr. Nelson.

Tiffani surmised the tall, tan man wearing the green scrubs with cheerfully bright headwear over long dark hair bound at the nap of his neck was her soon-to-be PR project, Dr. Maxwell. Despite her distaste for his profession she couldn't deny that he was attractive. In fact, he might be the most interesting man she had ever seen. She couldn't let herself be distracted by that, though, he was still a doctor.

Ten minutes later, Dr. Nelson's assistant caught her attention and said he was ready to see her. Entering the office with confidence, Tiffani saw Dr. Nelson still seated behind his desk and the doctor in scrubs slumped in a chair with his hands in his lap. She could feel defiance radiating from him even though his expression was professionally polite.

Dr. Nelson stood, arms wide and palms up. "Come in, come in, Ms. Romano. I'd like you to meet Dr. Rex Maxwell."

The doctor had the good manners to stand and extend his hand. His long fingers circled hers. The clasp was firm, warm. His dark brown eyes searched hers intently for a moment before he released her hand.

"Please, both of you, sit down," Dr. Nelson said, taking his seat again.

Tiffani took the chair beside the doctor. He glanced at her before turning those sharp eyes on Dr. Nelson, who said, "I've explained the situation to Dr. Maxwell and he's willing to give you his full support."

Dr. Maxwell shifted in his seat. She glanced at him. His attention seemed focused on a small statue on the shelf behind Dr. Nelson's desk. He didn't look pleased.

The older man continued as if he hadn't noticed. "Both of you are professionals. I know you'll handle this project discreetly. With great aplomb. I expect a report in a week that I can give the board." He paused to look at each of them. "I'm here to help and I look forward to this being a meaningful, productive and very successful project. Please, call on me if there are any issues."

Dr. Maxwell stood, passing behind her chair on his way out. He was already in the hallway before Tiffani could gather her purse and bag. She looked at Nelson but he merely watched as she raced after the most important element to her plan. Her timetable required transforming her ideas into reality right away. That meant immediately getting better acquainted with Dr. Maxwell. He, however, was a good way down the long hall and using a stride she found difficult to match.

She called his name but he didn't slow or even look back as he briskly continued. The rapid tap, tap, tap of her heels echoed off the walls so he had to know she was behind him. As he slowed in front of a closed elevator door she finally caught up and grabbed his arm. To her amazement, he looked surprised to see her and glanced at where her hand rested.

Tiffani released him and said breathlessly, "I've been trying to get your attention since we left Dr. Nelson's office."

"I have a patient waiting." He pushed the button for the elevator again. The doors opened.

"We need to talk. I have plans to implement."

He stepped into the elevator, his gaze meeting hers.

She pursed her lips, hitched her bag strap more securely on her shoulder and stepped aboard just as the door was closing.

His eyes widened. "This is a staff-only elevator."

"Then I'll get off when you do. Right now, I am going to talk to you." She was determined to pin him down to a time they could meet. Timing was everything in this campaign.

He gave her a pointed look. "Ms. Romeo, I don't have time to waste right now."

They faced each other like two bulls in a box. She had no intention of letting this man dismiss her. Meeting his obstinate expression with one of her own, she said tightly, "It is Ms. *Romano*. How soon can you meet with me?"

"I don't know how long this surgery will take. You handle things without me."

The elevator stopped. There was a ding before the doors opened. He almost jumped in his haste to get out. Tiffani didn't hesitate to follow. "So I'm to make the decisions and give you the details?"

He kept walking. "Works for me."

She stayed with him, saying in a stern voice, "This project will only be successful if you play a significant part."

They soon faced closed double doors.

Eyes locked on those doors, he removed his badge

and swiped it over an ID pad as he announced, "Look, I have patients to see. I have neither the time nor the interest in being a part of your PR campaign."

The doors opened. He went through.

She did too. "Dr. Maxwell, Dr. Nelson told me you're willing to give this campaign your full support. Did you lie to him or was he lying to me?"

He stopped so suddenly she almost bumped into his backside. "You can't be in here."

"What?" She didn't understand the abrupt change in the conversation.

"This is the surgery suite. Didn't you read any of the signs?" he asked, as if she were a four-year-old.

"Uh, no, I didn't."

"Are you planning to follow me into the OR?"

"No." She certainly had zero interest in doing that. She'd seen enough gore to last her a lifetime, having had to help care for her father. She had started cleaning and bandaging his wounds while she'd been in middle school.

"It was nice to meet you, Ms. Romano," he said stiffly, before he turned and walked away, dismissing her.

Furious, Tiffani backtracked her way to Dr. Nelson's office. The return trip calmed her and she sighed. Somehow, she had to gain Dr. Maxwell's cooperation. Without Dr. Maxwell there was no successful PR crusade, no promotion and no escaping her past.

Rex had been fairly certain when he'd entered Nelson's office that he wasn't going to like whatever the meeting topic was, and then Nelson had caught him off guard with the stupid PR project. Rex had barely been able to conceal his disgust. He hated being forced to be part of another dog-and-pony show at this point in his life, his career. The hospital would survive the recent bad press, just as he had. All that was needed was time. That was what it had taken after the bubble had burst when he'd been a kid. He'd gotten over the lies and what he had believed about his family. He was a better man, a bluntly honest one, thanks to the experience.

No, participating in a cover-up to make everything squeaky clean was something he refused to do. Shouldn't have to. Proving his abilities as a surgeon was unnecessary. He already knew he was good. The people he'd saved before and after Royster were proof enough.

Late that evening, with his patient doing well, he finally got back to his office. The voice mail light was blinking. Ms. Romano's, stating she would like to meet with him first thing in the morning, was the third message. Rex harrumphed. He'd bet she had no idea that his day started at five thirty. She could figure that out on her own. He didn't feel like dealing with her nonsense.

With her dark hair twisted tightly and her expensive-looking navy blue business suit, Ms. Romano struck him as an uptight bit of fluff. Someone trying to project an aura of authority, with her don't-mess-with-me attitude. The only hint that she might have a softer side had been the glimpse of cleavage in the V of her white silk blouse.

Long ago he'd gotten beyond being impressed by what a person wore. Still, something about Ms. Romano's attire made him think she was trying to make a point to the world. He wasn't interested in being a part of her road to redemption or whatever she was after.

His allegiance lay with the free spirits of the world, those willing to live their lives without worrying about public opinion. Ms. Romano's job alone said she cared too much about what people thought. He'd leave making the hospital look good to her and go on about his business.

The next evening it was well past dinnertime when he finally made it back to his office. Intent on grabbing his jacket, finding a hot meal and going home to bed, he opened the door and froze as he reached for his coat. Ms. Romano sat in one of his two visitors' chairs.

She jerked upright in her seat. The file that had been in her hands fell to the floor, scattering papers everywhere.

Had she been asleep? "Ms. Romano?"

"Uh...yeah." She pushed a loose tendril of hair back from her face. "The cleaning person was coming out when I arrived. I told him you were expecting me."

Rex would have to speak to the housekeeping staff about letting people into his office when he wasn't there. Obviously Ms. Romano didn't mind doing whatever it took to get her way. Ignoring her wasn't going to be as easy as he'd thought.

She bent and started gathering her papers. "You didn't return my calls."

Rex went down on his heels to help her. "I've been here since 2:00 a.m."

Lowering her chin, she said, "I thought you were just dodging me."

Guilt pricked him. Ms. Romano said what she thought. She was honest. He respected that. Continuing to pick up the fallen pages, he was adding them to the growing stack in his hand when he glanced down at one of them and saw his name. He looked at her. "Is this your research portfolio on me?"

Her dark green eyes rose to meet his. "You're an important part of my plan. I need to know all I can about you." She took the papers from his hands and stood.

Rex did as well, snapping, "The hospital should be the focus, not me."

"This is about you too. I can drag you in kicking and screaming but you're still going to be a part of the campaign."

He took a deep breath and exhaled through his nose. "And just how do you plan to do that?"

"As I said before, Mr. Nelson assured me you would cooperate with me." Her obstinate expression didn't waver.

Rex detested her threat of blackmail, but he didn't want Dr. Nelson aware of his determination to take as small a role as possible in this PR nonsense. "Look, I've had a long day. I'm tired and hungry. Can't we do this later?"

"No. We've already lost twenty-four hours. We don't have time to waste."

He let out a deep sigh of disgust and sank into his desk chair. "Then let's get on with it. I'm hungry and need some sleep."

She apparently wasn't in the least bit sympathetic that he'd been at the hospital for eighteen hours.

She placed the folder on his desk in front of her, opened it and sorted papers with precision.

Maybe all he'd be required to do was to listen while she talked. He had naught to contribute, except that he wanted nothing to do with this complete waste of his time and the hospital's resources.

"I need to go over a few things with you so I can make calls first thing in the morning. We have such a small window of opportunity we've got to immediately start pitching ideas to the media."

Rex watched her continue to organize her papers. At this rate, it would be a long month.

"I have some very exciting ideas I want to run by you," she said in a swift, cheerful manner.

Rex knew better than to ask but did so anyway. "Such as?"

"I'd like to do an 'in-your-face' campaign. I want to show the hospital trusts you enough to make you their ambassador. Put it right up front. 'Neither I nor the hospital was guilty of malpractice. You can trust us with all your health needs.'" She pointedly looked at him. "If you gain people's trust then the hospital will be trusted too. It all works hand in hand. I have in mind you doing a couple of medical segments on some morning talk shows. Maybe talk about sports health. Hopefully put an article in *Memphis Magazine*. But time might be against us there." She was talking fast while flipping through her portfolio. "A newspaper ad on Sundays might be very effective. People need to get to know the real you."

The PR woman was in her zone. A sour taste formed in his mouth. She seemed to no longer be aware he sat across from her.

Any hope of not being overly involved was waning fast. He had to put the brakes on this madness. A little louder than necessary, he announced, "People who have met me do know the real me. I have nothing to hide or be ashamed of. I'm not about to rub elbows and smile ingratiatingly at the same people who were burning me at the stake a month ago."

She kept her attention on her file, which was now tightly clenched in her fists. "Yes, you will! Not everyone trusts doctors and hospitals. To have any hope of swaying public opinion in your favor, we need to get the media on our side ASAP."

Rex narrowed his eyes and watched her closely. "So, what's in this for you?"

With a startled jerk, she looked directly at him. "What do you mean?"

"I know why I should be so interested in improving the hospital's rep, and even mine, but why're you so enthusiastic about it?"

She studied him for a moment then said with a harsh note in her tone, "Because it's my job."

Had he hit on something? "It seems to me you're going beyond the call of duty to sit in my office, waiting on me for who knows how long, working overtime on just another job."

"If I pull this off, with your help, I have a real chance at a promotion I really want. Need, in fact."

There was her blunt honesty again.

"I see."

"I'm pretty sure you don't but that isn't the issue." She looked away. "I want to have a couple of billboards put up around town. Have people see that the hospital is here for them and that you are part of what makes it… great." She faltered on the last word. As if she weren't sure it was the correct one.

"Me?"

"I want you on the billboard, standing in front of a picture of the hospital. With a healthy, happy patient. You know that kind of thing." She absentmindedly waved one hand in the air.

Rex's insides tightened. His hunger had vanished. This was starting to sound like what his parents had done when he'd been a kid. Make their family look all perfect on the outside. He turned his head to the side and looked down his nose at her. "You want my picture on a billboard?"

"That's right."

He shook his head. "No."

"We need to put you out there in front of the public. Let them know who you really are."

Rex leaned back in his seat and crossed his arms. "I don't think me being on a billboard is going to tell them anything."

Her expression was stony. "Dr. Nelson thought it was a good idea."

She was playing hardball again. Rex felt the walls closing in. He was being left no choice. If he wanted to keep his job, or any chance of becoming department head anytime soon, he would have to go along with this. But he wouldn't make it easy. "I don't have time for these extracurricular activities. My surgical practice and responsibilities to my patients monopolize my time."

"We'll work around your schedule."

His refusal, his objection hadn't even slowed her down.

She studied him a moment. "One more thing. We need to work on your image."

His gut tightened. This was getting worse by the minute. "What's wrong with my image? My appearance is part of my identity."

After looking him over for a moment, she answered in a quiet but steely voice, "You have a bad-boy image. One that has to be softened up a little bit."

"And just how do you plan to do that?"

"A haircut here, some clothes there."

This was going too far. "Not going to happen. I don't do makeovers. You can talk to Nelson all you want but that's stepping over the line."

She slipped the now organized papers into her folder. "After this campaign, you can go back to your slouchy, unkempt look, but you *will* look sharp and reliable for the media. You think about it. From what I understand, this is all sanctioned by the board. I'm not telling you your business but can you really afford to go against them?"

He hated this. Everything about it brought back memories he'd thought he had gotten beyond. "Again, where do I find time for this makeover to happen?"

"Don't you have a day off?" She sounded as if it wasn't a big deal for him to get away.

Yeah, but not one he wanted to spend her way. "Tomorrow, in fact."

"Perfect. I'll make an appointment with my hairdresser for tomorrow afternoon. First we'll do a little shopping. So, I'll be on my way. Goodnight." She stood, put her bag over her shoulder and turned toward the door.

"Hey, wait a minute. You don't need to be going to your car alone at this time of night." Rex picked up his jacket.

She had stopped and was looking back at him. "I'll be fine. I'm in the main parking lot up front."

"I'm still going to walk you out."

She shrugged and walked away. He followed. They said nothing to each other as they went down in the elevator and stepped out into the parking lot. The silence wasn't so much uncomfortable as it was mutual.

"This is it," she said when they reached a white compact car. With a click, she unlocked it with her fob. "Why don't you get in? I'll take you to your car."

Rex wavered a moment, fearing that if he managed to get his long body in he might not be able to get it out. "My bike is in the back. I don't mind walking."

"You ride a motorcycle?" The unusual high note in her voice irritated him.

"Yes. You mean that wasn't in your notes?"

Her perplexed demeanor was almost comical. Had she really thought that everything there was to know about him was in black and white in her folder? "Actually, it wasn't, but it should have been."

He was tired of being under the microscope. First the malpractice suit and now this. He liked his motorcycle. Liked the freedom. The lack of restriction. The fact that he was snubbing people like the ones in his past social circle made it even more fun. "Is me riding a bike a problem?"

"It could be," she said, as if pondering the issue, climbing in and closing her car door, leaving him with the unfortunate feeling he had just become the dog in her dog-and-pony show.

CHAPTER TWO

WHERE IS HE? Tiffani asked herself more than once as she paced in front of the men's store in downtown Memphis. She had texted Rex the address and the time earlier that morning. He'd sent a terse response.

I'll be there when I can.

She hadn't heard another word from him since and his scheduled appointment time with her hairdresser was growing ever closer. Moreover, her father was expecting her later this afternoon. He'd worry if she was late. Rex needed to hurry.

It wouldn't have surprised her, though, if Rex was keeping her waiting on purpose. Wasn't that what doctors did? Made people wait? It proved what she thought about them must be true—little worry for how they affected others—and so Rex not being courteous enough to tell her he'd be late shouldn't have astonished her.

Fuming over her assumption that he'd show up at the time she'd told him, her hopes rose at the roar of a motorcycle. Was that him?

He'd made it clear he didn't like any of her ideas, but she wasn't sure he understood the big picture. He kept insisting he wanted nothing to do with the effort to improve the hospital's reputation. Then he'd flat out balked at her insistence he needed a makeover. Something deep was behind his protests and stubbornness. What had he said about his appearance? He'd said it was part of his identity.

She watched the motorcycle rider pull into a parking spot not far from hers. He wore a plain black T-shirt, worn jeans with a hole in one knee and black ankle-high boots. When he pulled his helmet off, dark hair fell around his broad shoulders. Rex was impressive in a wild sort of way. She almost regretted insisting his hair be cut. Somehow it made him more fascinating. Her opinion, though, didn't matter. What mattered was his image in the eyes of the residents of this city if her plans were to succeed.

Her gaze met his.

"What's wrong?" he asked.

Had she been staring? She went on the defensive. "I expected you here thirty minutes ago. Maybe your patients understand you not showing up on time but I don't."

Climbing off his bike, tucking his helmet under his arm, he stepped into her personal space, claiming all the air around her. She could hardly breathe, let alone hear him quietly inform her, "Something came up at the last minute but I'm here now."

Tiffani took two steps back and inhaled. "You could've at least texted me."

"I didn't have a chance. Sorry. My patient was having difficulty breathing. I didn't have time to message you before I started operating, repairing her lung. Afterward I was too busy rushing here to text you."

She'd firmly been put in her place. Somehow sorry didn't cover it but she said it anyway.

"Now that I'm here, let's get this over with." With a grim look on his face he looked at the storefronts.

"The manager is waiting for us." She led the way to the specialty men's shop.

"I still don't understand why all of this is necessary." He followed close behind her.

Over her shoulder she replied, "That biker gang look might work just fine in your everyday life but in my world a more professional appearance is called for."

"What if I want nothing to do with your world?" Stepping ahead of her, he opened the door.

His manners couldn't be faulted. At least that area needed no work. As she passed him she retorted, "Right now, you have no choice."

He said softly, "We'll see about that."

The middle-aged store manager greeted them and directed them to a row of suits.

"I'd rather not." Rex shook his head. "If I must dress up, I'd prefer jackets and jeans."

"You need a suit. I have a TV interview set up for next week." The opportunity to show Rex as qualified and trustworthy was too good to pass up.

"No suit. It's non-negotiable." The firmness in his tone stated he meant every word.

"You don't make the rules here."

"I do about what I wear," he shot back. "I won't be dressed up and paraded around like a preening bird. Complain to Nelson if you like."

She took a deep but discreet breath, counting to three before she said in her most soothing tone, "We'll try it your way, but I get the final say. If I don't like the look you choose then you may have to try on a suit."

"Won't happen." He turned back to the manager and started pointing at jackets. "I'll try that one, that one and that one." Moving to a wall with cubby holes filled with stacked shirts, he pulled out several. "Here," he said, piling them in her arms. Moving to a rack of pants, he sorted through them until he had chosen a handful. The manager took the pants from Rex, who all but growled, "Where's the dressing room?"

"This way, sir," the older man said, appearing perplexed.

"Just call me Rex."

The man nodded and led the way to the back of the store.

Tiffani followed, feeling a little dazed. Rex had taken over. She needed to regain control but was unsure how to do it.

Rex dropped his helmet on top of the last display table before the dressing stall. Immediately he pulled his shirt over his head.

Tiffani was given a spectacular view of his back muscles shifting under bronzed skin. That expanse of pure masculinity tapered down to a trim waist.

Her step faltered.

Surely it was from the shock of him stripping so freely. Not from the delicious view she'd been given. She should want nothing to do with men, doctors in particular, but she wasn't immune to a good-looking male. Rex Maxwell had a very fine body to go with his handsome face. If he affected her this acutely, surely other women would also be attracted to him. Smiling to herself, she nodded. Tiffani would use his raw virility to her advantage during the campaign.

"Hand me the shirts and pants first. I'll try the jackets on last," he said from behind a wooden door that stopped a couple of feet from the floor. She watched with a skip of a heartbeat as his jeans puddled around his feet.

The manager hurried to give him the pants. Rex opened the door far enough to take them. Seconds later he opened it again and stuck out a hand. "Shirts?"

The manager moved out of Tiffani's way so she could hand him her armload of shirts. She did her best to keep her eyes off the almost naked man before her. When Rex chuckled softly, she instinctively met his gaze. The twinkle in his smoldering eyes made her discomfort intensify. He was playing with her. But she had endured enough cat-and-mouse games for a lifetime.

She quickly turned but not before her downward glance had registered his navy sport briefs barely concealing his manhood. Trying to hide her sexual attraction, she said in as flat a voice as she could muster, "Let me see you when you're dressed."

Minutes later he came out wearing a light blue shirt and navy pants. The manager held up a tan jacket. Rex slipped it on with a grace Tiffani couldn't ignore. He'd been toying with her earlier. Had known he was embarrassing her. Yet here she was, ogling him again. Whatever was going on with her body had to stop. He was a client and one she was determined not to like or trust. All doctors were self-centered and so far Rex Maxwell hadn't proved himself any different.

He put his arms out and slowly turned around. "What do you think? Will I do?"

She studied him intently, hoping to find a flaw. There wasn't one. So she promptly ordered, "Let's see the others."

"No. You can choose what you like out of my selection. I'm done here." He shrugged off the jacket.

She stepped in front of him, ignoring the garment he held out. "You need to try them all on. I want to make sure they create the right image."

He took the stance of a man in a gunfight, letting the jacket sweep the floor when he lowered his arm. His stare was hard. "They're all the same size, just different colors. Mix and match 'em. I've done all the fashion-show stuff I'm going to do. Period."

Everything about him warned she shouldn't push any further. So she looked down at his boots. "Okay. Now for shoes."

Rex lifted a foot, moving it one way then another. "What? You don't think these go with everything?"

Relieved his mood had mellowed, she retorted, "I think traditional footwear would be more appropriate. The boots work for your motorcycle but I don't think they're the best choice for TV interviews or social situations."

"Social situations? What social situations am I going to be in?"

She could feel the appalled aura envelop him.

"The hospital is planning a small cocktail party and dinner for the accreditation committee. It'll be a great opportunity for you to talk to influential members of the community, while impressing the committee. Let them get to know you." She smiled, hoping to encourage him.

His jaw tensed. "I won't be attending. That isn't my thing."

Time to try coaxing. "Sure you will. You'll be the face of the hospital by then. The surgeon everyone wants."

"If that happens it'll be because I'm a great surgeon, which by the way I am, and not because you dressed me up and paraded me around." He headed toward the dressing room.

She called to his back, "It'll be good for you and the hospital."

Rex turned and confronted her. "I have no interest in

being linked to the hospital forever. I've agreed to help because Dr. Nelson strongly encouraged it, but with this I draw the line. I don't do social."

"Your social appearance might mean getting top marks from the accreditation committee. You know they're overly conscious of the malpractice case. We're trying to rebuild some public goodwill as well." She couldn't back down on this. It was the cornerstone of her plan.

"Do you really believe changing my wardrobe and showing me off to people who value appearance over substance is going to make that much difference?" There was a snide tone to his words.

She fervently hoped so. This project was her ticket out of town and away from Lou. "I make a living seeing that it does."

He leaned close and looked her directly in the eyes. "Don't you think honest people see beyond all your publicity? I know I'm more interested when I get to know the real person, not the one putting on shiny shoes and a smile, trying to be someone they're not."

Stepping closer and lowering her voice, she hissed, "You need the shiny shoes and smile so people will want to take the time to get to know you. Do you think black T-shirts, holey jeans and biking boots exude medical professionalism? It's important the community has confidence in you. Believes they'll get the quality of care they expect."

Surprise and then something she wasn't sure she could name flickered in the depths of his eyes. He said, just as quietly, "Their quality of care hasn't changed. Mine or the hospital's. Just because a family wouldn't accept I couldn't save their father's life doesn't mean my skills are any less competent or professional than they were before the malpractice suit."

Tiffani flinched. This conversation was treading too close to the personal. She had promised herself that she would see this job through without letting what had happened to her father intrude. The only way to do that was to go on the defensive. "Just what is your issue? After all, you're getting a new wardrobe at the hospital's expense and you're an intelligent man, so you know how important what I'm trying to achieve is. Why all the pushback?"

"Like I can't afford my own shoes and my own clothes," he spat. "Clothes I have no interest in wearing."

"I still don't understand the problem. It looks to me like you'd want to help." Why couldn't he just not fight her on this?

"The problem is, I'm not going to pretend to be somebody else." He dropped the jacket on a stack of causal shirts and gestured toward the clothes she and the manager still held. "I'm a skilled surgeon, regardless of what I wear. I don't care who is or isn't impressed by my appearance."

She believed him. He was his own man and he was brutally honest. Unlike virtually all the people around her. She had to admire that about him.

After Lou's lies she appreciated the honesty. She was glad that, with Rex, she was certain she wouldn't misread his feelings. He would make them clear. In an odd way, it was refreshing.

But his stubborn insistence that his appearance ought not matter to people would be the ruin of her campaign if she couldn't make him see reality. With his biker appearance came negative connotations, no matter what type of person he really was. With secret desperation she coolly asked, "If you won't present the image the public has of a gifted, confident, trustworthy surgeon, just how do you expect to convince them you *really are* gifted, confident or trustworthy?"

He gave her a seething glare. "And you think this dog-and-pony show you have planned will do that?"

Tiffani raised her chin and shrugged with all the indifference she could muster, sensing victory. "It's done all the time."

Rex seemed at a loss for words. Abruptly she was aware of the manager's intense interest in their disagreement. What was going on between her and Rex wasn't good PR. Taking a cleansing breath, she tried to appease Rex into compromising. "It's just for a little while. I'll try to make it as easy as possible."

"I don't care how long it is. I won't pretend to be somebody I'm not. Ever again."

Again? So there *was* something in his past driving his illogical refusal to admit she was right. "Then I'll make an effort not to ask you to. Agreed?"

Juggling her armload of clothes, she extended her hand. He looked at it for a moment then took it. Inexplicably, a shiver went up her spine at his touch. She pulled her hand free.

"Agreed." His voice was calm and sincere.

She smiled. He was going to try to meet her halfway. Tiffani made her tone appeasing. "Now, I know you don't want to hear this but it's time we get to your hair appointment."

His lips puckered and jaw tightened. Was another fight coming?

To her surprise, he finger-combed his hair back from his face and said, "Okay. But only because I'm due for a trim." He picked up the jacket and returned to the dressing room.

Relief washed through her. The tightness between her shoulder blades eased. A least he was going to go along with her plans regarding his hair. Trim? She needed him to have more than that. She'd let Estell handle making that happen.

While waiting for Rex, she made arrangements with the manager to pick up the purchases later. As they left the store she announced, "The shop isn't far from here. Should we walk?"

"Do you think biker boots will be okay for that?" he asked with a smug smile, tucking his helmet under his arm.

She glared. "Yes, but I don't think they're suitable for every occasion. The hairdresser is this way."

Rex, although familiar with this area of Memphis, had spent little time there. As he examined the small businesses with cute storefronts he noted many of the other people on the street were fashionably dressed and clearly wealthy. It all reminded him too much of his childhood where nothing had mattered but where you shopped and what brand you could afford.

The boutiques lining the street looked just like the ones his mother used to frequent. But then the terrible truth had come out.

At least now he didn't care what he wore as long as it was comfortable. He'd spent half his life going in one direction and the other half hell-bent on another. No way was he returning to the old lifestyle his parents had pretended they could afford. He had no reason to prove himself to anyone through his appearance, zero interest in outside trappings. He knew with bone-deep certainty who he was and for the rest of his life there would be no more pretentious facades.

Still, damn it, he had agreed to help with Tiffani's PR nonsense. His plans for his future actually rested on it to a certain degree. If a few wardrobe changes and a haircut could gain him what he wanted, then was it such a big deal?

Yes! It was a very big deal. He had set his boundaries all those years ago for very real, vital reasons and had successfully, happily lived by them ever since. He had no intention of ignoring them now. Not for Tiffani. Not for anyone. Nor for any reason, regardless of its appeal.

But walking down the street on a sunny day with a pretty woman beside him somehow made all the ridiculousness of this makeover less disturbing to his peace of mind. He glanced at Tiffani. She still wore her hair up but not quite as tightly as before. Her attire was more casual as well. A simple purple knit shirt, black pants and flat shoes unleashed her subtle sex appeal, which floated around her like honeyed perfume.

He didn't care for her high-handed ways and wasn't even sure he liked her, but it was a nice change to argue with someone who gave as good as she got. Few people in his life dared to talk back to him. He'd found his disagreements with Tiffani invigorating, something he'd experienced rarely with a woman. The women he tended to date were only interested in a good time or were in awe of what he did for a living. There was no challenge. Tiffani was definitely that. She wasn't impressed by his looks and certainly not by his position.

They stopped in front of a store with flowers painted on the windows and a sign above the door that read Cute Cuts. He felt his eyes involuntarily roll in disbelief. Maybe he should have ridden his bike and parked it out front. Letting out a low groan, he informed her, "I'm going to have to give up my man card if I go in here."

"It won't be all that bad. I promise." A bell tinkled as she pushed the door open. "Come on in, be brave."

Rex didn't miss the humor in her voice. "It's not courage I lack but desire."

A woman with short, spiked green hair tipped in red looked away from the client she was working on and said to Tiffani, "Hey, girl, I'm almost done here. I'll be right with you."

Rex gave Tiffani a speculative look. She shrugged in response. What had he gotten himself into? This place looked nothing like his barbershop. Instead of a group of balding men sitting in the back, talking and playing checkers, there was a rock station blaring on the sound system and an over-the-head hair dryer going.

The only place to sit in the tiny place was a wicker settee with floral printed cushions.

Tiffani settled on it. Unsure if the wicker was strong enough to hold them both or if he wanted to sit so close to her, he chose to stand.

"She'll be done in a sec, I'm sure," Tiffani offered. "Estell's the best in town."

Rex nodded, but really didn't care. He just hoped one of his male colleagues didn't see him leave the place. The jokes would never end. Had Tiffani been polite enough to ask, he'd have preferred to have gone to his regular guy. Rex's urge to leave grew. Too much of his day off had already been wasted.

Soon the customer was gushing over her new look and leaving.

"I'm ready," Estell called.

He approached her with a tentative smile.

"Well, hello, handsome. What can I do for you today?" Estell purred, low and throaty.

Rex chuckled, liking the "out there" woman. It surprised him that Tiffani used her as her hairdresser. Estell seemed too eccentric to appeal. Tiffani acted so closed off and all business. Was there another side of her he'd not seen?

While he pondered her, Tiffani said, "Estell, I was thinking cut it above the ears. A little longer on the top—"

"I can handle this," Rex stated in his "surgeon-in-OR" voice that tolerated no argument. "Why don't you go get us some drinks? We're good, aren't we, Estell?"

Grinning, she nodded. "Yeah, Tiffani, we're good."

"I need him to look professional, clean cut." Tiffani looked concerned, almost as if she was unsure they could be trusted to be left alone.

"Will do," Estell said, and returned to her cutting chair.

Rex pulled from his pocket a few bills and handed them to Tiffani. "I'd like a soda. Get yourself one too. How about you, Estell?"

She grinned. "Sure."

"Make that three," he added.

Tiffani stood immobile, looking rather bewildered.

He winked. "Take your time. Estell and I might be busy a while."

Estell snickered. Tiffani's eyes narrowed. She muttered as she left, "I don't know about this."

Estell had just finished with his hair when Tiffani returned. With the turn of the chair he faced her as she crossed the threshold. She stopped short, gaping. Heat simmered through Rex. He knew well the pleasure of a woman's admiration, but he'd never experienced one devouring him with her eyes. He shifted uncomfortably as hot blood-hardened parts made themselves known.

"So, what do you think?" Estell asked from behind him.

Tiffani blinked, appearing to struggle back to the here and now. "Uh, I wanted it…much shorter."

"I didn't," Rex announced, his gaze still locked with hers as he slipped out of the chair.

A long second later she fluttered her eyelids. "Okay."

He took the plastic bag she held. Checking its contents, he pulled out a soda and tossed it to Estell, who caught it neatly. He handed Tiffani one before withdrawing and opening his.

As if coming out of a daze, Tiffani straightened her back and glared at him. "You had me go buy these to get rid of me."

Shrugging his shoulders Rex set his drink down and pulled his wallet out. He paid Estell, giving her a generous tip along with a kiss on her cheek. With a wink, he said in a confidential tone Tiffani could hear, "You know what's said at the beauty parlor stays at the beauty parlor."

Tiffani snorted behind him.

Estell giggled and replied, grinning, "I had fun too. Nice to meet you, Rex."

"I'll wait for you outside," he told Tiffani as he stepped around her.

Tiffani wasn't sure what had just happened. She rarely ogled men, especially not one who was her client. Or one she considered egotistically self-absorbed, not to mention argumentative. Yet she'd been literally unable to take her eyes off Rex when she'd reentered the beauty shop. He was gorgeous. All virile male at ease in a den of feminine décor. Confidence oozed from him. To make matters worse, like an idiot she hadn't been able to put two words together.

Estell had taken a few inches off his hair and tamed it around his face so that it complemented his rugged features. It looked healthy and free, just like he was. Tiffani had never been a big fan of men with long hair, but Rex was a definite exception. Her first instinct had been to touch it, to caress his scalp and let the strands flow through her fingers. A totally inappropriate impulse for a professional such as herself.

The worst thing about those first agonizing moments had been his obvious relish of the effect he was having on her. Enjoying it. She mustn't allow that to happen again. She had to remain in control of the situation, and herself, at all times around him. That was the plan.

"Honey." Estell shook her head as if thinking, *Yum, yum, yum.* "You've got a real man on your hands. I hope you can handle him."

"He's not my man. We're business associates." Tiffani almost snapped, wincing at the edge of defiance she heard in her voice. She wasn't interested in a relationship. And certainly not with someone like Rex Maxwell. Her breakup with Lou had guaranteed she'd think long and hard about allowing herself to become intimately involved with another man. Besides which she didn't need one. Heartache was all the opposite sex offered.

"Well, if it was me, I'd sure figure out a way to make him mine," Estell said as she opened her drink.

Rex was standing by a light pole when Tiffani joined him outside. Virtually every female walking by gave him a second look. Obviously, Tiffani's reaction to the new Rex wasn't unique. His image on the billboards would certainly captivate most women. An ambassador

who was a handsome surgeon with sex appeal practically assured a positive rise in the hospital's reputation.
She was tickled. The campaign was fast becoming far
more effective than she'd first hoped. The only thing that
might ruin it was Rex inexplicably fighting her every
step of the way.

He shifted impatiently from one foot to another. "Is
there a café or something around here?"

"Yes, there's one just around the corner." She pointed
up the sidewalk.

"Would you like to join me?" Rex asked.

"I guess so." Tiffani didn't make a habit of socializ-
ing with clients but she couldn't think of a good excuse
not to. She was hungry and had time for a quick meal
before she had to leave to see her father. Plus, she had
one more thing she needed to discuss with Rex. He'd
be more receptive to it if he heard her proposal with a
full stomach.

He fell into step beside her. "The women I dine with
usually sound more eager to share my company."

"This isn't a date," Tiffani retorted, a little more
stiffly than intended. "And I only have time for something quick." She felt his dark eyes on her.

"You have a problem with dating?"

"No," she said slowly. "And you are my client."

He stopped. She did too and looked back at him.
People walked around them. He said, as if choosing
his words carefully, "And if I wasn't your client? How
would you feel?"

"I don't do business and pleasure in the same place."
She'd more than learned her lesson there.

"That was a loaded statement. Care to elaborate?"

"I do not. It's too long and too ugly a story." And too
humiliating to repeat. Especially to a man who probably

never had a female turn him down. "And it has nothing to do with us. The PR campaign, I mean."

"They say talking it out with someone makes it better." He continued along the sidewalk.

She couldn't believe his arrogance. Did he really think confiding in him was going to make anything better? He was a doctor. One she didn't trust. And definitely not a confidant she'd trust her embarrassment to.

"I know you're very sure of your bedside manner but do you really believe I'd spill my life story to you?"

"Not really. But it sounds like it might be interesting."

She looked at her reflection in the glass front of the restaurant. "You should save your charm for the TV interviews."

"Now you're trying to ruin my meal." He opened the door to the small sixties retro café.

They were shown to a table for two in the middle of the dining room and handed menus. After studying the menu, Rex asked, "Anything you can recommend?"

"I've only been here a couple of times. The pork chop and potatoes or the spaghetti is good."

He nodded sagely. The waitress took their drink orders on her way to another table. After a moment he questioned, "Have you decided?"

In principle, sharing social time with a client wasn't a good idea, but the raw truth was that being seen with a good-looking man gave a much-needed boost to Tiffani's damaged ego. Being told you're not wanted by someone she'd thought had loved her had been devastating. After that catastrophe, having any male attention was like a much-needed salve.

Against her better judgment, her mind started to chew over her past love life. Learning Lou didn't return her love had nearly destroyed her. To make matters worse, he'd made a show of announcing to their coworkers that he wanted nothing more to do with her. Had arrogantly declared he was now available during an office meeting. Tiffani had wanted to melt under the table. She'd never been more mortified. In her despair, she'd vowed never again to share herself completely with a man. All the males in her life had always wanted more from her than they had ever been willing to give in return.

The waitress returned with their drinks and took their orders. Tiffani settled on a salad and Rex asked for a pasta dish. With that done, Tiffani said, "I wanted to let you know that I have a photographer coming tomorrow to take pictures of you."

"I have surgeries planned."

"I know. I got your schedule from Dr. Nelson. We'll work around it. The photographer will be at the hospital to take pictures so he can shoot you between your cases."

Rex thumped his fork on the table. "You have to be kidding."

The noise accompanying his disbelieving tone startled her. If she showed weakness now, she feared all would be lost. "Dr. Nelson said we could use a conference room to take formal portrait shots of you."

"You've got it all worked out, haven't you?"

She could tell by the way he clenched his jaw that he was holding back what he would like to say. "It's my job."

"I don't think much of it." His words were heavy with contempt.

She looked him straight in the eyes. "The feeling is mutual."

"How's that?" He looked confused.

"It doesn't matter. We don't have to like each other, or

each other's professions. We just have to work together long enough to repair the hospital's public reputation."

Crossing his arms on the table, Rex leaned toward her. "You expect me to accept that cryptic explanation?"

"You don't get a choice." She took a swallow of her drink and let the ensuing silence between them speak for itself. Thankfully the waitress brought their food in short order. They said little as they ate.

"Someone, help!" cried a woman on the other side of the room. "She's choking."

Tiffani's eyes jerked in the direction of the desperate plea. Even as she did so, Rex shoved his chair back and hurried to the distressed woman, who was beating a child's back, dodging tables as he went. Tiffani followed.

"I'm a doctor. Let me have her," Rex commanded with unquestionable authority.

The woman stopped her movement in midair and handed the gasping child to him.

Rex took the girl's arm and turned her round, pressing her back against his chest. He wrapped his arms around her, clasping his fists together and positioning them under her ribs before giving her a tight squeeze.

Nothing happened. The girl's lips were turning bluer.

Rex pulled the girl tight again and landed an audible blow to her abdomen. Something popped from her mouth. The child gasped, taking deep breaths. The mother descended on her, crying and pulling her from Rex's hold into a tight hug.

Clutching her daughter, she raised a tear-streaked face to Rex. "Thank you, thank you, thank you."

His smile was one of relief. "You're welcome. What's your name?" he asked the girl.

"Lucy."

"Lucy, I'm Dr. Rex. Will you let me give you a little check just to make sure everything's all right?"

The elementary-school-aged girl gave her mom a questioning look. The mother nodded, her sobs subsiding.

"Why don't you have a seat right here?" Rex asked, pulling out a chair.

Tiffani couldn't deny he was good. She shouldn't have been surprised. After all he was a charmer. It occurred to her that this was the type of stuff she couldn't manufacture with billboards and TV interviews.

"I'm going to sit right here." Rex pulled up a chair in front of the girl, ignoring the other patrons crowding around them. "Why don't you open your mouth and let me have a look?"

The girl did as he requested.

He unclipped his keys from the belt loop of his jeans. There was a small penlight on the ring. Turning it on, he examined the girl's throat. "Looks good in there. I'm going to check your neck. Tell me if it hurts."

The girl nodded.

"That was pretty scary, wasn't it?" Rex said to the child as his fingers worked over the outside of her neck.

This was PR that Tiffani couldn't pass up. She had been terrified for the child but now that the drama was over she had to think about her job. This was perfect material. Dr. Rex, The Respectable Good Samaritan. She hurried back to their table and pulled her phone from her purse. Seconds later she was taking pictures of Rex and the girl. Maybe some of the others had gotten video of him saving her.

He glanced up at her, his eyes narrowed, before his attention went back to the girl.

Tiffani continued taking pictures.

"Take a deep breath for me," Rex said to Lucy. She inhaled and exhaled. "I think you're going to be just fine," he pronounced, and stood.

The mother hugged him. "Oh, thank you. Thank you so much. I don't know how to thank you."

"Just make sure she takes small bites. And pass up on the hotdogs when you can." He smiled at Lucy. "I'm glad you're all right."

Tiffani had believed all her life that doctors were only interested in themselves and how much money they could milk from someone in pain. Yet Rex Maxwell had just proved he was a doctor with a tender side and wasn't concerned about making money in a medical emergency. Her realization somehow made her feel unsure about a lot of things. Had doctors *really* been at the root of her family issues? Or could it have been something else? Thrusting the uneasy feeling aside, she forced herself to center on what really mattered here. She had some perfect material she could work with to pull off this job, get the promotion and finally escape Lou's ever-hovering presence in her life.

As they returned to their table Rex said, "Are you done with your meal?"

"Yeah."

"Then I'll pay." He picked his helmet up off a nearby chair and walked to the cash register.

She called after him, "While you do that I'm going to see if anyone got video of what happened."

He stiffened and said emphatically, "Please, don't." His response shocked her to the point of not arguing.

When they stepped out onto the sidewalk he glared at her. "What was that about?"

"That was good social media material. Stuff I couldn't

have planned." She couldn't keep her bubbling excitement to herself.

His face twisted in anger. "I didn't help that child to further your pointless campaign."

"I know that. But that was still great PR. I didn't start taking pictures until the girl was okay." She really hated to pass up this opportunity. "Oh, man, I need to have the mother sign an agreement to let me use Lucy's picture." Tiffani swiftly spun about, intending to go back inside.

He grabbed her phone as she turned.

"Hey, what're you doing?" To her horror she saw he was deleting the pictures.

"What happened in there is off the table."

Tiffani stared in frustration. "I have a job to do. The girl is fine. The public would love seeing you in action."

"Not going to happen. I didn't help the girl so you'd have something to put on social media," Rex spat out. Dropping her phone into her hand, he walked away.

By the time she reached her car, he was roaring away.

CHAPTER THREE

TIFFANI WAS STILL feeling the sting of Rex's reaction to her wanting to use the café emergency when she entered the assisted living home where her father lived. Rex's reaction had been so over the top. The girl was fine. The people in the café had seen him as a hero. They'd even applauded. She had too. So why couldn't she use it to their mutual advantage? He was the only one who seemed to have a problem with it.

The least he could do was understand she had a job to do. An important one. Maybe he didn't like the idea that he must be involved in the campaign but he had grudgingly agreed to help. Now he at least had some marginally professional-looking clothes and a hairstyle that both showed the real him yet made him look like a qualified surgeon. However, he'd skillfully manipulated those decisions to his advantage. Fighting with him at every turn was getting old. She sighed. It was like her entire life was built on difficult men. Her father, her ex and now Rex Maxwell.

Entering the extensive one-floor brick building, she walked down the wide hallway. Her father's room was close to the back. She wasn't sure if it had been his or the staff's choice to place him there. He could be difficult, but she loved him. She was old enough to remember well when he'd been in the car accident. Her mother had cried for days, driving them back and forth to the hospital to visit him. Her brother and sister, being younger than she, hadn't understood the tragedy as she did. It had been a long time before her father had come home. While he'd been gone, all kinds of people had come and gone at their house. First it had been friends, then workers, who'd made the doors bigger, rebuilt the bathroom and replaced the front stairs with a ramp.

Nothing had been the same again. Her father hadn't been home long before her mother had taken a job to help support them. That had left Tiffani alone to care for her father and her siblings. She'd learned to change her father's bandages, give him his medicines and assist him in any way he'd needed. He'd depended on her and she had been there for him.

Despite the loss of his legs he'd remained the commanding force in the family. Being with him, she'd heard daily how the doctors had taken his legs rather than save them. Had ruined his life. She had been taught to mistrust and second-guess anyone even remotely connected to the medical field. He was her father and she'd believed him without question.

She hadn't recognized it at the time but her father had begun growing more demanding and miserable. He drank regularly. Years had gone by before she'd discovered he'd taken too much of his prescription pain medicine too soon. He had been good with computers and electronics before the accident, but had made little effort to hold down a job afterward and had refused any vocational training. Their home life had deteriorated to the point that her mom had announced she was moving out, taking Tiffani's sister and brother with her.

Devastated, Tiffani had cried but couldn't go with

them and leave her father alone. He'd needed her. Who would take care of him?

It had taken work on her part when she had grown up, but she'd continued to visit him. She was the only one of her siblings who did and she saw him regularly. She even helped pay the difference between what it cost to live in the home and what he could afford.

Reaching the last room at the end of the hall, she knocked lightly on the door.

"Come in," came a gruff response.

To her amazement, her father sat in his wheelchair instead of being in bed. On more than one occasion she'd begged him to try the chair. Sadly, he had never made any real effort to use his prosthetic legs. His statement had always been, "If those damn doctors hadn't taken my legs, I wouldn't need those."

"Hello, Daddy." She pushed the door open. "How're you doing today? It's nice to see you out of bed."

"Hey, baby girl. Where have you been? I expected you thirty minutes ago."

As usual her father wasn't pleased she was there but was equally concerned about her being late.

"I was busy. I have a new client and a new campaign I'm working on." She hoped he wouldn't ask about her job because she didn't want to reveal her new PR project was a hospital and, worse, one of its doctors.

"I've been waiting for you to come so you can change the bandage on my hand."

He lifted it so she could see. There was white gauze wrapped around it, with tape holding it in place.

She looked at it with concern. "What happened?"

"I've been trying to use this wheelchair, like you wanted. Because of you, I have blisters," he accused.

As if she were the cause of the pain. Nothing was ever his fault.

But at least he was trying. "You know there're people here who can change a bandage for you."

"They don't do it right," he growled.

He'd become so dependent on her in those early days that he still demanded her care whenever he could get it. It wasn't unusual to have him call at any time of the day or night, begging her to come and do something for him. "Well, let me see what I can do."

"Baby girl. You're the only one that cares about me." His voice softened.

Tiffani sighed and kissed him on the forehead. "I love you, Dad." She gathered the supplies she needed from a drawer nearby, pulled a chair close to him and went to work. From years of practice she efficiently wrapped his hand. Seconds later she secured the bandage. "There you go. All done."

Her father raised his hand and waved it around. "It'll do."

That was all the praise she would get.

"You are having dinner with me," he said, wheeling backward one roll.

It was a demand, not a question.

In her most apologetic tone she informed him, "I've already had an early dinner so I'm not staying tonight."

"Why did you do that? You knew I'd want you to stay." The whiny tone had returned.

"I was with a client. We needed to talk over some things." This was a subject she did not need to go into detail on.

Yet he was watching her closely. "Like what?"

It was odd timing, but this was the most interest he'd ever shown in what she did for a living. Mostly she told him about what she was doing to distract him from complaining about something. Reluctantly she answered, "About what I needed him to do."

"Him? You're not back with that jerk you were seeing, are you?"

Her father had at least been concerned and supportive when she had told him about what Lou had done. For once the topic of conversation hadn't been her father. So why the interest this time? "I said he's my client."

"I hear something in your voice. What're you not telling me?" He wheeled closer, squinting at her suspiciously.

Her father had always been good at reading people. Even when he was drinking heavily he could catch a lie when she or one of her siblings told it.

"Nothing really." She put the bandaging supplies back in the drawer.

"Then why're you avoiding the question?"

She turned and looked directly at him. "Because I'm doing an image campaign for Metro Hospital."

Tiffani watched the shock, disbelief and then anger flow across his face. He flushed red. His hands went to the arms of the chair as if he were going to lift himself up. He barked, "You are what? That's where they took my legs. How could you do that to me?"

"Daddy, I'm not doing anything to you. All I'm doing is my job."

"But you're helping the hospital look all wonderful. Covering up what they really do to people there," he snarled.

"When your boss tells you to do something, you do it." She needed to calm him down or someone would come and check on them. She didn't want him to be thrown out of the center.

His voice rose with each word. "But you know what doctors do. You know how they treated me. You're helping the enemy."

Tiffani reached out to him. "I'm sorry, Daddy. I knew you wouldn't be happy but this campaign is important to my career."

He rolled away from her as much as the tiny space would allow. "I bet you're having to make doctors look and sound good. You know you can't believe what they say."

"I'm working with just one."

"Do I know him?" He gave her a pointed look.

It had been so long since her father's accident that most of the doctors he was familiar with were probably retired so she felt comfortable saying, "Dr. Rex Maxwell."

Her father pursed his mouth in thought before he blurted out, "Isn't that the name of the doctor involved in the malpractice suit that was all over the nightly news?"

Great, her father had been watching the news. She didn't look at him. "Yes. That's him."

"How could you, Tiffani? After what they did to me. My legs, my life." He waved his arms around, trying to express his furious frustration with her.

There was a knock on the door and one of the staff members stuck his head into the room. "Is everything all right down here?"

"Nothing's wrong except my daughter is a traitor," her father snapped.

The next day around mid-morning, having finished a case, Rex checked his phone messages. As he'd expected, there was a text from Tiffani, notifying him that she and the photographer were in the hospital. The text ended with her requesting he call the moment he was available. What if he ignored her? No. Tiffani would track him down. He wouldn't put it past her to show up in surgery. She'd not slowed down the last time she'd been after him.

The episode in the café the day before had not improved his opinion of her. The very idea of using pictures of that child's medical emergency to further Tiffani's agenda left him with a nasty taste in his mouth. He hadn't helped Lucy because it was a good PR move. He'd done what any dedicated doctor would do. His job was to save lives. Tiffani's opportunistic attitude appalled him.

Her comment about not caring for his profession struck him as odd. What did she have against doctors?

And still all this PR stuff painfully reminded him too much of his childhood. Dressing things up so they looked perfect and idealistic violated the promises he had made to himself. Straightforward honesty at all times was his motto. Yet here he was in a situation he wasn't completely comfortable with. The hospital provided exceptional care and he was who he was, an experienced physician. Neither of them needed some PR campaign to prove their worth. Still, he had agreed to participate in Tiffani's program.

Finally he texted back.

OK.

She replied.

We are in the conference room of the administrative suite.

Rex groaned and responded.

Only have thirty minutes till next case.

As he entered the conference room Tiffani made a beeline toward him. Today she wore pants emphasizing her curves and a flowing, ultra-feminine blousy shirt. To his disappointment, her hair was still worn up, this time tightly twisted behind her head. They might not agree ideologically but he had to admit he was intensely attracted to her and sought to know more about her. If nothing else, he wanted to see what she looked like with her hair down.

The meeting room had been transformed into a photography studio. The large table and chairs had been pushed against the walls. In their places stood a camera on a tripod, lights, a large backdrop that depicted the front of the hospital and a few other props. Besides Tiffani there was a man with a scruffy beard, wearing a vest, and two other people working at positioning props. Rex assumed they were the photographer's assistants.

"This is a bigger production than I anticipated," Rex murmured when Tiffani was at his side.

"We want to get pictures conveying confidence and trust," Tiffani informed him with an excited note in her voice.

The bearded man in the vest came over.

Tiffani took his arm, pulling him closer. "Dr. Maxwell, I'd like you to meet Luke Johnson, the photographer."

Rex offered his hand. "Make it Rex."

Luke nodded. "Nice to meet you. I'd like to get some shots of you dressed as you are before you change."

Rex looked through narrowed eyes at Tiffani. "Change?"

"Into one of the outfits we bought yesterday." Her expression was unyielding.

He did not have time for all this nonsense, but he'd given Nelson his word. The board would look dimly on it if he didn't cooperate as requested.

"Why don't you stand right here?" Luke suggested, indicating a spot in front of the backdrop.

"This is turning into more hoopla than I agreed to," Rex muttered, as he made his way to where Luke directed.

"I can assure you it's important," Tiffani replied.

Over the next few minutes Rex turned this way and that as instructed. Held his hands to his sides, crossed them over his chest and put them behind his back, all while smiling or not. Tiffani made comments here and there to Luke, occasionally placing her hand on his shoulder or looking into the camera before she gave Rex instructions to position himself a certain way.

Tiffani's obvious closeness to Luke deepened Rex's displeasure. Just how well *did* they know each other? Luke was a business associate, just like him, yet she paid him attention. She made it clear Rex was off limits. More perplexing and annoying was why he would care? He wasn't even sure he liked her.

It didn't take long until he'd had enough. Enough of having his picture taken. Enough of watching Tiffani so close to another man. Luke finally looked up from the camera said, "That was great. Now we're ready for the street clothes."

Perfect. There would be more of the same. Them using him as a mannequin while they huddled together and whispered.

Tiffani pointed to a screen in the back corner of the room. "You can change there."

"I don't have any more time for this. I'm expected in

surgery." Rex didn't even try to keep the irritation out of his voice.

Tiffani glanced at the clock on the wall. "It won't take long. According to the schedule Dr. Nelson provided, you have another twenty minutes."

Rex glared at her. "You should already have what you need."

"I need you in street clothes as well. It's better to do all the pictures at once than to have Luke come back later. When you're ready, we are. The clothes are behind the screen."

She was relentless. Like he cared if Luke was inconvenienced. It didn't matter to her that she was inconveniencing his surgical patients, let alone what he thought or wanted. Her job took precedence. Like yesterday with the choking girl.

More than that, he was unable to intimidate Tiffani. He wasn't used to that. His word was usually law. He wanted to assert his dominance over the irritating woman. At the moment that woman's and Luke's heads were almost touching as they studied the just-taken photos. Disgusted, Rex headed for the changing screen. The sooner he changed the sooner he would be done here.

He donned a sky blue shirt and khaki pants. To his great relief, there was no tie. There was a brown belt on a hanger, though. When he stepped from behind the screen Tiffani studied him before nodding, apparently satisfied.

"If you'll stand in front of the backdrop again," Luke said, looking through his camera on the tripod.

Rex took his spot once more. Luke clicked the button on the camera rapidly before asking Rex to turn another way. This entire ordeal was becoming more exasperating and frustrating by the minute. He was quickly reaching his limit on this silliness. Even so, he managed to give a pleasant smile on request.

When Luke stopped taking pictures and straightened, Rex's hopes rose. Maybe they were done with him. But a glance at Tiffani dashed his hopes. Her head was tilted and mouth drawn up in thought.

"Something's missing." A bright smile lit her face seconds later. "I know what it is. Anna," she said to one of Luke's assistants, "can you bring me that stethoscope?"

The girl picked it up from a chair and rushed to hand it to Tiffani.

Rex watched Tiffani approach. She was all business, viewing him as a figure she could manipulate this way and that. She didn't care about him. To her he was just the model for her damn PR crusade. For some reason that pricked his male pride. He didn't consider himself a vain man or expect every woman to find him appealing but he didn't appreciate Tiffani treating him as an object. The need to rattle her grew.

Reaching him, Tiffani held the stethoscope in both hands and raised it over his head. He didn't offer her help by bending so she could put it around his neck. She went up on her toes, causing her breasts to press against his chest. He burned where she made contact. Without any apparent reaction on her part, she slipped the tubing around his neck.

Watching her concentrated expression closely, he said soft enough that only she could hear, "My heart rate's up. How about yours?"

Her eyes widened and fixed on him. She stumbled. Rex put steadying hands on her waist. Her fingers gripped his shoulders. Hot seconds of awareness raced between them before Tiffani blinked and pushed away. His dented ego was bolstered by the red tint on her cheeks.

She kept backing away until Luke snapped, "Hey! Watch the camera."

Tiffani jerked around and sidestepped the equipment before going to the photographer's side. He immediately started taking pictures once more.

A minute later she said, "Anna, would you adjust the stethoscope so it doesn't hang quite so evenly? Pull it down a little on the right side."

Rex challenged Tiffani with a silent look, smug with the knowledge she was afraid to do it herself. He'd gotten to her. He smiled, emphasizing his unspoken invitation.

Tiffani averted her gaze.

Once Anna was out of the way, Luke resumed rapidly clicking, enthusiastically declaring, "That's it. The one we want."

Soon Tiffani announced, "That's all we have time for."

"I think we got what you wanted in that last batch, Tiffani." Luke started showing her the images.

Rex swiftly ducked behind the screen and dressed again. He left the "costume" piled beneath where he'd originally found it hanging. Tiffani didn't say anything as he left, but that was all right. He smiled as he strode down the hall. There was no doubt in his mind that she'd remember this photo shoot for a very long time.

CHAPTER FOUR

Two DAYS HAD slipped by since Tiffani had last seen Rex. During that time she'd relived that instant between them at the photo shoot, when his breath had warmed against her skin. He'd had her so aware of the sexual tension between them she'd almost knocked over an expensive camera, trying to escape.

The man was outrageous. She must not let him get past her self-control. This campaign was too important. Rex was attractive but she could not afford to react to him like that. Nothing but pain followed that kind of arousing interest anyway. He was merely toying with her for his own amusement. Just as Lou had.

Yet in those few seconds she'd felt outrageously alive. Once again she had to admit that having a handsome man notice her bandaged her secret, still-raw wound.

Even with the heated thoughts running laps in her mind over the last few days, she'd managed to accomplish a great deal of work. So far, her plan was coming together nicely, in spite of Rex. Luke had promised to get pictures to her as soon as possible. The billboard company had three available and by the beginning of next week Rex would be on them, larger than life in front of a gorgeous shot of the hospital. She had also booked him on two morning shows. Now all she needed to do was continue to generate positive press and social media action, some of which would happen this weekend.

She sent Rex a text.

Can you meet me at nine in the morning at the hospital? I've arranged for us to visit a local clinic for a photo op.

Half an hour later her phone buzzed, notifying her of his answer.

Yes, but I pick the clinic.

What clinic? I need to let the photographer know.

Rex wrote back.

No cameras.

She didn't even try to change his mind. Any pictures she got she'd have to take on her phone. They would look less staged anyway. Perfect for what she had in mind.

The next morning, Tiffani arrived at the hospital at nine. As she walked across the parking lot toward the main entrance, a horn honked. An old orange truck was coming toward her. She hurried out of the way. At another short blast, she took a closer look. Rex was driving.

He pulled up beside her and leaned out the window. "Hey, good-looking, hop in and I'll give you a ride."

Rex thought she was attractive? Her stomach fluttered at the idea. She gave the truck a long disapproving look. In the movies, when a man used that old line he was usually driving a nice sports car. Grinning, he lifted one shoulder. "You're the one who told me to get something beside a motorcycle."

She quirked her mouth. "This isn't exactly what I had in mind."

"Don't be thinking bad thoughts about Bessie." He patted the dash. "She can get you where you need to go. Come on, have a little sense of adventure. Lighten up a little." He revved the engine. "See, she's raring to go."

Tiffani barked a laugh. "Okay. Just this once."

Rex leaned across the seat and pushed the passenger door open. She climbed in, grateful she'd worn jeans. "So Bessie is your spare vehicle?"

"Nope. I borrowed her from a buddy just for you. I knew from the way you turned up your nose the other day you wouldn't ride on my motorcycle."

She wouldn't have. After what had happened to her father, she had no intention of getting on one. Rubbing her hand over the old but clean seat, she said, "You're right about that. Where're we going?"

"To a clinic over in High Water," Rex replied, as he pulled out of the parking lot.

She couldn't keep astonishment out of her voice. "Really?"

"Yep."

High Water was an area of the city known for crime and poverty. Why had he picked there, of all places? For whatever reason, it would certainly make for good PR. She envisioned the headline: "Metropolitan Hospital's surgeon spends day off helping out in High Water." She couldn't go wrong with this material. Even so, she had to know. "Why there?"

"Because they need the help." His tone was flat and his eyes never left the road.

She studied him. He had both hands on the steering

wheel. They were capable and strong, which she was well aware of because they had been on her body. For some reason that thought sent a zip of heat through her. Firmly instructing herself not to go there, she asked, "What do you usually do on your days off?"

"Is that question work related or personal?" He gave her a brief glance.

"Maybe both. I just wanted to get to know you better." She really meant it.

"Mostly I work at the clinic."

"What?"

He changed lanes and headed toward an exit. "Don't sound so surprised. I work at the High Water Clinic. I helped start it, along with a couple of other doctors in town."

"You're kidding." She maneuvered in her seat so she could easily see his profile.

"You really don't have a very high opinion of me, do you? You've been reading what the newspapers have to say. Tiff, you do know you can't believe everything you read, right?" he asked in a singsong voice.

Tiff? Since when did he call her by a nickname? More important, how had she missed such a crucial PR point? "Nowhere in my research did it say anything about you being connected to that clinic."

He exited the interstate, stopped at a traffic light then turned to look at her. "Because it isn't public knowledge and I'd like it to stay that way."

"But this is perfect PR material. The morning shows will eat it up." Anticipation flowed through her. This campaign had a real chance of succeeding beyond her wildest dreams.

He grimaced. "Please, don't do that. These people are hard to win over. If you bring in news crews and they start asking all kinds of questions, it might take some of them years to trust the clinic again."

She tilted her head to the side. "Then why're you taking me?"

"I guess I wanted you to see the real me. That there's more to me than a pointless publicity project or the wild doctor who rides a motorcycle."

Why would that matter to him? A disturbed expression came over his face. Had he intended to say that out loud?

"Maybe, because you wanted us to go to a clinic and I was already coming here," he was quick to add. "All I ask is that you respect these people."

"Of course I will." What type of person did he think she was? Where had he gotten the impression she didn't care about people?

Silent minutes passed before Rex entered a neglected section of the city Tiffani had never visited. Many homes were abandoned and stores closed. Grass grew through the cracks and paper littered the gutters. Tiffani tried not to think about the fact that this was considered the highest drug and crime area of town, or the fact that it was frequently a main topic in the news. She should be feeling nervous but inexplicably Rex's presence made her feel safe, confident he could handle himself as well as take care of her.

A few blocks farther he pulled into what looked like an old grocery store parking lot. There were people mingling around the glass front. Paper covered the windows halfway up. On a cinder-block wall facing the parking lot were the words: High Water Clinic.

Rex climbed out of the truck and walked around to open the door for her.

Tiffani smiled gratefully and took his hand. It was

strong and sure. She was too aware of his touch. There was no place in her life for that reaction. He was a client, and moreover she had no intention of being hurt again. "You really do have nice manners. Thank you."

"Let's just say they were drilled into me." He smiled, easing the words. "Come on. They'll be waiting for us."

Tiffani couldn't decide if his disclosure was positive or negative. But it made her think about something besides her growing fascination with him.

He closed the door and remained close as they went to the front of the building, circling behind the people at the door, waiting to enter. Several of them spoke to Rex and he greeted them by name. Maybe he wasn't the self-centered doctor she'd originally judged him to be.

"The clinic generally doesn't open until nine thirty on Saturdays but there's almost always people lined up waiting before then," he informed her with a note of pride as he again held the door for her.

Inside was a large, dim room. Mismatched chairs lined the walls and a gray metal desk that had seen better days stood directly in front of the entrance. Behind it sat a heavy-set, middle-aged woman.

"Louise, you're looking ravishing this morning," Rex teased.

To Tiffani's amazement the older woman blushed.

"Don't you start with me, you charmer, you. Our day's going to be too busy for your nonsense."

"What's up?" Rex was all business now.

"We're short a nurse and doctor today. Dr. Bruster and Ronda both couldn't make it in today. Dr. Bishop is already seeing a patient and Amanda is assisting him."

Rex groaned. "I wasn't scheduled for today. I just came to show Tiffani around." He faced Tiffani with an apologetic expression. "I guess I need to get to work. I'm sorry about this."

He didn't sound put out or discouraged, just willing to do what was necessary. There was nothing of the prima donna she had expected to see. He continued, "I'll take you back to the hospital as soon as I can, but for now you're going to see how an all-volunteer clinic works. Smooth and efficiently." He chuckled, touching Tiffani's arm briefly.

Louise laughed. "Something like that."

There was nothing sexual about his touch but the awareness lingered long after he'd removed his hand. She was so distracted she didn't immediately realize he was speaking.

"Tiffani Romano, this is Louise Townsend, the glue that holds this place together."

"We both know that isn't true," Louise snorted. "Nice to meet you, Tiffani." She looked at Rex. "Now stop gabbing and get busy."

"Tiffani, you can wait here or there's a table in the back. Again, I'm sorry."

If she just sat around she wouldn't have any material to use. She wanted to see him in action. "Can I watch what you do?"

Rex's brows went up as if her request had astonished him. "You're sure you want to do that? You might be bored."

"More than I would be, waiting in the back room?" She gave him a direct look.

"Okay, as long as the patients are okay with it."

Louise waved a paper at Rex. "Here's your first patient."

Taking the paper, Rex gave it a once-over, opened the door to let people in and called, "Mrs. Guzman?"

A silver-haired Hispanic woman struggled through the door, a piece of cloth wrapped around her leg. Rex hurried to helped her. "Come with me. We'll see if we can get you fixed up."

Tiffani followed them to a hallway created by business office cubicles. Rex directed his patient to the first one on the right. After getting the okay from Mrs. Guzman, Tiffani followed them in. She wasn't sure she hadn't made a mistake by asking to watch Rex.

She was really stepping out of her comfort zone. She could count the number of times she'd seen a doctor on one hand—she avoided them unless there was no other choice—so this clinic was a foreign land in more than one way. What she *did* know was that doctors didn't know everything. She'd seen the devastation a wrong decision could make in a family's life. She wouldn't wish that on anyone.

Her plan had been to go to the clinic, take a few pictures of Rex tending to two or three patients, then leave. Never in her wildest dreams had she imagined she'd be in an exam room with him. At least she'd be getting a lot of material she could use. Maybe she could sneak a few pictures...

To Rex, Tiffani didn't look happy with the situation but she hadn't demanded to leave. For that she got positive points. At the clinic, she would get a close-up of his life as a physician. Guilt pricked him. He glanced behind him and spotted her standing in the far corner of the room. She really was a striking woman, but more than that she was intelligent, persuasive, most of the time too much, and today far too agreeable for his comfort. He might find he liked her more than he should if this continued.

Tiffani returned a weak smile in response to his reassuring one. He just hoped she wouldn't try to use the people here as part of her campaign. It had taken years for the clinic to build community trust. An overzealous PR person could mess that up. He should have gone to the clinic she'd planned on but he'd let his ego get the better of him.

"Mrs. Guzman, have a seat right here." He helped the woman to settle on the lone chair in the space they used as an exam room. "Tell me what the problem is."

"I burnt my leg."

"Let's remove that bandage and see what damage you've done," he said to Mrs. Guzman. "After I have a good look I'm going to need to make some notes."

"I can do that," Tiffani said.

Surprised, he almost forgot what he was about to say. "That would be helpful. Just write what I tell you. You can find a pad and pen in the top drawer of that box." He pointed to the red metal tool box the clinic used as a supply cart.

Tiffani nodded.

He turned back to his patient and removed the cloth. He heard Tiffani's slight intake of breath. It was an ugly burn. The skin was red and angry and a large blister had already developed. To Tiffani's credit, the slight sound was her only reaction.

"Mrs. Guzman, how did this happen?"

"I was up early this morning, canning tomatoes. I moved the hot pot to the sink and hit the counter and spilt scalding water down my leg." The woman shook her head. "I should have been more careful."

"Tiffani, please write down, 'Mrs. Guzman, second-degree burn to right shin.'" He trusted her to do as he asked and continued with his patient. "I'll need to clean this and then cover it in clean gauze. I'll get the supplies and be right back with you."

"I can do that if it'll help," Tiffani offered. "Tell me where to find the supplies."

He hadn't expected her to say that. "You sure?"

She nodded.

"Down the hall and around to the right you'll find a sink and cabinets. The liquid soap and bottles of saline will be sitting on the counter. There's a plastic tub under the sink you should bring too."

Tiffani stuffed the pad and pen into her back pocket and left.

"Mrs. Guzman, now tell me how you've been besides your leg," Rex said. Over the next few minutes he gave the woman a basic physical.

Tiffani soon returned, carrying the soap and bottle in the tub.

"Good. Put it all down here," Rex said, indicating the floor next to Mrs. Guzman's foot. No doubt soon Tiffani would be calling a cab so she could leave. Rex wouldn't blame her. He hadn't planned on her getting roped into being his nurse. "Now, Mrs. Guzman, just put your foot in here." He indicated the plastic pan. "I'm going to clean your leg." He patted her hand and she gave him a drawn smile. "Tiffani, please write on your notes, 'Cleaned with soap and saline.'"

She nodded then slipped out the door. Had she had enough?

He took plastic gloves out of the supply box and pulled them on then took out a small pile of four-by-four gauze pads. "Now, Mrs. Guzman, I'm going to pour the saline over your leg." Rex talked as he worked. Seconds later he was lightly applying soap with the pads, being careful not to damage the blisters. Done, he said, "We'll let that dry then I can I cover it."

"I could do that," Tiffani said from behind him.

She'd returned so quietly he hadn't realized she was there. He looked at her, trying to conceal his disbelief. "You sure?"

"Trust me, I've got it. I've had a lot of experience."

He could use the time to see more patients. "All right. Is that okay with you, Mrs. Guzman?" When the woman nodded, Rex stood, telling Tiffani, "The supplies are in the box. Third drawer down."

"Your next patient is waiting next door." Tiffani pointed as she moved toward the box.

She was full of surprises. She'd gone to get another patient while he worked? He admired her efficiency and forethought.

"Mrs. Guzman, I want you to keep this clean and wrapped until you come back next week and see the doctor. Tiffani will give you a couple of rolls of gauze to use. Can you do that for me?" He smiled at the woman.

She nodded.

"Good." He patted her shoulder. "Clean and dry is the ticket."

Again, the woman nodded. He left, with Tiffani chatting with Mrs. Guzman as she gathered the supplies she would need.

None of this scenario would he have ever imagined. Where had she learned to bandage to give her such absolute confidence she could handle Mrs. Guzman's injury? Rex was impressed. He couldn't think of another woman he knew who was outside the medical field but still would have stepped in to help.

His next patient was a two-year-old child whose mother looked fearful.

Rex went down on his heels and said to the mother, "Can you tell me what has been going on with Johnny?"

"He's crying a lot, pulling on his ears. Wants me to hold him all the time."

"Have him sit on the table and you hold him. I'm going to take a look in his ears."

Rex turned to his small patient, who now sat on the portable exam table. He hated the clinic's inexpensive furniture, but that wasn't the important thing. There was solid care here. He found the otoscope in the supply cart.

"Johnny, I need to look in your ears," Rex said, touching the boy's shoulder gently. After studying the ear's interior, he said quietly, "Now the other one." When done, he informed the mother, "He has an ear infection. He'll need an antibiotic. I can give you a few samples but you'll need to go to the pharmacy for more. Will you be able to do that?"

The mother nodded.

Just minutes later, Tiffani hovered by the entrance with paper and pen in hand. She was fast. *Good girl.*

Rex backed away until he stood close to Tiffani. There was that fresh floral scent he'd first smelled when she'd climbed into the truck. It was one he would remember long after he and Tiffani had parted ways.

"You need to write down—"

"I've already got it."

He stepped out into the hall. Tiffani followed him. "Thanks for the great help."

She seemed to glow under his praise, but then she appeared unsure, as if he might have said something wrong.

"It's better than being bored. Plus, I'm getting to see you in action." She continued to scribble.

"While I'm getting the medicine for Johnny, would you mind calling the next patient for me?"

"Already done. They're in the exam room next to this one."

He shook his head in disbelief and looked into her eyes. She was his type of woman. The kind willing to do what needed doing. "Thanks. You really have been great about this."

She shrugged and smiled.

"A PR woman on the way to being a nurse."

Her eyes flicked up to him. "That won't happen," she said, a hard note to her voice, and then returned to writing.

As he fetched the antibiotic samples, he pondered Tiffani's statement. She didn't seem to care much for his profession. There had been her look of uncertainty a moment ago. Yet she was doing a great job. Maybe her hang-up had to do with blood or needles? After giving the pill packs and instructions to Johnny's mother, he went to his next patient.

He saw Tiffani in the hall a few minutes later.

"I need to clean Mrs. Guzman's exam room," she said. "Tell me a few things about your last patient and I'll jot them down."

They worked seamlessly over the next hour, seeing five more patients. It took another couple of hours before there was no one else waiting. For what should have been a difficult clinic, Tiffani had managed to make it much smoother. At least for him. She walked down the hall toward him after dropping off some papers he'd asked her to take to Louise.

"I can run you back to the hospital now," he said.

"Don't we need to go over the patients' notes?"

A lock of her hair had come loose. He fingered the

glossy strand before he brushed it over her cheek and tucked it behind her ear. Tiffani stared at him. She looked vulnerable, approachable, all that PR business-woman stuff suddenly missing. His gaze dropped to her mouth. What would she do if he tried to kiss her?

"Uh, you might not be able to read my writing." There was a hitch in her voice that let him know she hadn't been unaffected by his touch.

He grinned. "You do know you're talking to a doctor about penmanship."

"You do have a point."

"Let's go back here and make ourselves comfortable and see what you've got on those pages." He directed her toward the back of the building.

"My excuse is I had to write fast. What's yours?"

"I'll have you know I have better than average writing skills. Are you sure I don't need to be getting you back to the hospital, though?" He followed close behind her as they went down the makeshift hallway.

"No hurry," she said absentmindedly.

"What? No date on Saturday night?"

"No. Or any other night, for that matter." She looked stricken, as if she hadn't intended to make that confession out loud.

"I'd think someone as attractive as you would have a busy weekend planned." He directed her toward a fold-ing table the staff used for breaks. "Would you like a soda? Some crackers? All out of a machine, I'm afraid, but the upside is I'm buying."

She put the small notebook and pen on the table. "Both, if you don't mind. My breakfast gave out hours ago."

Guilt niggled at him. She been stuck here, helping him. He would have to make this up to her. Rex dug in his pocket for some cash. "I'm sorry. I didn't intend to tie up your day. I owe you one."

"Well, I wasn't too happy at first but what kind of person would I be if I demanded to leave when you needed help so badly?"

"Now I really feel bad," he said over his shoulder as he headed to the vending machines.

"Don't. I've learned a lot more about you today than I ever would reading my research," she said across the room.

"I hope it was positive." He put his money in and made his choices.

"If you promise not to remind me I said this, I happen to be impressed. The wild, unconventional, push-the-limits doctor you'd have the world believe you are actually has a really big heart. And a nice bedside manner as well."

Why did he enjoy hearing those words so much, coming from her? Smiling, he turned around and put his hand over his heart in a mocking gesture. "Stop, you're making me blush."

Tiffani laughed. Big, full-bodied laughter that did something to his insides. He joined her. It felt good to joke with a woman. Few, if any, of the women he'd been in relationships with had enjoyed sharing witty banter. With them, the interaction had always been a prelude to sex.

It was nice to have a conversation with a woman who tested his mental sharpness. Getting to know Tiffani was turning into fun. Something he was sure she needed more of, and which he knew he could use too.

When their laughter subsided, she pointed her finger at him. "Now, don't you make me regret admitting that."

"I can't make any promises. Have a seat and we'll

look at those notes. If it's not too busy, maybe we can get out of here after I do some quick dictation."

Tiffani was glad to put her feet up, propping them on the chair next to her. The last time she'd done that much walking and standing on a hard floor had been during her college years when she'd worked at a chain store one summer. Despite her aching feet, the morning had been interesting and enlightening. She'd never considered how adaptable a doctor must be. Each case was different. Helping at the clinic had given her a whole new perspective on the medical profession, and Rex in particular.

She'd seen nothing of the uncaring, unresponsive person in Rex that her father had for decades accused doctors of being. Rex hadn't displayed an attitude with his patients. He'd acted as if he genuinely wanted to help them. His compassion and concern when interacting with his patients had seemed genuine. Even in Mrs. Guzman's case, which had been particularly unpleasant, he had tenderly cared for her leg with aplomb and concern.

There was none of the *I don't care* or *I'm more interested in getting you out of here* arrogance she'd believed. Had she taken her bitterness over what had happened to her father and, in turn, her family, too far by blaming *all* of the medical community?

Rex worked hard without complaint and never appeared irritated when there was just one more question. That she was impressed with him was an understatement. He was nothing like the doctor she had envisioned him to be. Just how fast Rex was growing on her pushed her outside the boundary of her comfort zone.

He put a couple of packs of crackers and drinks on the table then took a seat across from her. "May I see those notes?"

Tiffani pushed the notebook toward him. He flipped through the pages. "We don't keep extensive medical records here. Mostly notes we can pull out just to see what has happened before. Or how much medicine we've dispensed. Many of our patients have drug-dependency issues and we don't want to contribute to the problem. I'll get these dictated quickly."

"Does Louise type them up for you?"

He chuckled. "No. We have a lady who volunteers her time."

"Does anyone get paid who works here?" She opened her crackers.

Rex shook his head, his hair swinging around his head. "It's an all-volunteer clinic."

"Amazing."

"We're only open two Saturdays a month. I often think we'll not have enough workers and can't open but it hasn't happened yet. Almost happened today, but you saved the day." He gave her an approving smile before his attention was back on what she had written.

"That's me, Wonder Woman. Not." She made a self-deprecating sound.

"As far as I'm concerned, you were."

It was nice of him to think so. She had felt so humiliated after the fiasco with Lou that it was affirming to have a man appreciate her, even if it was just for stepping in to help.

Waiting for Rex to finish looking at her notes, she crossed her ankles, which were still propped up on the seat of the chair next to her. "This is an amazing place and obviously much needed."

"You can say that again," he replied, sounding almost absentminded, but then he gave her his full attention. "There are very few Saturdays when they're not waiting two and three deep to be seen. Today's cases were roughly normal but we have gotten some gunshot wounds and knife injuries. It was hard in the beginning to get people to come in, so many of them didn't trust us, but now we're flooded." His attention had gone back to her notes.

"I can well understand that," she remarked.

He looked at her. "Huh?"

"I grew up not trusting doctors." Her gaze met his as his mouth thinned.

"Why?"

She shrugged and took a cracker from its wrapper. "My father was injured in a motorcycle accident when I was in elementary school. He lost a leg almost at the hip and the other below the knee. He believes the doctors didn't do enough to save his legs because he didn't have adequate insurance. Even sued." She almost held her breath while waiting for Rex's reaction.

"He did, did he?" There was a bitter note in Rex's question.

"Consequently, I saw doctors as people to question. That you couldn't trust them. My father's accident broke up my family. He convinced my mother his opinion was truth. He didn't allow her to take my brother or sister or me to doctors. Thankfully we never had something serious happen. As the oldest I learned to be a pretty good home nurse. I had a lot of experience bandaging."

"I guess you did. I can't imagine getting through childhood without seeing a doctor, much less mistrusting them to the point you don't take your children to one."

When he said it out loud, it did sound rather awful. "I know it seems strange but when you know nothing different, you don't think much about it."

He picked up his drink and took a swallow. "So

when you said you didn't care for my profession, you weren't kidding."

"No."

"It must've been really difficult for you to accept this job once you learned what you were going to have to do for the hospital. And worse you would have to work with the doctor with a black mark by his name."

She fiddled with the cracker wrapper. "It wasn't difficult. Let's just say it was a concern. Especially since my father lost the malpractice suit."

"Why did you take the job, then?" He crossed his arms on the table, watching her with unnerving intensity.

"Because, unfortunately, making you and the hospital look good gives me a chance at a promotion I really want."

He clicked his tongue and set back. "Tough spot to be in."

"Not anymore. After seeing you in action today, I feel better about telling the world you're a great doctor."

Rex nodded. "I take that as high praise after what you've just told me." His hand grazed hers as he took the package from her and removed a cracker.

There was that tingle again she got every time he touched her. "Have you told your father what you're doing?"

"I have." She kept to herself the fact that she hadn't stayed more than a few minutes after he'd announced she'd betrayed him. But had she really?

"How did that go?"

"About as well as you'd expect." She tried to keep the sadness out of her voice.

"I'm sorry that hanging out with me has made things difficult between the two of you." Rex took a long swallow of his drink.

"That's not your fault. It's my job and my choice."

He pushed the chair back and stood. "Well, it seems we've both had wrong views of each other for the last few days."

Tiffani couldn't disagree with him about that.

Rex gathered up his half-full cracker wrapper and can, putting them in a garbage can. "I'd better get busy or you'll be stuck here all day. There's a small dictation room over there…" he indicated another cubicle "…where I'll be. It'll take me twenty or thirty minutes. We should be able to leave after that. Sorry you have to wait. You might find a magazine to read up front."

"I'll be fine. I'll see if Louise needs help with something after I finish my crackers and drink."

"I'll make this up to you, I promise."

She sat up and gave him an eager look. "Like letting me take pictures?"

He twisted up his face as if to refuse, yet compromised with, "I'll agree to one. Of my choice."

She sank back into her chair. "You aren't feeling *too* guilty, are you?"

"It's more that I need to respect these people." He headed off without another word.

After finishing her snack, Tiffani walked to the front of the clinic. Louise was busy filing papers.

She smiled at the older woman. "Can I help with something?"

"Put these in alphabetical order. Then file them here." Louise touched the filing cabinet behind her. "What's Rex doing?"

"He's busy working on reports."

"He's pretty special, isn't he?" the old woman asked.

Yes, he is. Too much so for Tiffani's comfort.

CHAPTER FIVE

REX FOUND TIFFANI elbow deep in papers after he'd completed his dictation. "You didn't have enough to do this morning so now you're doing paperwork?"

She glanced at him. "I'll be finished here in a sec."

"We could use her around here all the time," Louise said.

He doubted that would happen. Tiffani had only been there that day because she hadn't known what she'd been getting into. He said to Louise, "I'm going to run Tiffani back to her car and get some lunch. You want me to bring you anything?"

"I'm good. I've eaten lunch."

A few minutes later Tiffani said, "I'm ready. See you later, Louise."

"Thanks for the help, honey," the woman called as they went out the door.

"I'll see you in an hour," Rex said. "You sure made an impression on Louise."

"I can usually get along with most people. You're the only one who's had a problem with me in some time."

Rex stopped and she did too. He looked at her as they stood in the parking lot. "Is that so? What issue did the last one have?"

"One I don't want to talk about. You know, I haven't

gotten that picture you promised. How about you under the clinic sign?" She pointed to the one on the wall above his head.

When he didn't immediately agree she narrowed her eyes and said, "You promised."

"Okay." He turned his back to the wall and faced her.

"I need a smile." She gave him an example.

"I am smiling."

She grinned. "That's more of a grimace."

"Will this do?" He gave her his best pleasant smile.

"I guess so, but I would've much preferred one like you gave Johnny this morning after you checked his ears."

She'd been watching that closely?

"I only have one of those a day to give away." He opened the truck door for her. As she was getting in she looked back at him, their faces almost at the same level.

"That's a shame," she said softly. "It's such a nice one."

A warmth he wasn't familiar with filled his chest. What *would* she do if he kissed her? For some reason, that thought kept coming to mind. He wasn't interested in teasing her anymore. He wanted to really kiss her. Hold her against him. Hear her sigh with pleasure. See if her lips tasted as soft and delicious as they looked.

Before he could act on that desire, she gave the door a tug to close it. He stepped out of the way. The moment was lost. He would regret that missed opportunity.

As he drove away he said, "I'm going to get a drive-through burger. You want one before I take you back to your car?"

"No, thanks. I've got to go home and cook a meal for my father so I'm good."

Rex certainly wasn't going to get an invite to that,

knowing how her father felt about doctors. Why would he even be interested in going? He wasn't a meet-the-parents type of guy. He'd just go to one of the clubs and catch some good jazz music. After all, he and Tiffani were in a business relationship. Nothing more.

On the way to the hospital they chatted about their morning. Soon he was pulling up behind her car. He hopped out and went around to open her door.

"You do know that I'm capable of doing that for myself, don't you?"

"It's not about you being capable but about me being polite." Watching her closely, he held the door wide but stood so she couldn't easily get around him.

"Is something wrong?" Her gaze met his.

"I was just wondering if I tried to kiss you, would you let me?"

He didn't wait for an answer. His lips found hers. They were just as soft and inviting as he'd imagined. When she didn't move he placed his hands on her waist and pulled her to him. Tiffani felt so good. She didn't push away, she just accepted. But he wanted her to reciprocate. He moved his mouth over hers in hungry invitation. She returned his kiss. Rewarded him with that sigh he'd wished for.

Seconds later she pushed him away, her look having turned cold and distant. "Please, don't do that again."

He didn't know if he could promise her that. "Why not?"

"I don't like to be played with."

Why would she think he was doing that? "Who said I was?"

"Like you really want to have a relationship with me. Up until today we barely tolerated each other."

"Whoa, it was just a simple kiss, not a shot fired

across the bows of your boat or a marriage proposal."
He backed away. "I didn't mean to insult you."

Her glare burned into him. "You didn't insult me.
I just came out of a bad relationship and don't wish to
repeat it."

"So you're saying that by kissing me you almost
started another bad relationship?"

Tiffani moved farther away from him. "Right now,
I need to concentrate on my job. Our interactions have
to remain professional."

"Based on that kiss, which was far too short, that
might not be possible." He took a step toward her.

"Then you'd better figure out how to make it so.
Thanks for an informative day. I'll be in touch." With
those words, she presented him with her back and hurried to her car.

"Tiff." He waited until she looked at him. "It might
be you who has to work at that."

Looking stricken, she climbed into the car.

What had just happened? He'd given a girl he was
attracted to a simple kiss and she'd made it plain she
wasn't interested. But there had been a second there
when she'd returned his kiss that proved she wasn't immune to him. Tiffani was just scared. But was she scared
of him or herself?

When Tiffani started her car, he came out of the daze
she'd left him in. He slammed the passenger door closed
and went around to the driver's side. Getting in, he put
the truck into gear and drove off.

He wasn't afraid to go after what he wanted.

Tiffani's hands shook on the wheel of the car as she left
the parking lot. Rex had kissed her. She'd liked it. Better than liked it. But it must *not* happen again. It was

wrong on a professional level. A personal one too. She couldn't handle someone with such a large personality after what had happened with Lou. She wasn't prepared for humiliation again. Nothing more than a fling could happen between Rex and herself anyway. They were too different. She refused to let herself be played with again. Once was more than enough.

She'd made the right decision to push Rex away. Yet a part of her wished she hadn't. She wanted him to kiss her again. Wanted the chance to run her hands through his mess of hair. His lips hadn't demanded; instead, he'd teased and tested as if telling her he could be patient. That he would wait for her until she was ready, until she could trust him. When she had given in and kissed him back, she'd found pleasure she hadn't known existed.

Being kissed wasn't new to her but even the almost chaste one from Rex left all the others lacking. But she was going to have to forget about it and put all her energy into earning that promotion. If she did get it she'd be moving anyway. There were too many ways that Rex Maxwell was wrong for her.

At least she had no reason to interact with him again for a few days. That would leave her time to get her mind going in the right direction. She'd make sure she was back in professional mode before she saw him again.

On Monday morning, she opened her emails to find that Luke had sent over the proofs of the pictures of Rex for the billboards. She searched through them. The camera had captured Rex's masculine attractiveness. When she'd been putting the stethoscope around Rex's neck Luke had continued taking pictures. He had caught that moment Rex had whispered to her. She hardly recognized herself. The wonder on her face. Even now warmth washed through her.

Tiffani swallowed and clicked the picture off the screen.

She'd trust Luke's opinion on the best picture to use for the billboards. By the weekend Rex's picture would be up around the city. She pulled out her phone and searched for the picture she had taken at the clinic. In a few minutes, she would have that out on social media. Hopefully it would generate some positive buzz.

Later that day, she reported to her boss about her progress with the campaign. He seemed pleased. Tiffani returned to her desk and picked up her phone. She'd been putting off the necessary phone call all day. Had Rex been thinking about her as much as she'd thought about him? She didn't need to go in that direction. There was business to attend to and her objective focus was required.

She punched in Rex's number. With any luck he wouldn't answer and she could just leave a message. On the third ring disappointment set in.

"Rex," was barked in her ear halfway through the fourth ring.

Her heart jumped in panic at the sound of his voice. "It's Tiffani."

"Hey, Tiff. Give me a second. I'm right in the middle of something." He seemed distracted.

"I'll call back." There was no response. Instead, she listened as he spoke to someone else. A minute later he said, "Sorry about that. I'm just coming out of surgery."

"This can wait."

"No, I can talk now. How've you been?" His voice relaxed on the last three words.

"I'm fine."

"I've missed seeing you." His voice was soft and deep.

He was flirting with her. If he kept that up it would be difficult to resist him. "I wanted to let you know I have an interview set up for you on WMEP *This Is Memphis* on Thursday morning."

"I may have surgery scheduled then."

The Rex she could handle was back.

"I can't rearrange my schedule," he continued. "My patients come first. What is it anyway?"

It was progress that he even asked that. "It's the most popular local morning show."

"I haven't seen it. I'm usually in the OR before those come on."

"Rex, this is an important interview. We'll work around your schedule. I need you to do this one," she pleaded.

"And what's in it for me?"

She didn't miss the suggestiveness in his tone. "Making the hospital look good."

"Come on, Tiff. You can do better than that," he teased, but there was a hopeful note in there as well.

Every time he called her Tiff she quivered. "I've already asked Dr. Nelson if we can set up in one of the consult rooms near the OR. You can do the interview in your scrubs. It'll look more authentic anyway. When the interview is over you can go straight back to surgery. How does that sound?"

"Like you're being all business. I'd still rather not do it. Again, what's in it for me?"

"It'd make me happy." Tiffani kept her voice even.

"That's better but still not good enough."

There was the faint sound of his name being called before he said, "I've got to go. I'm looking forward to seeing you Thursday."

Even over the phone Rex had her thinking of things better left alone. Thursday couldn't come soon enough.

It was around mid-morning when Rex entered the small consult room just steps from the surgery suite. Once again the table and chairs had been moved against the wall. This time there was a great deal more equipment than there had been for the photo shoot. Two large light stands, glowing brightly, faced two tall chairs situated close together, almost facing each other. Heavy-duty electrical cables ran along the floor. Two men stood behind two different cameras on tripods.

He'd walked into another world. A world he didn't understand and where he had no control. The urge to leave grabbed him.

Tiffani wore an expensive suit with matching shoes that made her look as edgy as she acted while she conversed with a blonde woman he recognized from billboards around town. As the women talked, they kept referring to a piece of paper. He didn't turn on the TV or often listen to the talk stations so he had no idea if the woman had given the malpractice case a lot of air time.

Tiffani glanced his way, said something to the woman and came to meet him. "Hey, there. Glad you're here." Her smile was hesitant.

Had she been nervous about seeing him? He liked that idea. If he had her uncertain then he had a chance. She would be more open to getting to know him better. He hadn't had to chase a woman since high school. Doing it now was both exciting and daunting.

"I've missed you."

"Rex!"

He grinned. "Well, it's true." Glancing around, he noted, "There sure is a lot of stuff here just for a short interview." Weren't these the same people who'd had nothing kind to say about the hospital weeks ago? "I don't have much time so can we get started?"

"They've almost finished setting up." She moved toward the set chairs on the set and he followed. "All I want you to do is answer questions honestly and positively. Remember this is about improving the hospital image."

"I always answer honestly."

She looked at him. "Don't forget the positive part."

The blonde woman joined them. She wore makeup so heavy she appeared cartoonish. Extending her hand, she announced, "I'm Maggie Martin. You must be Dr. Maxwell."

"Please, call me Rex." He took her hand. It held no warmth.

Maggie's smile was syrupy. "It's nice to finally meet you."

Rex nodded acknowledgment then gave Tiffani a winsome smile.

"We'll be ready in just a minute," Maggie said as she hurried away. Over her shoulder she added, "I'm glad you're wearing your scrubs. I like a touch of authenticity."

"I'm in scrubs because I am an authentic surgeon," he muttered through gritted teeth, watching her go.

Tiffani touched his arm lightly. "Be nice. Also, would you mind taking off your head cover? And you'll need to see the makeup person."

This was getting worse every second. "Why do I need makeup?"

"Please, Rex. It won't be much. This is too important. Please, just go along with it," Tiffani begged.

He leaned in close so that only she could hear him. "You know, I like the sound of my name on your lips."

Her blush was his reward. "Stop," she hissed. "Come on over here."

Rex wasn't sure the hospital's image was worth this aggravation as Tiffani led him to a young woman. "She'll do your makeup and brush your hair."

Rex narrowed his eyes and tightened his lips to let her see his disgust before she hurried off. Five minutes later the woman pronounced him ready for the camera and directed him to the chair on the right. He took the seat. One of the assistants hurried over and attached a tiny microphone to the V of his top and clipped the power pack to the waistband of his pants in the back.

Maggie joined him, settling in the other chair. Tiffani stationed herself beside one of the cameramen in front of a monitor.

"Rex, I'll be introducing you then we'll just talk. Easy-peasy," Maggie quipped.

Something warned him not to believe it would be that simple. This couldn't be over soon enough.

"Okay, here we go," Maggie said.

Rex straightened, eyeing Tiffani. She gave him a reassuring smile. He returned a less enthusiastic one. Because he had nothing to hide he wasn't nervous, but it was nice to have Tiff on his side.

"Good morning, Memphis," Maggie announced with professional enthusiasm. "Today we have a very special treat for you. We're coming to you live from Metropolitan Hospital. We're going to highlight the hospital and share a little bit about what happens in the daily life of the staff here. A staff made up of many dedicated and special people. This morning we're talking with Dr. Rex

Maxwell, a surgeon here at Metro." Maggie turned toward him and beamed. "Welcome, Dr. Maxwell."

"Good morning." He answered with all the pleasantness he could muster.

"I'd like to start off by asking you to tell us what a usual day would be like for you."

He glanced at Tiffani. Her expectant smile reminded him how important this interview was to her. He'd agreed to do this, so to please her he would play the game and play it well.

"I'm a general surgeon. Most of my cases are people who come through the ER. My typical day starts at five thirty in the morning and I'm at the hospital by six. I do paperwork and see patients until seven, when my surgery schedule starts. After that I see patients in ICU or on the floor." How he could have said more and told less, he didn't know.

Maggie nodded, wearing a thoughtful expression. "Wow, that sounds like a busy day."

He'd leaned forward a little, tilted his head. "Some days more so than others." A covert glance at Tiffani made him think she was pleased with his efforts.

Meanwhile Maggie gave him a practiced smile. "I understand that recently you and the hospital were involved in a malpractice suit. Would you care to comment on that?"

There it was. What his gut had told him was coming. His gaze found Tiffani. She wasn't moving a muscle and her expression implored him to give a positive answer. Was she afraid he was going to lose his temper? Taking a page from Tiffani's playbook, he went on the offensive.

Leaning closer to Maggie as if he were going to tell her a secret, he said, "I can't say much but I'll tell you this. I use every skill I have to care for and save lives.

Every time I, or my fellow surgeons, enter the OR our priority is saving patients' lives. Our livelihoods are the last thing on our minds when we're operating. This hospital puts its patients first in every case. Sometimes we simply can't win the war between life and death, but we do everything within our knowledge and with our experienced skills to fight the battles."

Maggie blinked, as if she needed a moment to regroup, then asked, "So you're telling me there was nothing to the malpractice suit?"

Rex sat back and clasped his hands in his lap. "When your loved one dies, it's only natural to seek a source of blame."

"Does that mean you're not guilty?" Maggie's look bored into him.

Rex squared his shoulders. He wasn't going to rehash old news for anyone. "No one likes being accused of doing something they didn't do. How many stories have you had to retract? Or weather forecasts have you issued that turned out to be wrong? Should you be fired for acts of God?"

Maggie's head jerked back as if she was astonished. "I guess we've all faced that at one time or another."

"That's true. But most people don't have to live with the accusation they caused someone's death or the fear they might lose their job because of something completely out of their control." Rex held her gaze with confident humility.

Maggie's eyes softened and her voice became sympathetic. "I imagine you do have some days when it's hard to go to sleep."

He smiled. "Yes, I've had more than a few. But I love my job and find being a doctor rewarding." Sneaking another look at Tiffani, he was relieved to see she no longer appeared worried.

Maggie's fake smile turned genuine. "Tell us why you wanted to become a doctor."

"Well, Maggie, I worked at a local nursing home when I was a teenager. I needed a job and wanted to do something where I could make a difference."

She nodded and leaned toward him. "So tell me, what does a surgeon do in his off time?"

"I don't know, what does a popular newscaster like to do?" He winked at her.

Maggie giggled. "You sure there's nothing you want to tell?"

He gave her his best grin, hoping it looked sincere. "It isn't an adventure if you know the destination." He then relaxed against the back of his chair.

"Before you get back to work, I'd like to know if you're participating in the Walk with a Doc event sponsored by the hospital and this station this weekend?"

Rex looked at Tiffani. She put up her hands in a praying manner and nodded her head.

"I wouldn't miss it." He tried to sound eager.

Maggie looked at the camera. "So everybody come out and join Dr. Maxwell and I this Saturday for a chance to Walk with a Doc in Tom Lee Park. As well as the walk, there will be qualified medical professionals providing free health checks." She turned back to him. "Dr. Maxwell, thanks so much for being here with us today."

Rex nodded, relieved it was over, and as the cameras cut out, the assistant quickly came over and removed his microphone. Tiffani's smile was wide, happy. It was nice to have her pleased with him. To have earned her genuine pleasure.

* * *

Tiffani couldn't believe her eyes or ears. Rex had actually had Maggie flirting with him. He'd used his charm to get around her probing questions and had come out the winner. The hospital had as well. The interview could have been a train wreck but he'd turned it into a PR triumph.

She watched as he stood, speaking to Maggie one more time, then came over to her. She met him halfway. Without thinking, she threw her arms around his neck and hugged him. "You were great!"

His arms encircled her, pulling her against the hard wall of his body. "Thanks. I'll take a rain-check on your enthusiastic expression of gratitude because I have to go. They're waiting for me in the OR."

Tiffani quickly released him, feeling heat flushing her face.

He whispered, for her ears only, "Don't ask me to do that again."

"But I had another in the works for next—"

"I won't do it. I'm not explaining my actions. Especially when I wasn't guilty of anything." He walked away and out of the room.

Was he going to fight her on every front? He'd done an excellent job and now he wanted to quit. Today's interview was the type that changed people's minds. It helped them to see him as a person, a dedicated doctor, significant. Was there something more than the malpractice suit eating at him?

She would be seeing him on Saturday for the Walk with a Doc event. At least he'd committed to it and she wouldn't have to blackmail him into going. Maybe while they were there she could work on convincing him he needed to do more interviews. He'd been a natural on-camera, and discussions like those were the perfect outlet for her PR campaign.

Really, though, with his charm, anything that involved a woman was his forum. Maggie wasn't the only one captivated by Rex. No matter how Tiffani tried to deny it, she too was quickly falling under his spell.

CHAPTER SIX

RINGING WOKE TIFFANI early on Friday morning. She rolled over, grabbed her cellphone and glanced at the number. Rex. Her heart skipped. Thoughts of him had been circling in her head all night and none had to do with the campaign. Why was he calling now? Had something happened?

"Hello."

"Hey, there, sleepyhead." He sounded far too cheerful. "If you don't want me to arrive on my bike tomorrow I'm going to need you to come by and pick me up. My buddy needs his truck."

By the tone of his voice he was enjoying the idea of making her his chauffeur for the day. Regardless, she didn't want him arriving on his bike for the Walk with a Doc event. She didn't want any opportunity for negative publicity about Rex to present itself, not when the campaign was going so well after his interview. There had been a huge amount of positive feedback on social media regarding the "cute doctor." She didn't need any damaging press right now.

"What's your address? I'll be around to get you about seven thirty tomorrow morning."

"Great, then I'll see you bright and early." Rex gave her an address that she recognized as being in the historical district, then said goodbye, leaving her alone with her thoughts about him.

On Saturday morning, Tiffani was up and out of bed earlier than normal. For reasons she refused to examine, she took longer than usual deciding what to wear, refusing for a second time to think about why she felt a deep-seated need to look nice for Rex. She decided to forgo the PR attire in an effort to appear more feminine and casual. After careful consideration she chose a short-sleeved, red button-down shirt and black skinny jeans. As a final touch, she pulled her hair up into a loose ballerina bun.

Rex's neighborhood had recently gone through rejuvenation. Young families and professionals were moving back. Trendy restaurants and jazz bars were in abundance. The famous Beale Street was only a few blocks away. If she could afford it, the area would be a place she would enjoy living.

Tiffani pulled up in front of the address Rex had given. It was a red brick building with the type of tall windows she'd always found especially appealing.

She pulled to the curb and texted him.

I'm here.

In less than a minute he came out of a dark wooden door and headed toward her. His hair was pushed away from his face and held by a ball cap worn backward. The T-shirt he wore fit him well enough to reveal his muscular chest. She acknowledged to herself, with a bit of guilt, that his jeans and tennis shoes suited him better than the "business" clothes she'd coaxed him into wearing for the photos. However, she had no choice but to present him as a polished, competent professional on the billboards.

His smile was broad as his eyes met hers through the windshield. It was refreshing to have someone glad to see her. Her father was only happy to see her when he wanted something and Lou had never exhibited such a look of joy when he'd seen her.

"Mornin', Tiff," Rex said as he climbed in. "Man, I forgot about how small your car is." He worked to get his long legs inside. "Will you help me out if I need it?"

She giggled. "That would be a good clip for the media. Me bent over your lap."

His look caught hers. "Sounds interesting to me."

She felt the rush of heat from head to toe.

Although he'd turned her remark into a naughty image, he might really need her assistance in getting out. His knees pressed against the dashboard even with the passenger seat as far back as it would go.

Rex remarked, "If I hang out with you much longer, you're either going to have to get on my bike or buy a larger car."

Was he thinking about them spending more time together? She had been. Despite his attitude about the campaign, she'd discovered she liked him. Liked how he had challenged her in the past few days to step out of her secure world.

She mustn't let herself think about such things. If, no, *when,* she got the promotion, she was moving out of town. She certainly didn't need a long-distance relationship that would no doubt end in another ugly breakup. She had sworn to herself she wouldn't go through that hell again.

It had rained near daybreak and the early morning streets were still damp. There were no clouds in the sky now, but in their area of the south it wasn't uncommon to get storms late in the afternoon.

Finding a parking spot near Tom Lee Park, she pulled in. Rex did have some difficulty getting out but, thankfully, he didn't request her help. They walked toward the staging area near the entrance of the park with the wide flowing Mississippi River on one side. She would miss it when she left. Tiffani glanced at Rex. He might be something else she'd miss as well.

Tents were set up in a grassy area with tables and chairs under them. People mingled while others worked to prepare for the event. As she and Rex moved toward the starting/finishing line, marked by a high arch of balloons, she overheard one woman say to another, "Isn't that the doctor on the billboard?"

"What're they talking about? Have the billboards already gone up?" Rex immediately demanded.

Tiffani stopped. He did too. She turned and pointed toward a billboard just barely visible in the distance on which Rex was bigger than life, standing in front of the hospital in his dress shirt, stethoscope around his neck, arms crossed over his chest and smiling with self-assurance. Everything about the picture generated an impression of you-can-have-confidence-in-me.

"I'm sure they're talking about that one, but there are others around town."

Rex groaned as if in pain. "The people I work with are already making fun of me about the interview. This isn't going to help things. How many are there?"

"Three, and I hope to put up a couple more. I wanted them in the most prominent places so I'm having to wait until space becomes available."

"You're killing me, woman." He started walking again.

Grinning, Tiffani caught up. "I told you I planned to do billboards as soon as possible."

"Yeah, but I didn't really think it through." He looked disgusted. "I'm so…large."

"But at least you're handsome." Tiffani realized too late what she'd said.

Rex smirked his pleasure. "So you think I'm handsome?"

"You're not going to pull me into that conversation." She walked faster.

He called after her, "You can't run and hide. I heard you."

She was glad when they reached the starting area. The WMEP crew was already setting up.

If she could manage it, Tiffani planned to have Rex do another quick interview with Maggie. Tiffani was certain it wouldn't be a problem after Maggie's reaction to him on Thursday. He'd charmed her without a doubt, but Tiffani knew convincing him to do another interview would be difficult.

"Hey," she said, as if on impulse, "I know you don't like all this limelight but I really do appreciate you working with me. I reported how things are going to Dr. Nelson yesterday. He seemed pleased and implied that the board would be as well."

"I'm glad someone's happy," Rex grumbled.

"Today would be another big boost if you'll just be agreeable. Would you do a short interview with Maggie about the event today?"

"I'm always agreeable," he said in a snide tone.

She gave him a dubious look and put her hands together in a praying manner. "Will you, please?"

He sighed deeply, giving her an uncertain look. Just

when she expected him to refuse, he said, "I'll do it if you really think it's necessary."

"I do. I'll go see if I can find Maggie." Tiffani hurried off with a smile on her face.

Rex watched Tiffani walk off in the direction of the TV van. She had a sweet little tush. One he wanted to cup and pull against him. Yet she behaved as if she had her elbows locked to keep him at arm's length. All she seemed to think about was her campaign. He consoled himself that at least they would have some personal time during the walk.

He liked these types of events, even though he didn't often get to participate in them. Most of his time was tied up at the hospital or the clinic. This morning was pleasant and the crowd was animated, clearly eager to have a good time, so he was going to make the most of it.

"Rex."

He looked in the direction of the call. Tiffani was waving at him. He strolled over to her.

"Maggie said she'd love to talk to you."

At least one woman was interested in him, just not the right one. "If I must."

Tiffani gave his arm a light slap. "Be nice. You were great last time."

Before he could respond, Maggie and a cameraman descended on them. "Hello, Rex. It's so nice to see you again."

Tiffani's eyes narrowed but a smile remained on her face.

"Maggie, it's a pleasure to see you too." He used his most pleasant voice, thankful for his perfect manners.

Over the next few minutes she asked him about why he was participating in the Walk with a Doc event and about what he did to remain healthy. A couple of times she rested her hand on his arm. The first time he happened to glance at Tiffani and found her lips pursed as she watched them intently. When it occurred again he made a point of looking at Tiffani. Her brows had narrowed and she took a step forward before she stopped.

Did she not like Maggie touching him?

Maggie finished the interview and the camera was off when she gripped his forearm and cooed, "Call me sometime. You can reach me at the station."

A second later Tiffani said, "Rex, we'd better go. It's about time to line up."

As if on cue, an announcement that the walk was beginning could be heard loud and clear.

Rex said in his best syrupy voice, adding a smile, "Thanks, Maggie. Bye." He called after Tiffani, who was stalking away, "Hey, what's the hurry?"

She stopped and looked at him. "What?"

"Why the rush? We have time."

"I was afraid that if I didn't get away from you two I might go into a diabetic coma with all that sugar piling up," she answered in a sarcastic tone.

A slow grin came to his lips. "I don't think I've ever felt more flattered."

Perplexed, she demanded, "What're you talking about?"

"You're jealous." He couldn't stop his huge self-satisfied smile.

"I am not!" she huffed, then hurried off.

"I thought you wanted me to be nice to her." Rex continued after her.

She stopped and glared at him. "I wanted you to look like a professional that people could trust, not a man looking for a date."

Rex burst out laughing. "I was carrying on a conversation. She was the one doing all the touching."

"And from what I could tell, you were eating it up." Tiffani huffed a second time and disappeared into the crowd.

Rex found her waiting near the starting line. He grinned and she looked away. Here he was, thinking he wasn't getting through to her and, lo and behold, she was jealous. That was a giant step in his favor.

The crowd gathered around them. As they did so, Tiffani took pictures of them and several of Rex.

He asked, "What're you doing?"

"I'm getting some shots to put up on social media, the hospital newsletter and website. They might not be as engaging as Maggie's interview but they'll be more about the hospital and less about flirting." She raised her chin. "Plus, these you can't forbid me to use."

His nose almost touched hers. "I bet I can."

She lifted her head haughtily. "But I'm not going to listen."

A representative of the hospital, using a microphone, demanded their attention. He welcomed everyone then asked all the doctors to raise their hands. Rex put his up. The crowd around them cheered. The man then said a few more words about the importance of wellness before he called out, "Ready. One, two, three, walk!"

The mass of bodies surged around Rex and Tiffani. For a second he feared he might lose her and grabbed her hand. Her head jerked around, her look rebellious as she tried to free her hand. He held tight. "I don't want to lose you."

With a trace of hesitancy in her eyes she stopped resisting.

They followed the route designated by arrows down

the path along the river. He'd reviewed a map beforehand and knew they were following a large circular path
through the park. Others strolled, deep in private conversation, around them. When the crowd thinned, Tiffani
pulled her hand free. He let her go without argument,
even though he missed the soft feel of her flesh next to
his. He set his pace to hers.

They hadn't gone far when a girl of about twelve
came up beside him, pointing to the billboard, which
was now easier to see. "That's you up there on that sign,
isn't it?"

Tiffani took a picture of them.

He wasn't going to enjoy having the billboards around
town. What had he been thinking to agree to it all? "Yes,
that's me."

"You're famous?"

Tiffani made a choking noise.

He glared at her then looked at the girl again. "No,
I'm not famous."

The girl seemed satisfied and ran off to join a group
ahead of them.

Through clenched teeth he warned, "Tiff, don't you
dare say anything."

Her giggles filled the air around them, eventually
fading away as they continued to walk.

The ensuing silence between them was comfortable.

Minutes later she said, as if talking more to herself
than him, "I love this city. I'll miss it when I leave."

His chest tightened. "You're leaving?"

"I hope so. If I get that promotion then I'll move to
the home office."

He looked at the railed bridge ahead across the river.
"Where's that?"

"Louisville, Kentucky."

He whistled low. "That's a long way away from here."

"It is. It'll be a big change but a good one." She sounded more resigned than excited.

Rex didn't want to scrutinize the uneasy feeling in his stomach. "How soon is this supposed to happen?"

"If this campaign goes well, I hope soon." She gave him a serious look then took pictures of people ahead of them.

The thought of her leaving had him suddenly thinking of ways to sabotage the campaign. But why was he overreacting? They hadn't even been on a date. A fact he decided to remedy right then. "Do you like barbecue?"

She gave him a look of disbelief. "Yeah. How can you live in Memphis and not like barbecue?"

"Wet or dry?" he asked as they made the turn and headed back the way they had come.

"Both, but dry is usually my pick." She clicked a few more pictures.

"Mine too. How about we go for lunch when we're done here? I know a great place that serves a special dry rub."

Her step faltered for a second. Rex grabbed her arm to steady her. When she was surefooted again he released her.

"I don't know if that's such a good idea," she finally said.

"Why? Two hungry friends can't share a meal?" What made her so reluctant to having anything to do with him outside her job?

"Put like that, it does seem silly to say no." She smiled at him.

"Then we have a plan." This type of campaign he could get into.

They were almost back to the starting line when

someone called, "Help! Someone, help!" Rex broke into a run. He came up on a few women on their knees beside another woman, who was lying on the ground.

"I'm a doctor. What's wrong here?" Rex went down on his heels next to the woman.

"She just collapsed," someone said above him.

He checked for a pulse. Finding none, he quickly said, "Someone, call 911 and get the first-aid people." Tilting the woman's head back, Rex checked her airway.

"What can I do?" Tiffani asked from beside him.

"Do you know CPR?"

"Yes," Tiffani said with confidence.

He clasped his hands in the center of the woman's chest. "Then you do the breathing while I do chest compressions. Give her two breaths to start."

Tiffani did as he instructed.

He started chest compressions, Tiffani breathing deeply into the woman's lungs every time he rested, before sitting back as Rex started compressions again.

Tiffani had no idea how long she and Rex worked in unison before the first-aid people arrived. She was in the process of giving the collapsed woman another breath when another woman, carrying an automated external defibrillator bag in hand, knelt beside Rex.

Tiffani, with sweat on her brow, moved out of the way. The tension didn't leave her body as she watched Rex and the woman work.

Rex continued compressions as the first-aid person placed the leads while he talked on the phone. From what she could tell from the conversation, he was talking to the ambulance people.

"Clear!" the woman said, and Rex moved away. Seconds later she pushed a button, sending an electric shock through the patient's body.

Rex leaned his head close to the woman's mouth. "Nothing."

The first-aid woman reset the machine and waited for it to recharge. "Clear!" Once again, she pushed the button. The woman's body jumped.

This time there was a slight coughing sound and the woman's chest started to move.

Tiffani released the breath she hadn't realized she was holding.

The sound of an ambulance's siren filled the air.

The first-aid person slipped an oxygen mask over the patient's nose and mouth.

"Don't move," Rex instructed the patient. To the first-aid person he said, "I'm Dr. Rex Maxwell, by the way. May I use your stethoscope? I'm going to give her a quick check and then I'll get out of the paramedics' way."

The first-aid person handed it over.

Rex efficiently and expertly listened to the patient's heart and lungs. He then checked the pulse in her neck.

Tiffani pulled out her phone and took some pictures. Now that the worst was over, she couldn't miss a chance to capture Rex in action. By the time he was finished the ambulance had arrived. She stood and waited out of the way while Rex spoke to the EMTs.

As the ambulance left, one of the women who had been with the patient said to Rex, "Thank you."

He answered with a warm smile, "Not a problem. I'm just glad I was nearby."

"That's you on the billboard, isn't it?" the woman asked.

"I'm afraid so."

Tiffani smiled at his not-so-gracious admission.

"The hospital picked the right guy. You were a hero today," the woman said.

Looking humbled, Rex nodded and headed toward where Tiffani was standing.

She said as he joined her, "You know, you really are a good guy."

"You doubted it?" He raised an eyebrow.

"Yeah. But it just goes to show you can't believe everything you read." Or believe everything her father had told her about doctors, or what she'd come to believe as true from what had happened with her family. Not all of them were bad. Especially not Rex.

"I could have told you that," he retorted.

Rex had been amazing with the hurt woman. Kind and gentle. He hadn't hesitated to run to help. Giving was part of his nature. All her life, her father had, and still did, demanded her help, always putting his needs first. Rex was just the opposite, thinking of other people before himself. He was so different from what she'd had in her mind he would be.

"Come on," he said. "Let's finish this walk. I'm hungry."

When he took her hand, she let him. The feeling of being wanted, of feeling secure, even if only for five minutes, sped up the healing of her heart.

Half an hour later they were in her car, pulling out into traffic. He gave directions to the restaurant. A short time later they parked in a lot two blocks away and she was shutting her door before Rex could get his legs out.

"I beat you."

"You have me folded up in this clown car and now you're making fun of my manners." He grinned at her.

As they walked to the restaurant Tiffani asked, "Where did those manners come from?"

"My mom said good manners can get you anywhere." He winced as if it had hurt him to confess that but immediately went on, "She reinforced them at home from as far back as I can remember. Cotillions and dance lessons embedded them in me."

"I like them. I'm glad your mother cared enough to teach them to you. Manners make a person think of others before themselves." Something the men in her life had never done as they'd always thought it was about them. She liked having someone think of her first. Even if only to open a door.

As she pondered her new appreciation of simple good manners, he said, "I never thought about it like that." It sounded as if he'd come to an important realization himself. Then he asked, "You ever been to Mac's before?"

"No."

"Best-kept secret in the city." His fondness for the establishment was audible and visible as he stopped in front of a red brick building with a large wooden door. Above it was a sign that read Mac's in bold red letters. Rex held the door open.

She smiled her genuine pleasure as she passed him. "Thank you." Once inside, she turned in time to see his grin and nod of appreciation.

"You're welcome."

They both laughed. She enjoyed laughing with Rex. Hadn't done much of it recently.

They went down a few steps and made a left turn into a dimly lit dining room. Tables were covered in white cloths with small flower vases in the center of each.

"This was a speakeasy during the twenties," Rex informed her on the way to the hostess stand.

"I can imagine." Tiffani loved the place immediately with its warm old-world charm.

A short, heavy-set, balding man came around the stand to greet them, a smile lighting up his face. "Rex. This is a pleasure."

"Hi, Joe," he said, taking the man into a hug and patting him on the back.

They broke apart and Joe said, "Long time no see."

"Too long. I've been busy."

"I saw that. Glad everything worked out," Joe remarked.

Rex stepped back and put his arm around Tiffani's shoulders in a friendly manner, pulling her close. "Joe, I'd like you to meet my friend Tiffani."

Joe's smile deepened. "Hello, Ms. Tiffani."

"Hi." She felt unusually shy all of a sudden.

Rex removed his arm. "Are we too early for the ribs to be ready?"

Joe picked up a couple of menus from the slot on the stand. "Not for you."

"Are they any good?" Rex teased.

"All my ribs are good." Joe grinned as he showed them to a table.

"I'll be the judge of that," Rex declared, pulling a chair out for her.

Tiffani settled into the wooden seat and Rex took the one beside her. Why did he choose to sit so close instead of across from her? Trying to dismiss her uncharacteristic shyness, Tiffani opened her menu. "I'm guessing we don't have to earn his vote of confidence."

"Nope. Joe and I go way back."

"It makes you uncomfortable to talk about the lawsuit, doesn't it?"

A grimace flowed over Rex's face. "I just hate that

people feel they need to tiptoe around what happened. I didn't do anything wrong. I was trying to save the man's life." In the same breath he added, "You're welcome to get anything you want but I recommend the dry-rub rib dinner. You can't go wrong."

Obviously, he was done with that subject. Now that she'd seen him with all sorts of patients she knew there was no way he had ever been guilty of what he'd been accused of. He was passionate about his work, caring. He would have saved that man's life had it been in his power to do so. She shot a covert glance at Rex. Was he the same in other areas of his life?

A young waitress dressed in a white shirt and black skirt came to take their drink orders.

"You eat here often?" Tiffani asked as the waitress walked off.

"No. I wish I did. I stay pretty busy at the hospital."

"I know you're a dedicated doctor and all, but don't you ever do something for fun?"

He shut his menu and put it on top of hers. "Sure I do. Every day."

What was he talking about? "Like what?"

"You won't like my answer. I ride my bike."

Tiffani smirked. "And I'm ruining all your fun."

Rex grinned. "Yeah, you are. I think you should make that up to me."

"And just how should I do that?" She watched as a hint of a wolfish grin curved his lips.

"I have a few ideas." His voice held a provocative note.

Tiffani shifted in her chair. She was grateful when the waitress returned and they ordered the ribs Rex had suggested. When they were alone again she pulled out her phone and announced, "I got some great pictures today. In fact, as soon as we finish here I need to post them."

He ignored the picture on the phone she held out for him to see, keeping his eyes on her face. "You talk about me having fun. What about you? Let's talk about something besides our jobs."

She put her phone away. "Okay, what do you want to talk about?"

"How about what's your favorite movie?"

He kept the easy conversation flowing as the food arrived and they ate. To Tiffani's delight, they had more in common than either of them expected. They even laughed over Rex's story about his first attempt to ride a motorcycle.

"Hey, look this way," Rex said as they finished their meal.

She did as he requested.

He leaned in close and wiped her cheek with a napkin. "You have rub on your face."

Their gazes met, held. Was she imagining the heat swirling around them?

"Well, if it isn't Tiffani Romano," came a sarcastic tone she recognized.

A cold wind blew over her, removing the warmth that had been there only seconds before. The urge to groan grew. *Lou.* What was he doing here? Why was this happening to her? She didn't even want to look. Would it have been so bad for her to have stayed in the heavenly moment Rex had created?

Against her better judgment, she looked up.

"Isn't this a surprise?" Lou said in far too cheerful a voice, his mouth wide with a smile.

"I guess you could call it that." Why couldn't he have just walked on by? More than that, why did she let him get to her? She didn't mean anything to him. All he was trying to do was belittle her to make himself feel more important. He wanted to humiliate her. Again. He made a point of stopping by the office almost daily. She didn't deserve it on her day off as well.

"Funny meeting you here," Lou said.

Tiffani didn't think it was humorous at all. She glanced at the woman with him, who was apparently his newest conquest.

As if she'd given him a reminder to gloat, Lou put his arm around the woman's shoulders and pulled her in so tightly she came off one foot. "This is Monique. She's an up-and-coming model. You may have seen her in a couple of magazines."

Tiffani had. Almost all of her.

She looked at Rex, who must have noticed the anguish in her eyes because he put his arm across the back of her chair and leaned in close. "Honey, aren't you going to introduce me?"

She couldn't deny the pleasure she felt when Lou's smile drooped. "Uh, this is Lou Habersham. A co-worker." She put emphasis on the last word. "Lou, Dr. Rex Maxwell."

"Tiffani, we were more than coworkers," Lou said in a meaningful tone.

"And we aren't anymore." Tiffani felt sorry for Monique, having to listen to this.

Rex smiled and offered his hand. "Your loss is my gain."

Lou looked as if he were taking Rex's hand more out of duty than desire.

"I wish we could ask you to join us but we've just finished our meal and are on our way out. We have something special planned for this afternoon." Rex made the word *special* sound so suggestive that Tiffani blushed. That would give Lou his comeuppance. Thanks to Rex, it now looked like she had a hot doctor and didn't need him anymore.

Taking her elbow, Rex guided her to her feet. "Enjoy your meal," he said to Lou, who now looked baffled.

Tiffani gave Monique a reassuring smile. Lou said nothing. She silently cheered Rex for leaving the pompous man speechless. As they walked toward the door she whispered, "Thanks for that."

Rex moved his hand from her elbow to her waist. "You're welcome."

She appreciated his support. How had he known she'd needed it?

They paused at the hostess stand, where Rex handed Joe a few bills. "Ribs were great, Joe. I'll be back soon."

"I'm going to count on that. Bring your lady with you."

"I'll do that."

She wasn't Rex's lady, but after seeing Lou she needed to feel like she belonged to him, even if it was just for a few minutes.

They climbed the stairs and exited. A dark cloud filled the western sky. There was a roll of thunder before a shower of rain began.

"Do you want to chance it or wait while I go get the car?" Rex asked.

"I'll walk. I don't want to wait here."

"Okay."

Tiffani headed down the sidewalk. He kept pace with her but didn't try to take her hand or touch her. As they went, lightning streaked across the sky and the wind picked up. The rain grew heavier. He grabbed her hand and they ran the last of the distance to the car.

Inside it Rex finally asked, "You want to tell me what that was all about back there?"

"It doesn't matter. It was just Lou, being the jerk he is."

"It looked and sounded like more than that." He watched her.

She finally met his gaze. "Rex, I'm sorry. We were having a nice meal. I ruined it and now you're all wet. I'll get you home."

The thunderstorm roared around them.

"I hate wet jeans," Tiffani complained as she started the car. "They stick to you…"

Rex's mouth quirked. "But the view is nice."

Warmth filled her that had nothing to do with the heat coming from the dashboard. Rex had a way of making her feel good about herself, she admitted with reluctance. "I'll have you at your place in a sec. I've already taken up too much of your day."

They rode in silence. They were almost at his apartment when lightning lit the sky just before a heavy roll of thunder followed. The rain made it hard to see in front of them.

"You're not driving home in this. It's too dangerous. Come up to my place until it passes."

"I'll be fine."

"Where do you live?" Rex asked.

"Out toward Germantown."

"That's a good thirty to forty minutes away. More in this weather, and it's headed that direction." He squinted out the windshield.

Fear that if she went into his home she might not want to leave prompted her to protest, "I'm sure you had other plans for your day besides seeing after me."

"Doctor's orders. You're coming in with me."

She couldn't sit around in his house in wet clothes. "I'm a mess. I don't have any spare clothes with me."

"I'll find something you can wear. Stop arguing." When she reached his address he said, "Drive around the block and up the alley. I have a garage there. You can't park on the street in this area."

Tiffani did as he said.

Halfway down the row he instructed, "Let me out here. I'll raise the door."

She watched as he climbed out into the downpour and pulled up the large square metal door. He must feel as miserable as she did in his wet clothes. His back muscles flexed under the soaked, clinging fabric of his T-shirt. He wasn't the only one who could appreciate a view.

Seconds later he was waving her into the garage. His bike was parked there and she pulled in next to it and got out. She stepped into the rain beside him as he pulled the door down in one quick motion. Together they hurried to a single wooden door across the way. Rex pulled keys from his pocket and opened it. Swinging it wide, he let her enter ahead of him.

"Head upstairs. The door at the top is open."

A light came on as she took the first step. The space smelled of oil and lemon, as if the wood had been cared for with polish. She pushed open the door at the top into a spacious kitchen area with brick walls, stainless-steel appliances and an ultra-modern dinning set. The floors were dark hardwood that gleamed even in the dim light. One wall was floor-to-ceiling windows, and beyond that was a roof patio with plants everywhere, even a raised garden. More astonishing was a view of the river.

She turned to Rex. "This is an amazing place."

"I'll let you look around to your heart's desire after you get out of those wet clothes. Come this way and

I'll show you where you can get a shower." He headed down a wide hallway into a huge space that faced the street, visible through four tall windows that lined the front. True to his word, he didn't give her time to explore, leading her to a small hall with two doors leading off it. He went into the one on the right. She followed. He had stopped in the middle of a room that looked as if it doubled as an office and guest room.

He pointed to another door. "There's the bath. Make yourself at home. I'll put some clothes on the doorknob. There's lots of hot water so take your time." He circled her and left, shutting the door behind him.

Rex wondered what possessed him to insist that Tiffani come in. Maybe it was the sad look in her eyes when she'd seen that guy at the restaurant, or the drowned-rat look after they'd jumped into the car, or just that he didn't want her to leave him yet. Whatever it was, he had to live with the decision now.

Tiffani was undressing in his bathroom. He shouldn't have been concerned about having a hot bath because what he really needed was a cold one. Opening a drawer, he selected a T-shirt for her to wear and pulled sweat pants off a hanger in his closet. Going back into his spare room, he hung the clothes on the doorknob of the closed bathroom door.

A sound came from inside. He grinned. Tiffani was singing a pop song. If he didn't get moving, the temptation to ask if he could join her would overcome common sense.

Forcing himself to go to his own bath, he peeled off his wet clothes and stepped under the shower. Minutes later he, dried off and pulled on a fresh T-shirt and a pair of shorts. Gathering his wet clothes, he checked to see if Tiffani was done. Sounds came from the kitchen so he headed that way.

Tiffani stood in her bare feet, looking into a cabinet. She looked so cute, wearing his clothes, even though they were large on her. Her hair was down. The gorgeous tresses fell just below her shoulders.

"I didn't know what I should do with my wet clothes," she said over her shoulder, "so I found the washer and put them in there. Why don't you put yours in with mine and get them going?"

Rex went to the laundry room just off the kitchen to do as she suggested. There was something intimate, almost erotic about the image of their clothes circling and whirling around each other. Rex shook his head. He needed to get control of his thoughts. He returned to the kitchen to find Tiffani looking in a different cabinet.

"Where can I find a glass? I'm thirsty."

"They're over here." He moved beside her and opened a door, reached for a glass and placed it on the counter.

"Thanks."

"It's longer than I thought," he said before he thought.

Tiffani turned. "Uh? What is?"

She pulled self-consciously at the T-shirt he'd given her to wear. "Your shirt?"

Rex stepped closer. "No, your hair." He gave in to his desire to touch it. Though still damp, the smooth strands flowed over his fingers. "Nice."

Tiffani stilled.

He heard her soft intake of breath. His gaze met hers. Her eyes were wide with wonder.

"You've been thinking about my hair?" Her words were almost a whisper.

"Every day since I met you. I've wanted to take it down so many times." He let his palm caress her head.

"Why?"

He shrugged a shoulder. "Because I thought you might let loose some if you let your hair down."

"Why would you want me to do that?"

She really had no idea what he was talking about. As if she couldn't see that she was so wrapped up in her job and her father that she left no room in her life for fun... or a man. He ran his hand beneath her hair at her neck and pulled her toward him. "So you'd be more open to one of these."

His lips found hers. Her arms came around his neck, much to his satisfaction, and she returned his kiss. When she groaned low, he reached around her waist and pulled her against him. It felt right having her there, like he'd been missing her against him since the first day he'd laid eyes on her. His mouth teased hers then traveled over her cheek to nibble behind her ear. Tiffani leaned her head to the side, giving him better access. She purred as he left small kisses along her neck.

"You taste so sweet. Like strawberries and cream," he murmured as his mouth found hers again.

Her fingers traced his nape as she opened her mouth in an invitation that he accepted without hesitation. His tongue entered and greeted hers. She gave him a warm welcome.

She went up on her toes, her body sliding against his. Heat that had been simmering deep inside him boiled over. He hugged her tightly to him. The movements of their meshed mouths turned frantic. He ran his hand over her hip and down to cup one butt cheek. It was every bit as wonderful to touch as it had been to watch in anticipation. He squeezed it, bringing her even closer to his straining manhood. She squirmed with impatience against his length, making him grow harder.

Had he ever been yhis hot for a woman?

He moved his other hand along her side until he brushed her breast beneath the knit material. At her slight press forward of encouragement he cupped her. Tested the weight of the soft mound while running his thumb over her nipple. She wore no bra.

That's right. It was in the washer, mingling with his clothes. She pulled his head closer, her kiss growing more urgent.

He had been right. She was all raw woman beneath the expensive business dress and *appearance was everything* attitude.

Skin. He had to touch hers. His fingers found the hem of the shirt and slipped underneath to touch the warmth and smoothness of her. Had anything ever felt so perfect? Slowly he ran his palms over her back. Tiffani trembled, then deepened her kiss even more than he'd thought possible.

His hands glided up her sides until both hovered near her breasts. Moments later he tenderly followed the curve of a full orb with his fingertips. It was so perfect. Silky. His index finger circled her nipple, found the tip. It stiffened, pushed toward him. He rubbed his palm over it and was rewarded with the feel of it becoming even harder.

Tiffani shuddered.

So responsive. The desire to see her naked, all of her, roared through him. To taste her. To worship her. To have her.

In the back of the burning desire was the knowledge that if he didn't regain control of himself now, he was going to take her on the kitchen floor. But before he could react, Tiffani stepped back, ending their kiss and putting a calming amount of space between them.

CHAPTER SEVEN

WHAT WAS SHE DOING? Tiffani's heart was racing and her hands shaking almost uncontrollably. She'd never acted like a wanton before and here she was in Rex's house, close to begging him to take her. All he'd done was kiss her and she'd lost her mind. "I'm sorry. I really should go."

"Go?" Rex croaked. "What? Why?"

Still unable to meet his look, she stammered, "I… uh… I…"

Rex grabbed her, kissed her again. Hard. Released her. "Please, don't."

She couldn't look at him. What if he ended up treating her the way Lou had? She couldn't survive that kind of devastation again. If she made this step and became too attached and he didn't care for her the same way… But Rex wasn't Lou. He'd proved that over and over. Still…

"You are a client. This is unprofessional."

He lifted her chin with a finger. Her gaze met his. "That has nothing to do with what's going on here. Can't you tell what you do to me? I don't care about anything but that. The rest doesn't matter." Rex studied her for a moment before he adjusted her shirt so it hung around her hips, leaving nothing of her exposed. He tugged on her hand. "Come with me."

"Where are we going?"

"Not where I would like to take you," he said in a droll voice. He led her into the living room to one of the two sofas that faced each other. "Have a seat."

"I really should go. I can get my clothes some other time."

"I can't make you stay, but I wish you would." He stood waiting.

With reluctance, she sat on the edge of the sofa.

Rex came down beside her but not touching her. "I want you to talk to me. I want to understand why you're running from me. The client business is just an excuse."

Tiffani pulled a small sofa pillow into her arms and clutched it to her chest. How could she make him understand how badly she had been hurt? That she was scared to give him the ability to do it too? "Because... I can't—*won't*—let myself be hurt again."

"Where did you get the idea I would hurt you?"

"It's not so much you." How could she explain this to him?

"Does this have something to do with the guy at the restaurant?"

He was always so perceptive. She felt more than saw him watching her intently. "Yeah."

"Will you tell me what happened?" Rex encouraged in a soft tone.

Rex deserved an answer. Yet she hated that Lou was intruding on what had been some of the most wonderful minutes of her life, being in Rex's arms. "I was stupid. I thought I was in love. We'd been dating for six months. I thought we were getting serious. Or at least I was. I'd even taken him to meet my father. Marriage had been mentioned. Then I told him I loved him. That was the end. Turned out he didn't feel the same. What makes it worse is that now he seems to thrive on reminding me. Like today."

"And you think I'd do the same thing?" There was a note of hurt in Rex's voice.

"Yes, no, I don't know. Lou and I work together. You and I basically work together. This campaign is important. Even now our relationship has become more personal than it should."

"Do you trust me?" Rex asked, taking one of her hands.

She nodded.

"Do you think I'd ever do anything to intentionally hurt you?"

"No." And she was confident he wouldn't.

"Good. I can't guarantee what will happen in the future but I can tell you about the here and now. There is something special between us, something I haven't shared with another woman. I can't put a name to it because I'm not sure what it is, but I know it's strong. Worth exploring. I want to know you in all the ways I can. Enjoy you. I'm willing to see what happens, if you are."

Tiffani hesitated, so Rex carried on.

"I understand the campaign and the chance for the promotion is important to you. I respect that." He continued to play with her fingers as he leaned back on the sofa and twisted sideways to face her, bending his knee to bring his leg up on the cushions.

He was saying all the right things. "I promised myself I wouldn't have another office romance or let myself get carried away again…"

"It doesn't take much for us to get carried away," Rex said with a grin.

"No, it doesn't." She looked at him from beneath her lashes.

Rex gave her a sly grin. "I like it when you get carried away. Those sweet moans, your touches and kisses. Look at me, Tiffani."

She did, against her better judgment.

"If we'd kept going the way we were in the kitchen, I would've had you on the floor in two more seconds. You deserve better than that. I want to make sure we're on the same page. I never want you to regret being with me, or being honest about your feelings."

Despite what she had said about being careful, her half-healed heart opened and took him in. He was thinking about her. Not what he needed or what she could do for him, but what was best for her. She'd had that so rarely in her life. Since she'd been young it had always been about helping her mother, her father, her family. With Lou it had been all about him. "Thank you for that."

"I'm going to make you a promise right now. I'll always be honest with you and will never hide who I am from you. What you see is what you get. Okay?"

She nodded.

"Now, with your permission, I'm going to show you just how amazing I think you are."

If she took this chance, she was opening the door to pain—but if she didn't, what would she miss out on? The possibility of something wonderful with Rex. She was going to take the chance. "Okay."

He pulled her onto his lap, his mouth taking hers. Their tongues danced as his hand made a path through her hair.

Tiffani met him kiss for kiss. She wanted this. If there was fallout with her job she would deal with it.

Her heart would be hard to handle but she would face that when and if it happened. Rex had made her promises and she trusted him.

He released her mouth and sat back. "This has to go," he said, tugging at her T-shirt.

"The windows. Daylight," she muttered through her stupor. The rain was still pounding against them, but they were exposed nevertheless.

"No one is going to see us. And I can't imagine anything more beautiful than you naked in the light. Your body should never be hidden."

A shot of delight went through her to know Rex desired her so much.

He raised her hands, skimming the shirt off. Tiffani cupped his face, brushed his hair away and with a gentle tug brought his lips to hers. Into her kiss she put all her passion. He pulled back and gave her a wicked look that started a pulsating need deep in her center. "You keep that up and I might not be accountable for what I do next."

"I might like that."

With all the confidence she'd heard more than once when he talked to his patients, he said, "I can guarantee it. But right now I want to admire you."

He dropped his gaze to her breasts. His hands tenderly caressed them, making them tingle. She hissed in pleasure when the pads of his thumbs massaged her nipples. They rose hard and erect as if straining for more of his caresses. The pulsating in her center began to grow. She held her breath as his head moved lower.

His warm, wet mouth covered a nipple. Letting her head fall back, she closed her eyes and relished the wave of hot desire rolling through her. As Rex's tongue circled then softly tugged, her center contracted. She squirmed, needing more. So much more. And soon.

He lingered, her tip remaining in his mouth. The pressure between her legs intensified. Rex took the other breast and gave it equal loving attention. How he pulled such feeling from her was a mystery she didn't care to solve. The cool air on her wet breast sent a shiver through her that quickly became a quiver of increasing need.

She feared she was going to spiral off into space too soon. His arousal pressed hard against her hip. She shifted, rubbing against it, eliciting an animal sound from him. As Rex suckled, he nudged her back on the sofa. His hand returned to fondle her other breast as his mouth continued working its magic.

Tiffani opened her eyes and pushed his hair away so she could watch. A sense of wonder filled her. This gorgeous, intelligent and uncommon man was loving her. She'd never been this hot for a man's touch.

His hand slipped from her breast and caressed the outside of her thigh then up and over it. He shifted her so he could touch where she was hot and wanting. He rubbed the fabric covering the juncture of her thighs back and forth. She closed her eyes and savored the erotic sensation, heat bubbling within.

Rex raised his eyes. Their gazes met and held as he shifted on top of her, the ridge of his desire barred from her center by clothing. She writhed.

"Tiff, you are so amazing. Do you feel what you do to me?" He flexed against her.

She ran her hands over his chest and down to the hem of his shirt. Slipping her hands beneath it, she caressed his heated skin. Wanting more, she pushed his shirt up until he sat on his knees and yanked it over his head.

Tiffani reveled in the sight of so much of masculine flesh on view just for her. He lowered himself once more and she traced a fingertip over one of his ribs.

He hissed as she continued to explore the line of hair disappearing under the waistband of his shorts. His mouth claimed hers as their skin met.

No man before Rex had ever set her nerve endings on overload like this.

His kiss was gentle, almost reverent. Giving. Reassuring.

While he began dropping small kisses along her cheek, he pushed at the sweat pants he'd loaned her. She shifted, helping him to shove them from her hips and tug them to her knees. He rolled to his side and his palm found the plane of her belly. Leisurely, he moved his fingers over her skin, studying and surveying, slowly moving downward to brush the curls.

Tiffani watched as Rex explored her body. His eyes abruptly rose to meet hers. "So beautiful."

Everything he'd said and done in these last almost eternal moments were like a balm to her wounded soul. He made her believe she was significant to his world.

She guided his lips to hers. Kissed him with gentle appreciation.

His finger found her bare center and teased her entrance. She moaned. Every fiber of her being was focused on his next action.

With one smooth move he slipped his finger inside her. She involuntarily flexed toward him. He exited and entered, repeating it with increasing speed until Tiffani thought she wasn't going to survive the excruciating bliss. Heat built, flamed, until it roared in her ears.

Without warning, it back-flashed, spiraling into a tower that bore her high. Gently she floated in a cloud of ecstasy that brought her softly back to reality.

Blinking, she registered she was naked in the daylight on Rex's sofa while he smiled down at her.

He whispered, "That was the most stunning sight I've ever seen. Thank you for letting me be a part of it."

How could she not love a man like him? But she would never say that aloud.

The moment Tiffani had found her pleasure by his hand, something changed in Rex. No one had ever let go so totally or readily for him. She still had him tied up in knots of need for his own release but he'd found joy in just watching her. Something beyond his understanding was happening between them.

He didn't have women to his place. Didn't have sex in his living room in the daylight. Didn't bring people involved in his work life into his personal world. He was at a loss for what to think.

What had made him scrap all his standards and beliefs?

Tiffani.

He looked down at her, lying half beneath him. She was watching him with a shy expression. "Thank you, Rex. For that wonderful…" She waved her hand. Her fingertips brushed his chest and his manhood jumped. Her eyes widened for a fraction of a second. "And for making me feel special."

He shifted, letting her know he still desired her. "You are special."

Seconds later she pulled her legs from beneath him. Kicking off her pants, she stood before him. There was nothing unsure about her direct look. She reached out her hand. He took it. Tiffani led him toward the bedrooms. When she started into the one she knew he pulled her hand. "Mine."

She took the lead again, taking him to the edge of his bed and stopping. Looking him straight in the eyes, she pushed at the waistband of his shorts until they dropped to the floor. She stepped back and studied his manhood straining stone hard toward her. Her gaze wandered over his chest before her look met his again. The tip of her fingers caressed the top of one shoulder.

When was the last time he'd quivered with need like this? Had he ever?

"You're too much. Too male. Too gorgeous. Too sexy. Too caring," she whispered, as she took hold of his waist then came up on her toes to kiss him. The second he tried to take her in his arms she stilled him but continued to build the heat in him by nibbling kisses along his mouth. She took his bottom lip between her teeth, giving it a gentle squeeze.

Releasing his mouth and hands, she grasped his forearms and turned him so his back was to the bed. He started to wrap his arms around her but she pushed them away. "Not yet. It's still my turn."

That was the Tiffani he recognized. The one in control, who knew what she wanted and would get it. The strong, self-assured person, not the sad, beaten one he'd seen earlier. He liked her vulnerable side that needed him but this bold one was hot, set his blood on fire.

"Lie back on the bed." She gave his chest a gentle shove with the palm of her hand. He fell back onto the mattress. Seconds later she was beside him. Her hand roamed his chest as she planted kisses along the crest of his shoulder. Again he attempted to touch her but she wouldn't allow it. "No, this is my turn."

Frustration built in him like pressure in a volcano.

Her fingers found his hair and brushed it out around his head. "I love your hair. All wild and wonderful."

"I thought you wanted it cut short," he said with a grin.

Tiffani leaned back so that he could see her face clearly. "No. I think you're like Samson, you get your strength from it. It's a statement of who you are." She threaded her fingers through his and stretched her arms out. Letting her breasts sweep his chest, she gave him a wet, hot kiss.

Rex's restraint was close to his limit. She straddled him and every muscle in his body constricted. His manhood rested in the crease of her behind. Just one small movement...

She rose up on her knees. "Protection?"

"Drawer," he croaked, and pointed to his bedside table.

Tiffani leaned over him. After pulling the drawer open, she rummaged around until she came out with a square package. He took it from her, opened it and quickly covered himself. He fisted a handful of her hair and brought her mouth back to his.

As they kissed Tiffani positioned her moist, hot center over him. Slowly, agonizingly slowly, she slid down his shaft. Rex clenched his teeth at the exquisite pleasure. He couldn't have stopped the lift of his hips if he'd wanted to. With one swift surge she took his entire length. Her eyes closed as an enraptured look covered her face. She pulled upward and pushed down again. When she started to repeat it, he met her action with an instinctive reaction.

She pulled her mouth from his and straightened,

throwing back her head, hands braced on his chest as their pace became more frantic. He watched her breasts bobbing, keeping time with their joined rhythm. He would remember this view forever.

Tiffani's mouth formed a small O, as if this second orgasm had taken her by surprise. She shuddered over him.

Male satisfaction filled him. He felt like he should be standing at the top of a mountain, thumping his chest, letting all the world know how great a lover he was.

She eased down over his chest like melting ice cream in the sunshine and sighed.

He rolled her over and reentered her. Gathering his hair in her hands and wrapping her legs around his waist, she joined him in his frantic ride to the finish. With a low grunt of release, he was transported to paradise.

Rex didn't know what time it was when he woke but there was still daylight and he was sprawled out on the top of his bed with the most amazing woman he'd ever met curled into his side, sleeping.

It had been a surreal day. Nothing had been as he'd expected. Tiffani had made it different. There was movement beside him. He looked at her. Her eyelids rose slowly. She blinked and her eyes went round.

"Hey," she said shyly, and looked away.

"Hey, yourself."

She shifted away from him and climbed off the bed.

He reached for her and just missed her hand. "Where're you going?"

"I should find my clothes."

Rex watched her bare butt as she exited his room. This unsure Tiffani was a new side of her he found intriguing.

A few seconds later, as he was pulling on his shorts

he saw her dashing into the other bedroom with clothes in her arms. So much for the soft afterglow moments. Did she regret what had happened between them? He wasn't going to let the situation become awkward. What they had shared had been amazing, nothing to be was ashamed of.

He was in the kitchen when Tiffani showed up again, wearing the clothes he'd let her borrow. He informed her, "I put our clothes in the dryer. They should be done in a little while. I thought you might like a glass of tea while you wait." He sat the two cups on the table.

"I don't think I'll wait for my clothes. I'll get them later." She moved toward the door.

"Whoa." He grabbed her forearm. "Where're you headed?"

She looked at his hand and he let it fall away. "I just think it's time for me to go."

Rex stepped close to her. "Take a breath. Slow down. Why don't you have a seat and we can talk about any arguments you might have to me kissing you again." He grinned at her and pulled out a chair. "Because I'm certainly going to kiss you again."

She gave him an odd but endearing smile before she dropped into the chair. A few seconds later she took a sip of tea.

Rex sat at the end of the table to give her some space. She appeared to relax. The silence, to his surprise, wasn't tense but more like that of two friends sharing a few quiet moments.

"This sure is a nice kitchen," she said, looking around. "It looks like it's used regularly. Some woman isn't going to come home and find me here, is she?"

Her sense of humor was starting to return. "You're asking me *now* if I have a wife or girlfriend?"

"I know you don't. Remember I read your bio." She played with the condensation on the glass.

He nodded. "That's right, the big folder of doom."

She cracked a smile.

Progress. He wanted the fun and open Tiffani back. "For your information, I do the cooking here. I consider myself a gourmet chef when I have time to prepare a meal."

"Really?"

He smiled. "That wasn't in the folder of doom either."

Her eyes lit up. "No, but that's great information. I could really use it."

"Tiff, I didn't tell you that so you can use it for the campaign. Can't you be off work for a little while?"

"I'm sorry. It's really all I have and I sometimes get carried away." She looked both sincere and sad.

Rex turned serious. "If I tell you something few others know, are you going to tell the world?"

She wrinkled her nose. "I might want to but I'll keep it to myself. So what is it?"

Satisfaction ran through him. He'd captured her attention. "I grow most of my food."

"I noticed your garden outside. That's really wonderful." She walked to the glass door and looked out onto his rainy patio. "Did you learn to cook from your mom?"

"Hardly. We had a housekeeper. My mother was too busy spending her time at the country club and planning bridge parties to cook."

Tiffani's attention came back to him. Had she heard the bitterness in his voice? "My daddy wouldn't have a garden. He could have. People offered to build boxes high enough for him but he didn't want anyone's help."

"You would've liked to have had a garden, wouldn't you? I learned to cook by watching late-night cooking shows to wind down after a long day. The cooks talked about using fresh vegetables and herbs and I thought I'd give it a try. Turns out I'm good at it."

"You're good at a lot of things."

He gave her a lopsided grin and a pointed look. "I like to think so."

Tiffani blushed a lovely shade of pink. "I'm just going to get my clothes. If they're a little damp it won't matter. I'm sure the good-looking bachelor must have a date on a Saturday night."

She didn't wait for him to respond before she headed for the laundry room.

That was it! Rex followed her. "Let me get this right. You actually think that I'd have sex with you in the afternoon and go out on a date this evening? You think that little of me?"

Tiffani straightened from where she had been looking into the dryer. She clutched a couple of articles of clothing in her hands. "I don't know what I think. I hadn't planned on this afternoon happening."

Rex stepped closer. "I didn't either." His hands came to rest on her waist. "But I thought it was amazing. More than amazing." He placed kisses along her neck.

"I need—"

He brought her against his growing manhood, letting her know what he was thinking. He murmured, "What do you need?"

Her mouth found his. The clothes she held fell to the floor as her arms circled his neck. Rex lifted her and she wrapped her legs around his hips. Taking a step back, he set her on the top of the dryer. She let him go and shimmied out of her pants while he pushed his shorts down and kicked them away. His lips found hers again.

He could learn to love this Tiffani.

* * *

The next morning the sun streamed through Tiffani's bedroom window. The storm had passed. She moved and a sweet soreness reminded her she had used muscles for activities she hadn't enjoyed for far too long. Sex on a dryer. That was a new one for her. One she'd like to repeat.

Her lack of control yesterday still shocked her. But she'd loved every second of touching and being touched by Rex. Her body heated at just the thought of him. She didn't know how she would concentrate on the campaign now. Whenever she was around him all she'd be thinking about was finding a place where they could be alone.

He'd not asked her to stay the night. She was glad because she wasn't sure she could have said no. And the way she'd acted like a loved-starved ninny who had never had a man look at her was still horribly embarrassing. But she hadn't ever had a man look at her the way Rex had. He was the first *real* man she'd ever been with.

Intelligent, caring, attentive, as interested in her pleasure as his own, giving and fun. How had she been so wrong about him? Worse, how could she have let things between them become personal? A real relationship between them would never work. There were too many variables working against them. His job, hers. Him in Memphis and her wanting to move away. Her betraying her father. Rex had said nothing about ever wanting to settle down. He was, she assured herself, the love-them-and-leave-them type. All they'd done yesterday had been to create a big tangle.

From now on any interaction between them would be strictly business. Tiffani groaned in despair, but his kiss goodbye last night had been perfect. For a second, she would have sworn she had floated.

But no more thinking like that.

She climbed out of bed. Enough of the daydreaming. Her father was expecting her to visit. She wouldn't disappoint him. He had called, asking her to do some shopping for him.

If she didn't discipline herself, she'd stay in bed and relive every second of those moments with Rex.

The last few days were ones to remember, but not in a good way. They didn't improve when Rex's cellphone rang around seven that evening as he pushed open the hospital door leading to the parking lot with thoughts of calling Tiffani.

"Rex Maxwell," he answered, trying not to snap but just missing it.

"Dr. Maxwell, you're needed in the OR. Auto accident."

He sighed. "I'm on my way."

Despite his regular surgery schedule, he'd done his share of emergency surgery in the last few days. He hadn't even had time to call or see Tiffani. He only hoped she didn't think he had used her and forgotten about her. He didn't believe in being intimate with a woman and then ignoring her. The least he would do was explain how he felt if he didn't plan to see her again. In Tiffani's case, he had every intention of seeing more of her, as well as experiencing her.

The problem was he couldn't get away from the hospital. He didn't remember another time he'd resented his job but he did tonight. Tiffani pulled at him. Like a need he didn't think would ever be fulfilled. But right now he had a job to do.

He hurried up the stairs to the second floor. Pushing

through the surgery suite doors, he asked the unit secretary which OR.

She called as he continued down the hall toward the locker room, "Six."

Minutes later he was changed, back in scrubs and washing his hands.

His scrub nurse came up beside him with a hat and mask. He leaned down and she helped him finish dressing. "So, what do we have?"

In a solemn voice she said, "Teen. One-car accident. Rollover. Thrown out. Internal injuries."

Rex let out a string of expletives beneath his mask.

"I know what you mean," his nurse replied. "It seems like it happens every full moon." She looked closely at Rex. "When was the last time you slept in your own bed and not in an on-call room?"

"Three or four nights ago," he said, remembering how Tiffani had left and he'd wished he'd insisted she stay. But he hadn't wanted to push. She was skittish enough about them being together. He'd missed her all night long. "Anesthesia ready?"

"Will be by the time we get in there." His nurse finished tying his mask.

"Then let's go."

They headed into the OR.

"History?" he said to his physician's assistant, who was already standing beside the patient on the table.

"Sixteen-year-old male, good heath, no allergies. Only issue is that his car didn't win the war with the tree."

"Let's get him patched up. What're we going after first?" Rex glanced at the X-rays on the wall screen.

"Spleen," the PA said.

"Turn on the rock 'n' roll and let's get started." Rex

stepped to the table. The music filled the room as he removed the organ, stitched up two perforations to the boy's kidney, one to the stomach. He had hopes of closing when the monitors started beeping.

"BP's going down," the anesthesiologist said urgently from by the patient's head.

"There has to be a bleeder somewhere. Suction." Tension started to well in him. He needed to find it, and fast.

Over the next few minutes he searched frantically with no success. Rex was still looking when the anesthesiologist said, "That's it."

"Continue CPR while I look," Rex demanded.

"It's over, Rex." The anesthesiologist met his look over his mask and shook his head. "He was already too far gone when he came in."

That wasn't what the family was going to want to hear. Rex left the OR. In the locker room, he jerked off his cap and slung it to the floor. Sitting on the bench, he put his forearms on his knees and hung his head. Now he had to go tell the boy's parents he'd been unable to save his life. These cases took a bite out of his heart every time.

Had he done all he could do? What had he missed? Should he have made the repairs in a different order? For all his bravado about it, before the lawsuit he'd never questioned himself like he did now. It was hard to admit, but it was true.

Picking up his cap, he stood and headed for the waiting room. Talking to the parents couldn't be put off any longer.

CHAPTER EIGHT

IT HAD BEEN easier to avoid crossing paths with Rex than Tiffani had anticipated. Sunday she had spent with her father. It hadn't been pleasant. He'd harped on about her job being a betrayal of her loyalty to him. She knew she mustn't ever let escape the least hint of how she'd spent her afternoon the day before. Even so, her father noticed her mind wandered more often than usual.

The next three long days at the office she spent managing social media, a magazine interview and other details of the campaign. Rex must have decided, as she had, that what they had done couldn't continue, because he hadn't tried to contact her. She didn't have a good reason to call him so she left things well enough alone. Yet he was constantly in her thoughts. When she wasn't dreaming of being kissed by him, she was forced to speak his name in the course of her job.

Her doorbell ringing just before midnight woke her. Someone needing something this late couldn't be good. Her phone buzzed, indicating a text message. What was going on?

She looked at her phone.

The doorbell rang again.

The number was Rex's.

Let me in.

Her heart hummed. Her common sense balked. Why was he here? It didn't matter. He just was.

She didn't bother with a robe and hurried downstairs in her nightshirt. Flipping on the porch light, she checked through the peephole. He was leaning against the door-jamb. The doorbell rang again. She unlocked the door. "What's wrong? Are you hurt?"

There was a weariness that hung heavily around him. His shoulders slumped. Concern pushed away any excitement she felt over seeing him. "Tell me what's wrong. What happened?"

He wrapped her in his arms and buried his face in her neck. "I don't want to think about it. Talk about it. I just want us. To know again how good you make me feel." His mouth found hers. There was hunger, desperation and need in his movements. His tongue mated with hers, becoming more desperate with every thrust.

All her vows fled. The glow only he could ignite with his touch grew. Sheer joy filled her. Her nerves tingled and her heart hammered against her ribs. This was what being alive felt like! She had no fear other than that Rex might pull away. He was hurting and she was here for him.

He lifted her and carried her inside far enough to kick the door closed, holding her so tight her breath was erratic. His mouth found her earlobe and his teeth bit down until she winced. With a brush of the tip of his tongue, he eased the pain. He cupped her butt and jerked her against him. His manhood was thick, long and solid beneath the fabric of his scrubs.

"I need you," he growled, then kissed her neck. "Now." She sensed his desperate fight for control more than felt it. To know she'd driven him so close to his breaking point empowered her femininity, set her own desire to boil deep inside her. Blood rushed to her center, to where she urgently craved Rex.

He needed *her*. Had come to find her.

Happiness gushed within her. She brought her legs up around his hips. "My bedroom is upstairs."

His hands tightened on her hips before he walked toward the stairs.

"Too far." Those two words were a snarl of feral need.

He set her on a step and came over her, kissing her again while delving under her sleepshirt and giving her panties an urgent tug. Seconds later they were wrapped around her ankles. Rex let go long enough to pull a package from his pocket and pull his pants down. He rolled on his protection, braced his hands on the step her shoulders lay against. He looked at her, studied her a second as if asking permission. She nodded, and without hesitation he pushed into her.

She accepted all of him. Something horrible must have happened, because the caring man who had been so tender a few days earlier was gone. In his place was this frantic, wild man who had come to her for solace. The wonder of his transformation amazed and gratified her with a profoundness that made her steady herself against his forearms and accept his strong thrusts readily. She would be sore in the morning but that didn't matter. Rex needed her, and she wanted him.

With one final plunge, he shook and grunted his release. He came down on top of her, his head resting on her breast and sighed. "Tiff."

She wrapped her arms around him and held him tight. "I'm right here. It'll be all right."

Tiffani was slowly rubbing circles on his back when

he shifted off her. Rex now seemed embarrassed or ashamed, or perhaps both. She felt honored he'd chosen her to smooth away his pain. The self-assured surgeon had been vulnerable, and had come to her for acceptance.

He searched her face. She let her concern for him, for his wellbeing, shine through her eyes as she met his. Standing, he pulled up his pants. She wanted to say something but nothing appropriate came to mind. Rex offered her his hand and she took it. He helped her to her feet. Tiffani wobbled for a second and he put a hand on her elbow. Her panties remained hooked on one foot.

He went down on his knees and stretched the tiny piece of hot pink material. "Step in." She did as he asked. With careful, gentle movements, he pulled them up and into place. That was almost as erotic as what had just happened.

"Please, forgive me. There is no excuse for that kind of behavior." He put his back to her as he stood. "I...I should go. I was wrong to come here. To take my bad day out on you."

"Don't."

He looked at her. "I'm surprised you're not screaming at me. I barge in here, wouldn't tell you why, and took you on the stairs? A few minutes ago I was only thinking of myself. That's not how it should be between us."

"I could tell you were hurting. You would never hurt me, remember? I believe that. I was glad I was here for you. I understand." She paused and smiled. "And I liked it too."

Her words were like a balm to Rex's wounded heart.

This time she was the one who reached out a hand. He took it and she led him up the stairs.

He hadn't planned to come to Tiffani's. Somehow,

he'd found himself speeding through the streets and had ended up here. If he hadn't remembered the detail about the flower pot she kept beside her front door he might still be wandering the city. No, he would have called her. He'd needed Tiffani. She had made the devastated faces of the family of the boy he'd lost go away for a few minutes.

"The bathroom is in there." She pointed to a door off her room. "Go have a hot shower. Have you eaten anything?"

"Not since noon." He sounded tired even to himself.

"Then while you're getting a shower, I'll fix you something to eat." She headed for the door.

Some of the shame Rex felt eased. She should have put him out on his tail for the way he had behaved, but instead she had shown him concern.

Half an hour later, Rex went down her stairs wearing only his scrub pants. A soft humming told him in what direction to go to find Tiffani. She had her back to him as he stood in the doorway of the kitchen, watching the gentle movements of her hips as she worked at the counter.

This was a sight he could get used to. A sight he could look forward to coming home to.

"Hey."

She smiled over her shoulder.

"Thanks for the shower. I didn't leave any hot water."

"You weren't supposed to." She picked up a plate and put it on the table in front of the chair closest to him. On it was a ham sandwich, some apple slices and chips.

"Not a gourmet meal like you can fix but the best I can do this late at night. Tea will be ready in a minute." She stepped to the stove. "Have a seat. Don't wait for me."

Rex pulled the chair out from the small white table and sat. "This looks good."

The teapot whistled and Tiffani picked it up and poured water into the two mugs waiting on the counter. Each had a tea bag string hanging over the side. "My mother always said hot tea makes everything feel a little bit better."

She sat a mug in front of him then gingerly took a chair at the end of the table. Placing her mug on the table as well, she sat and cradled it with both hands, as if warming them.

Guilt swamped him. He picked up half of the sandwich. Tiffani had actually cut it in half. He'd not had that done for him since he was a child. She had a way of making him feel cared for. She'd demonstrated that more than once while working at the clinic and had certainly shown him in the aftermath of his self-induced shame a short while ago. It had been a long time since he'd felt special to anyone. Her generosity tonight was more than he deserved. He took a bite of the sandwich. "This is good. Thank you."

"Despite your gourmet cook status, I don't think you take good enough care of yourself. You miss too many meals."

"Now you sound like a doctor or a nagging wife."

She sat straighter, looking indignant. "I'm neither, thank you."

He liked the fire in her eyes. Finishing his sandwich and chips, Rex started on his apple slices, pausing for a sip of tea. The warmth did calm him somewhat.

Tiffani twisted the handle of her mug one way then

the other before she said, "Will you tell me what happened to upset you?"

Rex stopped crunching his apple. After the way he had acted he owed her some explanation. His gaze met hers. Everything about hers said she wouldn't accept silence. "I'm sorry about tonight. I shouldn't have done that."

"I'm glad I was here for you," she answered in a soft voice. "Please, tell me why I needed to be."

It took all that was in him to show his weakness but she deserved to know what had driven him to come to her. "I lost a teenager tonight. I hate telling parents their child is gone. There was nothing I could do."

She didn't touch him, just said softly, "You and I know better than most that not everyone can be fixed. You even said that during the interview the other day."

She was right.

"Yeah, but that doesn't make it better, or any easier."

"No, it doesn't." Reaching across the table, she gave his hand a squeeze. "Knowing how you feel, the malpractice case must have been especially tough on you."

It had been. More than he'd let on to himself, and nothing he would show the world. It had caused doubt to creep in. Made him second-guess, analyze every decision he made in a case. He went over and over them in his head, looking for something he could have done differently.

Tiffani continued, "I didn't read much about the case on purpose. I didn't want to judge you any more than I already had. You were the center point of the campaign and I wanted to think forward, but I did hear some of the media reports."

"They were neither flattering or accurate. Especially

with the Royster family doing all the talking." He pulled his hand from hers.

It might kill him to tell the story but he was going to anyway. After how he'd acted with Tiffani she deserved to know the monsters that chased him. "I don't know if it was the fates, the universe getting back at me or just the luck of the draw that my patient turned out to be Mr. Royster."

Without saying anything, Tiffani's look asked him to explain. He had her complete attention. She even stopped fiddling with her mug.

"Vic Royster used to be my father's best friend when I was growing up. He was also the father of my girlfriend in high school."

Tiffani pursed her lips and nodded. "I thought doctors avoided doing surgery on people they were friends with?"

"I had no idea it was him. I was called in. An emergency. I didn't know the patient's name until after I was out of surgery. He was already too far gone by the time I got to him. I couldn't have done anything more than I did. But I did try." Talking about that night started the sick feeling he remembered so well churning his guts once again. Would it ever go away?

"So why the lawsuit?"

He looked at her. "The problem was, my past came back to haunt me."

Tiffani regarded him with expectation.

He was going to have to tell her about his dirty laundry as well. She shouldn't have to hear it but it was part of his story. "When I was a kid I lived in a world of affluence. My family lived in the nicest neighborhood, had the best cars. Even traded each year for the newest model. I wore the best brands from the best stores in town. We were members of the most renowned country club. I attended the most prestigious private school. We were in the 'in crowd.'"

"So that's where the great manners came from," Tiffani commented.

"That had a lot to do with it. I attend cotillion classes and there were dances all the time. At home, the social graces were required. It was important to always look and act correctly. My mother was very particular. To her, manners were a reflection of breeding. Appearance was everything."

He took a sip of his now-cold tea. "I was a senior in high school when I found out that all my family lived on was nothing but a house of cards. I discovered that only when it collapsed. Big time. My father and mother had had us living a lie. They were living far beyond their means. We had been part of a lifestyle they couldn't afford and it finally caught up with them. My dad had to file for bankruptcy. Gone were the house, the cars, the clothes and the friends. Do you have any idea how fast so-called friends can disappear when you embarrass them?"

Tiffani didn't answer. Just looked at him with steady, almost unreadable eyes. Thankfully her gaze didn't hold pity. If it had, he might have left.

Shaking his head and focusing on his tea mug, he forced himself to continue. "The country-club life was over. We moved across town to a three-bedroom apartment in an area our old friends wouldn't even drive through. Mr. Royster wouldn't take my father's calls. My girlfriend, the one I foolishly hoped to marry, told me she couldn't associate with a penniless person. She had to think about the repercussions of even being seen with me."

Tiffani hissed in a manner that reminded him of the sound a mother might make when her child was in danger. Her knuckles were white from where she now gripped her mug.

"What we didn't do was change schools. The year was already paid for. It would have been better if we had. Those last few months for me and my brother were horrible.

"I came out of the experience promising myself that I'd never put on the pretense of being more important than anyone else. I swore to myself I'd never use my job, my house, clothes or what I drive to create a façade of self-importance. I was going to be me and no one else."

"So the long hair, jeans and calling you by your first name comes from that." Tiffani was speaking more to herself as if she at last had found answers to her questions.

"Yep, what you see is what you get. Like it or not."

"So how did you afford to go to medical school?"

He shrugged. "I had good grades. I was always good at math and got great experience working in the nursing home. I received some scholarships, took out some loans and worked like hell. I was determined not to give up my dreams because my parents had selfishly pretended to be different people without considering the consequences if the truth came out. I like knowing I earned what I had." He sighed. "Anyway, Mr. Royster just showed up in my OR. When I had to go out and tell Mrs. Royster and her daughter, my old girlfriend, that he had passed away, I hadn't seen them in over fifteen years. Unsurprisingly, it wasn't a happy reunion."

"I can only imagine."

"They couldn't accept his death was natural. Couldn't accept he'd not been taking good care of himself or that he should have seen a doctor sooner. They blamed me for his death. They had the money and status to bring the lawsuit. At one point, they even accused me of letting Mr. Royster die on purpose because I wanted revenge for how he'd turned his back on my family when I was a kid. I think that will hurt more than anything for a very long time. These were people who had known me for a significant portion of my life and yet they actually thought I was low enough to let him die out of *revenge*."

Rex shook his head. He was almost done. "With the lawsuit involving both me and the hospital, I wasn't able to say anything. I was told to keep my mouth shut. But the Roysters could say anything they wanted, and took every opportunity to do so. Even airing my own mother and father's bankruptcy and fall from high social grace all those years ago."

"Oh, no," Tiffani said.

"I didn't agree with what my parents did but I certainly didn't want to see them dragged through the mud because of me."

"I'm sorry all of that happened to you." He hated the sad look that now filled her eyes.

"Yeah, but it's over and done now. I've moved on."

She gave him a dubious look but didn't question him further, for which he was grateful.

Tiffani's heart hurt for him. He'd suffered. In her opinion, he still was, but he couldn't see that about himself. She stood and went behind him. Putting her arm around his neck, she put her hands over his heart. It beat strong and hard, just like he was. He was a survivor who could still give to others. She pushed back his hair and kissed his temple. "You know, you're the biggest-hearted person I know. I love you because you care." She realized what she'd said too late. "Uh, you know what I mean."

Rex clasped her hands just as she started to withdraw. "I know what you mean," he said, sounding profoundly grateful. "Thank you for being here for me. Listening." He turned in his chair and pulled her down to sit in his lap.

Her arm went around his shoulders and she kissed him.

Sometime later he whispered against her ear, "I know I probably don't deserve it, but I'd like to stay tonight if you'll let me."

Tiffani stood. Taking his hand, she led him toward the stairs. "Come on. You need your rest."

The sun was high in the sky when she awoke. Rex's head rested on her shoulder. When they had come to bed he'd just held her. It had been as if he'd needed to feel someone was there for him. She was glad he had picked her.

Although she needed to call work, she wasn't willing to take the chance she might wake Rex to do so. Running her hand over his hair, she marveled that he lay in her arms. Rex was fast becoming important to her. Too much so. Forever with him was easy to imagine. If it was only that simple. Their lives were here and now, only for the moment. They had no real tomorrows, were on two different paths.

She'd had such a negative view of doctors all her life. Rex had learned to mistrust people. Her job was to make people look better. He despised any pretense. She was buttoned up and he was let your hair down. She was leaving and he was staying. It was impossible. All she could do was enjoy this all-too-brief interlude.

The fingertips of his hand skimmed across the skin of

her waist. Her pulse quickened. Rex was waking up. He rolled over and kissed the top of one breast before looking up at her to murmur, "Softest pillow I've ever had."

"I need to call work. I'm late." Tiffani moved to untangle herself from him.

"Don't go in today. Let's do something fun. Laugh." He gave her an imploring look as his fingers brushed over her skin.

"I can't, I have to work." Tiffani hated telling him no.

"You can call it a day of work. I'll let you take pictures. I'll even help an old lady across the street so you'll have something for social media." He grinned, the one that could get her to do almost anything.

She returned it. "You're a funny man so early in the morning."

"Come on, Tiff, live on the wild side a little bit." He was serious.

This was another area where they were so different. He didn't take his life too seriously. Knew how to laugh at himself. Enjoy living. "Okay, funny man. What do you think we ought to do?"

He sat up and looked at her with a twinkle in his eye. "How about a visit to Elvis's house? Ever been there?"

"Yes, but it's been a long time." This was the last suggestion she would have expected from him.

"Then Graceland here we come." He popped out of bed. "Shower, my place for a change of clothes and breakfast, then we're on our way."

Tiffani couldn't help but laugh. He was a completely different person from the one who had shown up on her doorstep the night before. She liked both sides of Rex. The tough, hardened one and the one who reminded her of a kid looking in a toy store window.

Pulling on her hand, he gave her a wolfish grin and

raised his brows up and down. "Let's share the shower. Save time."

Twenty minutes later Tiffani stepped out on shaky knees from the most satisfying shower she had ever taken. Rex had sent her to the summit of ecstasy before he'd carefully bathed her then wrapped her in a towel. She was still floating on pleasure when she followed him in her car to his place.

"Let me get on something besides these day-old scrubs and I'll fix us something to eat." Rex was gone before she could answer.

She was outside, admiring his patio and garden, when Rex returned. He wore his usual T-shirt and jeans. His feet were bare. Tiffani had never seen a sexier sight. She had to get beyond this fascination with him.

"Would you like to eat out here?" he asked, joining her.

She fingered a plant. "That sounds wonderful."

"Then you enjoy the sunshine and I'll get us something to eat." He went inside.

Tiffani followed him.

"I thought you were going to stay outside." Rex looked up from where he was getting a frying pan out from underneath a cabinet.

"I'd rather watch you."

Rex grinned. "In that case, I'll try to put on a show."

He started by squirting oil into the pan with a couple of quick flicks of his wrist. Next he broke eggs with one hand while whipping them into a froth with the other. Tiffani wasn't only entertained but impressed. Was there nothing the man wasn't good at?

"This might be the best omelet I've ever eaten," she said a short while later as they sat across from each other at a café table tucked in a corner of the patio.

"That's the fresh herbs. Makes everything better. Eat up. We've got to go."

"You sure are excited about today." Tiffani forked into her eggs again.

"I rarely get a day that I just get to play. And to do it with a beautiful lady makes it extra-special."

That warm glow left over from the shower intensified again.

Half an hour later they were going to her car, again parked in his garage.

"Would you like to drive? It might give you more leg room," Tiffani suggested, offering him her keys.

"Sure. It's worth a try." He took them.

Soon they were on the interstate. Rex was whipping her car in and out of lanes as they sped down the road.

She held the handle of the door. "You do know this isn't a motorcycle?"

He grinned. "It's almost as good. Drives like a go-kart."

Tiffani put a hand on the edge of the seat. "Great. Now I'm riding with a daredevil."

"Just sit back and enjoy the ride," Rex said. "I've got this."

"I hope those won't be famous last words." She chuckled.

Rex pulled off onto a city street and his pace slowed.

"Are you a big Elvis fan?" Tiffani asked.

"Who isn't? But I'll have to admit I came to it later in life." Rex pulled into the parking lot across the road from Elvis's home, next to the large one-level museum. "How about you?"

"Yeah, I used to watch all his movies. Even sang along." She hadn't thought of that in a long time. She and her father had watched a number of them together.

As they were getting out of the car Rex asked, "You want to see everything? Museum, house and plane?"

Tiffani shrugged. "If we're here, we might as well."

He took her hand and gave it a squeeze. "That's the spirit. You're learning. After all, we're in no hurry."

"I do have to see my father this evening." The idea didn't hold much appeal.

"We can leave from here," Rex said, as they headed toward the ticket building.

That wasn't a good idea. She couldn't take Rex with her when she visited her father. "You don't have to do that. I'll have time to run you home."

"I'd like to meet your father."

She couldn't let that happen. "Didn't you hear me when I said he doesn't like doctors?"

Rex pulled her into his arms and gave her a quick kiss. "I believe you told me you didn't like doctors either. This morning in the shower you liked me pretty well, though, I thought."

She had. But just because she had changed her mind about one particular doctor it didn't mean it would make any difference to how her father felt about them. For certain he wouldn't like Rex even "pretty well" if he somehow found out Rex had spent the night with her.

"Come on, we can discuss that later. Elvis is waiting."

"Don't forget you agreed to pictures today." At Rex's snarl, she grinned.

He paid for their tickets and they entered the museum. They walked from one exhibit to another, watching videos of Elvis in concert, studying his cars, before they moved on to where one of his many costumes was on display behind glass.

"He dressed with flair," Tiffani commented.

Rex said as they looked at one display, "I remember my mom telling me about going to one of his concerts when she was a kid. She loved his music, still does. He would wipe sweat off with the bright colored scarf and throw it to the crowd. She got so excited when he came on stage, she made her way to within two rows of him, even though her seat wasn't anywhere near the front. A security guard finally told her to go back to her seat. She used to tell us that story all the time."

Done in the museum, they boarded a shuttle that took them across the road to Elvis's mansion. There they joined a small group of people waiting for a tour of the bottom floor of the house. Tiffani looked up at the tall columns of the brick antebellum-style house. "This had to be some place in its day."

When they were in the living room and the guide was telling them about the extra-long white sofa, Rex whispered in her ear, "I wish I had one like that. We'd have plenty of room."

Tiffani burned hot with memories and hissed, "Shh."

Rex grinned and hugged her close for a second. "By today's standards, this isn't all that large a place but at the time it must have been very impressive. Sitting up here on a hill with the white fence around it."

They strolled through the garden. Tiffani couldn't remember the last time she'd just walked hand in hand with a man with no real destination in mind. She really did need to let go more. Plan less, enjoy more. They worked their way to the area where Elvis and his parents were buried and stood there for a few moments.

"He really made his mark on the world, didn't he?" Tiffani said in a low voice.

"Yeah, he did." Rex kissed her cheek. "Not unlike what you have done in mine."

She looked at him in wonder. "Have I?"

"I'm riding around in a car, aren't I?"

"I guess I have." For some reason, that really mattered to her.

His smiling eyes met hers. "You've done more than that. It's been a long time since someone has been there for me like you were last night. Thank you."

"You are welcome." She couldn't resist kissing him.

They caught the shuttle back and went to visit Elvis's private plane. The day had been a perfect one so far and she couldn't think of anyone she'd rather be with than Rex. She was having *fun*. Something she had little of in her life.

The plane was decorated in the same style as the house, late nineteen-sixties and early seventies.

Taking a seat, Tiffani asked Rex, as if she were conducting an interview and he was Elvis, "So, what was your favorite movie part?"

"I liked *Girls, Girls, Girls*. Mostly because of the girls." Rex gave her a wolfish grin.

Tiffani laughed. "And your favorite song?"

"Oh, there were so many." Rex did a poor imitation of Elvis's voice. "'Blue Suede Shoes.'"

"Your favorite place in the world?"

"Graceland, of course."

They both giggled like kids.

Rex took her hand and helped her down the steps. "I heard that they have a café here that serves Elvis's favorite sandwich. Want to try it?"

"What is it?"

Rex rubbed his stomach. "A grilled peanut butter and banana sandwich."

Tiffani turned up her nose.

"Come on, Tiff, where's your sense of adventure?"

Put that way, she wasn't going to say no. "Okay, I'll give it a try."

They walked to the small café. Lining the walls were pictures of Elvis in his signature jumpsuits with rhinestones and a large collar. They found a table and a young waitress took their order.

Tiffani had to admire Rex. He was eager to try whatever came along. She'd spent so much of her life hesitating and questioning that it had never occurred to her she could live with fewer restrictions.

When their sandwiches were delivered Rex grabbed his and bit into it. He nodded at her. "It's really good."

She cut hers into quarters and picked up a section. Taking a tiny bite, she was pleasantly surprised. It was good.

"Told you so," Rex said, as he took another mouthful.

On the way to the car she said, "Thanks for bringing me. It really was a lot of fun."

"I'm glad we came too." In the car Rex turned to her. "What's the address to your dad's place?"

A knot of panic formed in Tiffani's stomach. She'd forgotten all about him saying he was going with her to visit her father. Somehow she had to convince him not to. "Why don't you just head to your place? You don't have to go with me. It really won't be pleasant."

"Surely it can't be that bad."

"You'd be surprised. Especially when he realizes you're a doctor." Why wouldn't Rex just accept she didn't want him to go?

"We just won't tell him. I'd like to meet him."

"Are you sure?" She didn't know how to keep him from going without hurting his feelings. Neither did she want her day with him to end. But visiting her father…

Rex met her look. "I'm sure. I'm a big boy. I can take care of myself."

"Head east on the interstate." Maybe she could convince Rex to wait in the lobby or car while she just checked in on her daddy. The closer they got to where her father lived, the more nervous she became. What if he recognized Rex?

He reached over and squeezed her hand. "It's going to be okay. I'll behave."

"It's not you I'm worried about. It's him." She knew how her father could act.

Rex pulled into a parking spot in front of the building. They walked together down the long hall. When Rex reached for her hand she pulled it back. Her father wouldn't like that. Rex didn't say anything but she felt more than saw his disapproval. Even so, it did feel good not to have to face her father alone for once.

She lightly knocked on the door. There was the expected growl of, "Come in."

"Hello, Daddy."

"Well, it's about time, baby girl."

Tiffani went farther into the room. "I brought somebody with me today."

Rex stepped up beside her and held out his hand. "Mr. Romano, I'm Rex. Nice to meet you."

"What'd you bring him for?" her father grumbled, ignoring Rex's proffered hand.

"He's a friend and wanted to meet you." She pulled a chair up close to her father and sat. "We've been to Graceland today."

"It's the middle of the week. You're not working on that awful campaign anymore? The one with the hospital?" he spat.

Alarm seized her. She had to steer the conversation in another direction. "Yes, but not today."

Her father twisted up his mouth. "I still can't believe you're such a traitor…"

Rex shifted behind her.

"How's your hand?" she said to change the subject. She could see the bandage needed replacing.

Her father raised it. "It hurts worse than ever."

"Did you let someone change it?" she asked automatically, suppressing a sigh of frustration.

"No," her father whined. "Only you do it right."

"Then let me change it." She went to the drawer where she stored supplies.

Rex couldn't believe what he'd just seen happen before his eyes. Tiffani had morphed into a child. Where was the tough PR woman he knew? The one who faced each of his complaints head on? It was like she was at her father's beck and call. Had she been taking care of her father for so long that she couldn't see the change? Tiffani had a big heart, but her father was taking advantage of her.

A loud intake of breath from Tiffani had him looking over her shoulder. Her father's hand was an angry red, with the look of infection setting in. He would require more help than a bandage.

"Daddy, have you told anyone how bad this is?" She glanced back at Rex.

"Why would I tell anyone? You were coming to see me. Maybe if you came more often it wouldn't have gotten so bad."

Rex was about to lose his patience. Nobody, not even her father, should talk to Tiffani that way. He went down on one heel beside her. "Let me have a look."

Tiffani continued to hold the man's hand in her palm while Rex examined it. It was going to require an antibiotic to keep the infection from spreading.

"What would you know about it?" her father snapped.

Rex looked him in the eyes. "I'm a doctor."

Mr. Romano reared up in his chair. "What? Get out of here! Get out of my room! Leave my daughter alone, you quack."

"Now, Daddy, he's only trying to help." Tiffani nudged him back down in the chair.

Rex hated to hear that placating tone in her voice.

"Doctors took my legs and now this one will probably want to take my hand," the old man ranted.

Rex stood and focused on Tiffani. "I'll wait for you outside."

"I'll only be a minute," she said over her shoulder.

Her father's face had turned red and he pointed toward the door. "Did you hear me? Get out! Leave my daughter alone."

Rex wanted to drag Tiffani away from the toxic man too. How had she lived with that hatred all these years? What must her childhood have been like? At least his parents hadn't taken out their pain at losing everything on him or his brother. Instead, they had worried about how their children were being affected.

He found one of the attendants and asked where to find the head of the nursing staff. Locating her, he identified himself and told her about Mr. Romano's hand, then called in a prescription for him. Rex was waiting in the lobby when Tiffani came down the hall, her shoulders slumped. The smiling and playful woman he'd known earlier in the day had disappeared. By the glisten of her eyes she was on the verge of tears. Rex put his arms around her and gave her a hug.

She buried her head in his chest. "I'm sorry. I should have insisted you not come in with me. He shouldn't have said those awful things to you."

"You warned me. Don't worry about it." He tightened his hold for a second before he said, "I called something in for him. His hand should be much better soon."

"That's if he takes it."

"The nurses around here know how to make that happen." He turned her toward the door. "Let's go home. We've had enough excitement for one day."

Tiffani looked at him. "Thank you."

"Not a problem." Where she was concerned, it wasn't.

CHAPTER NINE

BY THE TIME Rex had merged onto the interstate the sun was setting. "I didn't even think about the fact that we'd be driving into the sun this time of day."

"It does make it miserable and dangerous," Tiffani murmured.

They were the first words she'd said since getting into the car. Rex was glad she was coming out of the stupor that visiting her father had put her in. "You hungry? We could stop and get something."

"Not really. The sandwich filled me up."

He grinned at her. "It was good."

"I had a good time today. Thanks for making me play hooky."

"I had a good time with you today too." He took her hand and intertwined her fingers with his, lifting it with the intention of placing a kiss on her knuckles.

A bang filled the air.

"What the hell?" His look jerked to the road ahead.

Before him a car spun around. Another hit it and sent it into the path of a transfer truck. It flipped and rolled.

Tiffani released his hand and he quickly put it on the steering wheel. "Hold on." Glancing into the rearview mirror, he saw a car coming up on him fast. He whipped into the next lane. Slowing, he just missed the truck jack-knifing and came to a stop on the shoulder of the road.

"Do you have a flashlight in here?" he asked, already opening the door.

Tiffani didn't immediately answer.

"Tiffani!"

"Uh, it's in here." She unlatched the glove compartment and pulled out the light.

"I'm going to see who's hurt. Call 911 and report the accident. Tell them I'm here. Then I want you to find me. Don't get near any moving cars. Got that?"

"Yeah. Be careful. I don't want you to get hurt either," she called as he hurried away.

If they had been only a few seconds earlier it could be Tiffani and himself injured. His chest tightened. If he lost Tiffani... Had it come to that?

Debris covered the road. He almost tripped over a bumper. It had turned dark and this was the one stretch of road with little lighting. His first concern was the car that had rolled over.

Reaching it, he found a man struggling to get out. Rex went to his knees and shined the light on him. "I'm a doctor. Stay still, don't move any more than you have to. Help is on the way. How many people are in the car?"

"My wife. She's unconscious. My son and daughter are in the back." The man groaned.

Rex's chest constricted. Children. "I'll check on them. You stay still." He looked into the rear passenger window and was relieved to see two sets of wide eyes looking back at him.

Hurrying, he went around to the other side of the car. The door had been crushed. The woman's head was bleeding. Rex checked a pulse in her neck. It was faint but there. She needed medical attention right away.

Thankfully shrill sirens filled the air in the distance.

A person came up behind him. "Can I help?"

"Yes. I'm a doctor. I want you to stay right here with this lady." Rex pointed to another person. "When the paramedics get here I want you to show them where this woman is. Do not move the people in the car. Understood?"

The people nodded.

Rushing to the next car, he passed the truck driver. He was wobbling on his feet. "Hey, buddy, you need to sit down." Rex shined the light on him. The man had a gash on his forehead.

"Rex, I'm here. What can I do?" Tiffani came to a halt beside him.

"I need you to get this man somewhere he can sit down and see if you can find something to put over the cut. I've got to check that other car."

He jogged in the direction of the second vehicle. There was no need to worry whether or not Tiffani would take care of the trucker. Rex was confident she would follow his instructions. At least this car was sitting upright. A middle-aged man sat behind the steering wheel. Rex tried the door handle. Tapping on the window, Rex said, "Open the door."

The man didn't look at him.

Was he in shock? Dead? Rex knocked harder at the window. "Sir, open the door."

The man looked at him through glazed eyes. There was a click of the lock. Rex pulled the door open. "Can you tell me what's wrong?"

Someone came up behind him. "Let me hold the flashlight."

It was Tiffani. He could count on her to know what

was needed. Handing it to her without looking back, he checked the man's pulse. It was erratic.

"Tiff, help me. We need to get him out of here. Go around to the other side and climb in. Help me get him out far enough that I can get him on the ground. I'm afraid he's headed for a heart attack."

Tiffani did as he instructed. She grunted in her effort to push the heavy man out of the seat. Finally Rex was able to get his arms under the man's shoulders and pull him from the vehicle. Tiffani rushed back around the car and held the light for him.

He could kick himself for not putting his emergency bag in Tiffani's car. Normally he had it on his bike. Placing his ear to the man's chest, he listened to his heartbeat and checked his pulse. It was unsteady, but there. The man needed immediate medical attention as well.

There wasn't enough of him to go around. Too many seriously injured. "Anyone here know CPR?" he asked the crowd behind him.

"I do," a woman said, coming forward.

"Then you stay here with this man. If he stops breathing you start CPR. I'll be right over there. You…" he pointed to a man "…go meet the paramedics and tell them they have a possible cardiac arrest. Tiffani, come with me."

Not asking any questions, she followed him. She stumbled, and he caught her before she went down. "Careful, I don't need you hurt too."

They returned to the woman in the first car. To his relief, the ambulance pulled up with lights flashing and sirens blaring.

"Tiffani, hold the light right there for me. I need to examine this woman." Rex placed his fingers on the artery in the woman's neck. All he was getting was a faint response. It was lighter than before. He felt over her chest to her midsection.

A brighter light than the one Tiffani was using shone over his shoulder, giving him a better view of the woman.

The paramedics came up behind him. He stood. "I'm Dr. Rex Maxwell. The best I can determine is that she has internal bleeding. Her husband and two children are in there as well. The man over there..." he pointed "...is having cardiac issues."

Tiffani stepped back from the car so as not to block the light. It turned out it was the light from a news camera.

A woman she recognized as a reporter at a local station came up beside her. "Who is that guy?"

For a second Tiffani didn't understand what the woman was talking about. "He's a doctor."

The reporter said, "We were only a few cars back when the accident happened, and started filming as soon as we got here. He's been amazing. A real hero."

Tiffani's mind shifted gears to her job. "That's Dr. Rex Maxwell, a surgeon at Metropolitan Hospital."

"He's been a lifesaver here tonight." Tiffani didn't miss the awe in the woman's voice.

As if on cue, Rex carried a child over to the ambulance and set him down. Tiffani glanced at the cameraman. He was focused on Rex and the camera was rolling. What would it hurt to give the newswoman a few choice tidbits about Rex? He might not like it but Tiffani still had a campaign to run. "Did you know he's the go-to general surgeon for west Tennessee? They find him indispensable over at the Metropolitan."

"Really?" The woman was obviously enthralled with Rex. "I'm going to have to get an interview with him."

SUSAN CARLISLE 167

A policeman approached and told them all to get out of the accident scene area. Tiffani was almost to the car when Rex jogged up.

"All the injured are going to Metro. I'm going to ride in with the woman. She'll need surgery right away. You good to get home by yourself?"

"Of course." She liked it that Rex worried about her but she'd been taking care of herself for a long time. "I'll be fine."

He gave her a quick kiss on the lips. "I'll call you."

Tiffani watched as he ran back into the thick of things. She couldn't help but be proud of him. He was her hero. And tomorrow he would be the city's.

Rex pulled his surgical cap off and dropped it into the bag hanging on a stand. It had been a long night. He'd been asked to scrub in when he'd arrived at the hospital. The woman had coded on the way in. It had taken everyone to keep her alive long enough to get her into the OR. There was a slim hope she'd make it through the night.

Now he was going to go home and get some sleep, then give Tiffani a call and invite her over for dinner. He smiled. And dessert. The sweet kind only she could provide.

"Hey, Rex, how does it feel to be the man of the hour? You hiding a red cape under those scrubs?" one of the doctors coming into surgery asked.

"Uh?"

He grinned even wider, "You haven't seen the news this morning, have you?"

"No, I've been in the OR until ten minutes ago. What're you talking about?" Rex was starting to get a nasty feeling in his gut.

"Go out in the waiting room and have a look at the

TV. They're even talking about you on social media. My wife texted me to see if I knew the doctor everyone was talking about."

Rex strode to the waiting room. Thankfully it was empty. He didn't have to wait to find out what was going on. There, in living color, was a video of him carrying the boy to the ambulance. He had offered to help and the paramedic had handed him the kid. The next clip was of him on his hands and knees beside the window of the other car involved. How had they gotten those pictures?

A knot formed in his chest. Anger roiled, feeding his suspicion. *Tiffani.* Would she do anything to get the publicity she needed? The picture moved to a woman holding a microphone, who was talking to Tiffani. She was talking about *him.* She had no excuse for not knowing how he would feel about taking advantage of the tragedy. How could she have done it? Because all she could think about was that promotion, about PR, about *appearances.* Just like his parents. Do whatever you can to get what you want, even if it hurts others.

Less than thirty minutes later he pulled his motorcycle in behind Tiffani's car parked in the driveway of her condo. Jerking his helmet off, he laid it on the seat and stomped to her door, not bothering with the bell, instead hammering on it. He didn't care who he woke.

Seconds later the lock clicked. Tiffani, dressed in her robe, opened the door and hissed, "What's wrong with you? It's early."

Rex pushed his way in and slammed the door behind him. He had to give her credit. She didn't even step back. "How could you? Does your job mean so much to you that you don't care about anyone else? Not even a family who almost lost a wife and mother?"

"You saw it?" She walked into the living area where her TV was turned to the morning news channel.

He followed on her heels. At least there was some contrition in her voice. "You bet I did. After I've spent hours in the OR, trying to save the woman's life, I came out to that nonsense."

"How is she?" Tiffani looked at him.

"Like you care."

She flinched. For a fleeting second he had compassion for her. He lowered his voice. "All you're interested in is getting your promotion. What did you do? Call the news?"

"They were already there. Not far behind us on the road. The reporter came up to me. They had already been filming you. I just told them your name and where you worked."

His eyes bored into hers. "And you knew good and well how I'd feel about that."

"I had an idea, but it was too good an opportunity to pass up, Rex. You *were* a hero last night. If you hadn't helped those people, they could have died."

"You're just like my parents. Trying to dress things up to look a certain way when they're not. I'm a doctor, I care for people. That's my job. My calling. I don't do it so I can be a hero on the morning news. Don't make me into something I'm not."

She put her hands out, palms up as if pleading with him. "But the coverage was important—"

"Why? So you can get a promotion and run away from a jerk who was never good enough for you to begin with?" he spat.

"Run away?" She made a step toward him. "You're one to be talking. You run every day from who you were. You did a complete role reversal so you don't have to remember how much it hurt to be rejected from your old life. And you're blaming everyone else for feeling that way. I bet you don't even see your parents but maybe once a year! Yet, from all I can tell, outside of them trying to live the good life, they loved you. They cared for you."

"Don't put your issues on me just because you act like this strong, assertive woman, but when you get around your father you become a child who'll do anything to make him happy. The problem is you *can't*. He uses his disability to control you. You can't see he's eaten up with bitterness and that if you don't get away soon, one day you will be too."

Her shoulders reared back as if he had slapped her. "How dare you!"

"I dare because it's the truth. Have you ever thought that he might have learned to walk on artificial legs if you hadn't waited on him hand and foot? He demanded attention. You gave it to him. You're still giving it. Granted, you were a child, but he should've been man enough to know better than to put that guilt trip on you. All that stuff about doctors is to cover up his fault in the accident. You ask him. I bet he was driving too fast. Had been drinking. Not paying attention to the road. You and I both know his doctors saved his life."

"If you're done psychoanalyzing me and my father, you need to go." Tiffani circled around him and got as far from him as the space would allow. She held the door wide.

He gave her a pointed look. "I'm going, but I won't be anyone's pawn. I am through with your crusade. I'll let Nelson know. You do your thing without me. Good-bye, Ms. Romano."

CHAPTER TEN

REX'S FINAL WORDS had rerun over and over in her mind like a bad film for days. He'd called her by her last name. When he'd said goodbye that was what he'd meant. Not only to the campaign but to her. She'd thought she'd been hurt before by a breakup but that pain came nowhere near the searing agony she was feeling now. Just getting out of bed was torture. The only relief she found was sleep but there was precious little of that. The dreams were too intense. She woke aching for Rex. It was both a pleasure and a pain to see his smiling face on the billboards around town.

Dr. Nelson had called the next day to inform her Rex would no longer be required to participate in the campaign. She had no idea how Rex had explained the situation and she hadn't asked. Despite Dr. Nelson's announcement, he seemed genuinely pleased with her progress. That news coverage of the accident scene had boosted the hospital's image in the public's eyes—and destroyed any chance she had at happiness.

She had fallen in love with Rex.

But she had hurt him. Worse, disappointed him. She couldn't take it back. Didn't know how to fix it. All she knew to do was accept the promotion she had been offered for her successful campaign, move away and hope to start anew. There would never be another Rex. Just a hole in her heart where the piece he held belonged. Had he been right to accuse her of running away by chasing the promotion to the other office? She'd never thought of herself as a coward. If she could endure losing Rex, then she shouldn't have any difficulty facing Lou every day at work. After all, she *did* deserve better than him. She'd let Lou treat her like her father did. That wasn't a healthy relationship. For a boyfriend or a father. It was time to make changes in her life.

That Sunday when she visited her father she entered his room with her head held high. It was time for him to start taking responsibility for his actions and his life.

"Baby girl. There you are."

She didn't pull up a chair. Instead she chose to stand. "Hi, Daddy. How's your hand?"

He waved it at her. He no longer wore a bandage. "Much better. Even though that quack looked at it."

"You're not going to talk about Rex that way around me. If you do I won't be coming to see you anymore," she said tightly, holding her father's shocked gaze.

"But you know how those doctors are."

She did. The one she loved was giving, caring and dedicated. "Daddy, you never really told me what caused your accident."

Her father looked uncomfortable and turned his gaze away from her. "Why do you want to know now? That was a long time ago."

"It was but I'd still like to know." She used her most encouraging tone.

"I was on the way home from work. I came through

a curve and the bike came out from under me." He repeated the words as if it was a rehearsed statement.

"You didn't stop on the way home? You used to tell me you stopped by Charlie's for a drink sometimes." She watched him closely. His eyes shadowed.

"I might have. I don't really remember."

Tiffani could tell he did. "It had been raining that day."

"How do you know that?" he said with uncharacteristic quietness.

"Because I couldn't go out to play. I ran to the door when the policeman rang the bell."

"Ah." He nodded, still not meeting her look.

Rex had been right. There was more to the story than what her father wanted to admit to.

"Dad, I think it's time you think about getting some help. Use your wheelchair more. Get outside some. Talk to other people."

There was moisture in his eyes. "What's going on?"

"It's time for you to take responsibility for yourself. I'm not going to enable you anymore. I'm not coming to see you for a while. I think we both need a little time to think."

"That's fine with me. I don't need you," he spat.

"Bye, Dad." She sighed. "I'll see you in a few weeks."

Tiffani walked down the hall with her shoulders straight but that had been one of the hardest things she had ever done. She'd hated to do it but it had needed to be done. She and her father needed space from one another.

Tiffani stopped by the attendants' desk and told the woman there, "I just wanted to let you know I won't be coming in for a while. My dad needs to learn to deal with things on his own."

The woman gave her a wry smile. "I couldn't agree more."

"Thanks for taking care of his hand. It looks much better," Tiffani said.

"It does. I told Dr. Maxwell that as well just yesterday."

Rex had been checking in on her father? Even after the way her father had treated him?

"Bye," she told the woman, and hurried out of the building before she broke down in sobs.

Rex had worked himself to the point of exhaustion for over a week now. That was the only way he could get any sleep. Still, those hours weren't restful ones. He missed Tiffani. The worst thing he could have ever done was invite her up to his place. Now, wherever he looked he thought of her, even when washing his clothes.

As soon as he had made it home that morning after seeing Tiffani, he had phoned Nelson. He was excited about the TV report but his joy vanished when Rex told him in no uncertain terms that he wouldn't be continuing as part of the PR campaign. If the hospital didn't want him for his skills he would go elsewhere. Nelson assured him the hospital didn't want to lose him. When he asked what the problem was, Rex just told him that he and Ms. Romano could no longer agree on how much of his time could be diverted from surgery for the sake of the campaign.

He felt betrayed. She'd chosen her career over him. Once again, someone he cared about had placed their own wants and needs ahead of anything else.

His job was to help people, not create material for

great PR. He'd done his best by Mr. Royster and it had come back to bite him. He was trying to do the right thing for the people in the High Water neighborhood, but what if somehow that turned into a negative too? He hoped not. Surely Tiffani wouldn't use the clinic like that.

But now, after calming down, he couldn't help but wonder if she had been right. Was he doing the same thing as she was? Running? He wouldn't have ever believed he was doing that, but now...

Were his hair, clothes and motorcycle all a show? How was his determination to present a specific image to the world any different from what his parents had done? They'd worn clothes for who they wanted to be, had lived the lifestyle they'd wanted. Where they had messed up had been failing to create a plan to prevent it all from one day crashing down on them. Was his blind determination to be an individual with no pretensions causing him to push away the one person he wanted in his life?

Tiffani had been right. His parents loved him. They had cared about him when he'd been a child and even now they called regularly. He just hadn't returned the same treatment. They had asked for his forgiveness but he had yet to give it. They'd made a mistake, but their family had survived. What had he really lost? Nothing except a girl who he'd learned cared more about money and appearances than she did him. That wasn't a bad thing to know before it was too late.

He'd accused Tiffani of doing the same thing, but she'd abided by his request to keep the clinic out of the media. She could have used it. More than once he'd given her the opportunity to use her knowledge of him personally for the sake of the campaign, but she hadn't.

She'd explained what had happened at the accident. The question was, did he believe her? But why shouldn't he? Tiffani hadn't lied to him before.

What had he done? He'd overreacted. Lost the most wonderful thing that had ever happened to him. She brought out the best in him.

Tiffani had opened her arms wide and taken him in when he'd needed her that terrible night. There had been no questions or condemnation, just a warm, safe harbor for his wounded soul. Even when he'd told her about what his parents had done, she'd seen the positive side. Pointed out what they had done right. Tiffani knew how to care and what had he shown her? Disdain. Scorn.

Shame filled him. He'd spent much of his adult life acting holier than thou. The very thing he despised. It was time to apologize. His parents were first on his list. Then with his heart in his hand he was going to ask Tiffani for forgiveness.

And pray hard she would give it.

Two days later, Rex gathered enough courage to call his parents and ask if he could visit. His mother sounded both surprised and overjoyed to hear from him. That weekend he showed up at their house on Saturday morning. He hadn't even pulled very far into the drive before his mother and father came out to greet him.

As he put his helmet on the seat his mother embraced him with a hug and a kiss on the cheek. "Honey, this is a real treat. We're so glad to see you."

His father gave him a bear hug, bringing Rex in close and gently pounding on his back. Guilt washed over him. All these years he'd been pushing his parents away with his attitude, and by refusing to see them more. Tiffani had faithfully visited her father regularly for all her adult life and had probably never once received the warm reception Rex just had. He promised himself he would do better about being a part of his parents' lives.

"Come in and tell us all about what you have been doing." His mother wrapped her arm around his and walked close as they entered the house.

It was nothing like the one Rex had grown up in. Where his childhood home had been spacious and two stories with a pool in the back, this one was bungalow-sized and in an established blue-collar area of the city. Just big enough for two. He had to give them credit for trying to live within their means. Even their car was a basic four-door and secondhand, from the looks of it.

His mother led them into the kitchen. The table was laid with his favorite meal. "You know I'm not much of a cook, but I tried."

Rex gave her a hug. "It looks wonderful, Mom. Thanks."

Her father chuckled. "She's been working and worrying since you called."

There was something to be said for being loved. Rex hadn't realized what he'd had until he'd seen Tiffani's father in action.

They took seats at the table and chatted about what was going on in their lives and his brother's while they ate.

Then, as if his mother couldn't stand it any longer, she blurted out, "Tell us about that billboard."

"You saw that," Rex said, his appetite dying.

"Hard to miss." His father chuckled.

His mother's gaze met his. "I was surprised. I never thought you'd agree to anything like that."

"The person who talked me into it can be pretty

persuasive." Rex went on to explain his involvement in the campaign.

Both his parents looked at him, amazed.

"I knew the Royster business must have taken a toll on you but you never said anything, and, to be truthful, I felt responsible," his father said.

"You weren't. His family just didn't want to accept the truth," Rex assured him.

His mother's eyes held a sad look. "We should've been more supportive during that time but we were afraid we'd make it worse."

"It might have. I know I've been hard on you about what happened years ago. I was a kid only thinking about himself. I just want you to know that I'm grateful for your love. More than that, I appreciate you loving each other. Even though you've lived through tough times, you stuck together. You loved us. That's to be admired. I've always known you were there for me, even when I didn't show it."

His mother was openly crying and his father had moisture in his eyes. His mother said between sobs, "We thought you'd never forgive us."

"Thank you for telling us that. May I ask why you told us this now?" his father asked.

Rex gave him a direct look. "A woman."

His father nodded sagely. "That'll do it."

There was a sparkle of interest Rex hadn't seen in his mother's eyes in a long time. "When do we get to meet her?"

"Soon, I hope. I have some groveling to do first."

"It's like that, is it?" his father said with a grin.

"Yeah, I messed up."

"We all do that sometimes," his mother whispered, wiping her eyes.

"It has taken me too long to figure that out. For that I'm deeply sorry," Rex said, looking at his mother then his father.

As he was leaving his mother asked, "When're you going to get rid of that motorcycle? It scares me."

"Soon. I think it's time I make some changes in my life."

Tiffani stepped out of the taxi in front of the historic Peabody Hotel in downtown Memphis. She had chosen to come by taxi so she didn't have to worry about finding a parking place or waiting in line for a valet. She'd delayed dressing to the last minute, unsure if she wanted to even attend the cocktail party and dinner being held for the visiting accreditation committee.

Dr. Nelson had called and left a message at her office that she was invited to attend. She'd spent most of the last week and a half working on the campaign from a distance. She'd had numerous requests to interview Rex but she had declined them all. She wasn't going to ask and he wasn't going to agree.

She hadn't spoken to or seen her father since her last visit. Unable to stand it, she had called the home and asked the nurse how he was doing. She'd been told her father had become increasingly difficult the first few days after her last visit but that he was more agreeable now. The nurse assured Tiffani she had done a good thing by making her father face a few facts.

Tonight Tiffani had dressed in a light blue dress she saved for special occasions. It fit well and she felt she looked good in it. Not that she would see anyone that mattered. Rex would certainly not be there. This type of dinner wasn't his thing. She'd left her hair down and pulled it over to one side. Wearing it free was a habit now. Rex had been right. She had dressed to appear un-approachable. After Lou had dumped her she'd hidden behind her appearance, her job. Now she knew well what it was like to have a man truly appreciate who she was. The sad part was that she'd lost him, but she refused to let the lessons she'd learned about herself be overshadowed by negativity.

The time of the cocktail party had been arranged so that everyone attending could enjoy the Duck March beforehand. Twice a day, live ducks and their offspring, who had been trained in a unique tradition, trooped dutifully into the lobby of the hotel and swam in the beautiful lobby fountain. She'd seen it when she was a child but not recently. It would give her something to smile about, something she hadn't done since Rex had walked out her door. There was already a crowd forming along the red carpet stretching from the elevators to the fountain in the center of the lobby. All of this to watch five mallard ducks walk to a fountain for a swim.

Tiffani found an open spot near the fountain. A few minutes later the doors to the ornate elevator opened and out walked the ducks, followed by the Duckmaster. She couldn't help but grin.

"They're fun, aren't they?" a voice she knew well said from behind her. *Rex*.

Tiffani's insides quaked. He was here! And talking to her. "They are. I love them."

The ducks waddled past them on their way into the fountain.

Rex came to stand beside her, just touching. It was like the sun burning brightly along that side of her body. He wore a dark suit and shirt and a conservative striped tie. The only omission to looking like a professional in the traditional sense was his hair. The edge that had always drawn her to him was still there, making her glow hot in her middle.

The ducks swam a couple of laps in a circle, climbed out of the fountain, shook off and gathered to make the march back.

Rex whispered in her ear close enough his breath brushed her hair. "Can we talk?"

Tiffani tingled all over. This was her chance to tell him how she felt. She'd made the mistake of trying to share her heart with the wrong person once, but she had no doubt Rex was the man for her. She met his gaze. "Please. I'd like that."

Dr. Nelson said, passing them with a group of people, "Hey, you two. We're going to the Rooftop Bar."

"We'll be along in a few minutes," Rex said, taking her hand and heading in the other direction.

Hope flared in Tiffani. "Maybe we should—"

"We have more important things to do," Rex said, hurrying her toward the lavish lobby stairs. He started up them.

"Where are we going?"

"You'll see." At the top he guided her along the hall, turned right at the end and a few rooms down stopped in front of a door. Putting the key in the lock, he opened the door wide.

"You were that sure of me?" Tiffani didn't try to hide her suspicious tone.

His eyes took on a worried look. Was he anxious? Fearful she might reject him? She couldn't think of a time she'd ever seen Rex anything but confident. Even when he'd been upset, having done all he could have for a patient.

"No, I was that hopeful. And we needed a quiet place

to talk. You don't have to come in if you don't want to. And you're free to leave anytime you wish."

"I think I'll take my chances." Tiffani smiled and saw the tension in his shoulders ease.

She stepped to the middle of the room. It was decorated in a pale green. The walls, the window treatments, the carpet and the bedding were all a variation on the color, giving the space an elegant look. A large four-poster bed was the center of attention but there was a small sitting area near one window.

"Wow, this is a beautiful room. I've always wondered what one of the rooms at the Peabody looked like."

Rex shrugged out of his jacket and walked to the sitting area, where he put it over the back of the small sofa. He loosened his tie and said, "Why don't we sit? I need to say something to you."

He didn't touch her when she went past him. She took one of the two chairs and Rex sat on the settee, facing her.

"I have something I want to say first," Tiffani said.

"My meeting, I go first."

She sank back in her chair and put her hands in her lap. "All right."

"I owe you an apology."

That wasn't at all what she'd expected.

"For how I acted about the accident being on TV," he continued. "I know you were only doing your job. I trust you, and know you were telling me the truth about what happened. I've been so wrapped up in trying not to be who I used to be, I forgot to appreciate who I am now."

Tiffani began to say something.

He put up a hand. "I'm not finished eating humble pie. I want to thank you for making me see what kind of parents I really have. I've let one part of their personalities overshadow everything about them, including the good. I went to see them the other day and told them how much I appreciate them." He relaxed and watched her.

She waited for a few seconds. "May I talk now?"

He grinned. "Please do, before you explode."

"I want to thank you. Because of you, I now see what my father was doing to me. How I was enabling him. I told him I wouldn't be back to see him until he decided to take responsibility for himself. And about the accident being on the news, I'm sorry I hurt you. I didn't intend to. I let the thought of a promotion get in the way. But it wasn't worth losing you over."

"You haven't lost me." Rex went down on one knee in front of her and took her hands. "I was afraid you wouldn't forgive me."

Raw emotion as sweet as spring water flowed from Tiffani. She cupped his face. "That would never happen."

"I love you."

She had no doubt he did. "I love you too."

Rex lay back on the pillows piled against the headboard with Tiffani securely in his arms. He kissed her temple. His need for her had overwhelmed him to the point that talking was no longer possible. They had unfinished business. His future was with her and he needed to secure it.

"Shouldn't we be thinking about going to the dinner? Dr. Nelson will miss us," she murmured as she ran a hand over his chest.

"I don't care if he does. I had more fun here with just you."

"That was a nice thing to say. Speaking of nice things,

I meant to tell you how handsome you looked in your suit. You cut a dashing figure." She grinned.

"Don't get too used to me dressing that way."

Tiffani gave him one of those smiles he had missed so much.

"So have you heard anything about that promotion?" He needed to know. If she was moving he would be going with her, if she would have him. He would start his career over wherever she was.

"I got it." Excitement filled her voice.

Rex was both glad and sad. He was pleased for her but he hated to leave his practice.

She was quick to say, "But I got a better offer today."

Dared he hope?

She was already explaining. "Dr. Nelson wants me to come on board as the head of the Metropolitan's PR department. He was so impressed with the campaign he said he couldn't let me go."

"Is that what you want? I'll go wherever you are." He meant it. Life without Tiffani would be intolerable.

"That's the nicest thing anyone has ever offered to do for me, but I couldn't take you from the hospital or the clinic." She gave him a teasing smile. "And all your fans. The billboard company said your picture has been the most successful they have ever had."

"Yeah." There was no note of enthusiasm in his voice. "At least I have some claim to fame."

She kissed him. "You'll always be the most wonderful person to me."

"And you to me." He held her tight, secure in the knowledge he would never let her go.

* * * * *

TEMPTED BY HER
HOT-SHOT DOC

BECKY WICKS

MILLS & BOON

For my mum. Sorry about the sex scenes.
Don't tell Dad.

CHAPTER ONE

THE RAIN WAS coming down harder than she'd ever felt it. Sharp, wet pricks to her bare arms sent mini-lightning bolts through Madeline's flesh and deep into her bones as she hurried along the London cobblestones, holding her umbrella over her as best she could.

The bolts, of course, were mostly due to the man her agent had arranged for her to meet—America's wealthiest and most inspiring flying doctor and a man most women would surely kill to meet—Ryan Tobias.

His name, now rolling around in her brain, sent further spikes of adrenaline through her body, along with the goosebumps now settling in with the cold. She'd left in such a hurry she'd forgotten her jacket.

'Don't be late,' Samantha had told her. 'He doesn't like it when people are late.'

But Madeline had been so caught up in her internet research that she'd gone and made herself late anyway. She'd been determined to have as much background information on him as possible before their meeting, and it had been near impossible to tear her eyes away once she'd started.

The internet seemed to have its own busy corner of photos, articles, videos and GIFs made from *Medical Extremes* footage—the show Ryan Tobias starred in along with his team of GPs and surgeons. She'd watched a clip of him walking across the glacier in Alaska to reach a stranded explorer at least five times, pausing on the moment when the camera had gone in for a close-up of his bearded, rugged face in front of the whirring helicopter blades.

She had no idea at all about what Samantha had in mind for her to do with this man, but she couldn't deny it was exciting. And *terrifying*.

Madeline's phone beeped, making her jump. She almost tripped over the cobblestones. Damn, she *had* to pull herself together.

'I'm nearly there,' she blurted hurriedly into it, just as she rounded the corner into Trinity Buoy Wharf.

Samantha was standing there in the doorway, waiting. She was in high heels, too, Madeline noticed. Were they both dressed to impress a man they knew almost never looked impressed?

'He's already here,' Samantha said in a low voice, taking the umbrella and ushering Madeline's wet body through huge green doors into the sandy-coloured building.

A flurry of filming activity assaulted her eyes as she swiped at the raindrops on her skin. Men were everywhere: lifting crates, unscrewing lighting equipment, packing things into cases. It was a studio, as she'd expected, but the hectic feel of the place, plus the knowledge that a good few pairs of eyes were now on her, threw a spanner into her already frazzled works.

'Over here first,' Samantha said, putting a firm hand to Madeline's soaked white shirt and starting off across the room.

She was a little too quick for her to keep up, however, and before she could stop herself her heel was catching on a cable stretched out across the floor. She almost went flying.

'Are you trying to kill yourself?'

The deep voice sounded out in front of her, just as she put her hand to the wall to steady herself.

'I'm so sorry. I'm…' Madeline trailed off, realising it wasn't actually a wall she was touching.

It was hard, undoubtedly, but it was breathing.

'Dr Ryan,' she blurted, straightening up instantly.

She removed her flattened palms from his broad chest, scanned his face up close and felt her cheeks flare from pink to beetroot as her heart started pounding in her ribcage. For a strange moment she felt just as if she'd fallen asleep at her kitchen table and woken up on the YouTube channel.

Ryan Tobias wasn't in his trademark *Medical Extremes* white shirt and jacket. He was wearing a black waterproof coat and jeans. His hair, just as it always was on television, was wild and windswept—as though the breeze over London's River Thames had as little respect for him as the wind in a Patagonian hurricane.

She'd watched *those* clips twice or more. Somehow they'd airlifted a pregnant, sick lady to safety, even though Ryan and the brave pilot had been the only ones willing to risk a flight in the storm.

He was taller than she'd expected, somehow, towering over her with a look of amusement mixed with something she couldn't quite read in his familiar grey eyes.

Madeline realised with horror that he must be taking in her rain-drenched hair and the small but noticeable coffee stain on her shirt. A woman had splashed her latte on her on the tube. What must he be thinking?

She glanced around her. Samantha had been ushered off to another corner and was now apparently deep in what looked like an angst-ridden conversation with a guy waving a flowerpot.

Ryan was still appraising her, she realised.

He coughed and crossed his arms. 'I'm afraid I don't know your name.'

'Madeline,' she said, flustered.

'Where did *you* come from, Madeline?'

'From a *much* less embarrassing situation,' she replied without thinking.

Surprise flickered in his eyes before he uncrossed his arms and laughed. A proper laugh that revealed his teeth, as white as snow-capped mountains—a laugh she was pretty sure she'd heard only two or three times on the television.

'Well, they do insist on blocking the walkways like this,' he said, motioning to their feet. 'Good thing you didn't twist your ankle in those shoes. I don't know which box my emergency supplies are in.'

'Guess I got lucky.'

He threw her a surreptitious half-smile. 'I prefer to live life on the edge of danger, too.'

'I've never seen *you* in high heels.'

She adjusted her handbag on her shoulder as he laughed again. A part of her couldn't quite believe she was making Dr Ryan Tobias laugh.

'Anyway, my agent Samantha, over there, kind of surprised me with all this, so…'

'Your agent?' Ryan's expression shifted before her. 'What do you mean?'

Shards of ice were stuck in his eyes now, and it was as if Madeline was alone with him on the peak of a snowy mountain, or maybe trekking over that glacier to reach another lost adventurer who'd been injured and needed his help. Either way, she was suddenly much colder.

'Agent for what?' His arms were crossed again.

'My writing career.'

His forehead creased into a frown.

'Sorry—sorry.' Samantha bustled up behind her, breaking their locked gazes apart. 'I see you've met Madeline Savoia,' she said, putting a hand to Madeline's shoulder. 'She's almost set to be your new ghost-writer, joining you in the Amazon. What did you think of her portfolio?'

Madeline spun her head around to face Samantha. Ghost-writer? *Amazon?* It was the first she'd heard of it.

Samantha had called her to the TV set at the last minute, saying she had the perfect opportunity for her with none other than the selfless, compassionate and dazzlingly good-looking Ryan Tobias, but she'd assumed she'd be assisting in an interview with him—maybe sending some tweets for the travel and entertainment website Samantha sometimes had her freelance for.

Ryan was unreadable now, standing solid as a rock.

'I see. How much experience do you have with malaria and spider bites, Miss Madeline?'

He didn't sound as friendly as before.

Samantha squeezed her shoulder. 'Madeline is a phenomenal writer, Ryan. You might have read her geopolitical romantic thriller—the one set in Madagascar?'

'Can't say I have,' he said. 'I don't get a lot of time to read.'

He was reading *her*. Madeline knew it. Scrutinising her like a beetle under a microscope. She felt the urge to cover herself, but realised it was pointless.

'She's a keen traveller and explorer, like you, *and* she's a medical professional,' Samantha carried on as Madeline's cheeks flamed. 'I thought she'd be the perfect fit.'

'What kind of medical professional?'

'I used to be a nurse, but I'm not any more…' Madeline let her words taper off. She didn't particularly feel like explaining why she'd quit nursing. The thought of it still shamed her, but she doubted the time she'd spent on the wards of St David's Hospital would help anyone who'd been mauled by a jaguar or hugged by an anaconda in the Amazon.

'Is this necessary, Samantha?' Ryan said, after a moment.

His tone was irritated. His arms were still crossed, tighter than ever.

Something in his icy tone made Madeline recall with a flash the other articles she'd uncovered on the internet. Ryan had lost one of his team members five years ago on a sponsored expedition. He'd been twenty-seven at the time. She remembered thinking that she and Ryan were the same age—both thirty-two now.

No one knew the finer details of how or why the young physician Josephine McCarthy had died suddenly out in the jungle. Ryan had clammed up—never shared it with the media. And the medical team with him at the time had also never divulged what had happened—if they even knew.

The rumour mill had been spinning ever since.

Most of what had been printed was hearsay, of course, but Ryan had spent a lot more time in the wild since then, setting up an HIV awareness programme in Africa, arranging vaccinations at schools in Nepal.

Apparently he hadn't particularly wanted the camera crew to follow him when the concept of *Medical Extremes* had first been discussed, but the money they paid him helped thousands of villages get the medication they needed. And besides, the world needed to see the importance of doctors operating without borders.

That was what had been announced in the press release, at least.

'I'm sorry, Ryan,' Samantha said, interrupting Madeline's thoughts. 'A contract is a contract.'

'I know… I know.'

His jaw twitched in annoyance as Madeline stood awkwardly between them.

'If you don't take Madeline with you we'll only have to send someone else you haven't even met, and we're running out of time.'

'Time has a habit of running out,' he replied, somewhat mysteriously.

He's incredibly moody—that was what she'd read. Those rumours must be true at least. Ryan Tobias spent his life touching the lives of many in the world's most remote locations, but he himself was untouchable. And now Samantha was somehow asking *her* to accompany him on his next televised medical mission to the jungle?

She wondered whether her telling Samantha that she was now single had anything to do with this. She suddenly regretted telling her agent how Jason had decided to pursue his burgeoning relationship with a young zoologist called Adeline.

'How can he want an Adeline when he has a perfectly good Madeline?' she'd said at the time, enraged.

'Ryan!'

Someone was calling him back towards a camera. He didn't move. Instead he shot Madeline a narrow look that rattled every nerve-ending in her body. She fixed her eyes on his, determined not to let him know she had a lump in her throat the size of a cricket ball. He didn't break his gaze—not that she was about to break hers either. She was damned if she'd let another moody man walk all over her, even if he *was* rich and famous.

'Well, as you say, a contract is a contract,' he muttered after a moment, sucking in a breath and letting it out so heavily that Madeline felt her damp hair ruffle.

'It'll be great for your profile,' Samantha told him matter-of-factly, and Madeline caught him rolling his eyes.

'We'll see about that. Good to meet you, Madeline.' He thrust his hand out at her suddenly. 'We can always do with another nurse around, I suppose.'

'Oh, like I said, I'm not a—'

'Ryan! We need you over here, please.' That voice again.

His face was expressionless as he engulfed Madeline's hand with his own, and for some reason another episode of *Medical Extremes* was flashing in her mind. Cambodia. The one where he'd eaten a fried tarantula. It had been a gift from the family of a man he'd helped to save.

Ryan Tobias was fearless—that was what everyone said. Well. She was damned if she'd let him scare her.

'I'm looking forward to working with you,' she said calmly.

'Ryan!'

'I'm *coming*, damn it!'

He dropped her hand, turned and strolled across the studio, and Samantha took Madeline's elbow, leading her to a sofa and coffee table in the corner of the chaos. Both were covered in sheets of paper.

'You did good. I'm so sorry to spring this on you.' She poured them both a cup of coffee. 'But this opportunity wouldn't have waited. I suggested *you* the moment I heard what happened to the last ghost-writer...'

'What happened?' Madeline realised just how dry her throat was.

'Fell down some stairs—cracked three ribs, broke one arm. Ironic isn't the word. Would you like a biscuit?'

She shook her head, glancing to her right. Ryan was walking towards a guy packing a camera into a very large black box on wheels, talking about some supplies he needed but hadn't seen yet. His voice still sent chills…or was it thrills?…straight through her.

Was she *really* going to the Amazon?

'He seems…nice,' she ventured, sipping her coffee.

'He's *very* nice, when everything goes to plan. So, Madeline, the long and short of it is that Ryan's contract states that he needs to deliver a memoir and his publishers want it released for Christmas. Only as yet he's been too busy to write it.'

'OK…'

Madeline gripped more tightly onto her cup and bit into her cheek. Ghost-writing wasn't exactly something she was thrilled about doing. Her last book—written under her own name—hadn't gone too well, though, due to her publisher having no marketing budget, mostly. Her sales had suffered horribly while she'd been out writing the next one in the middle of nowhere in Zimbabwe.

Apparently bad things happened to books if you couldn't spend twenty-four hours a day on Twitter, telling everyone about them.

Bad things happened to relationships, too, if you stupidly left your boyfriend alone for two months…

Madeline pushed thoughts of Adeline from her head.

Samantha sipped her coffee, then put the cup down on the messy table.

'Ryan is about to go and shoot the third season of *Medical Extremes*, as you know, and what with all his appointments he hasn't got time for the memoir, too. We need someone to help him write the book at the same time as he's filming—gather quotes, insights, interviews, you know? Am I right in thinking you're still free to take a week or two, probably three, out of London at the moment?'

Madeline nodded blankly. Ryan was so tall and so commanding without even trying. Everyone seemed to be in awe of him. And although she was a little loath to admit it, after the way he'd just acted towards her, it wasn't hard to see why.

As well as being the sexiest doctor since George Clooney, Ryan was a millionaire who gave selflessly to charities all over the world. He didn't have a lot else to spend his riches on, apparently. His father was a heart surgeon, famed for working with those less fortunate in the US. Ryan had taken things one step further by setting up his own non-profit organisation and flying all over the world with his team, crossing borders to reach people who'd never get help otherwise.

Samantha lowered her voice. 'Ryan doesn't write. Obviously his skills lie in other areas. But with you on board, plus his celebrity status, this book could be a bestseller. Easy. The publishers have a very impressive budget.'

'And Twitter?' Madeline said. 'How many followers?'

'Over four hundred thousand. He never tweets a damn thing, of course, but we have Amy from Middlesex University who's his biggest fan. She won the competition to be his Twitter manager. He just got done with a news team covering the story… BBC, I think. How are *you* at being on camera? You've got great cheekbones— I bet it loves you. And you speak several languages, I recall? Always useful.'

Madeline's stomach lurched. This was turning out to be a lot more than she'd bargained for. But it wasn't as if she had anything else on the cards.

She mused over the offer as Samantha kept on talking. She vaguely registered her agent mentioning Rio, a remote tribe—*'none of those weird neck rings or anything'*—parasites, anaemia… But after a minute she was only half listening, because she could feel Ryan looking at her again from across the room.

She straightened her back again, so that he could see he wasn't intimidating her in any way, and tried to look enthusiastic and excited. She had to play her cards right. This chance was too good to pass up and maybe Samantha was right. It could be a bestseller by Christmas.

We can both get something out of this, she thought, sending the thought across the void and straight into Ryan's cool, iceberg eyes.

CHAPTER TWO

'DID YOU KNOW that CAN's first pilots were called the flag-bearers of the skies? That was in the early nineteen-forties.'

'I don't know much about CAN at the moment,' Madeline said. 'This was all a bit short notice, as you know. Maybe you could explain?'

She was trying her hardest not to let turbulence affect the way she was talking to Ryan. This plane was far too shaky for her peace of mind, but of course this man flew everywhere for a living and didn't even look as if he'd noticed they were bumping up and down in what felt like God's hugest tantrum since the last giant tornado.

'Correio Aéreo Nacional,' he said, picking up a packet of peanuts and running a tanned thumb over the seal without opening it. 'Their mission was to help integrate the most remote Amazon outposts with the rest of the country.'

'How did they do that?'

Madeline pulled out her notebook, wishing she'd put her laptop under her seat instead of up in the overhead locker. She could type much faster than she could write these days, but there was no way on earth she was climbing past Ryan. She'd rather not risk feeling his eyes on her again as she tripped, or did something else stupid as a result of her nerves.

There was something in his stare, she mused. It stayed with her even with her eyes closed. She'd seen it a thousand times in camera close-ups, of course, and it was part of what drew people in their thousands to watch him in action. It had the power to make you feel like you were the only person on earth. It also had the power to make you feel like an idiot.

Ryan smiled, apparently scrutinising her handwriting from his seat on the aisle. 'CAN transported isolated residents from riverside communities to places where they could be helped—usually the city. They had dozens of planes flying over the Amazon—more than they do now anyway.'

Madeline scribbled as fast as she could to get his words down, feeling thankful that she'd brought a Dictaphone for later.

When she looked up his grey eyes were fixed on her, and she found herself annoyingly self-conscious. At least she wasn't wet and covered in coffee this time—she'd put on a very respectable knee-length blue dress for the flight, one that accentuated her small waist, and she'd left her long hair down around her shoulders. Also, he seemed to be making a concerted effort to be friendly, for which she was more than grateful.

'The flying doctors were known as the Angels of the Amazon, is that right?' she asked him, reaching for her necklace.

'Correct,' he said, watching her fiddling with the silver chain as she slid the small crystal apple up and down on it. 'They *were* angels, Madeline. Still are. They deliver medical aid by aircraft. If they didn't these people

would only get help after weeks of travelling on foot
through the jungle, or by boat.'

'So, would you consider yourself an angel now, too?'

Ryan frowned, drumming his fingers on his tray
table. 'I just do what's necessary—like *they* do,' he said.
'These people live and breathe the Amazon—a place
most of us know little about, except that it's a living
pharmacy essential to billions of lives on earth, right?
They're the caretakers of the jungle and everything in
it. By helping them and looking after their health we're
helping the environment.'

The plane jostled them again and Madeline's tray
table jumped.

'Do you know where we're going?' he asked, catching her notepad before it slid off.

'Caramambatai,' she replied quickly, hoping she was
pronouncing it right. 'Your producer says it's an indig-
enous settlement...'

'The Ingariko tribe, yes. They're spread all over
South America, but this camp is pretty much hidden
on the border between Brazil, Venezuela and Guyana.
It's about as remote as you're going to get. Legend has
it people have been swallowed whole by thick morning
mists in these parts. They're more likely to have been
finished off by surucucu snakes, if you ask me. Highly
poisonous, by the way. If you see one it will probably
be the last thing you see.'

She realised, now that he was so close, that he had
lines around his eyes—proof of laughter, perhaps, more
than age. He'd been happy once. Happier than the media
made him out to be now anyway. He looked sexier in
person, too, she decided.

Then she caught herself.

Sexier? There was no way she was letting herself

think *that* again. She was here to do a job—and besides, as if *anyone* would go near her, let alone this guy. Her friend Emma had said she reeked of heartbreak, which wasn't particularly nice but was definitely true. Hardly surprising after what Jason had done.

Madeline could still recite every line of that love-struck email to Adeline she'd read by mistake after he'd left his laptop open.

I'm just trying to find the right time to tell her, baby. You know it's not her I'm in love with any more.

'So, how do we reach these people once we get to Brazil?' she asked, trying and failing to cross her legs properly under her tray table.

They'd been on the plane for four hours already, and she'd already counted at least nine things in her head that she'd forgotten to pack or research. She was hoping she'd have time to sort a few things out in Rio—where they were stopping for supplies before taking another flight to Saint Elena.

'We'll take a Cessna,' Ryan said. 'Either that or a Black Hawk—whatever the team have booked. Both are pretty good on the runways.'

'There are runways in the rainforest?'

'Well, they're mud strips, really.'

Ryan opened the peanuts and offered her one. She shook her head, trying her hardest to write without scribbling on the tray table instead. They were still bouncing up and down, as if the plane itself was on some sort of trampoline.

'The runways were carved out by the gold miners initially,' he told her. 'Illegally, of course, but they help us do our jobs so I suppose the *real* value of that gold just keeps on increasing—wherever it is. You can write that down.'

She realised her pen was hovering and that she was lost in thoughts of Jason again. But this time Jason was standing next to Ryan Tobias in the jungle, and being somewhat dwarfed by him.

She blinked to get rid of them both. 'Right, yes. Good idea.' She started to scribble, flustered.

'Whatever you do, stay close to us,' Ryan said suddenly, in a tone that pulled her eyes to his again like a magnet. 'People go missing out there all the time.'

Her breath caught as she saw an emotion she didn't recognise cross his face.

He continued without looking at her. 'Last time we found a burnt-out helicopter which must have crashed twenty years ago. No skeletons inside…who knows what happened to them? The jungle has a way of luring people in and keeping them.'

Madeline tried not to shudder. For some reason she knew he was thinking of Josephine McCarthy. What *had* happened to her, exactly?

'When were you here last?' she asked.

'Eight months ago. Five-day CAN mission. No cameras. We treated six hundred patients for minor infections, brought some ultrasound machines. We felt bad we couldn't help the guy who got shot, though.'

'Shot?'

'He did it to himself—his gun got all twisted. By the time we found him his leg had more larvae in it than a dead horse. We cleaned him out, worked on him a long time, but he didn't make it. So, like I said, don't go wandering off on your own, please.' He met her eyes, concern shining around his pupils. 'And watch what you do with your gun.'

Madeline realised she felt quite ill. 'Ryan, I wouldn't be comfortable with a gun, and I really don't think…'

She trailed off as she caught the smile creeping onto his face and felt her cheeks flush crimson. He was joking.

'Don't worry—you're safe with us,' he chuckled, nudging her gently with an elbow.

But just as quickly as it had appeared his smile was retracted, as if a memory had snatched it back again. Something stopped Madeline asking any more questions, though a million were fizzing on her tongue.

'I *feel* safe with you,' she said instead, meaning it. 'How could anyone not?'

Ryan leaned back against the seat, and looked past her, out of the window again. 'You'll be safe with me as long as you're smart. It's no one's job but your own to protect yourself out here, Maddy. Can I call you Maddy?'

'Sure.'

'The Brazilian military uses these trips to gather intelligence sometimes, so if we have any guests you'll know they're on to something and it's a sign to be on high alert.'

'What do you mean?'

'Cocaine trafficking, illegal gold mining—it's all going on in these parts. There were reports of drug runners in the area not so long ago.'

'Drug runners?' Madeline whispered quietly. 'They wouldn't touch you, though, those sorts of people— would they? Especially not with a TV crew… That would just be drawing attention to themselves.'

Ryan shrugged, pouring a handful of peanuts into his big hand as the clouds fluttered past their window. 'You never know *what* they'll do, but let's just say our carefully made runways are as good for transporting illegal drugs as they are for shifting real medicine. You wouldn't want to see the wrong thing by mistake.'

'Do you ever get scared?'

He seemed to contemplate this for a moment, popping the nuts into his mouth, running a hand over his dark stubble. She studied his lips as he chewed. She'd bet he had a million women after him. She wondered if he'd ever asked anyone out who wasn't some sort of celebrity...

'I wouldn't say I never get anxious,' he replied eventually. 'But if we don't take these risks, Madeline... Maddy...we risk a lot worse. We risk thousands of people dying unnecessarily. Sick people take risks when they hear about us. They walk for days, even weeks, to get our help in these places. If we suddenly decide *we're* too afraid we're failing them and we're failing ourselves. You can write that down, too.'

Madeline put her pen back on her notepad, realising with dismay that her handwriting was worse than a child's.

'So, is there anyone you need to stay in touch with while we're away?' Ryan asked her. 'You know there's no signal in the Amazon? Rio might be your last chance to check in for a while.'

'I'm single. My boyfriend and I broke up,' she said, tucking her hair behind her ear and trying not to let the anger register in her voice.

She'd bypassed the emotional phase a couple of weeks ago and transitioned smoothly into fury—an emotion that reared its head like a lion whenever she thought of Adeline's face. She wished she hadn't checked out the other woman's Facebook page now. It was worse being able to picture her.

'He started seeing someone else while I was away

working on my last book. He didn't exactly stop once I got back.'

Ryan was silent. When she looked up he appeared to be fighting a smile.

'I'm sorry to hear that,' he said, straightening his face quickly. 'But I actually meant for this book—do you need to send things to your editor while you're away?'

'Oh.' Madeline's cheeks were on fire. She kicked herself internally. 'Not for a while,' she managed. 'I just have to make sure we get our interviews in—and I'll shadow you, if that's OK.'

'However you think it would work best,' he said, resting his arm on the armrest and brushing hers accidentally. She moved as far away from him as she could, crossing her legs away from him.

'I really am sorry about your boyfriend,' he said quietly. 'It hurts to lose someone you're close with, however you come to part ways.'

Madeline closed her eyes. Something in his voice spoke volumes of his own loss.

'These things happen for a reason,' she said, as firmly as she could manage. She picked up her pen again. 'It'll be interesting to see your work with my own eyes. I've watched most of your shows—you really do amazing things for people.'

'Thanks…we try.' He nodded appreciatively. 'You're a trained nurse, as I recall?'

Her heart sped up. 'Yes, well remembered.'

'Why did you quit?'

She opened her mouth to reply, but shut it again quickly. She found it hard to vocalise exactly what had happened. She'd thrown herself into her writing instead; it was what her counsellor had told her to do.

'It's OK—you don't have to tell me.' Ryan put a hand on top of hers for a moment.

Two seconds, maybe three, of skin-on-skin contact and her heart was a kangaroo. She yanked her hand back—maybe too quickly. What had happened in the hospital almost poured out of her, but she bit her tongue. He was a relative stranger. And she was in no mood to go into the details of her past life—that was what it felt like sometimes anyway.

For the next few hours Ryan plugged himself into an action movie and left her to read her book. She couldn't help the odd glance in his direction, just to confirm she wasn't dreaming. And she was almost entirely certain he was sneaking a few at *her*. The next few weeks accompanying him and his *Medical Extremes* team were going to be 'extreme', to say the least.

CHAPTER THREE

RYAN STUDIED HIS face in the mirror. He liked to think he didn't really suffer with jet lag any more, but the truth was he probably threw himself head-first into every new time zone without giving his body the chance to react. This mission was going to be a particularly tough one—not least because he'd have Madeline Savoia on his trail.

He rested his hands on the sink, leaned closer to the glass and frowned at his reflection. His eyes looked tired. Madeline had distracted him from sleeping on the plane.

She looked a lot like *her*. The first time she'd all but ploughed into him in the studio he'd almost jumped out of his skin. His reaction had been poor, he knew. Angry... The way he always acted when confronted with something he really had no clue how to handle. He'd felt as if he'd seen a ghost.

Josephine.

The name popped into his head like a gunshot. He swallowed hard, jerked the cold tap on and ran his hand under it. Then he said it out loud, straight into the mirror, watching his lips make their way over the word in a way they hadn't for a long time.'

'Josephine.'

He rarely let her name past his lips. Every time he so

much as thought of her the guilt crashed over him like a tsunami. It had smothered him and almost made him tumble when Madeline's hands had pressed against him to steady herself. She hadn't realised, of course, but she'd kind of been holding him up at the same time.

Ryan splashed his face with cold water. The more he tried not to think about this, the more he *did*. It was something about Madeline's eyes. And her pursed lips. And the way she'd crossed her arms defiantly over that coffee stain she'd clearly been so embarrassed about. The way she'd lowered her head just slightly when she'd asserted herself, indicating her vulnerability.

A knock on the hotel room door made him jump again. *Dammit.*

'I'm coming,' he called, wiping his face on the towel and running a hand through his hair. It was getting long at the front again. He frowned at the few stubborn greys now making a permanent home in his stubbled chin.

Nothing he could do about it.

Salt and pepper looks better on you than on my French fries.
#DrRyanTobias

A fan of his had tweeted that the other day. He mentally rolled his eyes—such gushing usually went straight over his head. He had quite enjoyed that French fries reference, though. He liked to think years of torment hadn't marked him physically…at least not as much as they had on the inside.

He threw on a white button-down shirt and pulled on his smartest jeans as the knock sounded out again. 'Give me one second!'

He hopped across the patterned carpet, still doing his belt up, and pulled the door open.

'What's the emergency?'

'No emergency.' Madeline smiled. Her hand was still hovering in the air, as if she was about to knock on his face. 'Sorry to interrupt. You said to knock before I went downstairs.'

'What time is it?' he asked, flustered.

He was totally thrown now. She looked entirely different somehow in this light, with her round, beguiling eyes lined with kohl and a hint of green eyeshadow. His hand found his hair again, at the same time as the other started buttoning up his shirt.

'Almost five thirty,' she told him, with her gaze now fixed on his exposed chest. 'Doesn't the drinks thing start now?'

'Yes, yes—sorry, I got caught up. There was an issue with the supplies being delivered to Saint Elena, and I've been on the phone trying to fix it.'

'Is it sorted out?'

'Almost. I did all I could.'

'OK. Well, don't worry, I'm sure we can sneak you in late without anyone noticing. It's not like you're a VIP or anything.'

Laughter burst from his mouth as he hurried back into the room to pull his shoes out of his suitcase. The dryness in her tone tickled him. He'd always found the British sense of humour quite fascinating.

He grabbed his key card and wallet, turned the bathroom light out and let his eyes travel over Madeline's petite yet curvy figure as he walked towards the door again. She was wearing another dress, an emerald-green one this time, tied around her waist with a paler green belt. Her hair was up now, in a French braid draped over

one shoulder, and her lips were glistening in a shade
of burgundy.

'Were you writing?' he asked, for want of something
to fill the silence.

'In my room? A bit.'

He nodded. He'd fought the urge, on the journey, to
ask her more about her books, aware that he'd perhaps
been a little rude about her passion before. It was just
that when Samantha had first mentioned a ghost-writer
he'd imagined for some reason someone older, greyer,
crinklier. Perhaps an avid cat-lover or crochet aficionado.
He definitely hadn't imagined…well. *This.*

He cleared his throat. 'You look nice,' he said.

'Thank you—so do you.'

'So, you recognise me OK without the *Medical Extremes* outfit?' He smiled now.

'You're kind of hard to miss.'

'Is that right? I thought I'd been watching my weight.'

It was Madeline's turn to laugh now. 'As if you need
to. I meant you have presence.'

Ryan realised that her cheeks were redder than they
had been five seconds ago. He hadn't exactly intended
to get himself dressed in front of her…but, then again,
they *were* headed into the jungle. Tribal villages in the
Amazon rainforest weren't exactly renowned for their
privacy.

He stepped past her, closing the door behind him, then
put a hand to the small of her back as they walked towards the elevators, noting her shoes—summer wedges
with green straps.

'You're a little better at walking in those,' he said
without thinking, pushing the button.

'That tripping over in public thing? That was a one-
off—don't worry.'

'I'd only be worried in the Amazon,' he replied as the doors pinged and slid open. 'Big black cables on the floor of the jungle have a nasty habit of not being cables.'

She raised an eyebrow questioningly.

'Snakes,' he explained, and she pulled a face that made him chuckle.

In the elevator, Ryan fixed his eyes on their reflections in the full-length mirror. She was at least a foot shorter than him; that was shorter than— He clenched his fist. This was ridiculous. Madeline was not *her*.

He was determined to count the differences.

Some of her expressions were similar, sure, but Madeline had bigger eyes, wide and unnervingly quizzical— even more so now, framed with make-up. Her hair, long and dark and shiny, was the same…but she was slimmer, perhaps. He didn't know much about women's sizes, but he knew when he could hold a waist with both hands without leaving too much room between his fingers.

The elevator doors swung open. The music in the hotel foyer took the edge off his discomfort slightly as he guided Madeline towards the restaurant, past a crowd of tourists in matching floral shorts, speaking hurried German.

'I'm sure you've been briefed about this,' he said, trying to regain an air of authority if only for his own peace of mind.

'Not really.'

He frowned, looking down into her sea-green eyes, then cleared his throat again. 'Well, this is basically a getting-to-know-you event for the new people joining us and the suppliers. We also have a new cameraman from here in Rio, and a local paramedic. It's about building trust as a team before we get out there, you know? That's when the real work starts.'

'It's a good idea,' Madeline said. 'So I'll introduce myself as your ghost-writer?'

Ryan felt his brow crease. How had he forgotten her mission? He felt that tsunami again at the thoughts of having to regurgitate any of those moments he'd been trying his hardest to bury for so long—of seeing them laid bare on the pages of a book…a book he'd eventually see someday in a bargain bin, with the forgotten demons that would surely plague him for ever tossed aside by a reader who'd lapped them up and promptly let them go, in a way he never could.

His hand found his hair, swept it from his forehead. 'About this memoir… We need everyone to feel secure in the fact that our attention is fully on the patients. Our work always takes priority.'

'I know that.'

'You're there to write the memoir, of course, but we might need you to help out as a nurse from time to time—'

'I'd really rather not be a nurse while I'm here,' Madeline interrupted.

She paused halfway to the table, where he could see the team already waiting, chatting away. She looked nervous again now.

'Ryan, with all due respect, I didn't come here to—'

'Madeline, I get your current role, believe me, but people will be needing you out there. Do you really think, after everything you've trained for, that you could actually walk away from someone in pain?'

She opened her mouth to respond, but shut it again quickly. Annoyance was flickering in her eyes. He was concerned that this wasn't looking very professional; people were looking at them.

'It's going to be fine,' he whispered in her ear, getting

a whiff of her floral perfume as he did so. Dear God, she smelled good.

'Ryan, my man! Good to see you—and who's this?'

The tall, sandy-blond-haired guy approaching them in smart black trousers and a purple shirt was Evan Walker—a trusted friend and doctor from Wisconsin, and a firm voice of reason on the *Medical Extremes* team. Viewers loved him for his sense of humour and equally for his ability to take charge at a moment's notice. He had his own online fan club and was also popular because of his award-winning wife's efforts in setting up a domestic abuse helpline.

'Madeline Savoia is my ghost-writer…for the memoir,' Ryan said calmly as Madeline dutifully held out her hand. 'But she's a nurse, too. I've explained that it's all hands on deck at times.'

He felt her eyes burning his cheek as he spoke, but he didn't turn his head.

'Excellent,' Evan enthused, throwing him a look Ryan knew only he could read. Evan knew everything about Josephine. And he hadn't said a word.

'I'm a huge fan of your work, Dr Walker,' Madeline said.

'Thank you very much. So, have you been out to these parts before?'

A waiter approached and guided them all to their seats.

'No, I can't say I have,' she replied.

Ryan pulled a chair out for her and motioned for her to sit down beside him. He'd noticed the way Evan was looking at her now.

'You know, you really look a lot like…'

'What is there to drink?' Ryan put a hand up for the waiter and signalled for a menu.

Evan seemed to take the hint. He took his seat and started pouring the three of them water from a jug full of ice and lemon.

'You're in for a treat, Madeline,' he continued, 'these are some of the nicest people on the planet. Always so grateful and patient. It's harsh out there, you know?'

Madeline pulled her glass towards her. Ryan noticed her nails were drumming slightly on the glass. 'So I hear.'

'And they live pretty differently to how we do. Most have no idea that all this is even here, and even if they did they'd probably hate it.' He gestured around him now at the opulent restaurant, with Rio de Janeiro's Ipanema in their direct line of vision through the windows.

Ryan gazed out with Madeline at the swirling cormorants and emerald hills in the distance. The beautiful side of the jungle, he thought to himself, feeling a sudden twinge of familiar guilt.

He forced himself to think of something else.

He couldn't help but wonder yet again what the story was with Madeline quitting nursing. Whenever anyone brought it up she looked as though she might run for the hills. He kind of understood how that felt, though. He'd been running for years.

He'd hidden behind deadlines and responsibilities, creating more work for himself than one man should probably have to deal with in a lifetime. But now it had caught up with him in the form of this woman—sent to spill his secrets to the world.

He motioned to the waiter approaching with the wine. 'White, please,' he said. He turned to Madeline. 'You?'

'Red,' she said. 'Just a bit, though, I don't want to fall asleep at the table. I'm trying to outsmart my jet-lag.'

He smiled.

Evan was still talking. 'Last time we were here we helped a little baby—just nine months old, I think. She had a temperature of one hundred and two and climbing…and she wasn't getting enough oxygen. She had pneumonia…she was malnourished. If we hadn't been there…if *Ryan* hadn't been there…she would have been dead in two days.'

Madeline turned to him as a starter of fresh fruit was placed before her on the table, and he was surprised to notice the glistening of tears in her eyes at the mention of the baby.

Casual conversation about supply checks and sleeping arrangements at the camp kept them going as their starters were consumed and everyone's glasses were refilled, and then, just as the waiters hovered on the periphery with their main courses, Ryan tapped his fork on his glass to silence the table.

He rose to his feet, dropping his napkin.

'Ladies and gents,' he said, smoothing down his white shirt and holding up his glass. 'I'd like to thank you all for coming on this brand-new mission with *Medical Extremes*. Let's welcome Pablo, our new cameraman from right here in Rio, who'll be joining us where thousands wouldn't and hopefully not capturing *everything* on camera. No one looks their best after living on bananas and tropical rain for a few weeks.'

He paused for laughter, which flittered around the table as he'd known it would.

'I'd also like to introduce Madeline, here. She'll be working on some writing and lending a hand wherever possible, so I'd like you all to give her the *Medical Extremes* welcome we give everyone and make her feel like one of the family.'

He raised his glass higher, but before she or anyone

could say another word, a noise from the kitchen made
the entire room jump in their chairs.

'Fogo! Fogo! Fogo!'

The voice was female.

'Help!'

Ryan just had time to see Evan grab his medical bag
before they were both off their chairs in a flash, running
for the kitchen. He made it to the back of the restaurant
just in time to see the blaze of orange fire running up
a woman's sleeve—just before he plunged her arm into
a nearby sink, under a gushing tap. She was sobbing.

'What happened?' he asked, and was flooded with a
stream of Portuguese. The fire was gone, but a crowd
of people in white coats and chef's hats were all talking at once.

Evan was behind him, pulling out a sterile bandage
from his bag as Ryan moved closer to keep the woman's arm under the water. It was blistered and red, but
he could already tell she wasn't going to need hospital
treatment—thank God.

'I'll go tell everyone not to panic—you got this?'
Evan said.

'All good,' Ryan told him, and watched him shoot
back through the door.

'She was pouring pecans into the chocolate mix when
her sleeve caught on fire. That's why they're all over
the floor.'

Madeline.

Ryan had only just realised she was there, too. She
was holding the bandage Evan had given her and translating every word. He took the bandage from her, noticing the pecan nuts under his feet for the first time.

'She says she's worried the dessert is ruined. It's been cooking too long now without being stirred.'

Ryan listened as Madeline spoke in Portuguese to the crowd and someone moved to stir the pot she was pointing at. She reached for a clean dishcloth, soaked it under another tap and handed it to him. On autopilot Ryan placed it over the woman's arm for a moment, before wrapping the bandage around it and fastening it behind her wrist. Her tears were subsiding already and she really did seem more concerned about her dessert.

'Can you tell her I'll give her some ibuprofen, and that she should go home and get some rest?' he asked Madeline, who promptly did as she was asked.

Back at the table, when the ibuprofen had been dispatched and the drama was all but forgotten, the party resumed its happy chatter while the glorious Rio sunset made way for a sky full of stars.

'You were pretty impressive in there, Nurse Madeline,' he whispered, when he couldn't keep it in any more.

He hadn't been able to stop thinking about it—the way she'd sprung into action and known what to do, and say. His Portuguese was limited, as was his Spanish. He got by—but mostly on charm and miming, he had to admit.

'I didn't do anything,' she said quickly.

He frowned. 'Yes, you did. It was instinctive.'

She shrugged, clearly uncomfortable with his eyes on her. Her jaw started pulsing and he knew not to say anything else.

He also knew without question that keeping away from Madeline Savoia was going to be impossible. Not only was she impossibly intoxicating—whether she liked it or not—she wasn't just a writer.

If he had his way she'd be helping him with medical duties so frequently that the details she really needed for the memoir to be a hit would be the last thing on her mind.

CHAPTER FOUR

THERE WAS SOMETHING about Rio de Janeiro, Madeline decided, that was quite entrancing. The streets were alive with the sound of market stall fruit sellers, and tourists examined cheap patterned sarongs and vibrant paintings of ladies dancing under starry spangled skies. The smell of coconuts and sunscreen permeated the air, and she'd seen more thongs, she mused, in the space of twenty minutes than she'd seen in twenty branches of her favourite high street store back in London.

Madeline had been wandering around in the sunshine for a couple of hours alone, trying to get some last-minute bits and pieces before they were due to catch the plane to Saint Elena at six p.m. The rush of the ocean in her ears as she strolled along the mosaic-riddled promenade, coupled with the whoosh of rollerblades, was like a musical symphony. It was hard to believe that just twenty-four hours ago she'd been climbing out of a black cab in the awful London rain.

Madeline was grateful for this time to herself while Ryan rushed about filming another segment for *Medical Extremes*.

'Go enjoy yourself in the sunshine,' he'd said that morning at breakfast. 'And don't forget Sugar Loaf Mountain.'

She wasn't sure she had the energy for Sugar Loaf.

They'd stayed around the table till the early hours last night, discussing the mission they were about to undertake, and perhaps, on reflection, she'd enjoyed a bit too much wine after that incident in the kitchen.

She'd noticed that Ryan had stopped at one glass, and she remembered reading somewhere that Ryan didn't drink much. Something about never knowing when he might need to help someone. She smiled, remembering the look on his face in the kitchen. He hadn't realised she was fluent in Portuguese. Then again, how *would* he have known?

What Ryan had said about her actions being instinctive had been playing on her mind. She'd told herself a million times that her nursing days were over, but he was right. Someone had really needed her and she hadn't been able to turn those instincts off at all.

'Mango!' a fruit seller was calling from her tiny stall.

Madeline shook her head politely. She'd avoided eye contact with Ryan all night after that. She knew without him saying another word that he was planning to demand her nursing skills in the Amazon.

'Pineapple?' another fruit seller called out as she turned another corner.

She smiled once again, holding up the plastic bag of fruit skewers she'd bought earlier.

Ryan had escorted her up to her room at around two a.m. By then she'd been almost asleep on her feet. She'd been acutely aware of his hand on her lower back over her dress as they'd left the dining room, and the sound of him clearing his throat in the elevator as he'd pressed himself against the wall opposite her. She'd felt his eyes on her in the mirror.

She'd pondered at the time that he might be trying to

stand as far away from her as possible in the enclosed space. She'd been doing exactly the same thing.

'Try to sleep in if you can in the morning,' he'd said, stopping with her outside her room. 'It might be the best sleep you'll get for a few weeks. The sleeping arrangements won't be up to this standard in the jungle. But I'm sure you've probably figured that out.'

'I'm looking forward to it,' she'd said, trying to sound as if she meant it. 'Thank you for tonight.'

'Thank *you*,' he'd replied softly.

'We should pencil in some time for us to talk. I was thinking regular slots, maybe one every day...'

'Let me see what I can do once we're out there,' he'd said, cutting her off quickly. 'I mean, of course we have to get this memoir written, but things are going to be really hectic for the first few days at least.'

He'd been looking at the doorframe as he'd said that—not once at her.

'I'll see you tomorrow,' he'd told her, and with that he'd leaned in and dropped a quick kiss on her cheek.

It had been as soft as a moth landing on a shadow. She'd felt the brush of his stubble on her skin, caught a whiff of his cologne. Then he'd turned on his heel and Madeline had watched his undeniably sculpted butt in his jeans as he'd walked the whole way back down the corridor and turned the corner.

For the first time in months, with questions she wanted to ask this mysterious doctor galloping maddeningly through her thoughts along with jet-lag, Madeline had eventually drifted off to sleep without thinking once about her ex. She was grateful for that at least.

Armed with sunscreen and mosquito repellent, plus a new bright yellow sarong and several colouring books and sets of crayons for the children she'd inevitably meet in the Amazon, Madeline reached the hotel again at four p.m.

She'd just arrived back in her room and was planning on changing, packing and heading down to find the team, when a knock on the door made her jump. She went to open it in bare feet, expecting someone from Housekeeping. Her insides performed an impressive somersault as she came face to face with Ryan.

'Hi. Everything OK?' she asked, clutching the doorframe and hoping she didn't look terrible.

'We're still waiting on some of the ultrasound equipment we lost track of yesterday,' he said.

She ran her eyes quickly over his blue denim shirt. The sleeves were rolled up over his tanned forearms and his practical, multi-pocketed khaki trousers made her smile. It was still a surreal dream, being face to face with this man.

She didn't miss him looking her up and down in return, in her knee-length, red strapless sundress. She hoped she hadn't dropped any fruit on it.

'Some of it's already halfway here, so unfortunately it means I'll have to stay another night.'

'Just you?'

'It only needs one of us to wait. The rest of the team will leave today and set up camp as planned. I was just wondering if…'

He trailed off for a second, seeming to contemplate his words. She detected the slightest trace of hesitation.

'I was wondering if you wanted to stay with me? I realise I've been a bit…well, aloof about this whole memoir thing, but I do appreciate you have a job to do. Maybe we can get to know each other a bit better over dinner. If you like. Just us this time.'

Just us this time.

Madeline stood up straighter. 'Yes,' she said quickly. 'I think that would be a good idea—before things get too crazy. Good thinking. I have some questions prepared that will help me get a good head start. I'll think up some more. What time should I meet you?'

She hoped she was sounding professional in this moment, because even as she spoke she was mentally unpacking her suitcase, looking for the right thing to wear to dinner.

Ryan shifted his weight onto his opposite foot and folded his arms. 'I was thinking we'd get out of the hotel. I know a restaurant nearby that does great tapas.'

'My favourite. Huge fan of olives.'

He nodded. 'Good. Shall we say seven in the lobby?'

'Seven it is.'

'Great. Well…' He paused again, uncrossed his arms and let out a long, almost relieved sigh. 'I'll see you then, Maddy.'

She shut the door after him, turning back to her room in a panic. She had precisely three hours to prepare a set of questions that wouldn't make Ryan Tobias fear talking to her about the details they both knew she needed, and in that little time she had to make herself look worthy enough to be out in a restaurant with the world's most famous flying doctor.

She rammed her hands through her hair again.

By the time seven p.m. rolled around Madeline was more or less satisfied that she looked OK. She'd opted for her second-favourite green dress—a casual maxi-dress that plunged at the neck in a V without revealing too much. She'd paired it with a long beaded necklace and left her hair loose around her shoulders. Silver-strapped flat sandals completed the outfit, and a hint of peach lip-gloss made her mouth shimmer in a way she hoped made them look plumper, too.

Gathering her green and silver sequined purse, she put her notebook and pen inside and took one last deep breath before reaching for the door.

Ryan was already waiting for her in the lobby. She felt as if the jet set of the insect world was throwing a party in her stomach as she approached him. She hated being starstruck—if that was what this feeling was. But at least it was taking her mind off her break-up.

'Green is definitely your colour,' he said.

His smile reached his eyes and she could tell it was genuine.

'Thank you.'

Ryan was still wearing his khaki trousers, but had chosen another white button-down shirt that highlighted his broad chest and deep bronze tan. The kind of tan only a travelling man had, she mused in appreciation.

Madeline caught his eyes lingering for a split second on the hint of cleavage she knew she was displaying behind her beads, but instead of feeling self-conscious she realised she was feeling quite empowered.

'Let's go,' Ryan said, patting his flat stomach. 'I'm famished.'

They walked outside together, through the hotel's revolving doors and into the balmy night. The breeze picked up her long hair and tousled it about her shoulders as she walked alongside him.

'Any more news on the supplies arriving?' she asked.

'First thing in the morning, so they said. We'll fly at two p.m.'

They passed a shirtless guitar player on the street— a beaming guy with huge, chunky dreadlocks. Ryan pulled some notes out of his pocket and dropped them into his upturned hat. The guy's hands stopped moving instantly on the guitar frets and his eyes widened at what was clearly a significant amount of money, but Ryan didn't stop.

The palm trees swayed rhythmically to their own calypso as they walked along the street. Tourists strolling towards similar reservations were either hand in hand or holding selfie sticks between them, taking photos. She thought back to her friend Emma's gushing email that morning, posing a million questions and demands of what she wanted Madeline to ask Ryan.

Are you single? seemed to be top of her list.

They were welcomed into the restaurant by a beaming waitress the size of a toothpick, who flicked her long, styled auburn hair over her shoulder as she raked over Ryan with eyes as wide as Bambi's.

'I hope this will be OK for you, sir,' she gushed in a thick Portuguese accent as they were led outside to a table on the terrace. She made a big fuss over arranging Ryan's napkin on his lap.

'Fine, thank you,' he replied, seemingly oblivious to the batting eyelashes an inch from his chest.

Ryan took the wine list. A candle flickered in the middle of the table in a mason jar and Madeline studied his famous face, now bathed in a soft, flattering glow in a way she rarely saw on the television. The surgery lights were always so harsh.

She placed her purse under her feet, careful to keep the strap around her knee. She'd been caught out once by a bag-snatcher in Peru, and these days she was disappointingly quick to suspect passing strangers of crimes they probably had no intention of committing.

All around them people were chatting and laughing amongst themselves and Ryan leaned back in his seat.

'Drink?' he asked. 'You might not get the chance again for a while. They don't have much in the way of vintage wine in the Amazon. How about a cocktail?'

'If you're having one,' she said. 'Or maybe just a gin and tonic?'

'Great idea—make that two, please,' he told the waitress, handing back the drinks menu.

'Coming up. I'll be back to take your food order, Dr Ryan.'

She tottered off on her high heels, and Madeline watched as Ryan took his phone out of his pocket and flipped it to 'silent'.

'Is it not weird that everyone knows who you are?' she asked. 'We're in *Rio*!'

He put his phone back and folded his arms in front of him on the table, unwittingly causing his biceps to bulge in his shirt. 'It's less weird than annoying.'

'I read somewhere that you hardly ever drink,' she followed up, training her eyes away from his biceps.

'That's true. I usually stop at one.'

'In case somebody needs your help and you need to focus?'

He grinned, thumbing the corner of the menu. 'Did you read that online?'

'Maybe.'

'I don't really drink because I choose not to. I guess that's not exciting enough for some people. Anything you don't eat?'

Madeline liked the way he was talking to her. It was *easy*, somehow. She wondered what he'd been like before fame…whether he was different now.

She thought about his question. 'Just coriander. I think you call it cilantro where you're from.'

He smiled. 'Can't stand it either. Tastes like old books.'

'I think it tastes like metal pipes.'

'You've licked a metal pipe?'

'Maybe.'

He was laughing now—she could see his shoulders shaking. 'Well, *there's* a way to start the memoir. *I don't like cilantro and I refuse to dine with people who do—especially if they lick metal pipes, too.*'

She shook her head, laughing with him. 'It has best-seller written all over it.'

They ordered a selection of dishes, and as they chatted idly she scribbled a few notes about his childhood, memories of the years he spent in Chicago looking up to his ambitious yet workaholic father.

'Do you have any siblings?' she asked.

His mouth twitched towards a smile. 'I thought all the basics were on the internet?'

'Some of them, yes, but I'd still prefer to hear it first-hand, from you,' she replied. 'As we've already discovered, people stretch the truth a lot.' She crossed her legs under the table. 'Have you ever looked yourself up on the internet?'

He nodded slowly. 'But it wasn't my smartest move.'

'Why not?'

He pulled a face, leaned back in his seat and turned his glass on the checked tablecloth. '"As we've already discovered, people stretch the truth a lot",' he mimicked. 'But some truths you read and you wish you hadn't.'

'Like messages from your boyfriend to his other woman,' Madeline followed, without even thinking.

She felt her cheeks flush instantly. *Stupid gin.*

When she looked up Ryan was looking at her, his

eyes dark now…in shadow. 'Sorry,' she said. 'Still raw, I suppose.'

'Were you together a long time?'

She couldn't look at him now. 'Four years. I thought he was about to propose.'

He exhaled through his nose. 'Damn.'

'To be honest, I haven't had time to think about him since I found out I was coming on this trip. I think I just need to keep busy.'

'Keeping busy helps.'

His tone made her lift her head. As he shifted in his chair she caught that look in his eyes again: a slow burning that unnerved her. Madeline wondered if she should just ask him outright whether he was ready to set the record straight about his team member Josephine McCarthy, but she was forced to close her mouth when the chirpy waitress tottered back over with the first few plates of tapas.

Ryan gestured for Madeline to serve herself a helping of *patatas bravas* and skilfully steered the conversation back to his siblings—one older brother called David, who'd moved to New York and married an art curator, and a younger sister called Monica, who was studying dentistry. Madeline had the feeling Ryan wouldn't be spilling any of his own secrets as quickly as *she'd* just done, even if she asked him outright. Especially not now.

She popped an olive into her mouth. No matter how difficult the mission ahead of her, she refused to be deterred. To think this time last week she'd been wondering how on earth she was going to raise the money she needed to re-do her bathroom. Who knew ghost-writing a book while in the Amazon would wind up paying more than she'd ever earned by putting her own book up on the *other* Amazon?

All she had to do was stay focussed.

CHAPTER FIVE

PILLAR-BOX-RED SUITED Madeline's nails, Ryan thought—
although it was going to be pretty damn hard for her to
keep any element of her beauty regime going once they
got to camp. He'd never let on, but the shine of her hair
was also likely to be dulled after a few days of washing
it in murky pond water.

He'd felt for her when she'd mentioned her ex. While
she amused him with her quirky comebacks, the stabs
of pain he sensed in her with certain sentences had an
effect on his heart. It seemed that for all of Madeline's
bravado in public she was a tiny bit broken.

Not unlike me, he thought with a weary smile.

'So, when did you know you wanted to be a doctor?'
she was asking him now.

He leaned further towards her, saw the candle flame
between them flickering in her pupils. 'I think I was
born knowing I would be.'

'Really? Care to elaborate?'

'Not much—but something tells me I'll have to.'

Madeline raised her eyebrows, putting her pen to her
lips. Ryan replied to her questions in as much detail as
he could, helping himself to more chorizo and making
sure to keep Madeline's plate topped up with her share
of the food as she made notes.

He wasn't entirely certain she had the right idea about the food they'd be getting once they reached camp; he didn't know if she had any clue that they'd be on rice, bananas and, if they were lucky, fish the entire time. Either way, he was determined to have them both eat as much as possible now.

He told her how his brother's love of art and the metaphysical had led *him* only to contemplate a career in the physical, and yet the same empathetic streak still rendered them closer to each other than either of them was with their sister.

He explained the cluttered corners of their large family home—the way his mother had diligently cleaned while silently resenting the fact that she had to before wealth arrived and saw to it that she could hire a cleaner—a dumpy, smiley Mexican lady called Rose, who had always jangled with keys and tiny candies for the kids wrapped in foil.

He told her how his mother hoarded books of every genre, and always had a jigsaw puzzle on the go.

'Hmm… I see… I think this would be good in more depth,' Madeline would mutter every now and then. 'Tell me more about your backyard? What trees and flowers grew there in summer? Did you spend much time outdoors?'

He talked and talked, encouraged by her encouragement, until the waitress brought a brand-new candle to replace the one that had sizzled right down to a waxed lump in its jar.

While Ryan was putting on what he thought looked like a pretty good show of wanting to get to work on the memoir, it was really just for Madeline. If Madeline Savoia had turned out to be the crinkly old cat lady of his imaginings he doubted he would have been so accommodating. He definitely wouldn't have been sitting here, opposite her, spilling his family history in a Rio restaurant.

He would have emailed his thoughts in a string of misspelled sentences, probably—last-minute musings thrown together after she had reminded him a hundred times that he was supposed to be helping her. He would have barely seen her, and she'd have sat alone in her room, or in the lobby, drinking coffee and working on her crochet, perhaps.

He'd been selfish with his admissions, with his heart, for years. To the world Ryan was a giving man, generous and kind, but inside he was a tangled mass of secrets that he'd do anything to protect. When they got to the jungle he knew he'd have to remember to keep her busy. He had a feeling she already knew that was his plan. Still, he wouldn't crack.

He wouldn't talk about Josephine.

When the dessert menu arrived she was asking him about his relationship with his mother.

'Mary Tobias, sixty-seven, now married to the ex-head of the Department of Genetic Research and Bioinformatics in Oslo. Is that right?'

'Correct.' He nodded, then ordered a cappuccino from the too-skinny waitress who'd been orbiting them like a satellite since the second they'd arrived.

Even before the television fame and camera crews he'd had no problem attracting attention from the opposite sex, but he'd learnt to be discerning over the years. There had been way too many photographs and way too many tweets.

'Coffee?' he asked Madeline, ignoring the way the waitress was hovering a little too close to him yet again, with her apron ties practically dangling over his shoulder.

'Flat white, please, no sugar,' Madeline said, still scribbling furiously. 'So she still lives in Norway?'

'They travel back and forth. She's good friends with my father, thank God,' he said. 'They're better apart—they were both so driven, so ambitious, they never managed to head anywhere in the same direction. You can write that down.'

'I am. Do you think you're more like your mother or your father?'

He contemplated this, amused at the way she bit her lip or frowned as the sentences took shape beneath her pretty fingers. She was a woman who took great care and interest in what she did—he could tell that already. He wondered if she'd been the same as a nurse and almost brought it up. He decided not to.

'I guess I have my father's drive to help others, and my mother's ambition to see the world,' he said thoughtfully. 'Thankfully I've forged a career that lets me do both.'

'A very successful one,' she followed up. 'Tell me more about your team. How do you choose who comes with you on your missions? Would you say you're as close in reality as you seem on screen?'

He reached out quickly, took the pen from her hand and placed it on top of her notebook. She looked up, surprised.

'I don't think we're there yet, are we?' He held her gaze. He couldn't help notice how she flinched.

'Sorry.'

'I thought we'd go over things in chronological order—my youth, my family, college... Don't you want to hear about my days in the acapella club?'

Her eyes narrowed in amusement. 'Seriously? *That's* not on your Wikipedia page.'

'Of course that's not online. If it was, everyone would be asking me to sing. My job is to save lives—not to kill people.'

She picked up her pen again. 'I'm sure you're not that bad.'

'Let's just say you can worm your way into a lot of things on looks alone. It was a pretty short-lived experience anyway. I only joined because I had it bad for one of the girls in the group.'

'So you were this handsome in college, too?'

She flushed as she said it, hiding her face behind her hair for a moment, and he did his best to hide his smile. He'd noticed the way she'd been sneaking glances at him, maybe a little starstruck herself. Although he had to admit she was a lot more subtle than a lot of people.

When their coffees arrived he sipped at the hot foam, breathing an internal sigh of relief that he'd diverted her most prying questions and potentially bought himself some time to decide exactly how he was going to keep diverting them once they came around to the elephant in the room. *Could* he get away with a memoir that didn't mention Josephine?

Of course he'd been anticipating questions about her, and he knew he couldn't stop this memoir being written altogether. He didn't have to bare his soul completely, though, did he? He'd kept things light—telling her all about the blonde-haired soprano he'd followed about campus like a puppy dog, before she'd hooked up with the tenor and broke his tone-deaf heart.

By the time they got back to the hotel it was gone eleven p.m., and thankfully Madeline seemed content that her writing was off to a good start. He walked her to her room. The door clicked open at the swipe of her key card and she turned to him.

'Thank you, Ryan, for tonight. It was…fun.'

He kept his hands in his pockets. In this light she looked *less* like Josephine. In fact, with her unique style, Madeline had been morphing since yesterday into her own skin right in front of him. It was getting easier to be around her in that respect…and when their conversation was under control she was easy to talk to, too. She was also incredibly, magnetically beautiful. It wouldn't have taken much to let all his professionalism fly out of the window.

Just for one night.

He cleared his throat. 'It was my pleasure. I doubt we'll get as much one-on-one time once we're at camp.'

He noticed she looked despondent.

'We'll get the job done,' he added, 'and who knows? Maybe you'll have the chance to dust off your nursing skills again.'

'I don't think that will be happening,' she said, clutching at the beads around her neck.

He saw a flicker of a warning in her green eyes—the kind he was already getting to know.

'I know you think it will, but it won't. I'm here solely for the memoir, OK?'

'OK.'

Madeline stepped into her room, turning to face him again in the doorway. He could see her bed, all made up behind her. He rooted his feet to the floor, dug his hands deeper into his pockets.

'Anyway,' she said, 'thank you for dinner.'

'You're more than welcome. It *was* fun. I have to say you make for excellent company, Maddy Savoia, even if you do ask a lot of questions.'

'There are a lot more I *could* ask,' she said, pursing

her glossed lips for a second. 'But I have a feeling you're going to make me work for it.'

'It's no fun otherwise.'

He leaned in to drop a kiss on her cheek. He was about to tuck a few stray strands of hair behind her ear when Madeline stepped back from him, putting the doorframe between them.

'Goodnight,' she said curtly, and shut the door.

CHAPTER SIX

THE JUNGLE STRETCHED below them like a deep green blanket and Madeline could imagine a million pairs of eyes on their helicopter—from monkeys to jaguars, bats, rats and snakes, all plotting to lure them in and keep them.

'How are you feeling?' Ryan asked from his seat next to hers.

She turned her head away from the window, her lips a thin line. He put a hand to her arm to reassure her, and she was grateful for his presence. He was dressed in a light blue shirt with the *Medical Extremes* logo on the right pocket and another pair of khakis. She was dressed the same, all the clothes given to her by the producer—only *her* shirt was a tight-fitting tank top.

'You're looking like part of the crew already,' Ryan said loudly over the whir of the blades. 'Are you ready for some flying doctor Amazon action?'

'I don't know how to answer that,' she said honestly, noting the way his hair was sticking out adorably from the sides of his baseball hat. She clutched hard at the notebook on her lap under her seatbelt. Her hair was a mess and she'd long since given up trying to tame the flyaway strands that kept escaping from her ponytail.

She assumed she should probably get used to looking dishevelled from this point on.

The flight from Rio to Saint Elena had been fine, but the helicopter now juddering towards the camp was an entirely different story. It was only the second time she'd ridden in one. Jason had taken her on a surprise flight over Manhattan the first time they'd been to New York together, complete with champagne.

Her fingers found the apple on its chain around her neck—a present from her ex on that trip. This helicopter had zero champagne. The box of ultrasound equipment sat strapped in place beside Ryan's feet, and various packages, bags and boxes took up every other inch of space. There was even a box or two of bananas and another labelled 'solar power'.

'Chargers—so we can do it nature's way,' Ryan explained, seeing her studying them. 'We use the sun instead of batteries for a lot of things now…except our phones. Like I said, not much signal out here. Did you make your last-minute calls?'

'A couple,' she said, remembering the one she'd had to make to her insurance company, and also the one she'd sneaked to Emma, during which she'd told her all about the pair of them out in Rio, eating olives and talking about the intricacies of Ryan's childhood.

Emma had squealed so loudly down the phone Madeline had been left with a partially deaf ear for ten minutes.

'But, Maddy, is he *single*?'

'I don't know,' she'd had to admit.

Madeline still felt weird around Ryan. He didn't seem as if he was in a relationship. There had been a moment just before she'd left him lingering in her doorway when she'd suddenly panicked that he was going to kiss her—

and not just on the cheek this time. She'd moved away from his face as if she'd been dodging a baseball. It made her hot, just remembering.

But even if they had been flirting a little over dinner there was no way in hell she was about to become another one of his adoring female fans and start looking at him the way that waitress had. Besides, she hadn't kissed anyone like that...like Ryan Tobias...ever.

'We don't just eat those—don't worry—but I'm afraid there won't be too many tapas restaurants...'

'What?' Madeline blinked.

Ryan was still talking. He leaned in closer...so close his nose almost brushed hers as she turned.

'The bananas. Sorry, it's tough to hear over the blades, right?'

'Oh, yeah, a bit. Don't you ever fly these things yourself? I thought I saw you in the pilot's seat in one episode.'

'Sometimes—for kicks,' he said, leaning his head back against the headrest. 'I have my licence, but I prefer to let the professionals do their thing while I do mine.'

'I see.'

'Have you ever flown a plane, Miss City Girl?' he asked, cocking an eyebrow.

'Lots of times! My brother had a radio controlled one. It worked pretty well until he crashed it into a tree in Hyde Park.'

He closed his eyes, faking disparagement. 'Crazy Brits,' he muttered.

But she didn't miss his smile, nor the dimples that had taken to appearing more each time they talked.

At first Madeline had felt like a celebrity, being ushered on board the flight with Ryan Tobias. The new cameraman she'd met at that first dinner at the hotel had followed them, watching every move Ryan made through his viewfinder, his eyes shielded by the rim of his own *Medical Extremes* baseball hat.

She still didn't know how she felt about appearing on camera throughout this mission, but the producer had assured her they wouldn't be making a feature of her. She wouldn't have to talk like the rest of the team, and if she appeared in the show at all she'd appear in the background. All of which went some way towards comforting her, she supposed.

'What do you think of the view from up here?' he asked her. 'Better than Hyde Park?'

A rush of wind ruffled the trees below them like a Mexican Wave as they watched the shadow of the helicopter move like a black eclipse on the canopy.

'It's amazing…' she breathed.

Madeline had seen the rainforest before—in Costa Rica. A very handsome man called Ricardo had dared to capture a poisonous red tree frog, which he'd located by following the sound of its distinct croak. He'd held it in his hands to demonstrate that such frogs were only poisonous at certain times of the year, when they'd eaten a toxic kind of ant.

She'd been fascinated as they'd walked on rope bridges, stretching into the air from lush tree to tree at howler monkey height. She'd felt relatively safe there, above the jungle floor with an experienced guide. Here, however, with an infinite ocean of green treetops disguising what she was sure were a thousand death traps, she was having trouble stopping her stomach from knotting—and they hadn't even landed yet.

'We're heading in, boss,' the pilot called over his shoulder after a few minutes, and when Madeline turned to the window at her side she could finally see a clearing.

They flew in closer. Ryan placed a foot on the box closest to him to stop it moving. Madeline could make out what looked like a thin, long pathway, and two long boats waiting on the murky brown coloured river nearby. The pilot was talking to someone on the ground on the radio, and as the sound of the blades increased her hair whipped up into what she knew with utter certainty would be a mass of unmanageable knots and tangles.

The landing strip was in clear sight now. Two men in knee-length shorts and sleeveless T-shirts were running towards them as Madeline held her hair back out of her face. Three minutes later they were bumping onto the ground in the clearing, gliding to a stop, and Ryan was leaning over her, impossibly close, undoing her seatbelt.

'Home sweet home,' he said.

She watched his big hands on her seatbelt. Her heart-rate spiked even further and she held her breath as her insides tangled like her hair.

One of the men on the ground helped her out of the helicopter with the backpack she'd been given for the trip. It held considerably less than her suitcase. The other man walked with her quickly across uneven ground covered in mud and grass towards the murky-looking water. The swish of the helicopter blades created a welcome fan, but already Madeline could feel the heat closing in on her.

'*Sólo tiene que esperar aquí, por favor,*' another guy said to her, helping her onto a small boat on the river.

A local, Madeline noted, seeing the black swirling tattoo which stretched all the way up the inside of one arm. He was looking up at the sky.

She replied that, yes, she would wait right there, but when she turned around on her seat she saw Ryan with the pilot, another cameraman she'd been introduced to as Jake and the other man who'd been waiting for them, all lifting each box from the helicopter through a haze of heat wafting up from the ground.

She stepped out of the boat again, walking back towards them. 'Here—I can take those,' she offered, and the pilot shrugged, handing her a box of bananas.

Back at the boat she apologised to the local man whose command she'd disregarded, placed the box carefully to the floor and held her arms out for another, and then another, ignoring the beads of sweat that had started to trickle from her temples.

She didn't miss the look of approval Ryan threw in her direction as he fastened a radio to his belt, but neither did she miss the mosquitoes that were gorging themselves on her blood already.

She put the last box of supplies inside the boat and slapped at the top of her arm as Ryan climbed in beside her.

'You might want to get the DEET out,' he said. 'I trust you've been taking the malaria pills you were given?'

'For three days already—yes, sir.' She reached for the pocket of her backpack. 'Need some?'

Ryan shook his head as she sprayed her arms. 'They don't touch me any more. My blood's not sweet enough.'

She raised her eyebrows. Ryan was sweating, too, but it made *him* look sexy. He lifted the hat he was wearing and swiped at his forehead before stepping to the front of the boat. She realised she'd always loved seeing him all sweaty on the show, and then rolled her eyes at herself. Behind her, the last of the other boxes was being piled into the second boat.

'How far is it to the camp?' she asked, spraying her legs, then shoving the DEET back into her backpack.

'Not far.'

Ryan climbed back over the bench seats to sit beside her. A guy with a long pole stepped on and pushed off from the riverbank with it, quickly leaving the helicopter behind. Madeline couldn't shake the growing sense of apprehension coiling around her like a python. They were literally in the middle of nowhere.

'We need to get to camp soon—that storm's coming fast,' Ryan said beside her.

He was looking at the sky. In the sunlight his eyes were shining under his *Medical Extremes* baseball hat, but she noticed a thick black cloud on the periphery of her vision that definitely hadn't been there when they'd landed.

'I hope the helicopter gets out in time.' He leaned back to rest his elbows on the bench behind them. 'Can you hear that?'

'Hear what?'

'The jungle talking. Gets louder when a storm's on the horizon—they sense it. The insects and the birds... the cicadas and the frogs. The usual volume is loud enough—it sends me to sleep like a lullaby—but I wouldn't trust any of it for a second. Remember what I told you before?'

'I remember. No wandering off on my own.'

'Not even when it looks and seems like the most idyllic place in the world. Promise me?'

She touched a hand lightly to his arm. 'Trust me, I don't want to get eaten by a snake any more than you do. I promise you.'

And then lightning struck somewhere inside her as he took her hand and squeezed her fingers.

'Good,' he said.

His radio made a sound. Madeline watched more insects swirling around them as he dropped her hand and pulled the radio from his belt.

Evan's voice sounded out in the boat. 'How close are you to our dock?'

'Five…ten minutes—what's going on?'

'Emergency—fast as you can. I've called the helicopter back,' came the reply.

CHAPTER SEVEN

THE DOCK WAS a flurry of action as it came into view through the trees. Ryan stood up as the boat drew closer and waved at Evan. He was standing on the edge of the water, supervising the scene. The sky was a dark chalky grey and the wind was raging. The weather could change in a heartbeat in the rainforest—he knew that well— but the timing of this particular storm was supremely unlucky.

'Will we be able to help her?' Madeline asked from behind him.

She'd obviously overheard what Evan had said about a local lady who'd been hurt. She'd been stepping into a boat with a heavy bag of fruit when she'd slipped and hit the metal stairs of the dock with such force that she could no longer move. She needed to be taken to a hospital.

'I hope so,' Ryan told her as their boat pulled up alongside the grassy bank and several guys from the village and the camp helped to pull them in. He felt the rain start to spit on his arms.

'She's still in a lot of pain,' Evan said as Ryan jumped onto the bank.

He ran to the next boat with him and stepped carefully down to go alongside the woman. She looked to be in her fifties, pale and trembling with pain. A man, possibly her husband, was holding her hand beside the makeshift stretcher, looking equally pale. Another of Ryan's volunteers was holding her head and neck in place.

'We've stabilised her. The helicopter can't get to us yet—the wind is too strong.' Evan crouched down beside him. 'We're hoping it's not a herniated disc.'

'Can she feel her legs?' Ryan reached for the woman's other hand. 'I'm here...you're going to be OK,' he told her, before remembering that she probably only understood Spanish. He said it again in broken Spanish and she nodded, then howled out in pain.

'She can feel them, but she says she feels tingling, which isn't good. We've given her some anti-inflammatories, but we don't have any ice.'

'She'll need an MRI,' Ryan said, as the wind screamed like a banshee in his ears.

He was already having flashbacks to what had happened in Patagonia, when the aircraft hadn't been able to take off or land in the storm. He knew Evan probably was, too.

Before he knew it Madeline was stepping down beside him, carrying something—a plastic sheet from their boat. She handed him one corner, motioning for him to make a cover with it to put over the woman.

'Thank you,' he said, moving fast to tie it up.

Madeline took the other end, just as a cameraman appeared from nowhere and started capturing their every move.

'This rain's going to get worse,' he said.

'Can I do anything else?' she asked, as he watched a huge raindrop cruise down her nose.

'You can round up all these spectators and get them out of here,' Evan replied, pointing at the crowd, still watching, all agog. 'We need everyone out of here so the helicopter can land.'

As he spoke, the wind picked up yet another notch and rocked the boat, but Madeline was already climbing back up to the riverbank, calling out in Spanish.

'Is there any language she can't speak?' Evan said to Ryan, half laughing in spite of the situation. Ryan shrugged, but inside he was reeling. So much for the nurse who didn't want to be a nurse.

Evan's radio buzzed again. Ryan glanced up at Madeline, now herding people out of the clearing. He could see some of his crew moving quickly to help her. She didn't seem particularly fazed that they'd only just arrived in the middle of nowhere and a first-class storm was building up strength around them.

'The helicopter's managed to take off,' Evan said in relief. 'We'll have to take her to Manaus—it's the closest.'

A tree creaked close by in the wind and Ryan felt the woman grabbing his hand even harder as she wailed again. She was in so much pain but there was nothing more they could do right now. She needed ice—which they didn't have—and it was important to keep her conscious, so she could recount what she was and wasn't feeling. He prayed to God it wasn't a herniated disc, or worse.

Eventually the helicopter whirred into sight, scattering the leaves on the ground around them. Thunder crashed in the distance, and then came even closer, almost drowning out the noise of the blades. Ryan looked on in dismay as he realised it might be too windy for it to land.

Madeline was running towards them again now and his heart lurched at the sight. 'Get out of the way!' he yelled at her, realising how unsteady in the sky the helicopter was.

But Madeline was still running—right underneath it. His heart almost stopped as the helicopter lurched and then lifted again. She reached them, panting. She was soaked through, but was holding some cushions from the camp. Ryan grabbed her arm, pulling her into the boat, under the plastic shelter they'd created.

'What were you *doing*?'

'She'll need these—there was nothing else around here that I could see...'

'I said don't do anything stupid—weren't you listening?' His hand was still around her arm as the helicopter finally descended in the clearing behind them.

Her eyes were wide, incredulous. 'It wasn't anywhere near me! The pilot saw me!'

'Goddammit, Maddy.'

'I'm *helping* you! I thought that was what you wanted?'

'She is helping us,' Evan confirmed, before motioning to the volunteer and Ryan to help him lift the stretcher carefully out from under the shelter.

It was very humid and the thunder crashed again, just after a bolt of lightning lit up the sky. The pilot turned off the engine.

Ryan dropped Madeline's arm. 'Let's go!' he yelled at Evan, and together they moved as quickly and smoothly as they could, while the woman continued to moan, wail and whimper.

Madeline was with them, speaking in quick Spanish, trying to comfort her, hurrying beside them in the rain.

They were all but drowned rats by the time they made it to the helicopter, but Ryan noticed Madeline didn't flinch or look away from the woman once. They loaded her and her husband into the back of the helicopter in the thrashing rain, taking one seat out in order to make the stretcher fit.

'Are you OK to go?' Ryan asked Evan.

He knew he would be of better use to the people at camp, and he realised that he didn't want to leave Madeline. God knew what else she might try and do.

'Of course, doc,' Evan said, climbing into the back with another cameraman.

The volunteer got into the front and Ryan pulled Madeline back against him as the engine started up again, her hair whipping his face.

'Wait—take these,' she said, breaking free and handing Evan the cushions.

He took them appreciatively and used them as padding around the woman's side, still being careful not to move her. Ryan knew she'd be moved anyway, thanks to the juddering of the helicopter in this weather. He wasn't entirely sure it was a good idea to fly, but some risks were worth taking. The heat and humidity in the jungle tended to accelerate people's injuries.

He guided Madeline away quickly by the elbow as the blades began to whir again. They turned around just in time to see the helicopter rise, then drop back onto the grass.

Madeline gasped.

'Damn,' Ryan cursed. 'They can't take off in this storm.'

'She needs a hospital,' Madeline said.

'I know, but we'll just have to wait it out. It won't last long—these storms never do. Where's our stuff?'

'My bags and yours? They were taken to the camp.' She brushed her wet hair back from her face with her hand.

'Go find them and get warm and dry—there's nothing else you can do.'

He wanted her safe. Not out here in the middle of

a storm. He was already viewing her as a liability. He knew it was unfair of him, but Madeline Savoia definitely had a stubborn streak. He watched as she turned and did as he'd ordered, albeit reluctantly, and felt some modicum of relief as one weight at least was lifted from his shoulders.

It took what felt like an eternity to get the helicopter off the ground, and when Ryan made it through to his team he was wet and shivering himself. The camp was a frenzy of action, and as he signed some documents on a clipboard thrust suddenly under his nose he noticed Madeline helping someone to move the boxes of bananas and the other stuff that had obviously been moved in from their boat.

'Ryan, how did it go?'

It was Mark Bailey—up in his face, forcing his eyes away from her. Mark was a young doctor who'd been with them for three seasons of *Medical Extremes*. He was well liked around the place—and even more so on Instagram.

'They're en route to the hospital—finally. Fingers crossed the storm doesn't start up again.'

'Looks like it's stopping,' Mark said.

'No other emergencies so far?'

Ryan adjusted his hat as he walked with him, trying not to look at Madeline again. He was surprised she was out of her tent. She was talking to people and he hadn't even made any introductions yet. Then again, she did seem to be a person who took the initiative. Sometimes too *much* initiative.

'A couple this morning—one sprained wrist and a spider bite. Steady trickles for general check-ups and queries all day. We know the other villagers are making their way over now word that we're here has spread up the river, so we're leaving Maria stationed for any strays tonight and planning on an early start tomorrow.'

'Good call.'

Ryan was glad for Mark's organisational skills, as well as everything else. He noticed that the producer was approaching Madeline, leading her away behind one of the stations.

The camp comprised four stations. One was simply a raised platform, on which stood three foldable tables. There his team doled out vitamins and basic medication, and assessed the symptoms of those seeking other medical attention. Everyone who needed care went there first. With the rain and the storm there were only three people in the line now, waiting to be seen.

The other three stations were for treatment, so they held a couple of beds and chairs, with boxes of fresh sheets, gauze and other equipment stacked in all corners.

Would Madeline know what to do with all this, from her nursing days? he wondered. He knew he had to think of more tasks for her. He'd witnessed her instinctual need to help on more than one occasion now, and all this might make her tired…perhaps too tired to ask for many details for that memoir…

He clenched his fists to his sides as Josephine's face flashed before his eyes.

Don't think about it.

In one of the stations one of his volunteers from Chicago—a fifty-something half-Japanese lady called Maria—was talking to two young children on a plastic sheet on the floor. The kids were young members of the local tribe, no older than seven years old. Often the kids in these remote places gathered around out of excitement at having new people to play with.

'Good to see you, Ryan,' Maria called out, and the barefoot children giggled and waved in their ragged, faded clothing.

He waved back. Then, content that his staff had everything under control, he turned in the direction of the sleeping quarters. The rain was only spitting now.

He found Madeline unpacking her bags, hunched over on the floor of her small green tent.

'Did you find the mini-bar OK?' he asked from the canvas doorway.

She turned around in surprise, still on all fours. The tent wasn't exactly big enough to stand up in.

A sheen of perspiration was causing her face to glisten and her long wet hair was stuck in strands to the side of her face. She obviously hadn't yet found time to get dried off. She got to her knees, swiped at her forehead and gestured around her.

'Five-star,' she said, smiling. Then her expression changed. 'How's that patient? Do you think she'll be OK?'

'They're on the way to the hospital—we'll know more once they do some tests,' he said. He cleared his throat. 'Thank you for your help. I'm sorry if I sounded a little harsh back there. You...you freaked me out for a second.'

'Why?'

'You can't just run under helicopters, Maddy. You're not Indiana Jones.'

She grimaced. 'Sorry, I didn't think. And, yes, the mini-bar is well stocked, thanks.' She reached for a bottle of water that was poking out of her backpack and held it up.

Her tent, which had been set up prior to her arrival,

complete with sleeping bag, blankets and a prized inflatable mattress, was luxurious compared to where most of the people in the tribe and surrounding villages slept.

'We have someone covering emergencies for now,' he told her, 'but with any luck things will be slow until the morning.'

'Great—well, maybe we can work on the memoir some more?' She stepped out of the open doorway and stood beside him. 'Where are you sleeping?'

He looked behind him. No one was around. 'Want to see?'

'OK.'

He led them past a line of tents—all for the crew—and past the makeshift fire they often gathered around in the evenings. The rain was less impactful there, thanks to the thickness of the leaves and branches overhead, but the wind was still muttering all around them. He put his pack on the mossy floor, crouched down and pulled out his prized possession. Holding it in his hands he stood and looked around, studying his surroundings.

'Where to go...? Where to go...?'

'Where to go with what?'

Madeline looked amused. She also looked sexy as hell, he realised with some annoyance, in her *Medical Extremes* tank top and no make-up. She wore rain pretty well, too, he decided, remembering when he'd first met her. It seemed like months ago already.

He walked to a nearby tree and patted it, then shook it a little. It didn't move. Perfect.

'Help me with this,' he said, holding out one end of his hammock.

Her eyebrows shot up to her hairline. 'You're not serious? You're *not* sleeping in a hammock out here in the rain?'

He wrapped one end of it expertly round the tree, motioning for her to walk with her end to the next one. 'Probably not in the rain, but I like to have my spot set up.'

'But you can't sleep out here anyway, can you? What about snakes?'

'Snakes like the ground.'

'Snakes like trees, too. You're going to wrestle one for bed space, are you, Indiana Jones?'

He grinned. 'I'll be careful.'

She rolled her eyes.

'I like a quiet place to read. I might even read one of your books. Feel free to use it, too, if you need to get away. I'm afraid there's no socket for your laptop, though.'

He finished attaching the hammock to the trees, stepped back and crossed his arms, admiring his handiwork.

'Looks good, if I do say so myself. It's the best you can get. We don't mess around out here.'

Madeline was still looking at him as if he was crazy, tapping on a fallen branch with her boot. She looked away for a second, then, 'You have one of my books?'

He nodded, walking back to the hammock and sitting in it, facing her. 'Your "geopolitical thriller". It sounded interesting, and I got a good deal for it on my e-reader.'

She was blushing now.

'What's wrong?' he asked. 'Don't you want me to read it?'

'No, it's not that...'

'I felt I should know some of your work, seeing as you're here to observe mine. Fair's fair.'

He stood up. A gust of wind threw itself at the hammock and caused it to turn over on itself. More raindrops started to splatter on their skin and Ryan quickly zipped his bag up and hoisted it back over his shoulder.

'We should go. Have you seen the dining hall yet?'

'No, I've not seen anything else. The producer got called away.'

'OK—well, in that case, let me be your jungle guide, Jane.'

With his hand on the warm small of her back, Ryan guided her towards camp. On the way he noted without saying a word that his tent had been set up just one along from Madeline's, with maybe three feet between them...

The dining hall was a basic set-up, beyond the tents and makeshift toilets, which looked a lot like a giant chicken coop for humans. A wooden platform was covered only by a roof thatched with palm fronds to stop the rain getting in. Mosquito mesh stretched between wooden posts on all sides, creating walls.

He opened the mesh door, letting her step through ahead of him as she brushed the rain off her arms with her hands. Several people waved at them as they entered, but Ryan steered Madeline to where a volunteer was serving portions of white rice and boiled vegetables onto plastic plates from a huge silver pot. The boxes of bananas she'd helped to carry were stacked at either side.

'Gourmet cuisine from now on,' he said, handing her a plate.

'I don't mind rice,' Madeline said, signalling for another scoop from the kindly lady behind the table.

'You won't be saying that in three weeks' time. Better get used to these, too.'

He picked up a banana and balanced it on the side of her plate beside the rice. She didn't object.

Ryan guided her to the end of one of the long communal tables, where piles of cutlery had been dropped haphazardly into a pile in the middle. He noted Pablo and Jake in the corner, filming them as they took a seat on the bench. The rain was hammering hard on the roof again now, making a racket on the mesh. The air smelled of DEET and damp foliage and the space was filled with quiet chatter and the clanging of cutlery.

Madeline picked up a fork opposite him, and he was about to take a bite out of a piece of boiled carrot when something large and brown landed on the table—right between their plates.

Madeline screamed and jumped up from the bench. Her plate of food went flying.

Ryan jumped up, too, as everyone else started scrambling backwards. 'Tarantula,' he said, trying to sound calm.

Madeline was beside him now, and her face was a shade of white he'd rarely seen. She had both hands over her mouth, as though to muffle more screams, and was trying her best to hide behind him.

'Make that two tarantulas,' he said, peering closer at the fuzzy ball that was now untangling itself right by the condiments basket.

He felt her hand on his shoulder, clenching on his shirt.

'They nest in the thatch,' he said, pointing upwards as Jake zoomed his camera in on the hairy spiders, sitting dazed on the table where they'd fallen. 'They must have been mating and forgotten how to hold on! I'm surprised they're still alive.'

'That's one hell of a fall from grace,' someone said, and people started twittering amongst themselves again.

Ryan noticed Madeline still wasn't laughing. He also

noticed tears in her eyes, and the way she was glancing at the camera, which was pointed straight at her.

'That's enough,' he said quickly, stepping forward and putting his palm over the lens.

Jake stepped backwards, his face popping out from behind the viewfinder. 'Ryan, that was *gold*!'

'She doesn't want to be on film. We discussed this, didn't we?'

'I was told to film everything.'

'Well, *I'm* telling you not to.'

He turned around, but Madeline was gone.

'Don't follow me,' he said gruffly to the cameraman. He nodded at the tarantulas, still stationary. 'And get rid of those…before their friends come looking for them.'

He marched out of the dining hall into the rain, spun around, but couldn't see her. Then he spotted a blur of white tank top heading towards her tent.

Pulling his shirt up over his head, he sprinted across the grass. The sound of frogs and cicadas was almost as loud as the rain. He watched her unzip the door hurriedly, getting it stuck halfway.

But before he could reach her he saw the two local kids who'd been sitting with Maria running up to her.

'Miss! Miss!' they were calling.

'Oh, hi,' he heard her say in surprise as he moved closer.

He watched her swiping at her face to clear away what was obviously embarrassment and tears as much as rain. One of the kids in a yellow shirt threw his arms around her waist and she stood there for a moment, seemingly unsure of what to do.

'Can we see?' he heard the boy ask, pointing to her tent.

'Curious, are you?' Ryan said, walking up to them.

The kids thought nothing of running around in the rain—they were used to it.

Madeline looked at him. The kids' arms were still locked around her.

'You can see inside,' she said kindly, untangling the arms from around her and finishing unzipping the door. 'Actually, I have something for you.'

Madeline got to her knees and crawled to her backpack. The kids followed after her.

'Room for one more?' Ryan asked, squeezing inside. He reached for one of the boys—the one in the yellow shirt—tickling his feet until he was giggling wildly.

Madeline handed them each a colouring book, and a set of pencils between them. They looked elated.

Ryan was touched. He leaned on one elbow on the groundsheet beside her. 'You OK?'

She lifted her swollen eyes to the canvas ceiling, let out a long sigh and watched the kids roll onto their tummies and start to colour. 'He got all that on camera. I almost made a tree fall down with that scream.'

'He won't use it.'

'How do you know?'

'I told him not to.'

She met his eyes, and mouthed *Thank you* over the kids' heads.

The little boy looked up. 'Why you cry, miss?' he asked.

Madeline put a hand out to touch his damp hair. 'I saw something scary,' she said.

'A tarantula,' Ryan followed up.

The boy beamed, showing gappy teeth. 'Tarantula not scary.'

'To me they are,' Madeline said. She looked at Ryan, 'Especially when they fall an inch from your dinner plate.'

The kid put his pencil down, got to his feet and pulled his friend up. *'Vamos!'*

'What?' Madeline laughed now.

'Vamos!'

She got to her feet, followed him outside, and Ryan went with them. The light was fading fast but he had a vague idea what the boys were going to show her.

They took her hands, one on either side of her, and led her to the same area where he'd strung up his hammock. The rain was still falling, but covered by the trees it was less noticeable.

They pulled Madeline to a thick tree trunk and dropped her hands, busying themselves walking around the tree, peering at it closely.

'Home!' one of them exclaimed after a moment. 'Look!'

Ryan put a hand to Madeline's elbow gently, throwing her a warning look. She frowned and turned to where they were pointing, then walked as close as she could to the tree and peered into a hole in the bark.

'Wow!' She stepped backwards, then seemed to compose herself.

The kids were giggling again, pointing to another hole in the bark. 'Spider house!' The youngest one giggled, tugging on her shirt.

Each hole in the tree was indeed a house. Ryan knew it well. Nestled inside each cosy mossy crevice was a giant tarantula, just waiting for nightfall.

'They come out when it's dark and hang out on the tree,' he explained.

Madeline scrunched her face up just long enough for him to note her disdain, but he admired how she tried to look excited for the boys.

'Wow, that's great,' she said.

'They're not so scary when you see them like this, are they?' Ryan replied.

He couldn't help the smile stretching out his face.

CHAPTER EIGHT

MADELINE DISAGREED. THEY were tarantulas. They were terrifying wherever they were—not that she wanted to make even more of a fool of herself than she already had. She half expected the kids to reach into the holes and grab a few, start stroking them like cuddly toys just to prove a point.

She backed away and was surprised when Ryan held his shirt above their heads to shelter them both as he led them back to their tents.

'Probably should have brought an umbrella,' he said, catching her glance.

She smiled at the gentleman emerging in him now, with the more time they spent together, and walked close to him, letting the kids back into her tent with her to collect their colouring books and promising she would see them again tomorrow. Then she watched them scurry off into the jungle as Ryan took their place in the tiny space.

'Amazing,' she said wistfully, aware that he was filling up pretty much every inch of spare room in her tent; it was a thin canvas bubble for the two of them. His shirt was wet, as was hers, and the sound of the rain on the canvas was louder now than ever. 'The kids, I mean.'

'They're pretty amazing, yes,' he said, leaning on one arm and stretching out.

His feet were almost touching the door. He looked as though he was making himself comfortable…as though he had no intention of leaving just yet. Madeline hadn't laid out her bed sheets yet—which she was now pretty glad about. Otherwise he would literally be lying on her bed alongside her. The thought made her nervous.

'Extremely resilient. They literally have no fear. Sometimes gets them in trouble, though.'

'I can imagine.' She swallowed.

'It was great of you to bring the colouring books. You're going to be pretty popular round here if you're planning on pulling moves like that.'

'I bought a few in Rio.' She reached for her pack and pulled out her notebook. She didn't want to admit—even to herself—how she'd frozen the moment that little kid's arms had wrapped around her. All she'd seen was Toby. But she couldn't think about Toby now. She couldn't think about his little arms around her on the ward at the hospital, his big brown eyes, the look on his mother's face when…

She took a deep breath. While Ryan was here she was determined to get some more answers from him. She was pretty up to speed on his youth now, but the closer they got to the present day, the more he seemed to skate awkwardly around her questions. She'd warm him up, she decided, by asking him something easy.

But he was looking at her quizzically. 'What's wrong?' he asked.

'Nothing,' she said, too quickly. I was just thinking… about the spiders. Being on camera looking like an idiot.'

'I told you—they won't use the footage. What else is on your mind?'

She looked at him and shrugged, flummoxed. How could he tell she had been thinking about more than the spiders? Was it because he could read the pain in her eyes the way she could sometimes read it in his?

'Nothing. So—I'm guessing you're a bit better prepared for this kind of adventure than me. What do you bring with you in your pack? Aside from the usual equipment and your hammock, I mean? You must need a different kit wherever you go…mountains, desert, jungle…'

She watched him stroke a hand across his chin, then take his hat off. He was literally three inches from her damp skin, and in the silence the symphony of crickets, frogs and raindrops seemed to rush through her like another pulse. Everything around them and between them was alive.

'You're right—it's different every time. But some things stay the same. I never go anywhere without my multi-tool.'

'What's that?' she asked, scribbling it down.

'Only the manliest tool in the world!' He reached into one of his pockets and pulled out something that looked like a penknife, flipped out one of the blades. 'It has a million features—the manufacturers sponsored Season Two of the show, didn't you see that?'

'I wasn't watching it for the sponsors.'

She could hear the smile in his voice when he carried on with his answer. 'And I carry anti-venom, of course.'

'Of course,' she said. 'Over one hundred thousand people die every year from snakebites. I saw that on one of your shows, I think.'

'Impressive memory. Wait one second.'

He crawled back out of the tent, and seconds later crawled back in again holding another fabric case. He opened it, revealing a vial and two long, plastic tubes.

'I always keep these around. Hope to God I never

need them, but you should know how to use this kit if you don't already.'

'That's OK. I'm sure plenty of people here know how to use it,' she said, eyeing the tubes warily.

'You're right, but still… We have anti-venom for most snakes out here. Simple to use—just get as much info as possible about what bit, then inject the right anti-venom into the elbow crease right here.'

He squeezed her in the spot he'd indicated, gently, making her pulse quicken again.

'You've done that before, I'm sure.'

'Yes, but like I've already said I'm not here to—'

'I'm sure you wouldn't worry too much about making excuses if someone urgently needed your help.' He put the vial and tubes down and rested on his elbow next to her. 'You haven't so far, at least.'

She bit her tongue.

'I also have a fire stick and a sharpener somewhere— oh, and we all get given a sat phone push-to-talk in case we ever get separated. I have a roll of gaffer tape, too— you never know when you'll need that—and a water purifier. Someone usually has rice and a stove in their pack in case we have to stray from camp—takes no time to use, plus it's light.'

'You're literally prepared for everything?'

He nodded. 'Have to be. Here in the jungle, though, a good knife and my British army boots are compulsory.' He motioned to the heavy black boots on his feet. 'These are something you Brits do very well. Oh, and my hammock. Naturally.'

'Everything but an umbrella,' she teased.

'And the kitchen sink.'

'Ryan…'

She put her pen down, sat cross-legged and faced him.

He was playing with his penknife now, flipping things
open and closed absent-mindedly…the bottle-opener,
the wire-cutter. She felt as if the tent was closing in—as
though a flame had just been lit inside…one that could
at any moment become a fire.

She took another breath. Then she let the question
slide off her tongue. 'What's the most dangerous situation you've ever been in?'

She knew it was brave. Reckless, even. She just had
to see what he'd say.

He flipped the knife blade out and in again, loudly,
looking as though he was mulling the question over in
his mind. 'Most dangerous?'

'Yes.'

He smirked. 'Being in the middle of the Amazon with
amorous tarantulas falling from ceilings isn't dangerous enough for you?'

'I've seen you deal with worse,' she said, feeling her
heart thumping against her damp clothes.

'Well, there was the pair of hikers we had to treat for
hypothermia when they went off track in Iceland. Almost got screwed ourselves when the helicopter dropped
us down on the winch and couldn't lift us out again because of the wind.'

'I saw that one,' she said. 'What about…?' She
paused, wondering how best to phrase it—how far she
could push it. She was treading on eggshells now. 'What
about off-camera? Has there ever been anything so dangerous that you weren't allowed to broadcast it on television? Or talk about it afterwards?'

Ryan snapped the blade on his penknife closed one
final time, then shoved it into his pocket. His icy eyes
looked dark when he met hers.

He got to his knees. 'We show everything that happens, Madeline.'

'Except when *you* say not to, right?'

'What do you mean?'

'Like when women scream over falling spiders?'

He narrowed his eyes. 'The producers and editors have the final say.'

'Except when *you're* adamant that something isn't shown. Am I right?'

'I knew this was a mistake.'

He turned from her, started unzipping the tent, his fingers an angry blur. Madeline got on all fours and crawled closer to the door.

'Where are you going?'

'To my tent. We're done here.'

'What just happened?'

Ryan moved to step out, but turned at the last minute, bringing his face right up to hers. The trees were swaying behind him and the wind rushed in with the rain, making her shiver in spite of the heat.

'I told you we'd start at the beginning,' he growled.

'That's what we're *doing*!'

She'd blown it. She felt as if she was talking to a completely different person.

'I don't appreciate this hidden agenda. I know what you really want to ask me, Madeline, and I don't want to talk about it.'

Her insides were twisting more and more by the second at his anger and at his words, thick and cold like ancient lava.

She forced her face to stay neutral and mirrored his stance, sitting on her haunches. 'I'm sorry,' she said. 'But I'm writing your memoir, Ryan. You have to at least appreciate that your publishers are asking me questions about what happened that day…what you don't want anyone to know…'

'They're asking you to call me out. They want *you* to prove that the perfect, selfless hero you see on the television isn't real… They want it from the horse's mouth, don't they? So the world can get a kick out of how the mighty fall.'

Madeline was stunned. 'What? Why would anyone do that?'

'You tell me.'

'I would never write anything to hurt you or compromise your integrity.'

'We both know that's what they want so they can get more sales!'

'That doesn't mean we can't write it properly—say what *you* want to say…'

'Damn it, Maddy, I don't want to say anything at all!'

His hand was still on the tent's doorway and she watched helplessly as he unzipped the rest of it roughly and crawled out.

'Wait, Ryan—can we just talk about this?' she pleaded, sticking her head out into the rain after him.

But he was walking through the expanding puddles of mud, back towards the dining hall. She looked at the vial of anti-snake venom in its pack, still on the floor. Through the rain now striking viciously at everything in its path, Madeline could barely even see Ryan any more.

CHAPTER NINE

THE JUNGLE, RYAN thought from his place in the hammock, was merely a microcosm of the world in its entirety—a giant muddle of monsters trying not to look as if they'd eat you alive if they had to.

He sipped his coffee from the warm metal mug and thought that this might be something he'd tell Madeline for the memoir—after all, he'd seen a lot of the world, battled to save many of those harmed by the monsters in it.

But then he remembered with a small sigh that he was going to steer clear of Madeline for a while.

He'd seen her at breakfast, talking to Evan, who was just back from the hospital in Manaus with good news, thankfully. She'd glanced up and their eyes had met over the dining bench. He swore he'd seen her hand rise in cautious greeting, but he'd turned from her, grabbed his caffeine fix and some fruit and headed straight here.

He didn't want to make small talk and he damn well wasn't going to apologise to her either; he wasn't going to do *anything* with the cameras lurking like jaguars waiting to pounce.

'Ryan!'

A voice calling his name almost made him spill his

coffee. He sprung up from the hammock as Maria came into view, wearing her *Medical Extremes* uniform.

'Sorry to interrupt, but could we have your assistance?'

He was already walking towards her, annoyed with himself for hiding away too long. 'Of course, I was just finishing up. What's happened?'

'Skin condition and a fever with it. Evan and the other guys went back to the landing pad for the rest of the supplies.'

'I'm on it,' he said, walking faster with her towards the stations, kicking himself internally.

If he hadn't left the dining hall when discussions about fetching more supplies were underway he'd have known to be there already. Annoyance made his brow crease—Madeline was already affecting his work. All the more reason to stay away from her.

When they reached the medical stations bright sunlight was streaming into the clearing and a line of people had gathered, waiting to register. Three volunteers were taking their details, all of them in their trademark *Medical Extremes* T-shirts and hats. The rain had cleared in the night, and there were only a few fast-evaporating puddles to show for its appearance.

Madeline was talking to a small group of kids who'd gathered around her in a corner of the camp. Sunshine danced in her long hair. She was wearing a white tank and khaki shorts, exposing long, milky legs, and she was handing out the rest of the colouring books and pencils. Her eyes caught his as he passed her and he tried not to flinch visibly.

She was doing something good, of course, and having her do something practical around camp was better than her scribbling reams of notes about his shady past. But the sight of her caused something in his stomach to shift.

For a moment she looked as though she was going to say something, but he tore his eyes away before she had the chance, followed Maria into one of the medical stations and flipped the switch in his mind he always flipped when it came to focussing entirely on a patient in his care.

'What seems to be the problem here?' he asked as he approached a guy lying flat on one of the makeshift beds.

He was bare-chested, wearing faded red shorts down to his knees, probably in his mid to late thirties. His forehead was clammier than it should be, even in this thick heat, and several raised lesions on his legs and arms showed clear lines of demarcation at the edges.

Erysipelas lesions, he noted. It was a bacterial infection, common in these parts—simple to treat but dangerous if left too long.

He walked to the airtight container in the corner of the station, aware now of Jake in the other corner, filming him. He pulled out one of the kits inside as Maria translated the man's answers from his quick Spanish. He'd been feeling ill for two days, with headaches and vomiting, but had tried to push on without telling anyone. The muddy splashes on his legs showed he must have walked at least some way through thick jungle to get to them.

'We'll soon have this under control,' Ryan said, pulling on a pair of gloves and getting out the antihistamine. He'd have to be given prophylactic antibiotics, too.

He was explaining what his patient would have to do to ensure the lesions healed properly when a whirlwind seemed to sweep into the station. He turned and saw a little girl with braids in her long hair, no older than four or five, waving her arms around, bolting towards them.

'Daddy!' she shouted, reaching them in a flash and placing her little hands on the side of the bed.

Her cheeks were streaked with tears and her pale blue dress was covered in mud. His patient reached for her hand and started comforting her with soothing words in spite of his obvious torment. Ryan's heart broke a little.

Two seconds later someone else entered the station. Madeline.

'There you are,' she said to the little girl, walking over to her and placing a hand gently on her shoulder. 'Come on, they're treating your daddy and we have to let them work.'

She swept a hand through her own hair and Ryan was thrown for a moment—not least by the sight of her standing beside him. She switched to Spanish and, he assumed, repeated what she'd just said. The little girl gripped her hand.

This time he let his eyes linger on Madeline's as he pulled the packaging away from the hydrocortisone. He tried to ignore the rush of adrenaline he felt tearing through him as her sea-green gaze seemed to rip straight down the wall he'd been building around himself after their somewhat heated debate.

She stood there talking to the girl and ignoring *him* as he cleaned the man's wounds and bandaged the worst one, then made him promise to take it easy for a few days while the antibiotics did their work.

As he and Maria worked Ryan was aware of Madeline heading to the corner with the child, away from the camera, making her laugh, making her tears all but disappear. He wished he could hear and understand more of what she was saying.

By the time his patient was walking towards his daughter to receive a welcoming hug Madeline seemed to have become firm friends with her. Ryan tried not to give the impression that he'd noticed, but a part of him was more impressed with her than ever. What the hell had made her quit nursing? She obviously had a way with people—especially children. And hadn't she at one point during their extensive chats told him that she'd worked at St David's in London? The children's hospital? That must have been where she'd honed her skills at earning their trust.

He watched her step outside—saw the way she immediately became swarmed over by the kids. He was about to follow but another patient was being brought inside, this time by Mark. As the makeshift plastic sheet that served as a doorway fell down after him he heard her telling them all to follow her to the shade—that much he understood in Spanish.

'She's pretty good with those kids,' Mark said, sitting the patient—a lady in her mid-twenties—down on the chair beside the now empty bed.

'Who? Madeline?' Ryan said nonchalantly, stripping the paper from the bed and shoving it into a plastic bag.

'Yes, of *course* Madeline! She's got them all colouring under the trees out there like friggin' Mary Poppins. Usually they're running around under our feet by now and asking to wear the stethoscopes. Impressive Spanish, too. Did you know she was fluent in that as well as Portuguese? I think she said she lived in Colombia for a while.'

'Yes.'

Maria stifled a smile as she marked their last patient's notes on a clipboard.

'She's quite a hit out there,' Mark continued, oblivious

to Ryan's curt tone. 'I hope you don't mind, but I told her she could make a start on the dental hygiene project if she wanted something to do. Gave her the toothbrushes and worksheets. I figured Evan would have done the same thing. I know you guys are working on the memoir together, but—'

'The more hands on deck the better,' Ryan cut in, before the questions and the digging could start.

He had a feeling the team had all talked about the damn memoir behind his back already, and it made him uncomfortable to say the least. He caught Maria's sideways glance as he took his new patient's blood pressure.

'Everything OK?' she asked.

'Fine.'

He reached for a bottle of water. It was barely nine a.m. and already hotter than hell. The rain hadn't cooled things off for long, and there was undoubtedly more on the way. More patients, too.

It was several hours before he stuck his head outside into the sunshine. Evan and the others had fetched more antibiotics and yet more boxes of fruit. There was talk of a swim in the waterfall that he registered vaguely before Madeline caught his attention again.

He swigged from his water bottle, then stretched out his muscles, battling the urge to walk over to her. He'd been on form—performing routine duties one after the other, talking to the camera, trying not to let her creep into his thoughts. He was tired, he realised. And their argument was bothering him again.

From where he stood she seemed to be fully absorbed in what the children were doing, and he noticed that someone had stacked several cardboard boxes on the plastic sheets they were sitting on. She was laughing and smiling in the sunshine, her skin glistening with sunscreen and probably DEET. Maybe both.

He wandered over to her. Shutting her out was even more exhausting than letting her in.

'Colombia?' he said, clearing his throat, leaning on a nearby tree. 'You lived there for two years on and off? Is that right?'

The wind ruffled her loose hair, and from his stance looking down at her sitting cross-legged on the ground he could see her bra and the way it hugged her breasts beneath her tank top. He tried not to look as she fixed her gaze on him.

'Well remembered. Medellin, then Cartagena.'

A yellow and brown butterfly fluttered between them.

'I was writing a book.'

'Another geopolitical thriller?' he asked, folding his arms.

'A romance, actually.'

Her tone was blunt, and for the first time he considered that perhaps she was angry with him for what had happened yesterday. He *had* kind of turned on her out of the blue. Not that she hadn't deserved it after prying where she wasn't invited.

'It didn't really go anywhere. Guess I'm not too great with romance.'

He frowned, swallowed an apology before it bubbled out of him—she *had* to know there were lines she couldn't cross. And more that *he* couldn't cross, he added to himself.

'So, how do you feel about being involved in this?' he asked, gesturing to the dental hygiene boxes around them and the paper she had already handed out to the kids along with the colouring books.

'I think it's a great idea.' She got to her feet and faced him. 'Was it one of yours?'

'Actually, it was Maria's. It was kind of a joint wish for all of us to promote healthy eating, dental hygiene, basic first aid…all that as we go along. You start with the kids and it filters through to the elders, you know? How are those mosquito bites?'

He pointed to one on her arm—a small red welt. She covered it with her hand. 'I'll survive. Anyway, I think this is a good thing to be involved in. Teaching them basic health education while you're playing games—they think it's all fun.'

'Exactly. We wanted to focus first on helping them learn about brushing their teeth.'

Madeline nodded, looking at the fact sheets in Spanish about exactly that. Ryan noted one of the boxes was open, so she'd clearly seen the six hundred toothbrushes they'd brought with them.

'I've been colouring, then stopping to talk through the fact sheets, then colouring again…'

'Good start. And if you want to add songs at any point they love that.'

'Songs?'

'Evan plays guitar sometimes—makes up words. How are you at improvising?'

She shrugged. 'I guess I could give it a shot.'

Once again he was impressed. Having another pair of hands on the project would be a blessing. In other places where they'd tested the programme they had already seen an improvement in dental health and knowledge about how to prevent parasite infestation. It was one of their success stories, but they still had so much more to do.

Madeline shifted her weight from one foot to the other. 'Listen, Ryan, about last night…'

'It's forgotten,' he said quickly.

She let out a sigh. 'No, it's not, I can tell.'

He took her elbow, led her three steps away from the kids and lowered his voice. His hand tingled, just feeling her skin against his, and he withdrew it quickly, slightly shocked.

'Like I said, there are things I don't want to talk about, Madeline. *Ever.* I know you have a job to do, but if we could leave certain things out I'd appreciate it.'

'It's not going to work like that,' she said, frowning at him. 'You know the publishers will want answers about Josephine.'

A planet-sized rock shot up to his throat. Her name… *her* name…coming from Madeline's lips sent chills straight through him.

'We can write around it, but the stories…or the half-stories…are out there already.'

She reached for his arm. That spark again. He had to take a step back. His fists balled of their own accord.

'We can work this out,' she hurried on in a hushed tone, closing the gap again. 'You *have* to trust me, Ryan. Just trust me with the truth.'

Another butterfly caught on the wind beside her as he ran his eyes over her lips, her ears, the apple dangling on a chain around her neck. He wanted to trust her. He really did. She had some kind of strange effect on him… And maybe it was finally time for the truth.

He considered it for a second. Josephine and the real story behind that day had turned him into a walking wreck for the most part—shot a bullet through any real chance of a romance ever since. They'd all wanted to know what had happened and he'd flat out refused to say, building a wall up brick by damn brick till it was suffocating for all involved. Maybe it *was* time.

He opened his mouth, but one of the kids—a girl in a muddied shirt—jumped up and screeched with laughter, dragging a little boy with her over to Madeline. They both started talking to her excitedly in fast Spanish, pulling at her hands.

He closed his mouth.

'Sorry—you were saying?' Madeline said after a moment, breaking free.

The look of expectancy in her eyes tore him to pieces. He bit his cheeks. What the hell was he thinking? It wasn't time. It would never be time. He was letting his unnamed emotion and the heat interfere with his mental processes and it could never happen again.

'I don't trust anyone,' he said quickly, before his heart could hold him back.

He'd expected anger, and prepared himself to take the hit, but instead he watched confusion flood Madeline's eyes, then perhaps a hint of pity.

'That's a shame,' she replied softly. 'You must be really lonely.'

Then she sat down again with the kids, leaving him speechless.

CHAPTER TEN

MADELINE SAT ON the edge of the lake, drawing circles in the murky water with her bare feet. She clutched her coffee cup, turned the page of the book she was reading, but the words weren't sinking in.

She sighed, putting it down on the wooden deck, watching the dragonflies skimming the surface and leaving tiny ripples in their wake. One week in and she was growing to know each creature that dared to show itself around the camp—thanks to a book Maria had leant her.

She knew the iridescent *Rhetus periander* butterflies, with their vivid blue wings and red blotches, the black grasshoppers with their beady indigo eyes and bright yellow polka dots, the russet-coloured caterpillars which clung resiliently to leaves throughout every rainstorm and the sand flies that nibbled in invisible silence at her legs and feet, leaving marks she needed to remind herself constantly not to scratch.

Madeline knew a lot about her new surroundings already. But she still didn't know enough about Ryan.

Time passed slowly in the jungle. In seven days she hadn't once looked at herself in a mirror, but she could tell she'd lost weight. Her shorts were loose on her, as were her dresses. Even her bikini, which she was wearing now, wasn't as figure-hugging as it had been when she'd bought it. Rice and fruit were now the essentials to stop a rumbling stomach rather than something to enjoy.

Her phone had died three days ago. When Evan had offered her the solar charging kit she'd told him she didn't need it, instead charging her Dictaphone for yet another interview with Ryan that she knew wouldn't go anywhere.

In every awkward chat since that day under the tree he'd refused to step any closer towards the place she needed him to be—and that was the place where Josephine came into the picture.

She furrowed her brow at the shimmering water ahead. Madeline would only get paid if she delivered the kind of manuscript the editor had in mind. She was trying not to feel defeated but she couldn't really help it.

She couldn't help the chemistry still more than evident between her and Ryan either. Even thoughts of Jason were dwindling by the day. Their break-up had been a meteoric crash in her world, but she felt so far away from that now. Since coming out here she'd been swept into another existence entirely—one in which she was perpetually hot, sticky and dancing in dangerous circles around Ryan.

She shivered, even in the heat, remembering the night before.

Ryan had agreed to another interview on the condition that she accompany him fishing. Mark and Evan often went out on the river at night, and she'd been once, just for the boat ride and to clear her head. She'd never been off camp with Ryan. When he'd asked her to join him she'd been surprised, nervous and grateful all at the same time, because he'd chosen to spend most nights alone up till then, preparing equipment, stock-checking, talking to the camera or just hiding himself away in his tent.

She shivered again, twirling the water with her toes as her mind replayed what had happened in the boat.

'Ever tasted a piranha?' Ryan had asked, casting his line out into the blackness of the water.

The moon had been a bright yellow bulb above them, and with no other lights they'd been able to see a million stars. They'd also heard bats and monkeys in the tree-tops as they'd discussed his training days and a family vacation to the UK for the memoir.

Madeline had felt the Amazon closing in on them as he'd rowed them further away from camp. She'd sensed a thousand eyes and ears around them in the darkness—furry spies, she'd hoped, as opposed to any kind of drug runner.

She'd gripped the side of the small boat, watching his profile and keeping an eye out for caimans. 'Never,' she'd replied in answer to his question. 'What do they taste like?'

'A lot like sardines. They're pretty good when they're crunchy off the grill, but they're bony little things. Kind of a mission to get the meat off. Here—hold this.'

He'd thrust the fishing line at her then, and reached behind him to the small box he'd brought along and shone a flashlight into it. She'd seen raw chicken.

'They go crazy for this,' he'd told her, reaching for the line again.

His hand had brushed hers and he'd stood just an inch behind her, hooking tiny chunks of the white meat onto the end of the wire. She hadn't wanted to ask why *they* weren't being fed this luxury.

'Now, throw it in.'

'Me?' she'd asked, still processing the jolt she'd felt at his touch.

'This is a good spot. Don't panic—you'll be OK.'

He'd put the line back in her hands and moved up close behind her. Very close. So close that she'd felt his breath tingling over the nape of her neck below her ponytail. He'd put his hands over hers and lifted the line, helping her throw it into the water—hard.

Nothing.

Then everything.

The water had started moving around the end of the line.

'There they are!' Ryan had exclaimed excitedly, shining his light out ahead of them and putting a hand on her shoulder, over her clammy skin.

Madeline had gasped, feeling her face break out into a grin as a white-topped frenzy came into view. It had been as though someone had installed a tiny hot-tub in the middle of the river.

She'd felt the line tug as Ryan rested his flashlight on the bench, facing them.

'Don't let go—pull it in! Don't let the line go loose,' he'd urged as his hands moved to her quickly, gripping her waist over her thin blue dress to hold her steady.

'Don't let go of *me*—they'll eat me, too,' she'd said, leaning further into him.

'I won't. You've got it—you've got it…'

He'd been pressed against her in the boat. His head almost resting on her shoulder from behind as he'd helped her pull the fish in through the frenzy and over the side.

'Great job!' he'd cried, elated, holding up the line and moving away from her to reach for the flashlight again.

He'd shone it on their catch—a silvery fish about twice the size of a goldfish, with an orange tinge. It hadn't looked very scary, even as it wriggled and flapped. Madeline had reached for the line to get a closer look but Ryan had gripped her fingers and held them tight away from it.

'Not so fast!'

'Sorry.'

'You want to see what this thing will do if it gets a hold of your finger?'

His face had been so close to hers she'd practically been able to feel his stubble tickling her cheek. She'd smelled him: a raw, animal scent mixed with sunscreen that had made her a little wobbly on her feet. Luckily she'd been able to blame the boat for that.

He'd stuck a hand in his pocket, pulled out a thick green leaf. Holding the line with the fish still attached, he'd dangled the leaf in front of the piranha. Instantly the fish had opened its jaws, revealing an ominous row of razor-sharp teeth, and started chomping the leaf to pieces from bottom to top with ferocious zeal, as fast and as efficient as a chef's knife chopping a cucumber.

Madeline had watched with equal amazement and horror.

'Told you—you don't want to mess with these guys.'

Ryan had grinned, turned off the light and thrown what was left of the leaf overboard. His eyes had sparkled like ice cubes in the moonlight, and Madeline had sworn she'd never seen anyone so handsome in her entire life as Ryan when he was smiling, living in the *now*, not letting his past weigh him down like a hunk of lead.

'That's the most incredible thing I've ever seen,' she'd breathed, laughing with the sheer adrenaline of it.

She'd studied his lips, his mouth—so different from Jason's. She'd been so certain that she'd never even want to kiss someone else. But in that moment, awed by their primitive environment and slightly scared of the flesh-eating fish, she'd known she'd say *To hell with professionalism* and kiss Ryan Tobias if he'd initiated it.

As his eyes had raked over her lips under the infinite Milky Way she'd willed him to throw her down in that rickety boat and erase every last trace of her ex, and the others before him, from out of her for ever. At one point she'd been convinced he was going to—because Madeline had seen it in Ryan, too—looked it straight in the face.

That hunger. That unmistakable desire.

But he'd tossed the fish into the box under the chicken and rowed them back to camp in silence. Then, instead of sitting around the fire with her and the others, he'd given the piranha to Evan to roast, retreated to his tent alone and hadn't even said goodnight...

The trees shifted behind her, signalling that her time alone at the camp's only washing facility was almost up.

Madeline put her cup down by her book and jumped into the water with the small bar of organic soap she'd been given. It was one that left no trace of any chemicals behind. She swam for a few metres under the surface, popped her head up and looked back.

Her heart leapt like a rabbit as she saw Ryan standing on the deck, peeling off his shirt.

Had he seen her?

Her eyes glued themselves to his body. His muscles were rippling in the early-morning light; his unshaven face was shadowed around his jaw. He was fiddling with the button on his khaki trousers now, undoing it, sliding the trousers down his strong, lean legs and shrugging them off.

Madeline froze. If she moved he would see her. She considered closing her eyes, but it was too late. His boxers were already halfway down his legs and he was kicking them aside with his trousers and towel.

He was going for a swim. *Naked.*

Her breath caught in her throat. He lifted his arms and stretched up to the sun, as though expecting Mother Nature herself to stand and applaud her own fine work of art. Perhaps she was. The wind was riffling through the trees around the little lake, causing the cicadas to up the volume of their hum.

Madeline swallowed, digging her feet into the squelchy mud below her. She'd never seen a man with a body like his before. Ryan Tobias was pretty much perfect—the quintessential 'hot doc' calendar contender for the month of August, standing like some idolised enigma in shafts of yellow sunlight.

Bending over in the sunlight.

Pointing his hands at the water in the sunlight.

He dived in.

Madeline panicked.

She traced the line he was leaving on the surface with her eyes, as though he himself were a pack of piranhas. She considered swimming past him at full throttle and clambering out before he had the chance to see her. But, again, she was too late.

The water rippled out in front of her and his head appeared. Then his eyes sprang open, looking right into hers from less than a foot away.

'Hi,' she said, under her breath.

He shook his hair, sending a shower of droplets out around him. 'Good morning.'

'Didn't you see my book on the deck, with my cup?'

Her toes were still curling into the mud under the water. She couldn't see her feet, or anything else—a fact she was glad of as he stood there with a look of amusement spreading from his cool grey eyes down to his twitching lips.

He's naked, she couldn't help reminding herself, feeling the colour rise to her cheeks.

'Nope—didn't see. I was half asleep till I jumped in here. We had an emergency in the night so I didn't get much sleep.' He stepped closer to her, spreading his arms out on either side as though trying to gather the water between them. 'Nice surprise.'

Naked, naked, naked.

'What was the emergency?' she asked, stepping backwards slightly, aware that if she stayed where she was she might accidentally touch him with a very inappropriate part of her body.

'Poisonous caterpillar got to one of the kids and his finger swelled up so much the poor thing had a blue hand.'

He stopped right in front of her, his bare torso inches from her breasts in her purple bikini. She studied his face in the sun—the bronzed cheeks, the faint lines around his eyes—noticed how his eyelashes caught drops of water from his dripping hair before he blinked and set them on their downward path again.

Madeline felt as if she was under a searchlight all of a sudden, and another memory from the night before, of his hands on her waist in the boat, flooded her mind and her loins at the same time.

She turned onto her back in the water and felt his eyes on her breasts as they stuck above the surface like her toes. She studied the swaying branches overhead, and the darting dragonflies, reminding herself to breathe.

'Is the kid OK?' she asked without looking at him.

He floated on his back beside her. 'Yes, he's good now. Morphine always helps.'

'You must be exhausted.'

'All in a day's work. Or a night's. And I'm not the only one working hard—how's it going with your group of kids? You seem to really love them, and we can all see how much they love *you*.'

Madeline closed her eyes, swallowing as his fingers brushed hers under the water. She was still clutching her organic soap and he took it out of her hand gently, stood upright and then, to her surprise, took her left foot gently in his hands and ran the soap over it while she floated.

This was definitely not happening. Ryan was not going out of his way to touch her.

'I do,' she said in reply to his statement, though the words came out a little strangled. 'Love the kids, I mean.'

She tilted her head to look at him, but he seemed to be willing her not to say a word about what he was doing. In silence he trailed the soap between each and every one of her toes and massaged them with firm fingers... slowly, sensually.

Madeline's insides were on fire. Ryan wouldn't let her stand, though. He kept her feet against him, pulling her soles to his solid chest as he continued his massage, then worked the soap up her legs softly, firmly, then softer again.

If she hadn't been lying in a lake she'd be wet for other reasons by now, she realised, groaning inwardly.

'I don't know why you gave up nursing, Maddy,' he said softly, breaking into her thoughts.

He let her feet go but moved to her side, placing one hand under her back. He started to trail the soap softly in a circle around her navel.

'We've spoken about me a lot, but why don't we talk about *you*?'

Madeline was struggling to maintain an air of calm,

and she somehow levelled her voice, closed her eyes and allowed him to wash her. No one had ever done anything like this to her before.

'There's nothing to say. I'm happy to leave all that stuff to you guys while I write.'

He ran the soap between her ribs, up to the string at the front of her bikini. He pressed it against her flesh, released it and slowly ran the soapy trail up, up, *up* over her collarbone and neck. Then, with nimble fingers, he moved the hand that was beneath her in the water to the back of her bikini top and pulled it undone.

Every part of her was throbbing with desire.

'Is this what they call a medical extreme?' she whispered daringly as he pulled the flimsy fabric from her body, leaving her top half exposed to the sun and the sky.

She thought she caught a smile on his face. He trailed the soap over her nipples, taking his time, seemingly relishing the equal amounts of thrill and torture he was causing her. She could still sense his silent urging for her not to mention what was happening, just to let him continue. It was the most erotic situation she'd ever been a part of.

His body towered over hers, blocked the sun, and from behind her eyelids she could see him taking her in. She could feel his own longing mounting by the millisecond as he trailed the soap down over her midriff, down, down to her bikini bottoms.

'My God, you're beautiful,' she heard him say hoarsely.

She couldn't take it any more. She put her feet to the ground, moved her hand under the water to feel for what she had no doubt would be standing to attention like a soldier—but he grabbed her fingers, held them tight.

'Not yet.'

'Ryan…'

'Someone's coming.'

An enormous splash by the deck made her jump. She ducked under the water up to her shoulders and Ryan thrust her bikini top into her hands beneath the murky surface, sprang away from her side. Someone was swimming out in their direction, but she couldn't make out who it was.

With trembling fingers she rushed to tie her top up and noticed Ryan swimming four feet away from her, as if nothing had happened. As if they were just two strangers in a lake.

Her insides were doing cartwheels, and so were her thoughts. *Did that just happen?* What the hell were they thinking? They were here to work…not to romp about in the jungle like two wild animals. She wasn't another one of his lovesick fan girls—she was a professional writer on an assignment. And she was too heartbroken over her ex to notice anyone else anyway…*wasn't* she?

She rolled her eyes. She wasn't any more, and she knew it.

Whoever it was who'd come for a swim wasn't from the camp, she realised. The masculine figure swam right past her and carried on. She turned back to Ryan but he wasn't there. He was already swimming back to the deck.

He was climbing out, wrapping a towel around his waist, scooping up his clothes as if he'd already forgotten she'd ever been there. Then he walked quickly back the way he'd come through the trees, leaving her alone and still trembling.

CHAPTER ELEVEN

IT WASN'T AS if he could have stopped himself, Ryan thought, buttoning up a fresh white shirt outside his tent and raking a hand through his hair as he walked quickly back towards the medical stations. His hands had moved before his head had even been able to begin to process what he was doing.

Madeline had been floating there next to him with the sun in her beautiful green eyes, wearing next to nothing, and he'd been completely naked. He was only human, for God's sake.

A stupid human.

He'd been careless, and that had been a close call.

'Ryan!'

It was Maria, calling him over to one of the stations. He strode across the grass towards her, past the line of people waiting to register for treatment. He kicked a football that flew at him from the group of children clearly waiting for Madeline and waved at them, putting on a happy face.

His heart was pounding harder by the second. What if one of the camera guys had caught sight of them just now, with a telescopic zoom and an eye for making some seriously dramatic television? Not that anyone *here* would do that, he realised thankfully, but still, nothing would stop them talking amongst themselves about him and Madeline.

He clenched his fists at his sides. He couldn't keep away from her. Even being angry with her didn't help. Madeline Savoia was a bomb threatening to detonate right in front of him, and she was all the more dangerous for the way she was sliding into his conscience, getting under his skin.

All he'd wanted to do last night in that boat was lay her down and feast on the look of wonder and excitement in her eyes as he showed her even *more* new things. Hell, the things he wanted to show her...

He loved how empathetic she was, how readily she'd adjusted to her new environment, never once complaining about how harsh and hard it was to be out here. The kids adored her and lined up for her in the mornings, bringing her fruit and flowers and any other present they could think of to make her smile. Maria was lending her books.

She was the saint of the whole damn camp already.

'Ryan,' Maria said, leading him inside. She looked agitated. 'We just had a radio call—there's a patient on the way from the village. Mark and one of the volunteers are bringing her in on the boat right now.'

'What's the problem?' he asked, glancing at another volunteer, who was wrapping a strip of gauze around a teenage boy's forearm in the chair beside him. The air was thick and hot and smelled of antiseptic spray and disinfectant. He scrubbed his hands at the basin of water.

'Seventeen-year-old girl, name Abigail, severe abdominal pains. Mark's already diagnosed her with an ectopic pregnancy, ruptured tube...'

'We have methotrexate close if we need it?' he asked,

drying off his hands on a paper sheet. It was the safest and quickest way to induce abortion.

'Already on it,' Maria said, doing up her scrubs as he prepared the laparoscope. 'This kid sounds like she's been through a lot already, from what Mark says. She's been hanging out here the past two days with her little brother and Madeline—she probably didn't even know she was pregnant.'

'Madeline?' Ryan turned around, pulling on a pair of surgical gloves.

As he spoke her name the plastic sheet over the door was swept aside and Madeline came rushing in, this time beside Mark and a volunteer, followed by Jake with his camera.

The canvas stretcher they were carrying held the pregnant girl in question, and he recognised her immediately from the village. Long-haired, chatty Abigail, lying on her back with her belly exposed, letting out the most horrific howls. It wasn't clear at all that she was pregnant, but the blood on her skirt made his heart sink.

Madeline was clutching the sweaty girl's hand, talking fast in Spanish. As they brought the stretcher up to the bed he didn't miss the tears in her eyes. Her hair was still wet, tied in a bun on her head and she met his glance for half a second—a glance that said nothing but, *Help this girl.*

Ryan could see that her nursing instincts were primed once again, probably pushing all thoughts about what had just happened at the lake completely out of the window.

He was already in action. As the camera circled he helped Mark and Maria get the sobbing Abigail gently off the stretcher and onto the table. Her skin was damp, and had a greyish tinge that concerned him. A crowd of people had gathered at the opening to the medical station, but Mark walked over and ushered them all away.

Madeline looked as though she was going to leave, too, but Abigail reached for her arm, clutched it and gripped on as if her hand was a metal vice.

'No quiero que te vayaso,' she was begging in Spanish. 'Don't go, please.'

'We'll have to do keyhole,' Ryan told Maria, who nodded in agreement.

'What? Here?' Madeline looked shocked.

The girl sobbed, gripping her even tighter.

'It's better than open surgery. Quicker recovery, less blood loss. Maria—general anaesthetic…'

'Yes, Doc.'

Maria turned around to the trolley that held the equipment she'd prepared the second the radio call had come in. They were lucky to have a laparoscope—a long fibre optic cable system which allowed them to see the area in question on a monitor connected to a generator, which they charged via solar power. It wouldn't cause the girl too much extra trauma.

Madeline appeared traumatised enough in this moment for everyone, but Abigail was still latching on to her like a leech.

'Crap!' Mark exclaimed from the doorway. 'Lady out here with a hip fracture—we need you, Maria.'

'Now?'

Jake was having a field-day, zooming in on their expressions, Ryan could tell.

'Evan's tied up…'

'It's urgent,' Mark told her. 'I'll meet you next door.'

'I can't!' Maria protested.

'You guys get on it. Madeline's here,' Ryan declared,

reaching behind him quickly and grabbing some scrubs from a box. He threw them at Madeline.

Her eyes widened in terror. 'Ryan... Ryan, listen... I really can't do this...'

'Yes, you can—you're just helping me. Wash your hands.'

'I can't *just help* you.'

'You're a trained nurse—of course you can. Wash your hands and put those scrubs on.'

He'd made the decision on the spot. He knew she could do it. Whatever fear she'd convinced herself she had about being in a set of scrubs around an emergency was all in her head; he was sure of it.

'I need you, Madeline,' he said calmly as he prepared the cannula and reached for the girl's hand. 'Abigail needs you.'

'I don't want to do this,' she protested again, panic causing her voice to shake. 'This isn't why I'm here. I've told you this. Stop trying to—'

'If she can't do it, Ryan, she can't do it,' Maria said, flustered. Beads of sweat were glistening on her forehead and she looked exhausted.

Ryan put the cannula down. 'Madeline is going to help me,' he said firmly, in a tone that made them both fall silent. He turned to her and fixed his eyes on hers. 'I have every faith in you. You're a nurse, Madeline. You know it and *I* know it.'

Her eyes narrowed in silent defeat. She did as she was told—scrubbed her hands, let Maria tie the scrubs at the back. Then Maria squeezed her shoulder and hurried out of the station quickly with Mark, leaving them alone with the camera.

'Trust yourself,' Ryan said, as soon as they were gone. He heard her take a deep breath, seemingly psyching herself up. He watched her place a hand on Abigail's forehead.

'I won't leave you. I'm here,' she said in Spanish, and Abigail looked relieved, smiling weakly and muttering her thanks before Ryan administered the anaesthetic into the back of her hand.

'Muscles are relaxed, breathing is depressed, eye movements slowing,' he told her after a moment, wheeling the laparoscope closer. 'I'm going to make the incision right here.' He pointed to a spot below Abigail's belly button. 'Once the tube's in you're going to pump the carbon dioxide in for me, OK? It's really simple. I'm setting it all up. You just move your hands, slow and steady, OK?'

Madeline nodded, but didn't make a sound.

He turned the monitor around and pulled his mask up over his mouth. Madeline did the same, leaving only her eyes visible. He tried not to register the fear he saw in the wide green pools—his job right now was to make her feel as much of an expert as he was, so they could help this girl as quickly as possible.

Forty-five minutes passed, with Ryan explaining everything he was doing to the camera and making his usual trademark comments—the ones that never ceased to win him thousands of tweets from touched and inspired fans, and from wannabe medical prodigies around the world.

He could almost see them already.

Who's the new staff member? New romance? #DrRyan #MedicalExtremes.

He couldn't exactly tell them to edit this scene out as he had with the tumbling tarantulas. He blocked it from his mind. Having the camera lens on them meant he couldn't talk to Madeline either—not in the way he would have done without it—but slowly, as they worked together, he watched her fears seem to drain away, until all that was left was a determined young woman doing everything she was asked to do quickly, efficiently, in a way that made him proud.

Finally, after he'd closed the incisions with neat stitches, Madeline applied the dressing without flinching and by the time Abigail came round, groggy and confused, seemed completely calm.

Madeline pulled her mask down around her neck, stroked the girl's forehead again and held her hand, letting out a sigh.

'*Ahora está OK,*' she whispered. 'Dr Ryan fixed you up.'

'Nurse Maddy helped, too,' he added quickly, placing a hand on Madeline's arm.

Their eyes lingered on each other's perhaps a little too long, and when he turned to the camera he didn't miss the fact that it was directed straight at them.

Abigail was speaking now—softly, woozily. He could understand some but not all of what she said, and as she continued breathily Madeline's face was a picture of concern and fresh heartbreak.

She looked up at him, translating for his benefit. 'She says she got pregnant at fifteen, too. She went into labour for three days before coming for help, and then laboured for two more days before delivery.'

'What happened?' Ryan asked, remembering what Maria had said about Abigail's difficult past.

Madeline smudged a tear as it trickled down her cheek. 'She was induced, and then told that the baby had already passed away. A doctor from another village performed surgery, like you just did, but he wasn't a professional. So awful…'

A strange part of Ryan wanted to reach for Madeline suddenly, but he kept his hands firmly at his sides. He couldn't bear the misfortune this poor young woman had endured. Abigail was still a child herself.

'She couldn't walk for three months and was taken to the hospital in Saint Elena for physiotherapy,' Madeline said, still translating. 'She didn't know she was pregnant again, but she still wants a baby.'

Sympathy and despair for Abigail, and so many others like her, passed from Madeline to him like a secret note. Madeline's emotions were as tangible and hot as the jungle air. Her openness was rubbing off on him and she'd felt so good in his hands.

So good that in spite of being swept away again into another emergency, and trying his best to maintain focus, he still couldn't shift the image of her floating topless in the lake…of himself just moments away from making a mistake.

CHAPTER TWELVE

MADELINE HAD NEVER brushed her teeth so many times in one day. In the fading light, with her view polka-dotted by fireflies, she was sitting under the trees by the unlit fire, trying to demonstrate to the eight kids sitting around her how best to reach the backs of their mouths with their new 'toys'.

They seemed to think her sticking the toothbrush in her own mouth and making funny faces was the most hilarious thing they'd ever seen. It literally never got old. But they were learning fast, eager to impress her.

Truth be told, she was glad of the distraction, because every moment she wasn't busy she was back in that lake, being tenderly, sensually washed by Ryan.

Her cheeks flamed just at remembering, and she turned her attention back to helping the youngest child, a boy of just four, navigate his way around getting the paste out of a closed tube of toothpaste.

Her morning swim that had quickly turned into a semi-naked cleansing session at the hands of the in-famous Ryan Tobias had been only marginally over-shadowed by the surgery she'd helped him perform on Abigail.

Madeline was still shaking from it—picturing the blood, reliving the flashbacks that had struck like thunder as she'd pulled on those scrubs and put that mask over her face. How could she have stood there at that operating table and *not* remembered in vivid detail the last time she'd tried to help a child and failed?

She'd been so angry with Ryan that she'd almost stormed out, but the look in Abigail's eyes…it had been almost unbearable. That combined with the steel grip she'd had on her hand had given Madeline no other choice but to suck it up and follow his orders.

Ryan had forced her to face her pain today—even though he had no idea at all of what had caused it in the first place.

'Madeline, Madeline!'

One little girl called Alina was showing her a set of pearly white teeth and Madeline clapped her hands, then directed her to rinse her mouth out with bottled water and spit onto the grass.

She was annoyed with herself for being distracted. A small part of her was also annoyed at being putty in Ryan's hands after the way he'd handled her in the lake, but another part—a stronger part—was impressed that he'd called her out on her fears and, as a result, had shifted something inside her, somehow.

She smiled to herself as she watched a volunteer in knee-length denim shorts walk up with sticks and cardboard for the night's fire. Now she could think of Toby. Now she could compare the look of relief and thanks her young friend and patient had so often given her with the look of Abigail, a girl she'd been able to help. And now she could see that *both* times she'd done everything she possibly could have.

'Dinner!'

Someone called out the magic word from up at the camp, causing all the kids to start scrambling up, commencing their nightly routine of hugging her one by one, tightly. It was their cue to head back to their families and Madeline's to collect her boring rice and beans—not that she ever complained.

Seeing the way people lived in the Amazon, on whatever they could catch, or grow, or fetch in small supplies from towns after days of rowing upstream, was doing wonders for her gratitude levels in general.

'Night!' she said to the kids one by one, hugging them in return and watching them run off giggling into the twilight.

She was starting to forget she'd ever lived a life in which all thoughts of kids—of being around them, interacting with them—had been torture. Maybe she'd quit nursing too soon...

Ryan came in late to the dining room. Madeline was sitting beside Maria, finishing a second banana, when he walked in, grabbed a plate, filled it with food and walked back out again. He looked as though he was in a rush. Was there another emergency?

'Did he see another tarantula?' she joked with Maria, scanning the ceiling for a moment.

Maria smiled and shrugged, digging her fork into a boiled egg.

Disappointment, then annoyance swirled in Madeline's belly when she realised that Ryan might well be ignoring her after what had happened between them.

She couldn't help reliving the image of his well-endowed lower half, exposed to the sun on the deck right in front of her, the feel of his expert hands trailing the soap around her navel and down towards... Well... A mistake. Surely they both knew that?

She put down her banana peel, pictured having an early night—another torturous one with Ryan in a silent tent so close to hers—but to her surprise, when she walked outside through the usual flurry of buzzing insects trying to get to her flesh, she saw him sitting by the fire with Evan, unpacking what looked like a box.

Madeline stopped in her tracks, but Maria beckoned her forward. She was carrying two cups of tea for them in metal cups.

'Come on, honey—come and sit down. It's been a long day,' she said kindly.

Evan was playing the guitar that she remembered Ryan talking about. They each had a beer on the ground beside them.

Ryan stood up when he saw her, holding out another beer which he'd pulled from the box on the ground. 'For you,' he said, eyes twinkling.

He'd taken his hat off and his hair was sticking up crazily again, as though he'd wrestled with a bush. He looked as rugged and wild and ridiculously handsome as the first time she'd seen him on television—except that now, of course, she'd seen parts of him his regular audience never got to see.

'Thank you,' she said, taking the lukewarm bottle from him as Maria put her tea on the ground. 'I'll drink that after,' she told her, and Maria winked.

'We had it delivered especially,' said Ryan, offering Maria one. She declined. 'Figured we had a few things to celebrate.'

The light from the fire was playing in Ryan's hair, and although he looked tired he seemed relaxed, for once. He moved across the log he was sitting on so she could sit beside him.

'A *few* things to celebrate?' she said cryptically, and he raised an eyebrow in silent acknowledgement of their secret.

Madeline felt hot—and not just because of the fire Mark was now prodding with a long stick. She noticed Ryan's Boston Red Sox T-shirt, more casual than anything she'd ever seen him in, and his jeans as he stretched out his legs and feet towards the fire. He was still in his trusted British boots.

Others joined them as they trickled over from the dining hall. She felt Ryan's eyes on her every now and then, as hot as the sparks bouncing from the burning sticks, until eventually he leaned in to whisper in her ear.

'You did good today. You made me very proud.'

She turned to him. His face was so close she almost brushed his nose with hers, and the movement sent a familiar flight of butterflies coursing through her.

'What exactly are we talking about, here?'

He smiled, brushing her ear with his nose. 'You back in scrubs.'

She rolled her eyes, but he nudged her with his elbow.

'And out of them, of course.'

Madeline tried not to smirk as she took a sip of her drink. No one was looking at them, but she was more than aware of Jake, the camera guy, lurking not far away, no doubt waiting to catch anything juicy. She'd seen him zooming in on her before.

'That was a mistake,' she whispered, wishing she didn't have to say it.

'I know,' he said, brushing her ear again—with his lips this time.

She leaned away, her limbs growing weaker. 'I should thank you for what you had me do in surgery,' she managed after a moment.

Ryan took a swig from his bottle. Evan was strumming another song now and one of the volunteers, a lady in her thirties with straight red hair, had started to sing.

'I wouldn't have asked you to do what you did,' he said, 'if I hadn't thought all along that you could.'

'Well, you have more faith in me than I do,' she said, and sighed. 'But, seriously, you really helped me today, Ryan—more than you know. You've made me think about…things.'

'Like the thing that made you quit nursing?'

'Yes, I guess so.'

'Whatever it was, Madeline, you have to let it go. It's in the past.'

'You're right,' she said, nodding. 'Maybe *you* should remember that, too? Leave some things in the past?'

Ryan looked at the floor for a moment. A faint smile crossed his mouth as he shook his head. 'So what was it? *Who* was it that made you give up?'

'A boy called Toby,' she said, letting the words leave her mouth without giving them a chance to get stuck like they usually did.

She gripped her beer bottle in both hands, started picking at the label with her too-long nails.

'He was the first patient put in my care when I qualified—we got really close, you know? I would take him books and games, and I would tell him everything would be OK. Really, he was helping me as much as I was helping him. I was nervous, I was new, and he would say the right things… Like, "You're the best nurse, Madeline. I trust you, and I'm so glad you're here."'

'Sounds like a good kid,' Ryan said, putting his empty bottle down on the ground. 'What was wrong with him?'

'Leukaemia. Chronic lymphocytic leukaemia,' she said, feeling the familiar pang. 'He was strong for months, but one night on my shift he had sudden respiratory distress and I couldn't do anything…'

She trailed off, emotions rising.

'There was nothing I could do… He went into cardiac arrest and I couldn't even call his mother in time—'

'Of course you couldn't,' Ryan cut in, putting a big hand around her shoulder on impulse.

His voice was firm, as it had been in the medical station when he'd thrown her the scrubs. He pulled her in against him.

'You couldn't have done anything.' He shuffled closer to her on the log, moved his other hand to her knee. 'Toby never blamed you, Maddy—not for anything. And it wasn't your fault.'

'I know,' she said, putting a hand over his automatically in response. 'I know that now. But I didn't want to hear that for a really long time.'

'Because you missed him. And you felt like you'd failed him when you hadn't. You made his last few months so much better, and that was a parting gift he never would have had otherwise.'

Ryan's words were making her eyes turn to hot, wet pools again, and she blinked, not wanting to make a scene.

'Sometimes you *want* to feel the pain,' he whispered, 'because you don't believe you're entitled to feel anything else. Am I right?'

She could hear his voice crack just a little bit as he continued to hold her against him. He'd never touched her in public before. She was equally moved and afraid.

'You're so right,' she whispered back.

He looked down at his boots and after a while removed his arm from around her. She half expected him to stand up and walk away from his own feelings and the cameras yet again.

'Sometimes you think you'll just wallow in it for

ever, because you don't know how else to be any more,' she murmured.

He didn't get up. Instead he pressed his hot palm against her palm and laced his fingers through her own.

'God, Maddy,' he said on an exhale, 'I know exactly how *that* feels.'

CHAPTER THIRTEEN

HE DID KNOW. Ryan knew exactly how it felt to live under a blanket of insecurity and self-doubt. It was the exact opposite of the image he portrayed to the world.

He squeezed Madeline's hand, brought it onto his lap and looked down at their tangled fingers. The truth about Josephine seemed too big and too daunting to think about most days—even to himself. And he'd grown used to the ghosts that lived inside him…grown accustomed to the haunting taunts that had left him cold, even with a camera on his smiling face and four hundred thousand Twitter fans calling him 'hot'.

Madeline knew the bare bones of what was bothering him. He wanted to tell her everything—of course he did—because for the first time in a long time he realised he actually *needed* to talk about it.

He glanced at her profile, at the firelight bouncing in her eyes as she hummed along to Evan's music. He wanted to do so much more than talk with Madeline. She'd told him what had spawned *her* deepest insecurities. Couldn't he provide her with the same intimacy?

A frown creased his brow. Letting go of the past meant letting her in, and that was still a risk. Where would it end? Where would she stop with the information he offered her? How much would she put in a book to feed the vultures? She wasn't here to feed his ego, or his desires. She was here to write the book he'd been dreading and they both knew she couldn't give it less than her best.

'Mind if I play?'

Madeline's voice broke into his warring thoughts. She was talking to Evan. Everyone's eyes were on her so she dropped his hand back into the shadows. They'd probably seen anyway, he realised. After today, though, and the fears she'd faced in surgery, he had no doubt the producer would want to interview her about her back story, and him on why he'd been so insistent that she help him. Anything to make good TV.

At least he could pass their hand-holding off as affection between colleagues who'd saved a life.

With a slight look of surprise, Evan handed the guitar over to Madeline. He folded his arms across his chest as she pulled the instrument onto her lap.

'I only know a few songs,' she said a little shyly as she cast him a sideways glance.

Her fingers were already moving over the frets, though, creating a melody. Ryan noticed Mark and Evan grinning at each other like schoolboys, clearly impressed. Madeline had agreed to try improvising some songs for the kids, but she'd never admitted to being able to play like this. There was so much he still didn't know about this woman.

'Where did you learn to play?' he said into her ear.

'Colombia. I learned a lot there,' she replied.

Then she launched into a song he recognised immediately: *Moon River*.

Chills ran through his veins in spite of the humidity and the fire. He saw Maria's mouth fall open. Madeline could *really* sing. Her voice was like hot honey trickling over him, and he couldn't keep his eyes from her face. Her skin was glowing; her whole presence was pure light.

Ryan swore in that moment that he'd never seen or heard anything quite as exquisite as Madeline Savoia in his whole life.

When she wrapped up the final verse and chorus the circle broke out into rapturous applause—and *his* clapping, he realised, was the loudest. Evan shot him a knowing look, which he chose to ignore. For this one night, he decided, he was letting go. He was not going to give a damn what anyone thought.

'Can I keep this for tomorrow?' Madeline asked Evan, holding the guitar close against her. 'Ryan said the kids love to sing—we could probably do something fun around the dental hygiene stuff.'

'By all means, please do,' Evan said, holding his hands up. 'It sounds much better in your company than mine.'

Ryan smiled. 'I'm sure there's a tune in her about toothpaste.'

He heard Evan emit a snort—probably at the stupid words that had just slipped from his mouth. He stood up, rooted around in his pockets and pulled out his flashlight. Holding it up, he motioned for Madeline to hand him the guitar.

'I'll walk you back to the dining hall with that. No room in your tent, I'm guessing.'

She stood up herself and gave him the guitar. 'I was thinking of calling it a night anyway. It's been a long day, you know.'

'I know,' he said, feeling his pulse quicken suddenly. He had no clue where this was leading, but he knew he had to get them both away from the fire and all the prying eyes and ears.

They wished the group goodnight, and walked away into the shadows.

'You have quite a voice, you know,' he told her, shining his light into the dining room, opening the squeaky mesh door and resting the guitar on one of the benches before stepping out again and walking with Madeline towards the tents. 'I might have followed *you* around that university campus if you'd been there,' he said, 'instead of my acapella girl. She didn't even like me back.'

Madeline laughed, pushing her hands into her pockets as they walked across the grass and stopped outside her tent. 'How do you know *I* like you?'

The air was hot, even away from the fire, and Ryan couldn't help thinking that this would be the perfect night to be out on the river again. The fireflies were holding a glow-stick party in the trees around them and all he could think about was kissing her.

He turned off his flashlight, plunging them both into darkness.

'I know you like me,' he said in reply. 'You didn't exactly bat me off this morning.'

They were hovering outside her tent now. Her hands were still in her pockets. He stepped closer, reached for her arm and let his fingers slide slowly down from her elbow to the edge of one pocket till she was forced to set her hand free. He took it again in his, clasped his fingers around it, stepped even closer.

'This morning at the lake,' he said softly. 'I knew you were there the whole time.'

He could hear the smile in her voice when she responded. 'I thought about swimming past you and getting out, but I didn't.'

She was so close to him now. The crickets seemed to be serenading them. He reached for her other hand and she released it willingly, clasping it even tighter around his fingers. The tips of their shoes were touching.

Ryan leaned in closer. Their faces were an inch apart. He could feel her breath on his nose. Every bone in his body was weakening by the millisecond…except maybe one. He brushed her lips with just his shadow, but in a heartbeat Madeline was stepping backwards, swatting at something in the darkness and cursing.

'Are you OK? What happened?' He reached for her immediately in the darkness.

'Stupid mosquitoes. Just got me hard on the ankle.'

'Did you spray?'

'I forgot.'

Her hand was still in his as she scratched at her ankle with the other one, but the moment was gone—he knew it. He could feel it slipping further away into the trees.

He sighed to himself and shook his head. 'It's always the brightest lights that attract the most mosquitos,' he said, remembering a quote he'd read somewhere once.

'I'm not shining a light.' Madeline straightened up. 'And neither are you.'

He smiled. 'It's a metaphor. Your ex was a mosquito, drawn to your light. I was thinking about this earlier. Good thing you squished him.'

She stood still in the blackness. 'Very poetic. I should write that down. But he squished *me*, so to speak.'

'It's still a good thing that all the squishing went on… I think.'

'So do I. If I was still with Jason I wouldn't be here

now.' Madeline paused. 'Ryan, what's happening here?' Her question was cautious, but loaded.

'I have no clue,' he replied honestly, brushing his thumb against the side of her hand slowly.

He felt her shiver...practically felt her weaken alongside him as the moment they'd lost suddenly reappeared like a huge gaping window.

'I'm here to do a job,' she said softly, almost with regret. 'And I thought we agreed this morning was a mistake.'

He leaned forward so their foreheads were touching, feeling a zip through his insides at their closeness, at what they were surely about to do.

'Maybe it was. Maybe it wasn't. You're doing your job, Maddy, and more. So am I.'

'Not properly. I can't do it properly until you give me answers. Just now you told me you know how I've been feeling. What did you mean, exactly?'

He let out an anguished groan against her forehead. 'Why do you *do* this to me?'

'You know why. Ryan, I really don't think we should confuse this...'

'Screw thinking,' he growled.

Before she could say anything else he reached for the back of her head and pressed his lips to hers.

Madeline was almost flat against him in an instant, flowing into his arms like water as he bunched up her hair. She reached for his face, kissing him back just as hard. He felt his heart contracting and expanding in his chest as she flattened her hands against him, then clutched the material of his Boston Red Sox T-shirt as though she couldn't touch enough of him in one go. She tasted of beer and excitement, and somewhere at the back of his perpetually foggy mind he felt a cloud lifting.

Their tongues started a slow dance, then a faster tango as they kissed and kissed and kissed, and he found he was losing himself, losing his own tangled mind, for the first time in a really long time.

'We should move inside,' he whispered eventually against her lips, heart hammering, his flesh itching to touch more of hers.

Madeline's breaths were hot and heavy as her left hand reached for the button at the top of his jeans.

He motioned to the tent. 'Inside,' he said again, more urgently.

She turned around to unzip the tent, but a rustle behind them in the trees made them freeze. A flashlight appeared, pointing straight at them.

He stepped away from Madeline. 'Who's there?'

'Ryan? It's Mark. There's an emergency—we need you at the station.'

'Dammit,' he muttered, meeting Madeline's wide eyes in the flashlight as she stood up straighter. There was disappointment etched all over her face—and his, too, he was sure. Thank God Mark was standing too far away to see them clearly. 'Be right there!' he called, trying his best to sound as though he *hadn't* just spent the last five or ten minutes glued to Madeline's face.

Mark hurried off and Ryan closed the gap between them, snaking an arm around Madeline in the darkness. He kissed her again—hard and meaningfully.

'Duty calls,' he said with another groan. 'Get some sleep.'

'Will you wake me up later?' she asked suggestively. She was sliding a hand down his chest to his jeans again. He thanked the jungle for the darkness as something started standing to attention.

Pulling her hand away, he brought her fingers to his mouth and kissed them. 'Like you've woken *me* up?' he said gruffly. 'Madeline Savoia, you are officially killing me.'

CHAPTER FOURTEEN

WITH HER HANDS against Ryan's firm torso, even with his T-shirt between her and his bare flesh, Madeline had felt rocket ships launch inside her.

She rolled over in her sleeping bag, listening to the bugs outside and the growing wind ruffling the trees. They were here to do a job, she reminded herself once again. She also had to keep reminding herself that she wasn't about to start leaning on any other man to help fill a void in her life. Even if that man *was* Ryan Tobias.

She wished she knew what time it was. Sleep had been eluding her for hours, and Ryan still hadn't come back. It crossed her mind that maybe he'd realised the error of his ways and retreated to his own tent after solving whatever emergency problem had come up, but her ego told her otherwise. He wanted her, no matter what. Right? *He'd* been the one who'd initiated everything. He'd approached her in the lake…held her hand by the fire. He'd kissed her.

She put a hand to her lips, swollen and plump from those kisses. Her chin was still tingling in the wake of his stubble.

She pulled the sleeping bag over her head. So much for her being a professional. She needed him next to her *now*. She needed to feel his skin on hers. She wanted him to make love to her so badly she didn't think she'd be able to function otherwise. But where the hell *was* he?

When dawn arrived and she still hadn't slept a wink, she grabbed her toothbrush and water, pulled the zipper up on her tent and crawled outside, yawning. The camp was eerily quiet. Usually there were one or two people milling about, cleaning their teeth outside their tents, doing star jumps to wake themselves up.

She wandered towards the medical stations. The sky wasn't as yellow as it usually was at this time of day. It was a deep, ominous grey, looming large against the treetops like the roof of another dark tent. Rain was on the way again, she thought as she spotted a howler monkey leap from one branch overhead to another.

She saw Maria, walking from one station to another. Madeline followed her, pushing back the plastic sheet over the door. 'Morning,' she said.

Maria spun around in surprise, her hands full of the gauzes she was relocating from a box to a table. 'Oh, Madeline, hi—you're up early.'

'I couldn't sleep. Where is…?' She paused, realising she probably shouldn't ask specifically about Ryan. 'Where is everyone?'

'It was kind of a crazy night,' Maria said, and for the first time Madeline noticed the dark circles under her eyes. 'Guy got attacked by a black caiman up the river; the crew left about an hour ago to see to him.'

'Attacked?' Madeline realised she was still holding her toothbrush. She slid it into the pocket of her denim shorts.

'Five metres long, it was—apparently. Guy got too close to her eggs, we're guessing.'

'Is he OK?'

'If you count being alive as "OK" he's OK. They flew

him to the hospital and now they're back at the village. The crew wanted to do some filming there, I think. They'll probably be gone awhile.'

Madeline couldn't help the disappointment settling in her stomach like a lead balloon. She felt for whoever had been chomped on by a caiman, of course, but she also felt selfishly resentful of being kept from Ryan even longer.

'Oh, the producer wants to talk to you,' Maria said, making Madeline's heart falter for a second.

'Really? What about?'

She started to pray internally. Had Mark said something about how close she and Ryan had been standing outside her tent when he'd sprung up on them? Were they all writing stories of their own already? Was the producer going to tell her to back off—to be professional or not be there at all?

'I think she wants an interview about the girl you helped yesterday, if that's OK?'

Madeline tried not to sigh out loud in relief. She was way too paranoid. 'I'm sure that will be fine,' she said.

She left Maria sorting her gauzes and made her way back towards her tent. But the heat was already making the air intolerably stuffy and she knew that in a canvas bubble she'd simply sweat and feel uncomfortable.

At the last minute Madeline turned, passed the ashes from the fire and followed the path towards the river. She sometimes liked to wander down and chat in Spanish to the local guys who hung out there, waiting to row people up and down from village to village. Besides, she needed to wake up before the kids started gathering around her for the day. She was so tired. Now that she thought about it, she was actually still in a dream.

'Madeline Savoia, you are officially killing me.'

The longing in his voice as he'd said those words had made a pinball machine of her body, sending hot white sparks zig-zagging downwards from her ears, to her nipples, to her toes.

She'd never been kissed like that before. It had been like something from a movie, she mused, the way he'd reached for her and yanked her forward, pressed his mouth to hers as if she was some kind of lifeline. Maybe she was.

So romantic.

She was halfway to the river when a voice in the trees, slightly in the distance, caught her attention. Stopping in her tracks and yawning sleepily again, she listened closer and heard it yet again. It was a man's voice and it sounded vaguely familiar. One of the crew?

They were probably filming just outside the village. Or maybe there was another emergency. She frowned to herself, feeling stupid. She should be helping them. After what had happened yesterday Madeline was starting to feel she should probably be doing a lot more around camp than simply writing and teaching the kids about cleaning their teeth—much as she loved them.

Maybe she should be assisting in every medical procedure she could, to build her confidence up. Maybe she should even go back to nursing when she returned to London…

Another voice, closer now, yanked her out of her thoughts. She turned towards it, started walking the other pathway towards the noise. As she did so a crash of thunder overhead made her jump. She noticed with dismay that the sky was even darker. She could hear the voices, still ahead of her, and she sped up, clutching her water bottle.

Raindrops started thudding onto the leaves and foliage above her, a few of them slipping through onto her skin. Rain always sounded so much louder in the jungle.

The path was thinning a little. Some way ahead she heard what sounded like the whole team having a heated conversation about something. The rain was too loud for her to make any of the words out, but Madeline was sure there must have been another emergency. She hoped she'd be able to help.

She pushed through a wall of vines and came to a small clearing with what looked like several paths of flattened grass leading away from it in different directions. At the sound of a male voice she carried onwards, and when she turned a small corner she saw them, gathered in a circle, looking down at something on the leaf-strewn ground.

Madeline was just about to call out when she froze in her tracks.

It wasn't the crew.

Her heart leapt straight into her windpipe as she took them in. A group of guys—maybe seven or eight—olive-skinned and covered in black tattoos, some in black shirts, some in white, all studying what she was pretty certain was a dead body. They were speaking quickly amongst themselves, loudly in Spanish, and they hadn't seen her.

Slowly, so as not to make a single branch or twig crack, she stepped backwards, never taking her eyes off them. That was when she saw a flash of metal: an AK-47 being brandished about wildly by a shirtless guy who looked and sounded angry about something.

Drug runners, she thought, trafficking between Colombia and Brazil, no doubt…or planning to. She was almost paralysed with fear. She couldn't be certain that was what they were, but she couldn't hang around to find out.

Somehow she forced herself to move, thankful for the rain now coming down even harder, silencing her footsteps. She found herself back in the clearing, but in a panic realised in horror that she couldn't remember which way she'd come.

She cursed under her breath, hearing movement behind her. The group was getting closer.

Had they heard her?

Which way was the right way?

Feeling nauseous, Madeline started to run. In her hurry she dropped her water bottle, found the path, then ran even faster till her lungs began to burn and the branches slashed at her limbs like an evil army.

As she gasped for air in the suffocating heat she couldn't for the life of her figure out where she was. The path looked the same as the one she'd walked in on, yet it was totally different. She was lost in the jungle.

Fear flooded her veins. The rain pummelled punishingly at her head, arms and legs. Thunder crashed above her and the bugs upped their symphony, as though trying to compete with the noise. She turned and ran back the way she'd come. At least she *thought* it was the way she'd come.

She couldn't hear the voices any more, but then she couldn't hear anything at all—nothing but the rain, and the wind, howling all around her like tortured spirits.

Tears of helplessness brimmed in her eyes. She heard Ryan's voice in her head—the way he'd sounded back when he'd warned her: *'The jungle has a way of luring people in and keeping them.'*

No. *No!* How could she have been so stupid? She had to get out. She had to get back to the camp.

She picked up her pace, but in another second her sandal caught on something long and sharp and she fell hard to the ground, smacking her head. She barely had time to yelp or blink before blackness consumed her.

CHAPTER FIFTEEN

'WHERE'S MADELINE?'

Ryan couldn't keep the question in any longer. He'd been back for over an hour and hadn't seen her playing with the kids under the tree or anywhere else, like she usually was. The guitar was still in the dining room where they'd left it, seemingly untouched, which he found odd because she'd seemed pretty excited about playing it and starting to make up songs.

He'd gone for a swim in the lake the moment the rain had eased off, hoping she might be there, but she wasn't.

'I haven't seen her since this morning,' Maria told him, taking the thermometer from the mouth of the kid who was sitting on the table in front of her.

'This morning?'

'First thing. She was up at dawn, before the storm rolled in. Is she not in her tent?'

Ryan's jaw started to pulse. He didn't want to seem overly concerned but something didn't feel right. He left the station and walked across the wet, muddy grass, sparkling with the remnants of the storm. It was gone four p.m. and it would be dark in a few short hours.

Reaching Madeline's tent, he rapped on the canvas door. No reply.

Without hesitation he unzipped it and looked inside.

Her sleeping bag was in a crumpled heap on the mattress. A can of DEET was resting beside it. He straightened up again, swiftly scanning the swaying treeline.

He saw Mark appearing from his own tent, and walked over. 'Have you seen Madeline?'

'No, sir, not since last night.'

'Call everyone into the dining room, now.' Ryan was already walking towards it quickly.

It didn't take long for word to spread and for everyone on camp to gather in the enclosed space. All wore looks of concern, which unnerved him further. Jake, who'd been following him all day as they'd fixed up the man who'd been mauled by a caiman, was still rolling the camera, obviously sensing excitement in the air.

Ryan took off his baseball hat, dashed his hand through his hair as he tried to force his voice to stay controlled. 'Has anyone here seen Madeline Savoia since this morning?' he asked.

Silence.

He could see people looking around them in confusion. The way Mark was looking at Evan almost made him snap. Others were shaking their heads, looking at the floor.

He turned to Maria. 'Maria, did she say anything about where she was going when she left you?'

Maria shrugged, looked helpless. 'Not a lot…but I was busy. I told her the producer wanted to talk to her and—'

'What did she say when you said that?' he asked, hoping to God Madeline hadn't freaked out and let any paranoia over their…*situation*…get the better of her.

'Nothing, really, just that she was fine with it. She sounded perfectly normal—a little tired, maybe…'

'Tired?'

'She said she didn't sleep much.'

Ryan rarely panicked, but he was panicking now. Madeline was exhausted and had obviously wandered off somewhere. That could only lead to bad things in the jungle. Maybe she'd been caught in the storm. Anything could have happened.

'We're splitting up and we're going to find her,' he said resolutely. 'Evan, Mark—go back to the village. Take the sat phones. Maria, go with Pablo to the river, get on the boat and keep your eyes peeled. Take your sat phone, too—everyone take your sat phones…keep in touch…'

Ryan doled out responsibilities, then watched his people hurrying off two by two until he was the only one left—just him and Jake with the camera.

He grabbed some bananas, raced to his tent and lifted his pack, slinging it over his shoulders. 'I'll be right out,' he called to Jake. 'Actually, can you grab some more water and meet me back here?'

'No problem.'

Jake turned back the way they'd come and Ryan took his moment to flee alone.

Anger, fear and dread propelled him forward as he set out on the path, fixing his phone to the belt of his khaki trousers. He'd been in this situation before, and he did *not* need a camera filming his every movement. He did *not* need anyone seeing anything they didn't need to see, if that was what this was going to come to.

He hoped to hell it wasn't.

Josephine's face flashed to the forefront of his mind, bright and smiling, then pale and cold. He bit down hard on the inside of his cheek, fought to keep his breathing steady and his feet treading safely, quickly on the path.

This day wouldn't end up like that one had—not if he

had anything to do with it. It *couldn't*. He couldn't handle it again. He'd barely handled it before. And even now, with the faint glimmer of sunshine that was Madeline on the horizon, those demons were still dancing around him in the darkness, willing him to slip up or break.

He called her name. The air was thick, hot, suffocating.

Keeping tabs on his own whereabouts, he crossed the clearing. His phone buzzed and squawked. He could hear people talking over the radio. His crew were all out there, spread like a spider's web between the trees. The village had their people out now, too, but no one had seen her yet.

He was just about to take another step when he paused in front of an object. He bent down, picked up a toothbrush. It was one of the same branded batch they'd brought with them for the kids. One that Madeline would have had. He shoved it into a pocket.

A shape up ahead caught his eye next. He stopped in his tracks, waiting for it to move.

'Madeline?'

He stepped closer cautiously, adrenaline pumping through him. It was a person—a woman, he realised with sudden nausea—lying still on the ground like a fallen log, rain-soaked and lifeless in an unnatural heap.

Ryan's heart plunged as he hurried to her side. She was facing away from him, and he saw with utter horror the pool of blood spreading like a crimson lake from her stomach out onto the muddy, mossy ground.

He fell to his knees as his very soul seemed to splinter around him.

'Madeline?' A whisper now. His voice barely audible.

Long dark hair was splayed across the woman's face, hiding her features, and he felt like throwing up. He put a hand to her cheek. Cold, clammy. She was gone. He swallowed the sob that rose in his throat. He hadn't deserved her. He knew it. He never had.

He pushed the hair back from her face, ready to haul her into his arms and let grief consume him, but shock froze him as her features came into view. The rounded nose, the plump lips, the thick, bushy eyebrows.

It wasn't Madeline.

This poor woman had been murdered. There was no doubt about that. But she wasn't Madeline.

Ryan stood up quickly and almost stumbled as he reached for his penknife and readied himself to wield it against an attacker. He swiped at his tears, spun around, half expecting a Colombian drug runner to lunge in his direction. But all he could hear was the wind and the birds and the distant howl of a monkey.

With his eyes on the treeline he pulled his sat phone from his belt, radioed in his grim discovery, reading out the GPS location so the crew could come back for her and carried on, on his way, hope his motivation.

The light was fading and the wind was picking up again—like the rain. He knew another shower was on its way and prayed it wouldn't be as bad as the last one. He'd changed course now and was only a few metres back from the river. This was far enough away so that Madeline would never be spotted by Maria and Pablo from the boat, but not so far... Madeline might have gone just a little off track and thought she was further away from camp than she really was.

He let out a silent prayer. The rain started pattering more heavily on his hat and Ryan struggled to keep it together.

'Any luck?' It was Mark on the radio.

'Not yet,' he replied, trying to sound optimistic. 'She can't have gone far.'

But he heard his own voice crack in despair.

It was happening all over again.

He was just about to sink to the ground when he saw her. He almost dropped his phone. She was huddled under a tree, arms wrapped around herself, her eyes closed.

'Madeline!'

He was in front of her in a heartbeat, kneeling on the ground, letting the rain slam into him as he pulled his pack from his back, dropping it next to her.

'Madeline, it's me—look at me.'

He reached his hands to her face, hoping her cheeks wouldn't be as cold as those of the lifeless lady he'd just touched. To his utter relief her eyes fluttered open just a little. There was blood on her head, trickling down her right cheek and onto his hands. She looked dazed.

'What happened?' he asked, scooting even closer to her, inspecting the damage. 'Can you talk? Are you in pain?'

'Ryan?' Recognition flickered in her eyes before they flooded with tears. She reached out to him and wrapped her arms around his shoulders.

She could move, thank God. Her arms were weak but that hug, along with the sound of her voice, was everything he needed in that moment. He held her tight against him for a minute, swallowed more tears in private against her soft neck, then untangled her from him.

'I don't know what the *hell* you were thinking,' he blurted, sweeping her matted hair behind her ears, scanning her eyes, hearing his own voice croak again. 'Didn't I tell you *never* to go anywhere alone out here? Maddy, you could've been *killed*! Didn't I tell you…? Weren't you listening?'

'I'm sorry… I'm so sorry…'

'I could have lost you, too.'

He held her face, pressed his lips to her forehead for a long moment, letting them burn into her skin, breathing in her life at the same time.

'I didn't know what I was going to find.'

'Drug runners,' she whispered, clutching his hand and wincing as she tried to move again. 'I saw them. I think they killed someone, Ryan.'

'I think you're right about that. Now we need to get you cleaned up.'

It looked as though she'd fallen and hit her head at some point. She was covered in mud, too, and had probably dragged herself to the tree after her fall. She was clearly disorientated, and likely dehydrated.

He reached for his pack, pulled out a bottle of water and held it to her mouth. 'You need to drink, Maddy,' he said. 'As much as you can.'

With her eyes closed she did as she was told. Remembering the sat phone, he announced that he'd found her, and told the crew his co-ordinates. As he was talking he noticed that the insect bites on her legs and arms had caused her limbs to swell. She'd obviously come out without DEET on again. Either that or it had been washed off.

He was amazed she wasn't more hurt.

The rain was coming down hard again and Ryan knew it was going to be hell, trying to make it back to camp with her like this. He reached into his pack and pulled out the thin plastic sheet, stood and shook it out. It took him less than two minutes to hang it between three surrounding branches, creating a makeshift shelter. He pulled another sheet out and laid it on the ground, helped her onto it and sat close beside her.

At least they were dry, for now.

'What's that?' she asked, watching him pull tincture from his pack, along with some swabs and gauze.

'Iodine,' he said, holding it up. 'Here, let me look at you. You're still bleeding.'

He placed two fingers under her chin and she balled his shirt in her fists against his chest as he swabbed at the cut on her head, then applied antiseptic.

She screwed up her face. 'Stings,' she said.

'I'm not surprised. Did you pass out?'

'For a bit, I think. I was trying to get away from them. I heard them behind me, then I got lost. I feel like such an idiot. I'm so sorry, Ryan.'

'Not as sorry as *I'd* have been if anything worse had happened to you. You must have lost them, but there's a dead woman not far from here. I think they left her there.'

He started to apply a patch to the wound, but Madeline pulled back, putting a hand over her mouth.

'So they *did* kill someone?'

He nodded grimly. 'I saw her. We're retrieving the body.'

Her eyes were wide. 'I saw them standing around her. I saw a gun.'

'She was stabbed,' he said, grateful again for the miraculous fact that the same fate hadn't befallen her. He pulled a banana out of his pack. 'Eat this—you must be starving.'

He swabbed at some of the blood on her arms and legs with a cloth. Thankfully most of it had come from her head and the rest of her was unharmed except for the bites.

'We'll wait the rain out, then we'll get you back. Why did you walk off on your own?'

'I thought I might be able to help with a case. I thought I heard you talking, but it wasn't you. I can't believe... That poor woman. Why would they do that?'

'Any number of reasons. They make up their own rules out here.'

He pulled her to his side, wrapped an arm around her shoulders protectively as she ate and drank slowly, both of them listening to the rain. As the crickets chirped and the bats started swooping he felt the frantic thudding of his heart finally begin to subside.

'What happened with the guy who got attacked by the caiman?' Madeline asked.

Ryan stretched his legs out on the sheet. 'He wasn't as lucky as you—lost most of one arm. Luckily he had a friend with him who was able to call for help when it happened.'

She grimaced.

'We're just skin and blood and bones in the jungle, I guess,' he said, resting a cheek against her hair. 'We're all the same. We're all just food in a chain. Moving targets.'

'Terrifying, isn't it?' she said softly.

'Terrifying.'

He tightened his arm around her small frame, banishing the thought from his mind that Madeline might have been the one mauled or eaten or shot.

Ryan hadn't even known it was within him to feel so responsible, to feel so...*anything* about anyone, until today. The depth of his feelings now—the way they'd sprung upon him around this woman—was as terrifying as the jungle. But it also made him feel incredibly alive. More alive, perhaps, than he'd felt in five whole years.

CHAPTER SIXTEEN

MADELINE WATCHED THEM bringing the body of the murdered woman into the camp from her place on the bench in the dining room. Through the mesh of the walls she could make out Ryan, Jake and the producer, plus two volunteers carrying the stretcher across the grass.

They'd been informed it was a lady from another village, probably employed to traffic drugs up the river. She tore her eyes away as tears blurred her vision, pulling the blanket around her for comfort. Shock was sinking in now that she was finally safe.

She also felt impossibly idiotic.

She'd never been more relieved to see anyone in her whole life than she had when Ryan had found her under that tree. He'd been angry at first—that much she understood. She could hardly blame him. She'd gone against everything he'd told her when she'd stepped off that path and followed what she'd thought were her instincts.

She knew half of his anger was coming from a place of fear, though: fear of her being hurt. He'd shown her nothing but kindness ever since.

The ibuprofen Ryan had given her had taken some of her aches away, and a soothing gel had stopped her bites from itching. She'd eaten what she could of a plate of white rice and vegetables, but thoughts of what might have happened to her out there kept careening through her mind like a crazy carousel, making her feel sick.

She put her fork down, pushed through the thin mesh door and walked outside to the fire, now blazing.

Maria held an arm out to her, beckoning her to sit next to her on the log. 'Did you eat?' she asked.

'I did, thank you.'

'How are you feeling now?'

'Stupid,' she answered honestly, staring at the flames.

Maria rested her head on her shoulder for a second, then smiled. 'Honey, we all make mistakes. We're just glad you're all right. It's a good thing Ryan sent the search party out when he did. It's just so crazy busy here that things can sometimes get overlooked...'

'It was *his* call to get everyone out looking for me?' she asked. She'd had no clue.

'He was the first to realise no one had seen you in a while.'

When Madeline turned towards Maria she noticed something in the older woman's tired eyes that she hadn't seen before. A slight twinkle.

'You're good for him,' Maria whispered, conspiratorially. 'Whatever it is you're doing, keep doing it.'

Madeline flushed, shook her head, but she didn't have time to respond before she felt a firm hand on her shoulder from behind. The next second Ryan was stepping over the log, crouching down in front of her, his handsome face in shadow, blocking the fire.

'Hey, how's your head now?'

He reached for the bandage over her wound to check it, and instinctively she brought her own up to cover his hand.

'I'll live,' she said, moving his hand down to her lap as he smiled in what looked like relief. Gratitude overwhelmed her. 'I can't thank you enough for coming to find me, Ryan—for sending everyone out to find me. Don't think I'll ever forget that.'

She reached out a hand to Maria, too, and as she looked between them she was flooded with warmth and the purest of appreciation for everything she had. Everything that the poor woman who'd lost her life out there would never have.

'I'm going to go back to nursing when I get home,' she announced. 'I want to finish what I started. For Toby.'

Maria squeezed her hand. Ryan raised his eyebrows as he sat on his haunches and tossed a stick into the fire. 'Good to hear it,' he said.

'You have no idea how inspiring you all are.'

'Well, thank you, honey,' Maria said, sounding pleased and a little embarrassed. 'Who's Toby?'

Madeline ran a hand through her tangled hair. It was weird, but she didn't feel as uncomfortable talking about him any more.

'Toby is the reason I'm here.'

As the words left her mouth she realised it was true. That little boy's death had forced her to run away from her duties...possibly even from her destiny.

She loved writing—she'd stumbled into it and had been blessed to have had adventures all around the world because of it—but it was still a means of escape. And in escaping she'd wound up here.

How strange.

She tilted her head up to the sky, to the stars. Had Toby planned this out? Anything was possible, she supposed. The longer she spent in the jungle, away from technology and crowds and confusing messages coming at her from every which way, the more she felt connected to the universe. The more she resonated with the truths she *couldn't* see.

The only things that were real, she decided, were the things she could hold in her heart.

Ryan was looking at her when she opened her eyes. He got to his feet, helping her to stand. 'You should rest,' he told her, his grey eyes full of concern.

'Goodnight—sleep tight,' Maria said, after giving her a hug, and Madeline didn't miss the surreptitious little wink she threw her in the firelight as Ryan led her away.

'I need a bath,' she said, halfway across the grass, pulling on his hand in the direction of the lake.

He looked back to camp—for the cameras, she assumed. Luckily there were none in sight.

'Come with me? I can't sleep like this.'

'I probably shouldn't,' he said, looking around them again warily.

But she was already guiding him down the path, through the trees and onto the deck. The moon was clear now the rain had gone, sending bright white beams across the black expanse of water so there was no need for a flashlight. The trees rustled overhead and the bats were swooping, catching flies. So peaceful.

She peeled off her shorts, then her muddied tank top, dropping them at her feet. Ryan was standing in front of her, watching her in what looked like wonder while taking off his boots. She smiled at him with newfound confidence, then stepped closer, reached for his shirt and motioned for him to lift his arms. With ease she pulled it over his head, shuddering as his hands landed on her waist and his lips grazed the top of her head.

'You're amazing—do you know that?' he whispered into her hair.

'So are you.'

'Infuriating…'

She grinned. 'So are you.'

'I kind of think I need you, though.'

His bare skin so close to hers sent shockwaves pulsing through Madeline's body. She pressed her hands to his chest, tilted her head up for his kiss, let her fingers trail down towards his khaki trousers and undid them quickly. He slid them off his legs, followed by his boxers. Then, when he'd swiftly undone her bra and tossed it to the side, he got to his knees, naked in front of her, dropped butterfly kisses around her belly button and slid her underwear down past her knees, over her feet and to the floor.

She gasped as he kissed his way back up, lingering on her inner thigh, running his hands up her legs as he did so.

'Let's get in,' he said, reaching for her hand.

They slid off the deck and into the water. Madeline was careful not to dunk her head, and to keep her bandage dry.

The water was a cool, blissful blanket, wrapping around her hot skin as Ryan reached for the bar of soap someone had left on the lakeside. He guided her out a little further, then pulled her back to his chest, kissing her neck from behind as he ran the soap over her chest. She held her arms out and he did the same to them.

The insect bites all over her skin were extra-sensitive, but strangely she found his gentle touch turned the irritation into something almost sensual. Madeline turned in his arms, returning his passionate kisses, and wrapped her legs around his middle. He held her up with ease, kissing her hungrily, and for a moment she wondered what they must look like from afar, chest to chest in the middle of a lake under the moon.

Take the drug runners and the dead body and the fact that she herself might have died today out of the equation and she couldn't help thinking that this was the greatest day of her whole life.

She grinned against his lips in spite of herself.

'What are you thinking?' he asked curiously, trailing the soap up and down her back.

'How life is pure magic,' she said.

He smiled into her eyes. 'That, right there, Madeline, is why I…like you.'

Madeline pressed her lips to his again, drawing him into another deep kiss, running her hands through his wet hair. He'd left a gap before saying 'like'. Had he been going to say something else?

Her heart thudded against his. It was trying its hardest to jump out of her skin. Of course he hadn't, she scolded herself.

She thought about the way she felt about him, the giddy smile he left on her face. She thought about the way he'd held her and helped her today, the way he'd all but forced her to face her fears about performing any kind of medical duty. Ryan had changed her life already…maybe even *saved* her life. And now they were kissing madly like teenagers in a lake, and there was nowhere else on earth she'd rather be…

They gathered up their clothes, and Ryan gave her his shirt to wear. Clutching the rest, they sneaked back the way they'd come, making absolutely certain not to be seen. There wasn't any discussion about where they'd be sleeping. Ryan simply looked around one more time outside his tent, unzipped the canvas door and motioned for her to crawl inside.

He crawled in after her, zipped up the door again behind them, and in a second it was just the two of them in the tiny enclosed space. Madeline's heart was doing back-flips.

He flattened out the sheets on his mattress accommodatingly, so she could lie down, then leaned over her on one arm and inspected her head. Just his palm against her cheek, then against the back of her head, had her breathing more heavily again in a second.

'We should change the dressing on that,' he said, reaching behind him for his bag.

She sat up and he pulled her legs around him so she was straddling him, and in the light of his flashlight he carefully reapplied the bandage over her cut with the skill she'd seen a hundred times on all those on-line videos.

Starstruck, she thought, *and at the mercy of his nimble fingers*. She *was* starstruck, but it was more than that now. He was a different person from the man she'd literally fallen into back in London. To her he was anyway.

When he was done he turned the light off, plunging them into darkness once again. Madeline reached her hands to his stubbled jaw, stroked his face and dropped kisses onto the edges of his mouth.

'Thank you,' she whispered.

Her legs wrapped more tightly around him of their own accord. In less than twenty seconds he somehow removed his shirt from her damp body, and everything from himself. Carefully he lowered her onto her back on the sheets, traced his fingers around her collarbone and down her stomach with a touch so light it left her skin a mass of tingles.

'How are you feeling now?' he asked, replacing his fingers with his lips and trailing kisses along her skin, back up to her mouth.

Madeline wrapped her arms around him from beneath, pulling him closer. 'Better, Doctor,' she breathed. 'A little bit better every second, actually.'

He continued his kissing trail, teasing her, driving her crazy. By the time he reached her inner thighs she was practically about to explode, but he stopped every now and then, found her lips again, and then let her flip him onto his back and sit astride him.

Madeline knew she had him in the palm of her hands…literally.

He groaned.

'Shh,' she teased, pulling away and flattening her hands against his chest, tracing his muscles, relishing every sinewy stretch of his amazing body. She was conscious suddenly that the wall separating their antics from the outside world was a millimetre thick and not exactly soundproof.

'It's pretty hard to be quiet when you're doing that,' he growled, and she pressed her lips to his again, silencing him.

The tent was hot, and already their bodies were melding together as one with perspiration. The bugs were still singing in the night outside. The wind whipped about the canvas every now and then like a jealous lover trying to get in. Her head was starting to hurt again, where she'd fallen, but when Ryan reached for his bag again and unwrapped a condom Madeline was beyond caring about *anything*.

'You carry these?' she asked in surprise, taking it from him and rolling it on.

He put his hands to her waist, lifted her with ease and flipped her onto her back again.

'Not for me,' he said in a low voice, resting on his hands either side of her and sucking on her lower lip for a second.

She moaned quietly as desire rocketed through her.

'Sometimes the crew need them. Sometimes we give them to the teenagers.'

'How generous,' she said, kissing him deeply as her legs encircled him from beneath once more.

She lost herself in their kiss again, in their twirling tongues and clashing teeth and soft moans and groans, until she gasped, biting on her own hand.

'Does it hurt?' he said softly, pausing, stroking her hair against the thin pillow.

'No, don't be silly. I just don't want to scream.'

'They'll just think you've seen a spider.'

'Very funny.'

'Seriously, Madeline, you feel incredible.'

Tears sprang to her eyes from out of nowhere and she wished it wasn't quite so dark. She was beyond exhausted and yet she was making love to Ryan Tobias—slowly, gently, beautifully in their own little bubble. There was so much admiration in his words and in his tone she felt it settle into her skin, deep into her bones.

He took his time, being careful not to hurt her any further after her ordeal, she was sure, but the result of his concern was something so passionate, so sensual she had literally never made love quite like it. Whatever he wasn't saying he was showing as he stroked and caressed her, kissed her everywhere he could reach over and over and over.

She reciprocated, of course, limited only by the space in the tent, and when Madeline woke up the next morning with his arms wrapped tightly around her she couldn't even remember when they'd finally stopped—or how, or why, or in which position. All she knew was that she'd never felt so worshipped in her whole life.

She also knew she was probably in deep trouble.

CHAPTER SEVENTEEN

RYAN WAS STANDING outside the medical station watching Madeline strumming the guitar under a tree. Her made-up songs were proving a hit. He couldn't be sure but he thought that right now she was singing something about cars on motorways, in Spanish. At any rate, the kids were squealing and singing along as if they'd never heard anything so fantastic.

He smiled, quashing the urge to walk over and join in. Of course hiding their relationship...or whatever it was that had blossomed between them since their first amazing night together in his tent...had not been easy.

Luckily they spent enough time together professionally to warrant her hanging out with him in the lake, and in his hammock, and in the boat on the river without too much need for explanation.

The boat had become a favourite of theirs. They liked to take a couple of blankets out with them, fish for piranhas and talk under the stars. Then they'd spend long hours making love to the sounds of the jungle, with the sighs of each other's pleasure mingling with the wind.

He pushed his hand into his pocket, remembering that first morning he'd woken up with his chest glued to her back with sweat. Instead of feeling panicked, he'd felt remarkably calm. Maddy had entered his life like a hurricane, but somehow settled like a soft blanket of snow, silencing everything, instilling peace amongst the chaos of his busy mind.

The short weeks since they'd been strangers were blurred in his head now; all he knew was the curve of her smile, the feel of her soft tongue dancing circles with his, the sound of her laugher.

'She adores them,' Maria said, appearing next to him from the tent and nudging his shoulder. 'She's going to find it hard to leave them, I'll bet.'

He straightened, sipped from his water bottle, suddenly aware that he'd been staring at Madeline—probably with a sappy look on his face.

'I'm sure she will,' he said, clearing his throat and screwing the bottle cap back on. 'She'll miss them a lot.'

'They're not the only ones, it seems,' she added, nudging him again, and then slipping back into the medical station with a new patient before he could respond.

He frowned to himself.

No one had asked any questions—although admittedly he hadn't missed the looks and the little comments thrown his way by Maria, Mark and Evan.

Aside from their affair, though, Ryan was rather enjoying watching a transformation occur in Madeline. She was more determined than ever to return to her position at St David's Hospital once she got home, so was spending even more time with the kids, helping them read in English and assisting in as many medical duties concerning them as possible. She was soaking it all up like a sponge.

And at night they soaked each other up, wherever and whenever they could, for as long as humanly possible, until they fell asleep exhausted.

Last night had been no exception. She'd found him in the hammock after dinner in the twilight.

'Are you really reading my book?' she'd asked, taking the e-reader from his hands.

Her hair had been damp from a previous swim—a swim he'd had to let her take alone, thanks to a visit from the wife of the man who'd been attacked by a caiman—she'd bought him a thank-you box of fruit. More bananas...

'Of course I'm reading it. I like it,' he'd told her truthfully. 'You have quite a way with words.'

'Well, I should hope so. I'm a writer,' she'd said, taking the Kindle from him and climbing into the hammock alongside him.

It had stretched almost to the floor with their weight, and she had smiled contentedly with her head against his chest.

'Lucky this is the king of all hammocks,' she'd said.

He'd laughed, peeling the strap of her tank top away from her shoulder and kissing her soft, warm flesh. When darkness had fallen they'd made love right there in the hammock—a feat he hadn't even known was entirely possible.

Ryan had never been so turned on in his life than he had been by the sight of Madeline, sliding her underwear off beneath her sundress, raising her arms above him to clutch at the mesh, and she'd relished every moan he'd let slip from his mouth as she worked him up and then slowed her pace again, then sped up, driving him crazy.

He'd almost forgotten to keep an eye on the treeline for the crew, and for Jake with his damn camera, but they'd grown good at multi-tasking by now—and besides, he was in too deep to care.

He watched her now, putting the guitar down on the

grass between the kids, strolling over towards him. His heart leapt and he rolled his eyes at himself.

Way too deep, he repeated internally. There was no way out either.

He was considering asking her to accompany him on another shoot…in a medical capacity, of course. They were headed for Peru in a couple of weeks, and after that to Bali. Maybe she could extend her deadline for the memoir.

The memoir she still hadn't finished because of him.

He silenced the thought.

'Hey,' she said, stopping in front of him.

Her hair was pulled back into a ponytail and he saw the faint red outline of the mark on her head from where she'd fallen. It had healed nicely in his care.

'Hey,' he said back, meeting her eyes and feeling that familiar rush of adrenaline shoot through his veins. He was still getting used to the feelings she stirred in him—a reawakening of sorts.

'We're wrapping up for the morning. Now I need another interview with you,' she said, biting on her lip.

He raised his eyebrows, appraising her in her green dress, seeing the way it was already sticking to her sexily in the heat.

'Do you think you'll have time for a quick one?'

He knew what *that* meant, and as usual he was a moth to her flame. 'Can we do it in the waterfall?' he asked, stifling a smile.

She was struggling to keep the laughter off her face, but it was shining in her eyes. 'I'd *love* to do it in the waterfall.'

'Great.' He called out to Maria. 'I'm taking a break!'

Luckily he'd put his board shorts on under his scrubs…

They walked a metre apart from one another across

camp, until they reached another clearing. One of the local guys had introduced them all to the secret waterfall just a ten-minute walk along a hidden path the last time they'd been here, and as soon as they were out of sight of anyone from camp he wrapped his arms around Madeline, picked her up and ran the rest of the way, jumping over the branches and piles of fallen leaves on the way.

She laughed as her arms latched around his neck. 'You just *love* to feel like Tarzan out here, don't you?'

'What makes you say that?' he said, putting her down on the grassy slope that led down to the pool and beating his chest as he faced the water.

He watched her peeling off the green dress, revealing her purple bikini as she waded into the cool, murky pool. She was being careful not to step on the sharp rocks, just as they'd been shown. The pool was only ten or so metres wide, but the water rolling dramatically off the high rocks above it was pretty much the perfect disguise for the sounds of mutual enjoyment.

He knew that *she* knew that was what he hoped was about to happen now. She was teasing him, though.

'I meant it when I said I needed another interview,' she said, turning back to him and observing him ditching his shorts.

Her eyes never left his naked body in the sunlight as he followed her into the water.

'I know you've been avoiding the subject—putting me to work on other things, thinking I'll forget what I really came here to do. It's what you've been doing all along.'

She pulled her long hair from its ponytail and ran her hands through it. Then she dipped into the water and floated on her back. *Damn*, she was sexy as hell.

'That's not entirely true,' he said, meeting her in the

middle and running a hand up her leg, letting his fingers brush the soft fabric of her bikini bottoms.

He'd tease her for a few minutes at least, he thought, before lifting her up onto one of the flat, long rocks behind the falls and using the rest of their 'break' in a very constructive fashion.

She didn't move—didn't respond to his touch in the way he'd been hoping she would. Instead she spun round and wrapped her legs around his stomach, pulling him in. He was trapped, completely in her control, and he liked it.

'You know, it won't be long before we leave this place,' she said, moving her arms around his neck.

'You want to talk about that? What happens next… away from the Amazon?' he asked, ignoring the caution in her voice and what he knew was inevitably coming.

He moved his hands to her bottom and pulled her even closer, dropped a lingering kiss on her lips.

'I've been thinking about it, Maddy. You and me. The future.'

'You have?'

'Of course I have. In case you hadn't noticed, I think you're kind of OK.'

She smiled playfully. 'I think *you're* kind of OK, too—in a weird, moody way. But that's not what we need to talk about right now and you know it.'

He sighed, trying not to show his frustration. Something was ready for action, and he wanted to make love to her right here and now, but he could see he'd have to earn that privilege.

'Talk to me, Ryan. Talk to me about Josephine.'

His chest tightened at the sound of her name. He swam with Madeline's legs and arms still around him over to the waterfall, dipped them both under the surface and brought them up again behind the falls.

'I told you—I don't want to talk about that.'

She let him go, put her feet to the ground and swept her mass of wet hair back over her shoulders. The water was rolling off her eyelashes, down her nose.

'Ryan, not telling me what happened with her feels the same as you lying to me, somehow.'

He pressed his back to the rocks. 'It's *not* the same, I haven't lied to you, Maddy—not once.'

'It *feels* like you have. Why can't you talk about Josephine? *Why?* This has been going on long enough.'

'Don't say her name—and don't write her name in this memoir, please,' he said, closing his eyes again and raking his hands through his wet hair.

'Forget the memoir.'

'What do you mean, forget the memoir?'

'Ryan, it's *me* you're talking to.'

He curled his fists to his sides, dunked down in the water to his neck as Madeline floated in front of him with the cascade of the waterfall behind her.

So many damn questions. Why the hell couldn't she just be a nurse…a normal goddamn nurse with no ulterior motives…a nurse he could hold flat against these rocks and lose himself in completely?

He opened his eyes as he felt her straddling him again, sitting across his lap under the water.

'Forget the book,' she said again, against his lips. 'I'm going back to nursing anyway.' She bunched tufts of his wet hair in her hands.

'I see. So I tell you all my secrets off the record, and then what? You write them down anyway?'

Madeline was silent.

'They're pretty juicy. We'd definitely get a bestseller you wouldn't be able to resist.'

He put his hands to her waist, but she shoved them away.

'Do you *really* think I would do that to you?' Her voice was furious now.

She started clambering off his lap but he pulled her back to him.

'Plenty would. Think of the money.'

'Seriously? Is *that* the kind of person you think I am? You think I'd get involved with you to get some *secret* out of you for my own benefit? Let me go!'

She went to clamber off him again, but he reached a hand to the back of her neck and pulled her head against his, pinning her in place.

'You're sexy when you're mad.'

'That's insulting. Get your hands *off* me!'

'You *like* my hands on you—remember?'

He pressed his lips to hers and she groaned, kissing him back for a moment, letting her arms move around his shoulder blades. But all too soon she pushed him away again, putting a hand to her mouth as if to block him from trying anything else.

She shook her head, her face still only an inch from his. 'No. I can't do this. Do you think because you're some kind of celebrity I'll just take whatever part of you I can get?'

'Of course I don't… Come on, I was kidding.'

'This is *serious*. I want to finish this memoir for *you*—so you can be *free*, Ryan! So you can put this whole thing to rest the way *you* want to by telling the story. I don't have to write it at all—we both know I don't!'

'Then don't.'

'Fine, I won't. But will you still tell me what happened with Josephine?'

'I…' He closed his mouth. He couldn't read her.

'Tell me right now. Tell me because you *trust* me, Ryan. And because you want a future with me. You just said that's what you want. And I'd rather have you than some book that's not even in my name!'

His head was spinning. Josephine's face was right in front of him now, in his mind, laughing, smiling. Then crying. Then cold and lifeless. His fault. *His fault.*

'If you can't trust me we can't be together. There is no future for us. We can't do…*this*!' She gestured around them.

Her face changed—hardened as if she was battling something internally.

'I'm going to ask them to fly me out of here early.'

A laugh spluttered out of him suddenly. 'Right!'

Her expression hardened further.

He stared at her for a second, feeling panic start to rise. 'You can't just leave,' he said, watching her push through the falls. He followed quickly.

'There's no point in me being here one second longer. You've been pushing me and pushing me, Ryan, but you won't give an inch yourself!'

'I've given you plenty of inches,' he said, too quickly, but she wasn't laughing at his jokes any more. 'Maddy, listen. I want to give you everything, I really do. You deserve that. But…'

'But—there's always a *but*. You won't let me in— you won't tell me anything that matters. I feel like you won't share the *real* you! You can't keep leading people on and then pushing them away when closeness gets inconvenient for you, Ryan.'

'I just… It will change the way you think of me.'

'No, it won't.'

'Yes, it will, Maddy…'

'Then don't try and stop me when I go.'

She turned again and he watched helplessly as she gathered up her clothes and hurried up the path. He floated onto his back, breathing deeply, anger pulsing through his body.

If he followed, he'd cause a scene on camp.

Was she testing him?

He counted to ten. Then twenty. Anger turned to apathy. Then confusion. Then back to anger and then fear. He counted to twenty all over again, floated there, festering in his own thoughts, for what felt like hours.

In reality it was probably only half an hour. Then, feeling like a total idiot, he swam so hard back through the water he practically dislocated his shoulders.

The second he pushed through the trees to camp a young volunteer with a name badge reading 'Raul' ran up to him, looking panicked and out of breath.

'There you are! Everyone's been looking for you.'

Crap.

'What's happened?' He was only wearing board shorts—suspiciously dry, he realised, after his 'swim'.

He started walking towards his tent with Raul scurrying at his side.

'Emergency up river. They think it's the drug runners again. We heard gunshots and everyone left…'

'What?' He stopped for a second. This was insane. 'Everyone's gone?'

'Pretty much,' Raul said. 'I was told to wait here for you. We need to set up in case they bring people back. They could only take limited supplies with them.'

Ryan reached his tent, unzipped the door and threw his shirt inside as dread settled around him, making his stomach sink. 'I'll meet you at the station.'

Raul sped off and Ryan bent to crawl inside. He stopped almost instantly. Madeline was emerging from her own tent, complete with her bags. She was fully dressed—boots and all.

Panic seized his heart. 'Madeline?'

She ignored him, started walking quickly across the grass towards the path to the river, swinging her heavy pack over her shoulder as she went.

He ran after her. 'Where are you going?'

'I've arranged for a boat to take me back to Saint Elena.' Her voice was steely, cold as ice.

'Now?' He was incredulous.

'Yes, now.'

'Do you know what has just *happened*?'

'I do, and I'm sorry, but I need to get out of here, Ryan.'

He caught her arm. He was still just in his board shorts, no shoes on his feet, no shirt. He felt powerless. 'Don't go, Maddy. Not now.'

'Don't make this any harder, please, Ryan.' Tears glistened in her eyes but she swiped them away defiantly. 'This is the best time for me to go. No cameras…no one asking questions.'

They were on the pathway now. He could see the river through the trees. The local guys she often talked with were sitting in the boat, laughing about something, waiting for her. What the hell was going on? His world had folded in on itself in a matter of seconds. She couldn't just leave everyone…she couldn't just leave *him*.

'Madeline—'

He shut his mouth the second he'd said her name, let

out a yelp, then an anguished cry. He staggered backwards, then pushed her away so hard she fell down, weighted by her pack.

'Don't move,' he managed, and looked back just in time to see the long, thick-scaled, stripy brown and black snake he'd stepped on slithering away into the undergrowth.

'Did it bite you?' Madeline was scrambling to her feet in the dirt. Her eyes were on the tail end of the snake. 'Oh, my God, did it get you?'

Her voice was shaky. She shook off her pack and was at his side in a second, hands on his shoulders as he sank to the ground.

'Ryan!'

'It got me,' he said, sucking in a breath. 'Surucucu. Madeline, I need the anti-venom.'

He doubled over for a second. The pain was shooting up his leg already. Madeline stood up quickly, calling to the guys near the boat.

'Help! Over here, please!'

'They won't be able to help me…you need to go back to the camp…find Raul.' The guys were already running from the river towards them. '*Go*, Madeline!'

'OK, hold on—OK.' She kissed him quickly on the mouth. 'I'm so sorry…just hold on. I'll be right back!'

She pushed her pack towards him so he could rest on it and sped off back down the path.

On the ground, Ryan grabbed his bare foot and studied the two fang marks just above his ankle. He winced in pain. Sweat had broken out all over his body. The Surucucu's venom took less than two hours to finish someone off. He'd seen it before—the after-effects on soft tissue at least. The venom was a powerful haemotoxin and, thanks to some of the longest fangs on any snake, it had been injected deep into his bloodstream.

He sucked in another breath, tried to focus.

But he knew in his gut that he was running out of time.

CHAPTER EIGHTEEN

'HELP!' MADELINE RAN into the clearing. 'Raul! Anyone?'

She was panicked, desperate, but silence greeted her. Everyone was gone. Raul, too, it seemed. She spun around, calling out again, but clearly no one heard her because no one came.

Ryan's face flashed to the forefront of her mind. He'd turned ashen so quickly. The fang marks on his ankle had been deep and pronounced. It wasn't good and it was all *her* fault. She'd caused him to run after her barefoot, she'd been acting stupidly and melodramatically, and now... Now there was no one to help her or Ryan.

She called out again, shaking like a leaf.

Please, please, please...

Then she remembered something. Ryan had antivenom. He'd shown it to her the first night they'd got here. He'd even shown her how to apply it—not that she'd wanted to know.

She raced to his tent, pulled it open, threw herself inside and grabbed his bag.

Adrenaline propelled her forward, back the way she'd come.

'Hold on, hold on...' she said two minutes later, dropping to his side on the ground and resting her hand on his knee. He looked grey. He was leaning on her pack. 'Stay with me, Ryan! Can you hear me?'

Two guys from the river were sitting either side of him, holding his arms.

'We should not move him,' they told her in Spanish. 'We don't want the venom to spread.'

'OK, hold him steady.'

His eyes were heavy, drooping now. Sweat was glistening on his forehead and the snakebite was swollen, making his leg look twice its size. He clutched her hand for a second. He could barely speak, she could tell. She tried to stay calm, desperately channelling her inner nurse.

'I've got your bag,' she told him, pulling her hand away and opening it up in front of her. The contents spilled to the ground. 'Tell me how to help you, Ryan.'

'Anti-venom,' he mumbled. He was clearly struggling to keep his eyes open.

'I know, but which one?'

Madeline stared at the vials and tubes, the syringes and creams and containers. She recognised the anti-venoms, but there were several, all intended for different bites. She held one up to show him.

'This one?' she said.

He shook his head weakly, trying and failing to focus on the spread on the floor.

'This one?' she said, holding up another and reading from the label.

He shook his head yet again. The effort of not letting fear consume her was in itself threatening to make her crumble. He was deteriorating by the second.

'It's not there,' he managed slowly. He sucked in his breath, as if it pained him to speak.

'Then where *is* it?'

Madeline almost swore, but then realisation struck her like lightning. She cursed at herself. *She* had it— herself. She had put it in her pack that night to keep it safe, after he'd left it in her tent. She'd been intending to give it back to him but she'd forgotten. It was still in the pocket of her pack—which Ryan was now leaning on.

She reached behind him and motioned to the guys to keep him as still as possible while she pulled at the zippers on the pockets. Opening the one on the side, she pulled out the chain with the apple on it that Jason had given her. She'd forgotten to put it back on weeks ago. Then she found the vial she'd shoved in there that night and held it up to him, putting a hand to his clammy face.

'This one? Ryan, please tell me it's this one?'

'Yes,' he managed, wincing again. 'Do it.'

'Me? No, Ryan, you'll have to do it yourself.'

Madeline fumbled to unwrap a syringe. Her mind was screaming at her not to do this. What if it didn't work? What if she didn't do it properly and… God forbid…he died? He was semi-conscious, but *he* could do it. He knew how.

She pulled the top off the vial with trembling fingers and loaded the syringe. The guys were watching her with fear in their eyes.

Ryan reached for her hand. 'You have to do this, Maddy, Stick it right here.'

His breathing was laboured. His eyes kept closing as he held his arm out to her and pointed to a spot in the crease of his elbow. One of the guys held it in place.

'I trust you.'

She had no choice. He was growing greyer by the second.

Madeline took his arm, studied the place he was pointing at for the blue of a vein. 'OK, here goes.'

And before she could think any more about it she stuck the syringe into him and emptied the entire vial.

The next few minutes were a blur. The volunteer, Raul, appeared behind her, hot and flustered. He'd heard her calling, he said, but he'd had his hands full, shifting equipment around, and when he'd tried to find her she had disappeared. He radioed for help, explaining that they now had to get Ryan to the Cessna, which would be waiting for them on the runway when they got up river.

Along with the two local guys, Raul helped to carry Ryan to the boat. He'd passed out.

'Is he going to be OK?' Madeline asked, barely bothering to hide the devastation from her voice as she climbed in alongside them with her bag.

What if she'd got the anti-venom into him too late? What if he didn't make it? What if she lost him?

She couldn't bear it. This jungle was a nightmare—a total nightmare.

'He's just exhausted from trying to stay conscious,' Raul explained. 'We need to get him to the hospital. You probably saved his life, though.'

Tears of relief sprang to her eyes—but he wasn't out of the woods yet, she could tell.

Madeline clung to Ryan's hand as they laid him on the bottom of the boat. He looked like a shadow of his handsome self…so weak and vulnerable. 'I'm so sorry,' she whispered to him as her heart broke, and she crouched beside him, leaning over him, stroking his face.

Raul was frowning, looking at them as he spoke into his radio, and in the back of her mind Madeline knew she was raising suspicion—not that none had been raised concerning the two of them up to this point, she was sure.

She put a hand to his heart now, leant down and

kissed him. *Who cares? So what?* This was her fault. If anything worse happened to this man she knew without a doubt that she would never, ever forgive herself.

CHAPTER NINETEEN

PAIN. THAT WAS all he could feel. Pain and a tightness in his chest that felt a lot as if someone had stomped on him. A nurse was filling in some papers beside him when he opened his eyes, but a millisecond later he noticed someone else in the room, sitting on a plastic chair in the corner beneath the harsh, artificial light.

'Maddy,' he croaked.

He was weak. His leg and foot were bandaged, and he was wearing an ugly white gown, but he was alive. He had *her* to thank for that.

He saw her eyes flutter open, watched her rub them sleepily.

'She never left your side, Dr Ryan,' the elderly nurse said in a thick Portuguese accent, touching a hand to his shoulder as Madeline approached them. 'How do you feel?'

'Yes, how do you feel?' Madeline echoed, concern etched all over her features.

She was extraordinarily tanned, he realised now, in this brand-new setting away from the jungle. She was thinner, too, but so, so beautiful. He didn't deserve her.

'I'm OK,' he replied, looking into her sea-green eyes, feeling far from it.

Madeline reached for his hand and they both watched the nurse walk out of the room and shut the door.

'I owe you my life,' he said as soon as she was gone.

'Then I guess we're even.' She smiled, pulling his hand up to her mouth and kissing the back of it. 'I'm so glad you're OK.' Her eyes were tired and watery. Her hair was piled on the top of her head. 'You scared me, Ryan. I'm so sorry…if I hadn't been acting so crazy—'

'You had every right to act like that,' he interrupted, patting the bed at his side. 'I pushed you to it.'

She sat down. In the harsh light everything seemed clearer, somehow. His thoughts, her actions, the words he knew he had to say… She'd been right before. It had been going on long enough.

'Josephine was in love with me,' he said, before he could think any further.

Madeline's eyes widened, but she didn't let go of his hand. 'I had a feeling she might have been,' she whispered.

Ryan kept his voice steady and low, reliving the memories as he spoke and ploughing onwards anyway. 'But I didn't love *her*, Maddy, not in the same way.'

He moved his eyes to the spotless white ceiling as shame washed through him, as usual.

'We'd been dating in secret for a while—it was all kind of spontaneous and fun, you know? We argued about it…the fact that I could never admit we were a couple. We were arguing when she ran off…that's *why* she ran off.'

'What happened?'

Madeline's eyes were watery, he could see, but she wasn't clearing away her tears. Her fingers were gripping his like a vice.

'She ran into the damn jungle…got herself lost. We couldn't find her.'

'Oh, my God, Ryan…'

'It took four days. She didn't mean for it to happen… she was emotional and she got lost, ended up injuring herself, probably stumbling around in the maze of the jungle. By the time we found her there had been too much blood loss and no one could save her.'

He closed his eyes, feeling his hand grow hotter in hers. He couldn't even expand on the blood loss—it was still too raw.

'Mark and Even knew about us. They warned me to keep things quiet—they didn't want any extra attention from the media affecting the team—and of course I agreed with that. I didn't want the attention either. And then, when it happened…'

'I can imagine!'

'There were so many interviews, Maddy. Josephine didn't have any close family, or much of a life outside the crew, but obviously the world wanted to know what had happened to her. It was too late to tell the whole truth—that we'd been sleeping together and the reason she'd run away was because we'd been arguing about our relationship status, of all things… How could I admit that being with her in the first place had been a mistake on my part? I loved the fun we were having, but not enough to tell the world we were a couple. She thought we'd get married. But I was twenty-seven…she was twenty-eight.'

'Ryan, it's OK. I won't write any of this down, I swear.'

'I'm an asshole.'

'You're not—you were young. You just got carried away. You would have done the right thing in the end if you didn't want to marry her. You would have broken it off and gone your separate ways. Neither of you knew she was going to get lost, or what was going to happen in the jungle. People make mistakes. You have to forgive yourself. You *have* to let this go.'

'How can I?'

Madeline put a hand to his face, forced him to look at her. 'Just *choose* to, Ryan. Please. Just *choose* to forgive yourself. You get to start again. You get to be in love for *real*, if you want. You get to say I love you and mean it, and you get to hear it back. You don't have to deny yourself anything out of guilt or shame. I know that's what you've been doing.'

His heart lurched as she leaned in and kissed him softly on the lips, stroking his cheek and stubble. He leaned into her hand.

'I can imagine how awful that must have been for you,' she said. She touched her nose to his. 'It doesn't change the fact that I love you.'

He froze.

Madeline pulled back to meet his eyes as the silence stretched on and on and on. He watched her face change as the words played over and over in his head. Why couldn't he reply? Why couldn't he say anything?

He cleared his throat, searching her eyes. His head was spinning. 'Maddy, I…' He trailed off, letting the words hover in the space between them like heavy weights, waiting for someone to catch them.

And then he left those words to drop and burn themselves out as Evan and Mark entered the room with pretty much the entire crew of *Medical Extremes* and another cameraman.

They had balloons.

CHAPTER TWENTY

Three weeks later

MADELINE STARED OUT at the cold London rain. So different from the rain in the Amazon, she thought. The rain there had been harsh, but warm, and when it ended its assault it would trade places willingly with the sun, sending apologies down in hot white beams. Here it was just endless and mean, and the grey skies held no promise of swooping blue butterflies or lovemaking trysts with Ryan Tobias in waterfalls.

'Coffee?' the waitress asked, stopping at her table with a pot of sloshing brown liquid.

'Sure—thanks.' Madeline held out her cup.

Maybe coffee would cure her writer's block. She was stuck on how to end the memoir. She had over ninety thousand words already, and had thrown herself into writing pretty much the moment the plane had touched down in London. She'd had to—not least because Samantha was already on her back for the manuscript.

Typing about him every day, putting his history together like puzzle pieces on the page, was sheer torture. She missed him as she'd miss a vital organ—felt as if someone had amputated a limb. She couldn't get his face out of her head, nor his words when he'd finally opened up to her in that hospital room.

She remembered what he'd told her, word for haunting word, but knew she could never write it down. Of course she couldn't. Instead her mind played over the words she'd had to swallow when the team had walked in with their balloons.

Balloons. Ryan needed more than balloons to take his pain away. But he didn't *want* anyone to take his pain away—that was the problem. He thought he was destined to live out his days alone, racked with guilt about Josephine. He hadn't loved Josephine. And he'd refused to let anyone love *him* ever since.

Maybe he would never love anyone. Maybe he'd forgotten what love was.

She picked up her coffee, stared out at the honking traffic, thinking back over the flight she'd taken back home from Rio, knowing he was still there in that hospital the whole time. Knowing it was probably over between them. Knowing she was speeding further and further away from him in every sense.

Even so, she needed a better ending for him—something to inspire joy in other people the way he had in her.

Madeline had been accepted back at St David's and was already picking up where she'd left off. The same faces with the same smiles had been so understanding, so welcoming and helpful. She almost felt as though she'd never left.

Almost.

She put her cup down, sank back against the booth and let her eyes fall on the blank page on her screen. Her writing skills were all she had to give Ryan now, and she couldn't let them all be for nothing. She had no clue how she was going to finish the memoir, but she knew she had to find a way. She could write, and she could help others, and with more book deals at her fingertips—if she ever had time outside her nursing duties—she had the power to combine both.

She knew in her heart that she wasn't the same nurse who'd left St David's after Toby had died. An indelible line had been drawn between the old her and the new one. The new Madeline had taken risks and chances, had put herself in the line of fire and witnessed incredible things. The new Madeline had survived seemingly endless days on rice and fruit, learned how to trust in her own abilities and instincts, gained the respect of a tribe of children who sang from their hearts about the simplest of life's precious gifts, like butterflies and bananas and toothbrushes.

The new Madeline had felt love of the highest, most soul-splintering kind, spilling into her heart and filling the spaces there. She'd been lifted and bolstered by it—so much so that its absence hadn't killed her. She was still kind of floating. Perhaps a little bruised and unsure, but definitely grateful for a taste of what she now knew was out there.

Maybe she could find it again with someone else.

CHAPTER TWENTY-ONE

RYAN PUSHED THROUGH the door, feeling sweat break out on his forehead as soon as he stopped short under the bright, unforgiving lights. A woman in a tracksuit and neon pink sneakers seemed to recognise him instantly. Her eyes widened and she stopped in her tracks, looking as though she was about to race over to him in excitement.

Ryan held up his hand and hurried on past, pulling his baseball hat down further over his forehead.

He'd tossed and turned last night in his hotel room, debating whether or not to come, but Mark and Evan had finally sat him down at breakfast, shoved a black coffee under his nose and then given him another, perhaps even more effective wake-up call.

'She's the best thing that's ever happened to you!'

'With all due respect, Ryan, don't screw this up!'

'You *know*?' he'd said, feigning surprise.

You couldn't live that closely with people and not understand that they'd know when you were hiding something.

'It's been written all over your face ever since you first set eyes on each other. You're the smartest guy in the field, Ryan, but really you're an idiot.'

This room smelled of astringent fluids and the shiny

floor squeaked under his sneakers. Anxiety crept tighter around him like a rope. Seeing a reception desk, he made his way over. A girl of about twenty-one with a name badge reading 'Trudy' looked up, then did a double-take.

'Oh,' she said when he met her eyes. 'You.'

'I'm looking for Nurse Madeline Savoia. I was told she's here today?'

'Um…yeah…um…lemme just look that up…' Trudy trailed off, dropping a pen to the floor as she scrambled nervously for some papers.

Ryan tried not to smile and rested an arm on the counter. He was still getting used to people acting this way around him again. No one in the Amazon gave a toss who he was as long as he could help when someone needed him. If only the whole world cared more about those things…

He looked around him as a flummoxed Trudy scanned her computer screen. People in scrubs were walking alongside kids of all ages in gowns with dress-ings and gauzes. Parents and other relatives were mill-ing about, lost in their phones and magazines. An elderly man was wiping up a coffee spillage by a vending ma-chine. A young couple each holding a pile of kids' books looked at him with vague recollection, presumably try-ing to figure out where they'd seen him.

In his Red Sox shirt and jeans, Ryan looked like any other regular guy. Well, maybe an American. He won-dered what people would do when they found out what he was planning—just as soon as he could locate Mad-eline.

'She's on Peter Pan Ward… No, sorry…they moved her group to Elephant and Giraffe today.' Trudy was beetroot-red now, fiddling with the braid that she'd pulled across her shoulder.

'Sorry?' he said. 'Elephant and Giraffe?'

Was this some kind of zoo?

'It's the haematology/oncology department.' She stood up, pointing a manicured finger down the hall-way. 'She should still be there somewhere, if you go through those doors and take a right.'

'Right. Thank you.'

'Wait—Ryan, can you please sign this? I really love *Medical Extremes*…it's, like, my favourite show. And my mum's, too.' She pushed a piece of paper and a blue pen onto the desk, blushing even more.

'What's your mum's name?' he asked, taking the pen. He figured he needed all the good karma he could get.

'Sandy.'

He signed the paper—*To Sandy, love Ryan*—and added a heart, throwing Trudy a wink he knew would make her day.

Then, before anyone else could approach him, he walked quickly down the corridor and hurried through the double doors.

His thoughts were a washing machine on spin cycle as he walked the length of the ward, narrowly missing being struck by a toddler on a tiny tricycle. He'd never been this nervous in his life.

It had been the longest few weeks ever since she'd left him in that hospital in Rio. Her face had haunted him…that look in her eyes as he'd choked on his reply to her confession.

Fear had started rolling over him like waves from a tsunami the second she'd said what she had.

Did she *really* love him? Did he love *her*?

He'd watched her leave that hospital room, felt the ball of knots twist tighter in his stomach. Mark and Evan and everyone else had crowded around him with the balloons and he'd said nothing—just watched the back of her head and her hand sweep across her hidden face as she'd turned towards the door.

He'd needed to get his head around it. When they'd all gone, however, Ryan had felt as alone in that busy hospital as he had in the middle of the jungle at night. But in spite of the silence he had ached with the noises in his head.

He'd kept the truth locked inside some damn point-less Pandora's Box for so long that saying them hadn't felt real. Yet the words about Josephine had come out, no matter what Madeline chose to do with them. It hadn't been the thought of what she'd do with them that had plagued him, though. It had been the thought of losing her again.

All night he'd lain awake, his heart pounding as he'd healed. Visions of her smiling, laughing, floating in the lake had messed with his senses. He had almost smelled her, tasted her. Every movement she'd made in his arms, every molecule of Madeline, had seemed imprinted on his brain like a tattoo.

He'd wanted to get up and follow her, to catch her before she flew away, but as strong as his emotions were, and—dare he say it?—as strong as his love…his body was weak.

He loved Madeline, too. Of course he did. What was not to love? And who cared about a stupid memoir or what anyone else might think?

The people he was so concerned about were all just skin and blood and bones, living in the same jungle as him. He was just like everyone else in the world—doing his best to survive. Some survived longer than others, that was all. Josephine had run into trouble, but ultimately her death was not his fault—just as Toby's wasn't Madeline's.

He also knew he couldn't have forced love to exist where it hadn't back then. He'd been young and confused, of course, chasing adventure and fun. Josephine had made him happy in that moment—and perhaps he had been selfish. But what he'd felt for Josephine was nothing compared to what he'd grown to feel for Madeline.

Why should he deny himself happiness now? Why shouldn't he be allowed to say *I love you* to someone, and mean it?

He'd known even as he'd boarded the flight what he wanted to do.

Now minutes passed like hours as he searched the waiting room, the mini-cafeteria, the playroom.

Please, God, just don't let her tell me where to shove it.

Then…

It was the back of her head he saw first. He stopped and peeked through a window into the last in a long row of rooms leading off the corridor. He'd have recognised her anywhere. The soft slope of her shoulders in her blue scrubs…the knot of hair pinned to the top of her head.

He looked around him, then back into the room. There was one bed with a kid in it—no older than eleven or twelve. Madeline was talking to her, sitting on the bed, facing away from him. He could hear the TV on the wall, the faint, jovial preposterousness of a cartoon.

He put his hand on the door handle and before he could chicken out walked inside.

The little girl's head was bald, making her big blue eyes appear even wider as she gasped.

'Dr Ryan Tobias?' she exclaimed in disbelief.

Madeline froze. On the TV a cartoon mouse screamed with perfect timing.

'Is it really you?' the little girl asked, blinking and sitting up straighter in the bed.

He saw a card on the dresser that read *Get well soon, Camille.*

Madeline still didn't turn around.

His heart was thudding now. 'Yes, Camille, it's really me,' he said, letting his eyes fall on Madeline as he shut the door behind him.

'What are you doing here? Is this a dream?'

He smiled at her. Out of the corner of his eye he saw Madeline's face had turned pale, and she'd closed her eyes, lowered her head to her chest.

'It's not a dream,' he said softly, walking to the side of her bed. He was opposite Madeline now. 'I'm here to see your friend, and to tell her I've been really, really stupid.'

The girl giggled, seeming younger than eleven or twelve. 'You're not stupid! I've seen you on the telly!'

'Well, sometimes, Camille, I do stupid things that you don't see on the telly,' he said.

'Like what?'

He paused for a moment, then reached his hand across the bed to rest it on Madeline's shoulder. 'Like letting this amazing woman fly away on a plane without me.'

Madeline opened her eyes. She brought her hand up slowly to cover his and he swore he saw a tear trickle down her nose.

'Oh, my God, do you *love* Nurse Madeline?' Camille asked, eyes wide in excitement.

'Yes, I do,' he replied, conscious now of a group of people crowding at the window, looking at them from behind the glass. 'Very much. Nurse Madeline is a very special woman.'

'Yes, she is,' Camille replied quickly. 'But I can't believe it's really you.'

Madeline stood up and clocked all the people watching them. For a moment he wanted to yank the blind down, but then he figured, *What the hell?*

He met her at the end of the bed and took her hands. They were warm and slightly clammy. She had tears streaming down her cheeks now.

'What are you doing here?' she choked.

'Don't cry,' he whispered, wiping her tears away with his thumbs.

'I don't know what to say…'

'Don't say anything.'

He dropped to his knees, fumbling in his pocket on the way to the cold floor. He heard her gasp audibly. So did Camille, and the noise levels behind the window went up a notch.

'I love you, Madeline, that's all I came to say…and as well to ask you one important question.'

'Ryan, what are you…?'

'I knew I was in love with you the minute I almost lost you—when I thought that dead body was you. Probably even before that…'

'Ryan…'

'I can't live without you. I really can't. In fact, I refuse to. I want you to marry me. *Will* you marry me, Madeline Savoia?'

Madeline let out a sudden laugh as tears continued to stream down her face.

'Are you serious?'

He smiled up at her. 'Serious as a snakebite.'

'In that case I say yes!' She clutched at his hands holding hers. *'Yes!'*

He got up, took her hand in his, and she stared in disbelief at the ring he was sliding on her finger, its stunning diamond catching the light.

'Oh, my God—my friends will never believe this.' Camille was reaching for her phone, taking a photo.

Ryan didn't care. Let her Tweet about it.

'Ryan? Is this what you want?'

Madeline was looking from the ring to him, as if she might at any moment see a camera sweep in and pronounce her 'punked'.

He let out a laugh that felt like a dead weight falling from his shoulders and dropped another kiss on her lips—which she returned until they were kissing passionately in the middle of the room and everyone outside was whooping and cheering.

When he pulled away, holding a hand up at the window, he heard Camille clapping enthusiastically behind them.

'You know, I didn't exactly want to be in here,' she blurted from the bed, 'but I wouldn't have missed this moment for anything. So you're marrying *the* Dr Ryan Tobias, Nurse Madeline?'

Madeline shook her head for a second. 'I guess I am…' she said.

Ryan pulled her against him, once again breathing in the scent he'd missed. 'I hope that's true—because the second I walk out of this room I'll be mobbed, and I'll probably need my fiancée to save me.'

The words sounded strange coming from his mouth. He was planning a real future with Madeline and he was actually excited about it. There was so much he wanted to say, and even more he wanted to do… But not with Camille in the same room.

He cleared his throat. 'When do you finish your shift?'

'Not till seven…'

'Meet me at the Shangri La. We need to talk about things. We also need to talk about this memoir.'

'Ryan, I got pretty far, but then I stopped writing it…'

'Well, you need to start again,' he said, letting her go and putting his hand on the doorknob. He could hear more people outside gathering, talking, gossiping, gasping. 'I need you to get that story out there for the good of *both* of us. I'll call your editor and tell her why the manuscript is late. I'll explain that I wouldn't give you an ending, but now I'm going to write that part myself and send it to you. I want my memoir to have a *happy* ending—you hear?'

She shook her head, confused.

He kissed her lips, pressed his forehead to hers. 'I'm going to say that, thanks to an irritating, relentless but irresistible nurse, who saved his life in the Amazon, Ryan Tobias met the love of his life. And maybe a little bit more than that. But you can't edit that bit, OK?'

'OK…'

'Good. Now, I'm heading out there. If you hear a desperate scream it's just me.'

'I'll come and save you—I promise,' she said, smiling through her tears.

'That's what you do best,' he replied, and grinned.

EPILOGUE

Afterword from Flying High,
a memoir by Dr Ryan Tobias.

As I TYPE my way towards the end of this book—a book I urge you to remember I didn't even want written—I'm feeling a sense of peace I never expected to feel.

I've thought a lot about why this is, and I think it's because when you acknowledge why you don't want to do something…when you really face that demon head on…you realise that what is really bothering you is yourself—and yourself is something you can change in a heartbeat.

You just have to want to.

I'm making some big changes in my life, and I'm not afraid to say that falling in love has helped me make them. The wonderful woman you've probably seen me out with has changed the way I see myself and consequently the way I see the world! There was a time when I didn't dare think I deserved such a love, or such a wedding, filled with so many friends, colleagues and people I love. Maybe you saw the photos? Then you'll know I'm a lucky man indeed.

Oh, and if you didn't think it was possible for this flying doctor's life to get any more adventurous, believe me, you're not alone. Let's just say we've been busy painting one of our rooms a lovely shade of blue, and my wife has recently commented that she can no longer fit into her favourite jeans.

It's a beautiful thing, knowing a whole new life is about to begin, and I sincerely hope you'll come along with us for the ride.

Till the next adventure!

Yours,

Ryan Tobias.

PS Please note: all proceeds from this book's sales are to be split between St David's Hospital Elephant and Giraffe Wards and the Ryan Tobias Foundation. Thank you for your support.

* * * * *

MILLS & BOON

Coming next month

BOUND BY THEIR BABIES
Caroline Anderson

People joked all the time about sex-crazed widows, and there was no way—*no way*—she was turning into one! This was *Jake*, for heaven's sake! Her friend. Not her lover. Not her boyfriend. And certainly not someone for a casual one-nighter.

Although they'd almost gone there that once, and the memory of the awkwardness that had followed when they'd come to their senses and pulled away from the brink had never left her, although it had long been buried.

Until now...

Emily heard the stairs creak again, and pressed down the plunger and slid the pot towards him as he came into the room.

'Here, your coffee.'

'Aren't you having any?'

She shook her head, but she couldn't quite meet his eyes, and she realised he wasn't looking at her, either. 'I'll go back up in case Zach cries and wakes Matilda. Don't forget to ring me when you've seen Brie.'

'OK. Thanks for making the coffee.'

'You're welcome. Have a good day.'

She tiptoed up the stairs, listened for the sound of the front door closing and watched him from his bedroom window as he walked briskly down the road towards the hospital, travel mug in hand.

He turned the corner and went out of sight, and she sat down on the edge of his bed, her fingers knotting in a handful of rumpled bedding. *What was she doing?* With a stifled scream of frustration, she fell sideways onto the mattress and buried her face in his duvet.

Mistake. She could smell the scent of him on the sheets, warm and familiar and strangely exciting, could picture that glorious nakedness stretched out against the stark white linen, a beautiful specimen of masculinity in its prime—

She jack-knifed to her feet. This was crazy. What on earth had happened to her? They'd been friends for years, and now all of a sudden this uncontrollable urge to sniff his sheets?

They had to keep this platonic. So much was riding on it—their mutual careers, if nothing else!

And the children—they had to make this work for the children, especially Matilda. The last thing she needed—any of them needed—was this fragile status quo disrupted for anything as trivial as primitive, adolescent lust.

It wasn't fair on any of them, and she'd embarrassed herself enough fifteen years ago. She wasn't doing it again.

No way.

Continue reading
BOUND BY THEIR BABIES
Caroline Anderson

Available next month
www.millsandboon.co.uk

LET'S TALK
Romance

For exclusive extracts, competitions
and special offers, find us online:

📘 facebook.com/millsandboon

📷 @millsandboonuk

🐦 @millsandboon

Or get in touch on 0844 844 1351*

For all the latest titles coming soon, visit
millsandboon.co.uk/nextmonth